*Three bachelor cousins—male,
millionaires and they're very
marriageable!*

Tall, Dark &

Gorgeous

Three fabulous novels
from international bestselling author

CAROLE MORTIMER

CAROLE MORTIMER'S
TALL, DARK & HANDSOME COLLECTION

August 2013

September 2013

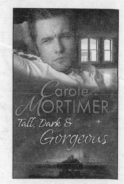

October 2013

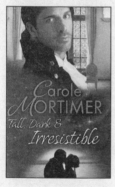

November 2013

December 2013

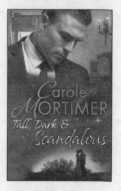

January 2014

A beautiful collection of favourite Carole Mortimer novels.
Six seductive volumes containing sixteen fabulous
Modern™ and Historical bestsellers.

Carole MORTIMER

Tall, Dark & Gorgeous

MILLS & BOON

Published in Great Britain 2013
by Mills & Boon, an imprint of Harlequin (UK) Limited, Eton House, 18-24 Paradise Road, Richmond, Surrey TW9 1SR

TALL, DARK & GORGEOUS
© Harlequin Enterprises II B.V./S.à.r.l. 2013

To Marry McKenzie © Carole Mortimer 2002
To Marry McCloud © Carole Mortimer 2002
To Marry McAllister © Carole Mortimer 2002

ISBN: 978 0 263 91024 7

024-1013

Printed and bound by
CPI Group (UK) Ltd, Croydon, CR0 4YY

Carole Mortimer was born in England, the youngest of three children. She began writing in 1978 and has now written over one hundred and eighty books for Mills & Boon. Carole has six sons, Matthew, Joshua, Timothy, Michael, David and Peter. She says, 'I'm happily married to Peter senior; we're best friends as well as lovers, which is probably the best recipe for a successful relationship. We live in a lovely part of England.'

To Marry McKenzie

CAROLE MORTIMER

CHAPTER ONE

CRASH!

'Damn!'

Logan looked up from the letters he was signing, his expression one of puzzlement as he heard first the crash of what sounded like glass, quickly followed by the expletive.

What—?

Crash!

'Double damn!'

Logan's expression turned to one of bemusement as he put down his pen to stand up, moving in the direction from which the sound of breaking glass was coming: the boardroom that adjoined his vast office.

He and a couple of business associates had lunched in there earlier, discussing contracts while they ate; Logan had found this to be a good way of doing business. The table was still partially set for the meal, he now discovered, but the room itself was empty.

'Damn and blast it,' a disembodied voice muttered impatiently. 'That's two glasses I'll have to replace now. I— ouch!' The last was obviously a cry of pain.

Logan was even more intrigued now, walking slowly around the long mahogany table, to find himself peering down at the top of a head of bright red hair. Ah, the puzzle was solved: this was the girl—woman?—who had served their lunch to them, an employee of Chef Simon. Logan hadn't taken too much notice of her during the meal, having been intent on his business discussions, but he did

5

remember the occasional glimpse of that gleaming red hair as she'd moved quietly round the table.

The girl straightened, frowning down at her left hand, where a considerable amount of blood had appeared at the end of one of her fingers.

'Did you cut yourself?'

Whatever reaction Logan had expected to his sympathetic query, it was not to have the girl jump almost six inches in the air in her nervousness, knocking over one of the water glasses as she did so!

Logan managed to reach out and catch the glass before it rolled off the table—to join the two he could see now were already shattered on the shiny wood-tiled floor.

'No point in your having to buy three replacements instead of two,' he murmured dryly as he righted the glass on the table. 'Is it a bad cut?' He reached out with the intention of looking at the girl's hand.

Only to have that hand snatched out of his grasp as it was hidden behind her back. The girl looked up at him with stricken grey eyes. 'I'm so sorry if I've disturbed you, Mr McKenzie,' she gasped. 'I was just clearing away, and—and—I broke the glasses.' She looked down at the shattered pieces. 'And—and—' Whatever she had been about to say was lost as she suddenly dissolved into floods of tears.

Logan recoiled from this display of emotion, frowning darkly. 'Hey, it's only a couple of glasses. I'm sure Chef Simon isn't that much of an ogre that you have to cry about it.'

The outside catering company of Chef Simon had been taking care of the occasional business lunches Logan had in his boardroom for over a year now, and Logan had always found the other man reasonable to deal with. Although he hadn't seen this young girl before, so perhaps she was new, and feared losing her job because of those breakages...?

'You could always tell Chef Simon that I broke them,' he attempted to cajole; weeping women were not his forte!

Well...not when they were weeping because they were worried or upset, he acknowledged ruefully as he remembered that last meeting with Gloria a couple of weeks ago. The frown deepened on his brow as he recalled the tears she had cried, tears of anger and frustration because he had told her their year-long relationship was over. She had even thrown a vase of flowers at him when he'd refused to change his mind, Logan remembered with distaste.

'Oh, I couldn't do that,' the girl instantly refused. 'Then he would put it on your bill, and that wouldn't be fair at all.' She shook her head.

Fair... It wasn't a word Logan heard too often, either in business or his personal life. Besides, the cost of a couple of glasses would hardly bankrupt his multimillion-pound, multifaceted company...

The girl reached up to wipe away the tears staining her face, inadvertently smearing blood over her cheeks instead. 'Oh, damn,' she muttered frustratedly as she realised what she had done, searching unsuccessfully in the pockets of her trousers for a tissue.

'You like that word, don't you?' Logan murmured, his head tilted as he looked at her properly for the first time.

She was a tiny little thing, barely reaching up to his shoulders, black trousers and a cream blouse emphasising the slenderness of her body, that shoulder-length bright red hair framing a face that, at first glance, seemed to be covered in freckles. On second glance, he saw the freckles only covered her cheeks and nose; her grey eyes were framed by thick dark lashes, her mouth wide, although unsmiling at the moment, her chin pointed determinedly.

Not exactly—

Where had that smile come from? Logan wondered dazedly as he found himself instantly reassessing the opinion he had just formed of this girl's looks being unremarkable. When she smiled, as she was doing now, those grey eyes became darkly luminous, dimples appeared in the slightly rounded cheeks, her teeth shone white and even in a softly alluring mouth.

Logan stared at her uncomprehendingly; he felt as if he had just had all the breath knocked out of his body!

'It's better than a lot of the alternatives,' she acknowledged. 'And, while I appreciate your offer concerning the glasses...' the girl continued to smile, appearing to have no idea of the effect she had just had on him '...as you said, it's not worth getting upset about,' she dismissed with a shrug.

'Then whatever were you crying about?' Logan rasped, angry with himself—and her!—for his unprecedented reaction just now.

The smile faded—and so did Logan's confusion. He shook his head. The girl was plain, for goodness' sake; just a load of freckles and smoky grey eyes!

'Well?' he snapped impatiently.

She was looking up at him reproachfully with those wide grey eyes now. 'I—I—I've cut myself!' She held up the damaged finger.

Logan scowled down at it. 'It appears to have stopped bleeding.' Which it had. 'And it doesn't look too serious.' Which it didn't.

And, he decided irritably, he had already wasted enough of his afternoon on this situation—whatever it might be!

'I'll have my secretary bring through a plaster,' he bit out abruptly. 'In the meantime, I would suggest you give that finger a wash. And your face,' he added with an impatient glance at her bloodstained cheek.

She put a hand up self-consciously to her cheek. 'I said I'm sorry for disturbing you.' She frowned, looking on the verge of tears once again.

She could have no idea how—momentarily!—she had disturbed him!

'What's your name?' he asked.

'Darcy,' she said miserably.

'Well, Miss Darcy—'

'Darcy is my first name,' she corrected, even as she sniffed inelegantly.

Oh, no, she was going to cry again! And wasn't Darcy a boy's name...?

'Your father wanted a son, hmm?' Logan murmured mockingly.

Those grey eyes flashed angrily. 'What he wanted, and what he got, are two entirely different things,' she clipped.

'It usually is where women are concerned,' Logan drawled derisively.

Darcy looked up at him beneath those long, dark lashes. 'Are you married, Mr McKenzie?'

Logan's surprised brows shot up beneath the dark hair that fell lightly over his brow. What did his married state have to do with anything?

'As it happens—no,' he answered slowly.

She nodded—as if she had already guessed as much. 'Women, I've invariably found, often respond in character to the men they are involved with. For example—'

'Darcy, I believe you were here to serve a meal and then depart, not to psychoanalyse the client!' Logan cut in scathingly, his jaw tightly clenched.

Until a few minutes ago he had been quietly pleased with his day; lunch had been a success, contracts were being drawn up even as he spoke to this young lady, and he had been looking forward to having dinner this evening with a beautiful blonde he had met at a dinner party on Saturday. That sense of well-being had now been lost in an increasing desire to strangle this young woman!

Darcy looked slightly flustered. 'I'm so sorry. I—It's just—I—I'm really not myself today!' she choked before burying her face in her hands as the tears began to fall once more.

Logan shook his head dazedly, once again feeling totally out of his depth in the face of the renewed tears. 'Oh, for goodness' sake!' he muttered before reaching out and taking her into his arms.

She felt so tiny as he cradled her against the hardness of his chest, that red hair feeling like silk against his fingers as he absently caressed it, her shoulder-blades so fragile to his touch she was like a little bird—

What on earth was he doing? This was the waitress who had come to serve lunch, for heaven's sake! More to the point, anyone could walk in on them and completely misconstrue the situation!

He shifted uncomfortably. 'Er—Darcy…?'

Her only answer to his tentative query was to bury her face even further into his shirt-front, the dampness of the material clinging to his chest now.

Logan felt totally out of his depth, beginning to wish that someone *would* come in and interrupt them—whatever construction was put on his actions!

'Here,' he prompted gruffly, handing her the snowy white handkerchief from his breast pocket, relieved when she moved away from him slightly to give her nose a good blow.

No wonder not too many women cried in his presence, he decided ruefully, if Darcy's unattractive appearance was anything to go by—she looked like a startled fawn: all eyes and blotchy cheeks!

'I really am so sorry,' she said miserably. 'It's just that I had some—rather disturbing news, earlier, before coming out. I don't usually cry all over perfect strangers, I can assure you.' She gave a watery smile.

Logan gave the ghost of a smile in return. 'That's okay—I'm far from perfect!' he attempted to tease, wondering exactly what sort of news this young woman could have received to reduce her to this state. 'Is it anything I can help you with?' he heard himself offer—and then frowned at this uncharacteristic interest in a stranger's— perfect or otherwise!—predicament.

Having originated from a large, Scottish-based family— consisting of his aged grandfather, his mother, a couple of aunts and numerous cousins—Logan usually found it all too easy to distance himself from the upsets that seemed to constantly plague his family. If he didn't he would spend most of his time caught up in one intrigue or another, and he preferred a much quieter life than that. Which was why he spent the majority of his time at his London apartment!

Why he should be showing this interest in the problems of a complete stranger he had no idea—especially one who had cried all over him and left bloodstains on his shirt!

Darcy's smile was slightly bitter. 'I doubt it.' She shook her head. 'But thank you for asking.'

He felt irritated because she wouldn't tell him what was bothering her! What on earth was wrong with him?

'A problem shared is a problem halved, so they say,' he encouraged cajolingly.

'I doubt you would be interested.' She shook her head again, beginning to look decidedly embarrassed now.

'Try me,' Logan prompted huskily.

Darcy shrugged again. 'It's just that— No, I really can't,' she decided firmly. 'Da—Chef Simon,' she corrected awkwardly, 'wouldn't appreciate it if he knew I had been discussing his personal life with one of his customers,' she admitted.

Chef Simon? *Daniel* Simon...? For surely this young woman had been going to call the renowned chef by his first name? And if her tears were anything to go by, it was a liberty that implied a much more intimate relationship between them than just that of employer and employee.

Daniel Simon and this girl, Darcy?

Logan couldn't hide his surprise. This girl looked no older than her early twenties at most, whereas from what Logan knew of Daniel Simon he was a man in his early fifties. Spring and Autumn. Not that it was an unusual arrangement, Logan acknowledged, he had just never thought of the other man in that particular light. In fact, he couldn't say he had given a single thought to Daniel Simon's private life!

As he didn't want to think about it now, either! 'You're probably right.' Logan nodded tersely. 'I'll send Karen through with the plaster,' he added dismissively before turning to leave.

'Mr McKenzie...?'

He turned reluctantly. 'Yes, Darcy?' he replied warily.

'Thank you,' she told him huskily, smiling at him for the second time today.

Once again causing that numbing jolt in his chest!

The quicker he got out of here, Logan decided grimly, the better! 'You're welcome,' he bit out harshly, making good his escape to the adjoining office this time.

Escape? he questioned himself once he was seated back behind his desk. From the woman Darcy? Ridiculous. He had just had enough of a woman's tears for one day—

especially as she had probably completely ruined his silk shirt with those tears and the blood from her cut finger!

What must Logan McKenzie think of her? Darcy groaned inwardly.

She had tried so hard to keep her worrying thoughts at bay this morning, concentrating on serving lunch to the client and his guests. But she just hadn't been able to control her chaotic thoughts once she'd started to clear away, and dropping the two glasses had seemed like the final straw on a day when she'd already felt as if the bottom were dropping out of her world.

But even so, she really shouldn't have cried all over Logan McKenzie's pristine white silk shirt. She very much doubted he would be able to remove those bloodstains!

She still had his sodden handkerchief, she realised as she looked down with dismay at the screwed-up item in her hand. Not that she could have given it back to him in this condition; she would have to launder it first and send it back to him. Not that she thought Logan McKenzie would miss one white handkerchief; it was just a matter of principle.

She—

'Here we are,' announced a bright female voice as Karen Hill, Logan McKenzie's private secretary, came into the room, laden down with disinfectant cream and plasters. 'Logan says you've had an accident.' She looked at Darcy enquiringly.

Logan—Darcy was sure—thought she was one big accident! She cringed with embarrassment now as she remembered the way she had sobbed all over the poor man.

'It's nothing,' she dismissed. 'Just a plaster will be fine,' she accepted lightly, the cut no longer bleeding, although it stung slightly.

But not as much as remembering her complete break-down in front of Logan McKenzie a few minutes ago! The sooner she got away from here, the better.

'Thanks.' She accepted the offered plaster. 'Er—do you have any idea of Logan's—Mr McKenzie's,' she corrected awkwardly, 'shirt size?'

Karen's blonde brows shot up in obvious surprise. 'Logan's shirt size…?' she repeated speculatively.

Mistake, Darcy, she admonished herself. If she intended replacing Logan McKenzie's ruined silk shirt she would just have to find another way of finding out what size to purchase.

'It doesn't matter,' she told the other woman brightly, avoiding Karen's questioning gaze as she put the plaster on her finger. 'I'll just finish clearing away here and be on my way,' she added.

'Fine,' the other woman answered distractedly, obviously still puzzled by Darcy's earlier question.

Well, she would have to remain puzzled, Darcy decided irritably; she had already embarrassed herself enough for one day!

Once on her own she cleared away in double-quick fashion, stacking everything into the baskets she had brought up with her, even the broken glass was swept up and wrapped in newspaper for her to take away with her.

It was just her luck to find Logan McKenzie waiting for the ascending lift when she struggled down the corridor with the two laden baskets!

He turned to glance at her, doing a double take as he obviously recognised her, a frown instantly darkening his brow.

Not surprising really, Darcy acknowledged with an inward wince; the poor man was probably wondering whether it would be safe to get into the lift with her, or if there was a chance it would break down the moment the doors closed behind the two of them!

'Hello,' she greeted inanely.

'Darcy.' He nodded tersely, glancing impatiently at the lights indicating the slow ascent of the lift.

Couldn't wait to get away from her, Darcy realised self-derisively, knowing he would probably make a point of asking Daniel Simon for her *not* to wait on one of his business lunches ever again! Well, he needn't worry on that score; she was only here today because they were short-staffed.

The restaurant, Chef Simon, opened in London by Daniel Simon five years ago, had become such a success that the customers often asked him if he was able to cater for dinner and luncheon parties in their own homes. The outside catering company of Chef Simon was a direct result of those requests. With numerous pre-bookings, already six months ahead in some cases, this secondary business was obviously doing very nicely, thank you!

Unfortunately several of the staff were off with flu at the moment, which was the reason Darcy had been roped in to help today. After the last disastrous half-hour, she wished she could have claimed a previous engagement!

'Here, let me.' An impatient Logan McKenzie reached out and relieved her of one of the heavy baskets.

Darcy blinked her surprise, having been taken unawares, lost in thought as she was. 'Thank you,' she murmured dazedly. 'But there's really no need,' she added awkwardly, moving to take the basket back out of his grasp.

Something he obviously had no intention of letting her do as his long, tapered fingers tightened about the wicker handle. 'Leave it,' he snapped impatiently as the lift finally arrived, standing back to allow her to enter first.

Darcy looked at him beneath lowered lashes as he

pressed the lift button for the ground floor. Aged about thirty-five, he was incredibly good-looking—in an arrogantly austere way, she decided slowly. His short dark hair was straight and silky, blue eyes the colour of the clear Mediterranean Sea, his nose slightly long, sculptured mouth unsmiling now, although Darcy had witnessed several charming smiles during the serving of lunch, his chin squarely firm. Tall and ruggedly muscular, he looked as if he would be more at home on a farm, than in an office wearing tailored suits and silk shirts.

Silk shirts…she remembered with an inward groan, the marks of her crying earlier clearly showing on the now-dried material. She really doubted that the traces of blood on the white silk would come off during dry-cleaning, either.

Darcy was relieved when the lift reached the ground floor, having found the silence between them uncomfortable, to say the least. 'Thanks.' She reached to take the basket from him, making no effort to follow him out of the lift.

Logan McKenzie stood in the doorway to stop the doors closing behind him, frowning again. 'Where are you going?'

'To the basement,' she told him lightly. 'I have the van parked down there.'

'In that case…' He stepped back into the lift, the doors instantly closing behind him as he pressed the button marked 'basement'.

'There's really no need,' she told him once again, completely flustered at having the owner of this world-renowned company helping her in this way.

'There's every need,' he rasped grimly. 'A little thing like you shouldn't be carrying these heavy baskets. And correct me if I'm mistaken, but was there only you dealing with the preparation and serving of lunch today?' Logan continued firmly, completely ignoring the fact that she had been about to protest at being called a 'little thing', blue eyes narrowed questioningly.

'Yes.' Darcy shifted the heavy basket to her other hand. 'We're short-staffed today, you see and—'

'No, I don't see,' Logan interrupted shortly, stepping out into the darkened basement that acted as a car park for the office staff of McKenzie Industries. 'Short-staffed or not, you shouldn't have been expected to deal with it all alone. A fact I will be passing on to Daniel Simon at the earliest opportunity,' he added grimly.

'Oh, don't do that!' Darcy turned from loading the van to protest, two wings of embarrassed colour in her cheeks. 'I managed just fine. You had no complaints about lunch, did you?' she pressed determinedly as Logan McKenzie still looked grim.

'No...' he answered slowly.

'Then there's no problem, is there?' she assured him brightly.

He looked at her consideringly. 'You know, Darcy,' he began slowly, 'you might find Daniel Simon less of a— bully, if you weren't so eager to please.'

Darcy looked up at him, but the subdued lighting in the car park made it impossible to read his expression clearly. Which was a pity—because she had no idea what he was talking about!

'It was only a lunch,' she responded, ready to leave now, the van loaded, the keys in her hand.

'I wasn't particularly alluding to lunch,' he rasped.

Then what was he talking about? Admittedly, she could have handled the latter part of this booking with a bit more detachment—in fact, a lot more!—but there really had been nothing wrong with the lunch this man and his guests had been served before her tearful outburst.

Logan McKenzie scowled at her slightly bewildered expression. 'I'm merely offering you some advice from a male point of view, Darcy,' he replied. 'It's up to you whether or not you choose to take it,' he ended abruptly, obviously impatient to be gone now.

'I— Thank you,' Darcy mumbled, having no idea what advice she had just been given!

It wasn't a question of being eager to please where Daniel Simon was concerned; she hadn't really been given too much of an opportunity to do anything else where this lunch today was concerned. She was upset, yes, in fact she was more than upset, but it would have been churlish to refuse to help out when they were short-staffed. Business was business, after all, she acknowledged slightly bitterly.

Logan McKenzie nodded tersely before turning quickly on his heel and striding back to the still-waiting lift, stepping inside, his expression still grim as the doors closed.

What a strange man, Darcy decided as she got into the van and drove out of the car park. Kind one minute, impatient the next, then offering fatherly advice—although anyone less like a father-figure, she couldn't imagine!

Oh, well, she decided lightly as she drove confidently through the early-afternoon London traffic. Logan McKenzie was the least of her problems at the moment. A frown marred the creaminess of her brow as she thought of what was her biggest problem.

Daniel Simon. *Chef* Simon.

And the fact that this morning he had calmly informed her that he intended marrying a woman he had only met for the first time three weeks ago!

CHAPTER TWO

'THIS has just been delivered for you,' Logan's secretary informed him, before placing a large square parcel on top of his desk, his name and the office address clearly printed in black ink on the brown wrapping paper.

Logan looked up with a frown, his thoughts still on the contract he had been studying; the legalese in these things became more complicated by the day. His legal team could obviously deal with it, but he would have liked his cousin Fergus's opinion too before anything was signed.

But his cousin's housekeeper had informed Logan that Fergus had gone to Scotland, to the home of their shared maternal grandfather. No doubt Hugh McDonald had a good reason for appropriating the services of the family lawyer, but, at this precise moment, Logan had little patience for those reasons!

He laid down the gold pen he had been using to mark his way down the pages, running one of his hands over the tiredness of his brow. Yesterday evening, spent with the blonde from Saturday night, had not been the success he had hoped it would be.

In fact, after only half an hour spent alone in the beautiful Andrea's company, he had already discovered that she giggled like a schoolgirl, talked incessantly, mostly about her modelling career, ate almost nothing, because of her figure—whatever that might mean!—and drank even less, for the same reason.

The evening had dragged on interminably for Logan, and he had breathed a sigh of relief when he'd finally been able to drop Andrea off at her apartment shortly before midnight. Without asking to see her again!

'What is it?' he prompted Karen now, glancing uninterestedly at the parcel she had put on his desk.

'I have no idea,' his competent secretary told him truthfully. 'I haven't opened it; it's marked "Private and Personal",' she pointed out, with a speculative rise of blonde brows.

Logan's mouth twisted wryly as he surveyed the paper-wrapped parcel. 'Have you checked it isn't a bomb? Or worse,' he drawled dryly, Gloria's shouted threats of 'you'll regret this' still ringing in his ears even after the passing of over two weeks.

Karen grinned, well aware, Logan was sure, that the telephone calls from Miss Granger had ceased two weeks ago. And was obviously totally unsympathetic to Logan's discomfort. Although that wasn't so surprising, Logan accepted ruefully; Karen had worked for him for almost ten years now, had seen several Glorias come and go in his life—and knew that he had remained unaffected by any of them.

'It was hand-delivered by a very reputable courier company,' she assured him teasingly.

He grimaced. 'That's no guarantee!'

Karen laughed softly. 'Go on, Logan, live dangerously for once, and open it.'

He frowned slightly at that 'for once' Karen had tacked onto her teasing statement. Perhaps his life did seem rather predictable to someone outside looking in, but that was the way he liked it. The way he deliberately organised it. Basically because he could remember far too many upsets and emotional scenes when he was a child to tolerate them in his own adult life...

He eyed the parcel once again before picking it up and

turning it over; no return address written on the back. 'Did the courier say who the parcel was from?' He frowned. It wasn't a very heavy parcel; in fact it felt so light it didn't seem as if there was anything inside the box...

'Nope,' Karen answered with a grimace. 'But if you really think it might be a bomb, do you want me to get Gerard to take it down to the basement and—?'

'No, I don't,' Logan assured her dryly. 'To both suggestions,' he added.

'Well, aren't you going to open it?' Karen prompted after several more long seconds had passed.

Logan sat back in his chair, the box still held in his hand as he looked across at her with narrowed blue eyes. 'I bet you were one of those little girls who crept down in the middle of the night on Christmas Eve and opened all her presents before anyone else had even thought of waking up!' he taunted softly.

'And I bet you were one of those infuriating little boys who opened each present slowly, barely ripping the paper, playing with each new toy before moving on to the next parcel!' Karen obviously felt stung into snapping back.

Logan gave an inclination of his head, smiling slightly. 'It seems we would both win our bets,' he said softly. 'You know, Karen, you aren't painting a very impulsive picture of me, either in the past or now!'

An embarrassed flush darkened her cheeks. 'I'm sorry, Logan.' She shook her head. 'I realise it's your parcel—'

'And I'm going to open it. Right now.' He grinned across at her. 'I was only teasing you, Karen,' he told her, even as he methodically unwrapped the brown paper from the parcel, opening up the box beneath to fold back the tissue paper. 'What the—?' He stared uncomprehendingly at the white handkerchief and white silk shirt that lay in the box.

Karen, looking over his shoulder at the contents, whistled softly between her teeth. 'So that's why she wanted to know your shirt size…' she mused.

Logan glanced up at her sharply. 'Who wanted to know?' he rasped.

But he already knew! The white silk shirt, well…with this particular label, that could have been an expensively extravagant present from any woman. But not the laundered white handkerchief. That could only have come from one woman—Darcy!

A quick glance before he folded back the tissue paper and put the lid back on the box showed him there was no accompanying letter inside. But there didn't need to be one; he was in no doubt whatsoever who had sent him these things. While he accepted that the handkerchief was his, and it was very kind of Darcy to launder it and return it to him, he had no intention of accepting the replacement white silk shirt. The girl was a waitress for goodness' sake, and he knew exactly how much a silk shirt of that particular label would have cost her.

His expression was grim as he glanced at his wristwatch: two-thirty. The restaurant would still be open. He glanced up at Karen. 'Could you get me the Chef Simon restaurant on the telephone, please?' he requested tautly.

'Of course.' Karen nodded, moving towards the door. She paused as she opened it. 'Be gentle with her, hmm?' she encouraged. 'She seemed terribly sweet, and—'

'Just get me the number, Karen,' Logan bit out impatiently. The last thing he needed was for his secretary to think Darcy had some sort of crush on him, and to react accordingly.

He knew exactly what this replacement shirt was about, and it had nothing to do with having a crush on him, but was more likely to be because the silly woman had a crush on Daniel Simon, and didn't want to risk losing her job working for him!

He snatched up the receiver as Karen buzzed through to him.

'Good afternoon. Chef Simon. How may I help you?' chanted the cheerful voice on the other end of the line.

Logan tightly gripped the receiver; he was angry at Darcy's actions, but there was no point in losing his temper with someone else over it! 'I would like to speak to Darcy, please,' he answered smoothly, realising that he hadn't even bothered to learn the girl's surname.

'Darcy?' came back the puzzled reply. 'I'm not sure if we have a customer in by that name, sir, but I'll check for you. If you—'

'She isn't a customer, she works there,' he cut in, his resolve to remain polite rapidly evaporating.

'I'm not sure… Just a moment, sir.' The receiver was put down, although Logan could hear a murmur of voices in the background.

Logan drummed his fingers impatiently on his desktop as he waited, a glance at the box containing the silk shirt only succeeding in firing his feelings of annoyance.

'Sorry about that, sir,' the cheerful voice came back on the other end of the line. 'It seems that Darcy will be at the restaurant this evening.'

'At what time?' he rasped.

'We usually arrive about seven o'clock—'

'Book me a table for eight o'clock,' Logan interrupted shortly. 'McKenzie. For one,' he added grimly.

'Certainly, sir. Shall I tell Darcy—?'

'No!' Logan interrupted harshly. 'I—I would like to surprise her,' he bit out through gritted teeth. Surprise wasn't all he would like to do to Darcy!

'Certainly, sir,' the woman accepted. 'That's a table for

this evening, for one, in the name of McKenzie,' she confirmed. 'We look forward to seeing you then,' she added brightly before ringing off.

Logan sat back in his chair, his expression set in grim lines. He very much doubted Darcy would share that sentiment if she were aware he was to be at the restaurant this evening—not when his greatest urge was to wring her slender neck for her!

This evening already promised to be a sight more interesting than yesterday's had turned out to be!

In fact, as he showered and dressed at his apartment later that evening in preparation of leaving for the restaurant, he actually found himself humming tunelessly to himself as he tied his bow-tie.

Because he was going to see Darcy again? he questioned himself incredulously.

Hardly, he admitted ruefully—not unless you counted—

He turned as the telephone on the bedside table began to ring. It was already seven-thirty, and if he was going to make the restaurant for eight o'clock he should be leaving in the next few minutes. But instead of the caller ringing off when he didn't answer, the telephone just kept on ringing. Persistent, or what?

Logan grabbed up the receiver. 'Yes?' he rasped his impatience.

'And a good evening to you too, cuz,' Fergus returned.

'Where are you?' Logan demanded. 'I have some contracts I need you to look at. You're never around when I—'

'Logan, as you are well aware, I am no longer a full-time lawyer. I only continue to act for the family as a favour to all of you,' Fergus cut in smoothly. 'Grandfather needed me in Scotland to discuss a few things with me. But I'm back in London now, so—'

'What sort of things?' Logan questioned warily; his grandfather had a habit of changing his will every month or so, depending on who was in favour at the time. Not that this bothered Logan on a personal level; he was wealthy enough not to be concerned with the McDonald millions. But his mother, as one of old Hugh's three daughters, was likely to be furious if she was cut out of the will yet again. Which meant Logan was sure to get dragged into the situation!

'That's what I rang to talk to you about,' Fergus answered evenly.

'I'm just on my way out, Fergus,' Logan told his cousin after a glance at his wrist-watch. 'Can't it wait until tomorrow?'

'It can,' Fergus answered slowly.

'But...?' Logan heard that hesitation in the other man's voice. It *was* that will again!

'But, I really would rather talk to you tonight.' His cousin confirmed there had been a hesitation.

'Okay, Fergus,' Logan sighed wearily, sure this had to be about his grandfather's will. 'I have a table booked at the Chef Simon restaurant for eight o'clock. Meet me there.' He was sure there would be no problem setting the table for two instead of one.

'The Chef Simon?' Fergus echoed sharply. 'But—'

'Do you have a problem with that?' Logan prompted, unsure whether or not his cousin was involved with anyone at the moment.

The three cousins, Fergus, Brice, and Logan, had been known as the Three Horrors by their family during their growing-up years in Scotland; the Three Macs when they had all gone off to Oxford University together at eighteen; now, in their mid-thirties, all of them having remained unmarried, they had become known in social circles as the Elusive Three.

But the fact that none of them had married did not preclude female involvement in Fergus's life...

'No, no problem,' Fergus answered thoughtfully. 'In fact, it's probably a good idea. A very good idea.' He was obviously warming to the suggestion. 'I have to change first, but I'll be with you as soon as I can.'

Logan slowly replaced his own receiver, frowning deeply. It would be good to see Fergus on a social level; it happened all too infrequently nowadays. Although in the circumstances, it was also a little inconvenient, he realised belatedly...

Never mind, with any luck he would have a few minutes before Fergus arrived to deal with the situation concerning Darcy and the silk shirt.

His mouth tightened grimly as he thought of the meeting ahead. Time for Darcy's surprise!

'The man on table eleven would like to have a word with you, Darcy,' a slightly breathless Katy informed her as she brought some dirty starter plates into the kitchen for washing.

Darcy looked up from what she was doing. 'Me?' She frowned. 'Are you sure he meant me?'

'Darcy. That's what he said.' Katy shrugged, picking up two plates of prawns nestling in an avocado nest before bustling back out into the main restaurant with them.

Darcy felt a sinking sensation in the pit of her stomach. A customer asking to speak to Darcy. She didn't like the sound of that. Not one little bit!

'Better go and see what he wants,' Daniel Simon advised dryly, busy making a sauce for a steak he also had cooking.

Darcy gave him a scathing glance even as she took off her apron and smoothed the black skirt down over her hips, her cream blouse tucked in neatly at her slender waist. 'Keep the customers happy at all costs, is that it?' she returned with barely veiled sarcasm.

He shrugged. 'Well... I draw the line at you selling your body for profit, but other than that...yes!' he answered teasingly.

Darcy's scowl deepened. 'Very funny!' she retorted. 'Can you manage without me for a few minutes?'

He smiled across at her, blue eyes crinkling with humour. 'I think I can cope,' he drawled. 'And, Darcy...' he called softly as she turned abruptly on her heel and flounced over to the doors that led into the restaurant.

She turned at the door. 'Yes?' she replied tautly, chin raised defiantly.

Things had been very strained between them since his announcement yesterday morning, mainly on Darcy's side, she had to admit. But she didn't intend letting him off the hook with a few teasing remarks. Not this time.

'Smile,' Daniel Simon advised ruefully. 'The customers prefer it!'

She only just managed to hold back her biting retort to that particular remark, instead shooting him another scathing glance before going out the swing doors that led directly into the restaurant.

Her footsteps became halting as she instantly recognised the man seated at table eleven. Logan McKenzie!

She had half guessed, because of the parcel she had sent him earlier today, and from the request to speak to 'Darcy', that it might be him—after all, he didn't know her surname. But actually to see him sitting there, looking ruggedly attractive in his black dinner suit and snowy white evening shirt, briefly took her breath away.

Pull yourself together, Darcy, she instructed herself firmly. He might be one of the handsomest men she had ever set eyes on, but she probably wasn't in the minority in that opinion. Besides, she doubted he had come here just to see her. In fact, as she saw the table he sat at was set for two, she was sure he hadn't!

He was looking out the window as she approached, obviously waiting for his dinner guest to join him. Good; that meant their own conversation could be kept to a minimum.

'Mr McKenzie,' she greeted huskily as she stood beside his table.

He turned sharply at the sound of her voice, those blue eyes narrowed as he looked up at her. 'Darcy,' he greeted smoothly, standing up. 'Join me for a few minutes.' He indicated the chair opposite his at the table. 'Unless you would prefer the embarrassment of my handing back your gift in full view of everyone?' He looked pointedly around the already crowded restaurant, his brows raised mockingly as he glanced down at the box that rested out of general view against the leg of his chair.

Darcy sat. Abruptly. Inelegantly. Oh, not because of his threat to embarrass her. It was the latter part of his statement that stunned her. 'Return it?' she confirmed.

'Return it,' he repeated harshly. 'Just what did you think—? I don't like your hair pulled back like that.' He broke off to frown across at her critically. 'It dulls that bright copper colour to a muddy brown,' he opined disapprovingly.

Darcy gave a ghost of a smile. 'That bright copper colour was the bane of my life as I was growing up. I was called Carrots at school,' she explained at his quizzical expression.

'Kids can be the cruellest creatures in the world,' he agreed. 'I'm sure the male population, at least, has been more appreciative of the colour since you reached adulthood.'

Not that she had noticed!

'Maybe,' she conceded dully. 'Mr McKenzie—'

'Logan,' he corrected sternly. 'You can hardly be so formal with a man you're on intimate enough terms with to present with an expensive silk shirt. In the right size, too,' he observed harshly.

Darcy moistened dry lips. 'I had a little help with that,' she admitted huskily, having looked at her father and assessed that he and Logan were about the same physical build. The size of shirt had been easy after that. It had been finding the right shop to buy the shirt that had proved more difficult.

Logan's gaze was cold. 'I'm not going to ask from where. Or who!' he rasped.

Darcy gave him an uncomprehending look. 'If the shirt is the right size,' she began slowly, 'and it's obviously the right colour, then I don't understand why you want to return it...?'

'You don't understand!' His expression became grimmer than ever. 'Darcy, you cannot go around presenting perfect strangers with pure silk shirts,' he ground out between clenched teeth.

She grinned at that, realising as she did so that it was the first time she had found anything to really smile about for some time.

Logan eyed her suspiciously. 'And just what is so funny?' he grated.

'The fact that you have already informed me that you aren't a perfect stranger!' she reminded, her eyes glowing luminously grey.

'I wish you wouldn't do that,' Logan exclaimed, shaking his head.

She raised puzzled brows. 'Do what?'

'Smile.' He looked at her darkly.

It seemed she couldn't win this evening; Daniel Simon told her to smile, because the customers preferred it. But this customer certainly didn't!

Darcy had no idea why Logan should prefer her not to smile—and wasn't sure she wanted to know, either! 'Chef Simon likes us to be polite and friendly with the customers,' she explained frigidly.

Logan studied her. 'And do you always take into account what Chef Simon likes?'

In truth, she was so angry with him at the moment, she really didn't care what he did or didn't like!

But Logan McKenzie had been kind to her yesterday, more than kind, and she owed him a debt of gratitude for the way he had helped her—as well as a new white silk shirt!

'For instance, do you think he would like the fact that you spent what must have amounted to a week's wages on buying a shirt for a man you've only just met?' Logan persisted, the softness of his voice doing nothing to hide his obvious anger.

She blinked. She hadn't thought about the buying of the shirt in that context at all—and now that she did, it still made no difference to the fact that she had ruined this man's shirt, and, as such, had to replace it. Even if it had cost what amounted to a waitress's weekly wages!

Logan sighed heavily. 'What I'm trying to say, and obviously failing to do so, is that I had no intention of telling Daniel Simon what happened between us yesterday—'

'Nothing happened between the two of us yesterday!' Darcy gasped incredulously, eyes wide. That cuddle had been purely platonic, and she dared him to claim otherwise.

'I meant the fact that your behaviour was a little less than professional—'

'It most certainly was not!' she protested, sitting bolt upright in her chair now, her expression indignant.

'Darcy, will you stop being so obtuse?' Logan came back. 'I'm trying to reassure you that I have no intention of telling your boss that you were upset and crying yesterday. In which case, you had no reason to buy me the shirt. Am I making myself clear now?' he asked her frustratedly.

'As a bell,' Darcy answered. 'You think I bought you the shirt in an effort to persuade you not to tell my boss that I was crying all over one of his private clients yesterday. Is that right?' she mused softly—dangerously...!

'Exactly.' Logan looked relieved that he had finally got through to her.

The arrogance. The damned arrogance—

'Sorry I'm late, Logan.' The man's voice was slightly breathless as he approached the table. 'I had trouble finding a taxi,' he explained as he reached them.

Darcy had glanced up as soon as she'd heard the newcomer speak. She had thought Logan was waiting for a woman to join him, but she had obviously been mistaken. The man who now stood beside their table was most definitely male, tall and dark, physically muscular in his black evening suit and snowy white shirt. Apart from the fact that his eyes were dark coffee-brown, and his dark hair was much longer than Logan's, the two men were enough alike to almost be twins.

Those dark coffee-brown eyes narrowed now as he realised Logan wasn't alone, that speculative gaze moving over her assessingly—and clearly coming to the conclusion that, in the black skirt and cream blouse, her hair tied back primly, with no make-up, she wasn't Logan's usual type at all!

That was because she wasn't with Logan!

'I suppose it should have occurred to me that you weren't here alone, Logan,' the newcomer drawled derisively.

'Oh, but he is.' Darcy stood up quickly. 'At least, he was until you arrived,' she informed the coffee-coloured-eyed man smoothly. 'Now if you two gentlemen will excuse me,' she said politely, 'I'll get back to the kitchen.' Where I obviously belong, she could have added, but didn't.

'Darcy!' Logan had stood up too, his hand moving with rapier speed to grasp her arm. 'We haven't finished our conversation,' he told her as she glanced back at him.

'Oh, I think we have.' Her voice was slightly tinged with bitterness, her gaze cold as she looked pointedly at his hold on her arm. 'You're attracting attention,' she warned him evenly, glancing over to where several of the other diners were staring across at them curiously now, as well as Katy and another of the waitresses serving this evening.

'I don't give a monkey's what I'm doing,' he rasped harshly, not sparing those people so much as a return glance. 'I have not finished talking to you—'

'Would you like me to leave, Logan?' the other man put in carefully. 'We can do this some other time.'

'Shut up, Fergus,' Logan snapped, his eyes locked with Darcy's. 'I—'

'Darcy?' the man, Fergus, suddenly echoed sharply. 'Did you say Darcy?' A sharp look in Darcy's direction accompanied his words.

The look Logan shot him was enough to wither a flower

in full bloom, Darcy decided; the effect on the other man was barely negligible, just a slight raising of dark brows.

'I asked you to stay out of this, Fergus,' Logan grated between gritted teeth. 'Would you just sit down at the table and I'll be back in a moment?' Without waiting to see if the other man complied with his instructions he pulled Darcy off to one side of the room, placing them behind a tall potted plant.

She glanced at the patchy green camouflage before looking up at Logan. 'Why don't you just take the shirt? Then we can both forget about the incident,' she pressed as he would have protested once again.

Logan drew in a hissing breath. 'Maybe because I don't want to for—'

'Everything okay, Darcy?' Chef Simon himself was suddenly standing beside them, his glance moving quizzically over them both. 'Katy seemed to think there was some sort of problem?' he elaborated with light enquiry, his eyes mild as they rested on the other man.

Great. Just great. After two days of feeling absolutely furious with this man, Logan McKenzie came along and put her in a position where she was the one put on the defensive! Which was the last place where she wanted to be at the moment!

'No problem,' Darcy was the one to answer tightly. 'Mr McKenzie was just about to sit down and enjoy his meal. Weren't you?' she added pointedly, giving him a glaring look.

'McKenzie?' Chef Simon echoed abruptly, his gaze sharp on the younger man now. '*Logan* McKenzie?' he prompted softly.

'And if I am?' Logan challenged.

Darcy, for one, had had enough of this. The situation had been ridiculous enough before, now it was becoming farcical, with the two men eyeing each other like contestants in a boxing match, apparently deliberating on who would be the one to strike the first blow!

She sighed heavily. 'Logan, will you just go back to your table and get on with your meal?' Her expression pleaded with him to comply with her request. 'We can talk about…that other situation, some other time,' she concluded soothingly as his eyes narrowed. 'If you really think we must.'

'Come and look at the menu, Logan!' The man Fergus had strolled over to join them too now. 'I don't know about you, but I'm starving!' he added with persuasive cheerfulness.

Logan looked ready to argue the point, but a glance at Darcy's rigidly set features seemed to be enough to make him relent slightly, although he still eyed Chef Simon belligerently, even as he answered Fergus. 'Maybe you're right,' he agreed slowly. 'After all, this is a restaurant,' he couldn't resist saying sardonically.

'One of the best,' Chef Simon answered almost as coolly. 'If you'll excuse us, gentlemen; Darcy and I have some food to prepare.' He took a firm grasp of Darcy's arm and almost frogmarched her back into the kitchen, barely waiting for the doors to swing shut behind them before grasping her other arm just as tightly and turning her to face him, effectively holding her immobile in front of him. 'Now perhaps you wouldn't mind telling me what you think you're doing, getting into cosy little corners with a man like Logan McKenzie?' he demanded forcefully, his teasing mood of earlier having completely disappeared.

Darcy stared up at him, not altogether sure how she should answer that particular question…

CHAPTER THREE

'HERE, have a look at a menu,' Fergus advised his cousin as he thrust one pointedly into Logan's hands. 'And for heaven's sake, sit down,' he instructed, already seated at the table himself. 'Then you can tell me exactly what is going on!'

Logan resumed his own seat, aware that several of the waitresses were still watching him curiously. Well, let them; he was more interested in knowing what sort of conversation was taking place in the kitchen between Darcy and her aged lover!

Because he was sure now that was what the other couple were; there was a familiarity between the two that was unmistakable, and a protectiveness emanating from Daniel Simon that Logan couldn't mistake as being anything other than a proprietorial claim.

He had to admit, he had been temporarily stunned by the realisation a few minutes ago, which was the reason Fergus had had to actually instruct him to sit down! He had thought Darcy's infatuation to be a one-sided thing, a crush on an older man, but now he realised there was much more to it than that.

And he didn't like it!

Which also shook him. He'd only met Darcy yesterday but even so, he felt a certain protectiveness towards her himself. The reasons for which he did not want to probe too deeply!

'I mistakenly believed you were on top of this situation

when you told me you were coming to Chef Simon this evening—'

Logan became aware that Fergus was talking to him. 'What did you say?' he asked tersely, his thoughts, if nothing else, still across the room in the kitchen.

Fergus sighed impatiently, putting down the menu. 'Let's have some drinks,' he advised as the wine waiter hovered near their table, obviously waiting to take some sort of order from them. 'I feel in need of one!' he added before turning to the young man and ordering a bottle of Chablis.

Logan pulled his divided thoughts back together, aware that he had no idea what Fergus had been saying to him a few minutes ago. Fergus's rapier-sharp brain was such that inattentiveness around him was not a good idea. During his earlier years as a practising lawyer, the prosecution had lost a lot of cases when coming up against Fergus's defence, for that very reason!

Besides, there didn't seem to be any shouting coming from the kitchen, and Darcy hadn't stormed out, so he could only assume the lovers were kissing and making up. Distasteful as that idea might be to him!

'You were saying…?' he prompted Fergus smoothly, once their wine had been poured and their food order taken; Logan thought he had ordered a fish starter and a steak main course, but he couldn't be sure!

Dark brown eyes studied him over the top of the glass as Fergus slowly sipped his wine. 'Exactly what are you doing here, Logan?' he finally asked thoughtfully.

'At the moment I'm drinking wine.' He held up his glass. 'And shortly, I hope, I shall be eating a meal. Isn't that what one usually does when one comes to a restaurant?' he parried dryly.

'Very funny.' Fergus smiled without humour. 'Might I

ask exactly what is your interest in Darcy?' Brown eyes narrowed speculatively.

'You might ask,' Logan gave an abrupt inclination of his head.

'Well?' Fergus pushed further.

Logan took his time answering, sipping his wine appreciatively, all the time his gaze remaining locked with his cousin's. 'What makes you think there is one?' he finally answered evasively.

Fergus's mouth twisted. 'She was sitting at the table with you when I arrived, the two of you were obviously deep in conversation about something.' He shrugged broad shoulders. 'I don't think that is the behaviour of complete strangers.'

'Or even perfect ones,' Logan returned dryly, lifting up a dismissive hand as Fergus seemed about to snap a reply at what he perceived as Logan's facetiousness.

Maybe it was, but the remark had reminded him too much of his conversations with Darcy for him not to have made that connection...

'She works for the outside catering company of Chef Simon,' he answered his cousin economically. 'We met yesterday when she catered for a luncheon at my office.'

'That's all there is to it?' Fergus pressed.

'Yes, that's all there is to it!' Logan echoed impatiently. 'But even if it weren't—since when have you been my keeper, Fergus?' he charged.

Fergus seemed about to bite out a reply himself, but then thought better of it, drawing in a controlling breath instead. 'When did you last see Aunt Meg? Your mother,' he added softly.

Logan's mouth quirked. 'I know who she is, Fergus,' he replied caustically.

'Well?'

He sighed. 'Fergus, I am not someone standing in the witness box suffering your own particular brand of cross-questioning!'

'I don't do that for a living any more, Logan, and you know it,' his cousin dismissed.

'Then you're giving a good impression of it,' Logan barked.

'I can assure you, I have my reasons for asking,' Fergus returned calmly. 'Have you seen anything of Aunt Meg during the last three weeks or so?'

Logan shifted impatiently. 'My mother is in her mid-fifties, and I am in my mid-thirties; neither of us feels the need to report back to the other on a regular basis!'

'Logan, I'm not criticising your actions as regards your mother—'

'I should hope not,' he rasped, eyes narrowed. 'Because if you were I would feel compelled to ask when you last saw Aunt Cate. Your own mother,' he added pointedly.

Fergus was prevented from answering immediately as the waitress arrived with their starters.

The fish Logan thought he had ordered turned out to be Chef Simon's pâté!

He was losing it, he decided, if he couldn't even re-member what food he had ordered. And all because of a young girl who reminded him of one of the deer on his grandfather's estate; extremely nervy, they had glossy red coats and huge limpid eyes, too.

'Do you want to get to the point, Fergus?' he asked his cousin more amiably after tasting the pâté and finding it was delicious.

'The point is, you haven't spoken to your mother re-cently?' Fergus also seemed more relaxed after tasting the deep-fried Brie that was his own starter.

Logan shrugged. 'Not for several weeks, no,' he confirmed.

'Then your being here this evening is just a coincidence?' His cousin grimaced.

'I've already said so, haven't—? What do you mean, coincidence?' Logan said. 'What does my mother have to do with Chef Simon?' He felt sure he wasn't going to like the answer to that particular question!

Fergus drew in a deep breath. 'Well, as you know, I've been to see Grandfather— Oh, no!' he groaned, glancing towards the door. 'That's all we need!'

Logan had turned too, aware that something momentous seemed to be taking place at the entrance to the restaurant. A short silence amongst the other diners was quickly replaced by the babble of excited voices as they easily recognised the woman who had just swept into the room.

The actress, Margaret Fraser.

At the very same moment, Logan easily recognised the woman who had just entered the restaurant, and also became aware of Darcy finally bursting out of the kitchen— perhaps he had been premature in his assumption the couple in the kitchen were kissing and making up...? Her eyes were glittering with unshed tears, her face was fiery-red— whether from anger or those unshed tears, he wasn't sure.

Darcy glanced to neither left nor right as she strode purposefully towards the doorway, although she stopped in her tracks as she too recognised the woman standing there looking so regally beautiful.

'You!' Darcy burst out with audible disgust, grey eyes definitely gleaming with anger now. 'Well, I hope you're satisfied,' she continued. 'You have what you want; he's all yours!' And with that she continued on her relentless way out of the restaurant, the door slamming behind her.

Logan turned dazedly to Fergus. 'What on earth—?'

'Go after Darcy, Logan,' his cousin told him economically.

'But—'

'For once in your life, will you just do what you're asked without argument, Logan?' Fergus told him sternly, standing up. 'While you do that, I'll try and deal with the situation here,' he offered grimly, looking pointedly across the room to where Margaret Fraser was continuing her entrance into the room.

Although the older woman had obviously been initially shaken by Darcy's verbal attack, she had quickly recovered her equilibrium, smiling graciously at the other diners as she strolled confidently through the restaurant, the three friends she had arrived with trailing behind her.

Of the two prospects, that of following Darcy, or coming face to face with the volatile actress, Logan had to admit he preferred going after Darcy; he would just also prefer to have a clue what was going on before he did so!

'Logan—darling!'

He cringed as, having finally spotted him standing at the back of the restaurant, Margaret Fraser swept across the room to envelop him in one of her theatrical greetings, her perfume overwhelming as she kissed him on both cheeks.

'And Fergus, too,' she recognised warmly, bestowing a similar greeting on him.

Logan watched her dispassionately as she kissed Fergus. Delicately tiny, her shoulder-length hair gleaming like ebony, her hourglass figure shown to perfection in a little black dress—that Logan knew would have cost a small fortune!—the beauty of her face completely unlined, deep blue eyes fringed by thick dark lashes.

There was no doubt that Margaret Fraser was a stunningly beautiful woman. Or, that she was the last person Logan wished to see here this evening!

'Darcy, Logan,' Fergus reminded him, once he'd surfaced from the actress's embrace.

Margaret Fraser gave them both a quizzical frown. 'Darcy…?' she echoed lightly.

Logan's mouth twisted. 'The young woman who insulted you as you came in,' he reminded her dryly.

'Oh, that Darcy.' She nodded vaguely.

'Will you just go, Logan?' Fergus urged in measured tones.

Gladly, Logan decided, nodding dismissively before striding out of the restaurant in search of Darcy.

It didn't take him too long; she hadn't gone very far. She was leaning against the wall outside, her slender body convulsed by desolate sobs.

After her earlier outburst, Logan had no doubt that Margaret Fraser was somehow involved in the desolation of those tears…!

The question was—how?

How could he? How *could* he! And with that awful woman too.

Oh, there was no doubting Margaret Fraser was beautiful enough. But the woman had been married twice already, had announced engagements to other men as many times. How could he even be thinking of marrying—?

'Darcy…?'

She froze at the sound of Logan's voice behind her. She had been so upset when she'd stormed out of the restaurant that she hadn't even noticed him. She doubted the same could be said for her own dramatic exit!

She quickly wiped the tears from her cheeks before turning to face him. 'Mr McKenzie,' she greeted shakily, unable to meet that piercingly probing gaze.

His mouth quirked humourlessly. 'This doesn't seem to be your night, does it?' he sympathised.

He could have no idea! She had thought the disagreement with him in the restaurant was bad enough, but the conversation in the kitchen that had followed had been even worse. And, then, to come face to face with that woman as she'd stormed out—!

'Here,' Logan encouraged gently, holding out a snowy white handkerchief to her.

She gave a watery smile. 'I've only just returned the last one you lent me,' she reminded self-derisively, making no effort to take the handkerchief.

'Which I've just left in the restaurant,' Logan realised. 'Never mind, my cousin will probably return it to me later,' he mused.

So the other man had been his cousin, Darcy noted, which obviously accounted for that strong resemblance between them.

'Take it, Darcy.' Logan continued to hold the handkerchief out to her. 'Your mascara has run,' he observed.

Darcy took the handkerchief with muttered thanks, mopping self-consciously at her eyes—before she remembered that she wasn't wearing mascara, that she hadn't worn any make-up this evening; the heat in the kitchen tended to make it cake! 'Very funny,' she replied, her smile rueful.

'That's better.' Logan nodded his approval of her half-smile. 'I'm sure—whatever it is—that it can't be that bad…?' He bent his head to smile back at her teasingly.

Darcy's own humour faded. 'Worse!' she said with feeling, giving an involuntary shiver. 'You can have no idea.' She shook her head, her expression bleak.

Logan tilted his head, dark brows raised questioningly. 'Want to talk about it?'

Did she? In one way, definitely no! In another way…it

might be quite nice to share this with someone. But was Logan McKenzie, a man she hardly knew, the right someone...?

Probably not, she acknowledged. But if she didn't talk to someone about this soon, she was going to burst! Besides, she had no intention of returning to the restaurant this evening...

She gave a heavy sigh, coming to a decision. 'Would you like to join me for a cup of coffee?'

'Darcy! This is so sudden.' Logan pretended to reel from the suggestion.

'I said coffee, Logan—er—Mr McKenzie—' She broke off, blushing at her own familiarity with a man who was, after all, a customer of Chef Simon. Although, in the circumstances, the formality of 'Mr McKenzie' did seem slightly ridiculous!

'Logan will do,' he assured her, obviously of the same opinion.

She nodded, her cheeks still feeling hot. 'And I was suggesting we go to a coffee bar, not my home!' she explained defensively.

'Aren't I a little overdressed for a coffee bar?' Logan looked down at his dinner clothes.

Of course he was, Darcy realised belatedly. But going to her home really was out of the question. After the heated accusations that had been made in the kitchen earlier, the last thing she needed was for Daniel Simon to return home and find her there with Logan McKenzie!

'We could always go to my apartment,' Logan suggested, his gaze narrowed, seeming to have read some of the indecision on her face. If not the reason for it!

Go to his apartment...! 'I'm sure you can't really be interested in hearing all this,' she burst out. 'I think it might be better if I just went home and—and slept on the whole thing. My mother always told me that things never look so black in the morning,' she went on with forced brightness, knowing this particular situation was going to get worse, not better.

'And my nanny always told me that a problem shared is a problem halved,' Logan came back dryly.

His nanny, not his mother, Darcy noted. But, then, he obviously came from a wealthy background, the sort where the children were cared for by a nanny. Nevertheless, it was very sad if, as it seemed, Logan had had a closer relationship with his nanny than with his own mother. Darcy's own childhood had been spent being cosseted and loved by a mother who had always been there for her. She had been dead just over a year now, and Darcy still missed her deeply.

'Maybe,' she conceded huskily. 'But my mother also warned me about the danger of going to the home of a man I don't really know.'

'My nanny warned me of the same thing where women are concerned,' Logan drawled, taking a firm hold of her arm, at the same time hailing a passing taxi. 'But I'll risk it if you will!'

For the second time in their acquaintance—despite the fact that she was deeply upset, and that she could see no solution to ending this particular misery—Darcy laughed.

Logan froze in the act of helping her into the back of the waiting taxi. 'I thought I asked you not to do that,' he ground out, his jaw clenched.

Darcy blinked up at him dazedly, shaking her head. 'I don't understand—'

'Never mind,' Logan replied tersely, climbing into the back of the taxi to sit beside her before leaning forward and giving the driver his address.

He really was a complete stranger to her, Darcy decided

during the drive to his apartment, Logan gloweringly silent beside her, one glance at his grimly set features enough to stop any attempt at conversation on her part, either.

What if her mother's warning turned out to be a correct one? What if—?

'Do I look like a man who has to drag young innocents off to his apartment in order to seduce them?' Logan suddenly rasped, turning to look at her with cold blue eyes.

Darcy's own eyes instantly filled with tears. He had seemed so kind earlier, so gentle, and now—

'I'm sorry, Darcy,' he said, turning fully towards her. 'One way or another, this evening has turned out a bit of a shambles for me too. But that's no reason to take it out on you! Forgive me?' he prompted, taking one of her hands in both of his.

To her embarrassment, Darcy found herself trembling at his touch. Of all the times in her life to find herself physically attracted to a man—!

She snatched her hand out of his grasp, instantly hiding it beneath the one that still lay on her lap. Although that did nothing to prevent that tingling sensation, just from Logan McKenzie's touch, from spreading up her arm…!

'Of course,' she dismissed sharply. 'But maybe this wasn't such a good idea. I'm sure I've already taken up enough of your time for one night. After all, it's still early enough for you to salvage something from your evening.'

'Too late, Darcy,' he told her teasingly as the taxi came to a halt outside an apartment building.

Apparently the one in which he lived, Darcy acknowledged slightly dizzily as, having paid the driver, Logan took a firm hold of her arm and steered her inside.

She wasn't unused to luxury, her own home being fairly comfortable, and the homes she visited on business for Chef Simon were often opulent, to say the least. But this apartment building—where Logan lived!—was something else.

The man sitting at the desk leapt to his feet as soon as Logan swept through the double glass doors, rushing over to call the lift after greeting him. Darcy's feet sank into the deep pile of the pale blue carpet as she walked at Logan's side. *Clamped* to his side by his firm hold on her arm!

It didn't surprise her that it was the penthouse apartment the lift whisked them up to—after seeing the reception downstairs, she didn't think anything about Logan's home would surprise her any more.

She was wrong!

Where she had been expecting chrome and leather furniture—ultra-modern decor—she found herself stepping into a sitting-room that, although it was expensively furnished, was clearly designed for Logan McKenzie's comfort and relaxation: a thick brown carpet, deep gold-coloured armchairs, mahogany bookcases along one wall, several small mahogany tables placed about the room, and the most amazing paintings on the walls.

It was to one of the latter Darcy was instantly drawn, picturing a deer grazing in the foreground, and a castle behind in the mist. 'A McAllister,' she breathed in awe-struck recognition of the artist, sure she didn't need to ask whether or not it was an original; she doubted Logan McKenzie would tolerate anything else in his home. 'It's beautiful,' she opined as she turned back to face Logan.

He gave a brief nod of agreement. 'It's of my grandfather's home. Can I get you a drink?' He indicated the array of bottles on a side-table.

Darcy was still reeling from the fact that the mellow-stone castle in the painting, shimmering mysteriously in the mist, actually belonged to this man's grandfather. Exactly what had she got herself into...?

'A small whisky, if you don't mind,' she accepted.

'My grandfather would certainly approve of that; he doesn't believe you can trust a woman who doesn't drink whisky!' Logan gave a slight smile as he poured the liquid into two tumblers, handing Darcy the one with the least in it.

With a name like McKenzie, this man's family must come from Scotland—which no doubt also accounted for Logan's grandfather's opinion about women and whisky!

Which was a pity—because normally Darcy couldn't stand the stuff; she just felt in need of a restorative at the moment. The whisky certainly was doing that, initially taking her breath away, but then it quickly gave her an inner warmth.

'Let's sit down,' Logan suggested, suiting his actions to his words, watching as Darcy moved to sit in an armchair across the room from his.

Her action was a bit obvious, perhaps, Darcy acknowledged, but the two of them were completely alone here in the privacy of Logan's home, and she doubted that obsequious man downstairs would come running to her aid if she decided to call for help!

'Now do you feel like telling me what all that was about earlier?' Logan ventured.

She took another sip of the whisky at his reminder of earlier. 'That woman!' she exclaimed with returning anger.

'Margaret Fraser?'

'Yes.' Darcy looked up sharply. 'Did you see her?'

Logan raised dark brows. 'One could hardly miss the entrance of an actress of Margaret Fraser's fame,' he drawled dryly. 'But, I have to admit, I have no idea where she fits into the scheme of things.'

Darcy wrapped both hands around her glass of whisky, wishing it were a hot drink now, so that it could warm her outside as well as in. 'She doesn't,' she replied with feeling. 'That's my whole point!'

Logan shook his head, smiling slightly. 'As clear as mud,' he responded.

Darcy gave a deep sigh. 'It's quite simple, really, my— Daniel Simon, Chef Simon—'

'I know who Daniel Simon is, Darcy,' Logan assured her.

'He's going to marry her!'

There, she had said it, actually had acknowledged it out loud. And it was no more acceptable now than it had been yesterday when she had first been told of the engagement.

'Going to marry whom?' Logan prompted, sitting forward in his chair now.

'Margaret Fraser, of course!' Darcy answered disgustedly.

'You can't be serious?' Logan said disbelievingly.

'Exactly what I said when he told me,' she agreed determinedly. 'But it seems that he is.'

'But I— She's—'

'Incredible, isn't it?' Darcy went on, standing up to pace the room. 'He only met her three weeks ago, and yet he's decided he wants to marry her!'

'Three weeks ago…' Logan echoed, looking thoughtful now.

'Ridiculous, isn't it?' Darcy continued. 'How can anyone decide, after only three weeks' acquaintance, that they want to spend the rest of their life with one particular person?'

'I believe it does happen sometimes,' Logan observed distractedly. 'Although I'm a little surprised—Darcy, are you absolutely sure of your facts?' He watched her with narrowed eyes.

'Positive,' she said with feeling. 'Why else do you think she's at the restaurant this evening?'

'The same reason as everyone else—to eat?'

'And that's another thing.' Darcy kept on going. 'The woman barely eats enough to keep a bird alive; a fine advertisement for a chef's wife!'

Logan's mouth twisted. 'I suppose she has to maintain that wonderful figure somehow.'

Darcy gave him another sharp look. 'Don't tell me you find her attractive too?' she said accusingly.

'No,' Logan answered. 'I can honestly say I am probably one of the few men impervious to her charms, physical or otherwise!'

'Good,' Darcy bit out flatly.

Logan stood up to pour himself another shot of whisky, holding up the decanter to Darcy, putting it down again when she shook her head in refusal. 'Tell me, Darcy,' he began gingerly, after sipping at his replenished glass. 'If—and, I have to admit, I still find it incredible to believe!—Daniel Simon *is* going to marry Margaret Fraser, where does that leave you?'

She shuddered. 'Out of there!' she told him with feeling, putting down her empty glass. 'There is no way I'm going to sit back and just accept all this.' She sighed heavily. 'I shall have to move out of the house, of course—'

'You *live* with him?' Logan interrupted harshly.

'Only for the last couple of months or so,' she replied. 'Since I finished uni. It was never intended as a permanent arrangement, just somewhere for me to stay until I take up a permanent post in September.''

Logan frowned. 'But I thought you worked for Chef Simon Catering?'

'Again, only temporarily. I'm actually a trained kinder-garten teacher.' And until yesterday she had been looking forward to starting her first real job, as such. At the moment, everything looked too black to be able to look forward to anything!

Logan paused, then admitted, 'I'm having trouble keeping up with all this...'

Darcy gave him a sympathetic smile. 'The job with Chef Simon is only a holiday job for me,' she explained. 'Oh, don't worry, I trained as a chef first, before I realised I liked working with children rather than feeding adults! I went back to uni to get the suitable qualifications.'

Logan's frown deepened. 'How old are you...?'

'Twenty-five,' she answered, knowing Logan, like many others, had placed her as much younger than that. She was sure as she got older that this was going to be an advantage, but at the moment it was only a hindrance to people actually taking her seriously.

He looked grave. 'Old enough to know better, then. Darcy, I realise this can't be easy for you, but what are you doing still staying around the man if he's told you he's going to marry someone else?'

She blinked her confusion. 'But he isn't married to her yet...'

'And you intend hanging around until he is?' Logan accused angrily, putting down his whisky glass to stride over to where she stood, and grasping her shoulders.

'Of course,' she assured him determinedly. 'The wedding isn't going to be immediately; I may still be able to persuade him to see sense.'

Logan gave a groan. 'Darcy, you're an attractive young lady yourself—'

'I'm not in Margaret Fraser's league,' she countered.

'Oh, damn Margaret Fraser!' Logan snapped.

Her eyes flashed deeply grey. 'My sentiments exactly!'

'Oh, Darcy...!' Logan muttered before his head lowered and his mouth claimed hers.

It was the last thing, the very last thing, Darcy had been expecting, standing acquiescent in his arms, her head starting to spin as the kiss deepened, became more intimate. Her body moulded against the hardness of his as his hands moved restlessly up and down her spine.

Emotions were high, Darcy's earlier anger turning to a passion she hadn't known she possessed, her lips opening beneath his, her hands beneath the material of his jacket, able to feel the warmth of his body through the silk of his shirt.

Her hair was loose about her shoulders now, Logan having removed that hated band that secured it at her nape, his fingers threaded in the silky softness as his lips sipped and tasted hers, hot breaths intermingled.

She had kissed men before, of course she had, but it had never been like this, feeling as if she were melding into Logan, their bodies a perfect match, her soft curves fitting into the hard hollows of his body.

But it came to a sudden end, Logan wrenching his mouth from hers, looking down at her, almost as if he were confused. 'What am I *doing*—? I'm sorry, Darcy.' His arms dropped from her as he ran the fingers of one hand restlessly through his own hair, his shoulders hunched beneath his jacket. 'I didn't mean to do that.' He turned away. 'I brought you here to try and help you, and instead I almost ended up making love to you. I just— The man is old enough to be your father, for goodness' sake!' he burst out as he turned back to face her.

Darcy took in a deep breath, barely able to think, her lips and body still tingling from Logan's kisses. 'What man?' She frowned her puzzlement.

'Daniel Simon,' he said aggressively.

She swallowed hard. 'I—' She tried to think, to remember what had already been said. But after Logan's kisses, she couldn't think straight at all! 'Logan,' she finally managed. 'I don't know—I don't seem to have explained— Logan, Daniel Simon *is* my father.'

Until just over a year ago, when her mother had died after a brief illness, Darcy's father had been happily married to her mother, their relationship a very loving one.

Which was the reason Darcy was so upset at his announcement he intended marrying again, to the flamboyant actress Margaret Fraser of all people, her off-screen affairs seeming to attract more attention than her actual acting career.

Darcy swallowed hard again as she saw Logan was staring at her, unmoving, a nerve pulsing in his tightly clenched jaw, seeming to be lost for words himself now. It wasn't too difficult to guess the reason why: he probably believed her attitude was an extremely selfish one. It probably was, Darcy accepted dully. But she couldn't help the way she felt...

CHAPTER FOUR

HER father...!

Daniel Simon was Darcy's *father*, and not the lover Logan had assumed him to be.

Apparently he had announced his intention to Darcy of marrying Margaret Fraser...

This was news to Logan, although he had an idea this could have been what Fergus had been intending to talk to him about earlier.

'I realise you must find my attitude—selfish.' Darcy began talking self-consciously. 'I just— My mother only died just over a year ago,' she explained in a sad voice. 'They were married for twenty-eight years. Twenty-eight years! We were such a happy family, too. I just don't see how my father can possibly believe himself in love with someone else after so short a time.' She looked across at Logan pleadingly.

Her father.

Every time Darcy said that, Logan gave an inward wince about what he had believed to be her relationship with the chef. It was his own fault for making such an assumption, of course, although, to be fair to himself, Darcy had never told him her surname—and he hadn't asked her for it, either—or addressed Daniel Simon as her father, or called him 'Dad'!

Although, looking back, Logan could see she had never really stated they had any other sort of relationship, either; he had drawn his own conclusions about that. Completely erroneously, as it turned out!

The problem was, how did he now tell Darcy—?

'I think I had better go,' she said suddenly, her gaze not meeting his as he looked across at her. 'I really have taken up enough of your time.'

'Darcy!' He moved to grasp her arm as she would have turned away, turning her slowly back to face him.

'I know I'm being selfish!' Those deep grey eyes were swimming with tears. 'I just—I can't even begin to think of that woman as my stepmother!' she cried emotionally.

Logan pulled her gently into his arms, cradling her against his chest as the tears fell hotly down her cheeks.

He seemed to be making a habit of this! Not that he was complaining, exactly, he just didn't like to see Darcy upset like this. Although, as far as his equilibrium went, it was probably preferable to her smiling at him.

Once again, in the taxi earlier, her smile had almost been his undoing. There was just something about Darcy's smile that took his breath away...

Which was incredible in itself. She was right when she said she wasn't in Margaret Fraser's league when it came to looks. It was like comparing an exotic bird to a garden robin: the actress was flamboyant, completely unmissable, whereas Darcy—unless she smiled!—would be all too easy to overlook in a crowd. Although Logan had no doubts which woman he—and apparently his inner senses too!—preferred.

'I know it's not much consolation at the moment, Darcy—' Logan stroked her back as the tears began to cease '—but I very much doubt that Margaret Fraser will ever be your stepmother!'

Darcy straightened, wiping away the tears. 'My father is adamant that she will.'

Logan shook his head with distaste. 'And I'm just as sure that she won't.'

Grey eyes widened, eyes that were slightly red from crying. 'But how can you be?' Darcy swallowed hard.

He looked serious. 'Believe me, Darcy, I—' He broke off as the intercom buzzed beside the lift.

After the way the evening had been cut short at the restaurant earlier, his visitor was likely to be Fergus—and his cousin was the last person he wanted to see at the moment. Well…probably not the last person, he conceded; Margaret Fraser had to take that honour!

'Shouldn't you answer that?' Darcy prompted as the buzzer sounded a second time, self-consciously wiping away all trace of her recent tears.

'I should,' he acknowledged reluctantly—because it was the last thing he wanted to do.

He needed time, and space, to talk to Darcy, to explain. But with Fergus waiting downstairs, now certainly wasn't that time. Except Fergus, if allowed up here while Darcy was still here, was sure to say something he shouldn't…!

'Darcy, will you have lunch with me tomorrow?' he found himself asking quickly.

She gave him a considering look. 'What for?'

His brows rose impatiently. 'Because I want to have lunch with you!'

'Why?'

'Good grief, woman, just say yes or no!' he barked, annoyed at her delay.

'If you're only inviting me because you feel sorry for me—' she began slowly.

'I don't feel sorry for you,' he bit out tersely. At least…not yet. If Margaret Fraser ever did become her stepmother, then he might have reason to change his mind! 'I just need to talk to you, okay?' he stated firmly, knowing Fergus would be becoming fed up as he waited downstairs, having no doubt that Parker would already have told his cousin that he was at home!

She gave a half-smile. 'Okay.'

'Good,' he said with relief. 'Now I'm going to take you downstairs, put you into a taxi, and I would advise you to go to bed when you get home and have a good night's sleep. As your mother told you, this won't look so black tomorrow.' Especially as Logan intended finding out exactly what was going on and doing something about this situation himself!

Darcy accompanied him into the lift. 'It certainly couldn't look any worse,' she surmised.

Oh, it could, as Logan knew only too well, but not if it was handled correctly. And he intended to see that it was!

Fergus levelled a look of cold criticism at Logan, for keeping him waiting, as Logan stepped out of the lift with Darcy at his side.

'I'll be back in a moment,' Logan told him as Fergus would have spoken, vaguely noting that Fergus did have the parcel from the restaurant with him. He could sort that out with Darcy tomorrow. 'I'm just going to put Darcy into a taxi.' He strode out of the building, Darcy held firmly at his side, before his cousin had a chance to make any sort of reply.

Darcy turned to him before getting into the back of the taxi. 'You really have been very kind,' she said almost shyly.

It wasn't a characteristic too many people would apply to him, Logan thought wryly, but if that was how Darcy saw him, he wasn't about to argue with her!

'Lunch tomorrow,' he reminded her economically. 'Twelve-thirty. At Romaine's. It's—'

'I know where it is,' she assured him, reaching out to touch his arm. 'And thank you once again.'

Logan stood and watched the taxi until it disappeared around the corner at the end of the road, his thoughtful expression turning to one of hard determination as he turned to walk back into his apartment building.

'Nice-looking girl,' Fergus remarked as he followed the glowering Logan into the lift.

Logan gave him a cold look. 'She's Daniel Simon's daughter,' he rasped. 'But then you already knew that, didn't you?' he added accusingly as the two men stepped into his apartment, Logan striding straight over to the drinks tray to replenish his glass, taking a grateful sip before pouring another glassful for Fergus.

'Thanks.' Fergus took the glass. 'Yes,' he sighed, bending his long length into one of the armchairs. 'I already knew that. This, apparently, is yours.' He held up the parcel.

'Thanks.' Logan took it and put it on the side without further comment. Fergus didn't have to know everything!

His cousin sipped the whisky. 'I know we were practically brought up on this stuff, but I'm not sure we should be drinking it at the moment; neither of us has eaten much this evening!'

'Come on.' Logan came to a decision. 'I'll cook us both an omelette—and then you can bring me up to date with exactly what is going on!'

It only took a few minutes to prepare the omelettes and a salad to go with them, the two men shortly seated at the breakfast bar; Logan had lived on his own a long time now, was more than capable of feeding himself. And anyone else who happened to be here. On this occasion, it happened to be Fergus.

Except it didn't really just happen to be Fergus...

He gave his cousin a sideways glance. 'Am I right in supposing that your recent visit to Grandfather was because my mother is about to announce her engagement to restaurateur and chef, Daniel Simon?'

His mother.

Margaret Fraser.

Although it was hard to believe—he chose not to believe it himself most of the time!—the actress Margaret Fraser was his mother. She was also Fergus's Aunt Meg.

With that cascade of dark hair, beautiful unlined face, youthfully slender body, Logan knew his mother didn't look much older than himself. But she was, undeniably, his mother. He knew—because he had lived with the unpalatable fact long enough!

He had been dumbstruck earlier when Darcy had announced her father's intention of marrying the beautiful actress. He and his mother had never been particularly close, but in the past his mother had at least told him—warned him?—when she'd intended either marrying or becoming engaged to someone. This time Logan had been taken completely unawares. Although he knew Darcy, innocent of the true facts, had misunderstood his silence. He intended explaining everything tomorrow when they met for lunch.

'It was,' Fergus confirmed with another sigh. 'Apparently she told him of her plans when she visited him at the weekend.'

'And, because the two of us have always been close, you were chosen to break the news to me,' Logan guessed.

His cousin shrugged. 'Ordinarily Aunt Meg would have told you herself. But in this case there seems to be a—complication.'

'Darcy,' Logan confirmed knowingly.

'Darcy,' Fergus confirmed flatly. 'Apparently she isn't too keen on Aunt Meg marrying into the family.'

'I wouldn't be too keen on having her marry into my family, either!' Logan exclaimed.

Fergus turned to give him a considering look. 'You know I've never tried to interfere in your relationship with Aunt Meg—'

'Then don't start now,' Logan warned him softly.

'I have no intention of doing so,' his cousin assured him calmly.

Logan gave him a sceptical glance. 'No?'

'No,' Fergus confirmed lightly, sipping the white wine Logan had opened to accompany their snack meal. 'Firstly, because there's no point; your feelings on that issue are your own business. Secondly,' he continued as Logan would have spoken, 'because I believe there is something of much more urgency for us to discuss.'

Logan raised dark brows. 'Such as?'

'Such as how you're going to break it to Darcy that you're Margaret Fraser's son? Without her hating your guts when you've finished, I mean,' Fergus added.

He had been wondering the same thing himself!

'I am right in surmising Darcy doesn't have a clue about that, aren't I?' Fergus mused.

'Maybe if you hadn't arrived here so precipitously—'

'Don't try and blame this situation on me.' Fergus held up defensive hands.

Fergus was right; Logan knew that he was. He should have told Darcy the truth the moment she'd mentioned Margaret Fraser. But, if he had, he also knew that Darcy would have looked at him with the same dislike she had looked at his mother. And that wasn't something he wanted from Darcy. He wasn't sure what he wanted from her, but it certainly wasn't for her to lump him in with the same antipathy she felt towards his mother.

He had less than twenty-four hours to think of a way of

telling Darcy the truth—without the end result being, as Fergus had pointed out only too graphically, her hating his guts!

She was late.

She knew she was late. Almost fifteen minutes, to be exact. With any luck Logan would have tired of waiting for her to arrive and already have left! After the morning she had had, she didn't feel up to this meeting, too!

She had taken Logan's advice the evening before, going to bed shortly after getting in, amazingly falling asleep too, not even waking when her father had returned home at his usual one o'clock in the morning. She had been exhausted, of course, from all the emotional trauma of the last few days.

Not that she'd felt any better when she'd woken at nine o'clock this morning, knowing by the sound of the radio downstairs that her father had already been up. Margaret Fraser was sure to have told him of her own parting shot as she'd left the restaurant the evening before.

She had been right about that; her father was absolutely furious that Darcy had caused a scene in the restaurant of all places. Her reply, that scenes were what Margaret Fraser enjoyed the most, had not gone down too well, and the argument that had followed had been far from pretty. With the end result that Darcy had told her father exactly what he could do with his holiday job, and that she would be looking for a flat of her own later today.

Darcy still cringed when she thought of that argument; until the last couple of days she could never remember being at odds with her father about anything. As far as she was concerned, it was all Margaret Fraser's fault!

But it was partly because of that argument with her father that she had been late changing into her figure-fitting navy-blue dress in readiness for joining Logan for lunch. Partly...

Logan hadn't left the restaurant!

She could easily see him as she entered the room, sitting at a window table. Very much as he had done last night. Except a lot had happened since she'd spoken to him at Chef Simon yesterday evening!

Logan was looking as arrogantly handsome as ever in a grey suit, and—unless she was mistaken—the white silk shirt she had sent to him yesterday...

He stood up as she was shown to the table, Darcy noting several female heads turning in their direction as he did so. No doubt those women had been wondering—as she had last night—who would be joining this attractive man for lunch; she doubted any of them had expected him to be interested in a mousy little thing like her!

Ordinarily they would be right...

'Darcy!' Logan greeted warmly now, indicating for the wine waiter to pour her some of the white wine he had obviously ordered while he'd waited for her to arrive. 'Unless you have to work this afternoon?' He quirked dark brows across the table at Darcy.

'I am, at the moment, what I believe is known in acting circles as "resting",' Darcy answered brittlely.

Logan gave her a sharp look. 'I wouldn't know,' he said dismissively.

'Neither does my father,' she scorned. 'But I have a feeling, when he marries Margaret Fraser, that he will very quickly find out!'

'Shouldn't that be *if* he marries her?' Logan replied hardly.

'Not according to my father,' Darcy muttered with remembered bitterness.

'Presumably, by your earlier remark, you're no longer working for him?' Logan queried.

'We've decided that a parting of the ways—in all areas of our lives—is probably for the best. Nice shirt,' she added dryly, looking at the snowy white garment.

'Damn the shirt,' Logan came back. 'No, I didn't mean that the way it sounded,' he continued a little less fiercely. 'It's a beautiful shirt. And I don't think I ever thanked you for it,' he admitted awkwardly.

Perhaps he wasn't a man who was used to accepting presents. Probably more used to giving them, Darcy decided.

'You're welcome.' She nodded. 'What made you change your mind about keeping it?' she enquired as she picked up the menu and began looking down the food on offer.

'The fact that you had obviously gone to a lot of trouble to get it for me,' he said quietly.

'I see.'

'Darcy—'

'Have you tried the lasagne here?' She looked over the top of the menu at him. 'I believe it's supposed to be delicious.'

'Darcy, I'm trying to talk to you,' Logan said wearily.

She raised auburn brows. 'I thought you invited me out to lunch?'

'I did,' he returned sharply. 'Because we need to talk.'

'And not eat,' she replied understandingly, closing her menu and putting it down on the table-top. 'Talk away,' she invited.

Logan paused. 'You seem different today somehow,' he said eventually.

'Do I?' she returned in that same brittle voice. 'Perhaps we should put that down to the fact that I'm a little—upset, that my father and I are no longer even speaking to each other because of his decision to marry a woman I can't even begin to like!'

Her voice broke slightly over the last. To her inner annoyance. She was rather tired of appearing immature and emotional in front of this man. In fact, she was more than tired of it!

'It will all sort itself out, Darcy,' Logan told her gently, reaching out to put his hand over one of hers.

She looked across at him with cool grey eyes. 'You seem very sure of that?'

'I am.'

'How can you be?'

His hand squeezed hers slightly. 'Because I—'

'May I take your order now, sir? Madam?' The waiter stood expectantly beside their table.

'No, you—' Logan broke off his angry retort, drawing in a deep, controlling breath, before turning to Darcy. 'Are you ready to order?'

She smiled up at the waiter to make up for Logan's previous terseness. 'Lasagne and a green salad, please,' she ordered—but wasn't absolutely sure she would be around long enough to eat it!

'I'll have the same,' Logan announced.

'Would you like any water with your meal—?'

'No, we wouldn't,' Logan interrupted the man gratingly, glaring up at him with icy blue eyes.

'Thank you.' Darcy smiled up at the young man again, receiving a grateful grin in return before he left in the direction of the kitchen.

Logan removed his hand abruptly from covering hers. 'I realise that until a few hours ago you were a waitress yourself,' he said harshly. 'But do you have to be so friendly with the staff?'

Hurt flared in her eyes at the unwarranted rebuke, making them appear almost silver. 'Good manners cost you nothing, Logan,' she returned briskly. 'Besides, why should I ruin his day, just because mine isn't turning out to be so brilliant?'

'Thanks,' Logan said sarcastically.

Darcy sighed. Why was she even bothering to go through with this? Because she was still angry? Or because she wanted to see just how far Logan was willing to go in this charade? The latter, probably, she acknowledged heavily. But this whole situation was grating on her already frayed emotions.

'Logan, exactly what is it you want from me?' she demanded suddenly, giving up all pretence now of this being a pleasant lunch together. Not that it had ever been that in the first place—on either side!

Logan looked startled by the question, eyeing her warily. 'What do you mean?'

She pursed her lips, her expression scathing. 'Stop treating me like an idiot, Logan,' she bit out disgustedly. 'I mean, what do you, Margaret Fraser's son, want from me?' she challenged, her eyes gleaming silver once again.

She hadn't been able to believe it this morning when, in the heat of their argument, her father had told her exactly who and what Logan McKenzie was, demanding to know what the two of them were plotting together.

At the time, she had even been too numbed by her father's revelation to defend herself properly against those accusations...

Logan McKenzie was the son of that—that woman?

Incredible as it seemed to her, it appeared that was exactly what he was. The actress looked barely in her thirties herself, and yet she had a son aged in his mid-thirties. And her son was Logan McKenzie...

Darcy had thought him so understanding yesterday evening. Hey, she had even thanked him for being so kind to her!

He had kissed her too. Worse, she had kissed him back…!

But she now realised Logan had had his own reasons for being so nice to her, and those reasons involved his mother!

She felt so stupid now when she thought of all she had said to him, all the things she had confided in him.

But most of all, she was angry. Furiously so. Which was the reason she had decided to continue with the arrangement of meeting Logan for lunch today; she wanted the pleasure of telling him to his face exactly what she thought of him!

'Well?' she challenged again at his continued silence, her expression mutinous.

He drew in a ragged breath. 'I'm not sure I know what to say…' he finally admitted.

Darcy bridled. 'An apology might not be amiss! What on earth you hoped to achieve by not telling me the truth from the beginning, I have no idea, but I can assure you that whatever it was you have failed miserably; nothing you could do or say would ever convince me to accept your mother marrying my father!'

She was breathing hard in her agitation, more angry with Logan McKenzie now than she was with her father. At least her father had been honest with her.

Logan frowned darkly. 'Let me assure you, Darcy,' he began, 'I am no more enamoured by the idea of the two of them marrying than you are. Until you told me about their plans, I had no idea it was even a possibility!'

She didn't believe him. He had to be fighting his mother's corner. Besides, if what he claimed were really the case, once he'd become aware of the engagement, aware of her own aversion to the relationship, he had had plenty of opportunity to tell her the truth about his own relationship to Margaret Fraser. If he had wanted to. Which he obviously hadn't.

Although, she did remember he had assured her that he didn't believe any marriage between the older couple would ever take place...

'My father, a mere restaurant owner, isn't good enough for your mother, is that it?' she retorted as the idea suddenly occurred to her, remembering that painting on the wall in Logan's apartment of the castle that was the Scottish family home. The home where Margaret Fraser had probably been brought up.

Logan waved the waiter away impatiently as the young man would have brought their meals to the table. 'Darcy—'

'That is it, isn't it?' she accused incredulously as the idea began to take hold. 'Exactly who do you think you are? More to the point, who do you think your mother is? Because from where I'm standing, she's nothing more than a—'

'Darcy!' Logan's voice was icily cold now, his expression glacial. 'There's nothing you could say about my mother that I haven't already said or thought of her myself. But that doesn't mean I'm willing to sit quietly by while someone else is rude and insulting about her!'

Darcy glared at him. 'In that case, you must spend most of your life getting into fights or arguing with people; I haven't met a single person yet with a nice thing to say about your mother!'

Logan's mouth twisted. 'Except your father, of course.'

'He's just besotted,' she defended. 'Knocked off his feet by the glamour that surrounds her.' She shook her head.

'I just hope he comes to his senses before he does something stupid—like marrying her!'

'Oh, he will,' Logan said grimly.

Darcy's eyes gleamed angrily. 'Because you intend seeing that he does,' she guessed. 'I don't know which one of you I despise more—you or your mother!'

Logan's throat moved convulsively. Whether from anger or some other emotion, Darcy couldn't tell. And she didn't particularly care, either.

'I've had enough of this.' She threw her unused napkin on the table before bending down to pick up her bag. 'Enjoy your meal, Logan—both portions of it!' She stood up to leave.

Logan's hand snaked out and grasped her painfully around the wrist as she would have walked away, looking up at her with darkened blue eyes. 'Darcy, I'm on your side—'

'I don't have a side, Logan,' she assured him contemptuously. 'Thanks to you and your mother, I don't even have a home any more, either!' Her voice broke slightly as she realised the truth of her words.

She mustn't cry. She would not give Logan the satisfaction of seeing her cry again. As far as she was concerned she never wanted to set eyes on Logan, or his mother, ever again!

'Let me go, Logan,' she ordered coldly, looking down to where his fingers encircled the slenderness of her wrist.

'And if I don't?' he challenged softly.

Her eyes returned slowly to the harsh arrogance of his face, her chin rising defiantly. 'Then I'll be forced to kick you in the shin,' she told him with determination.

Darcy watched as some of the harshness left his face, to be replaced by what looked to her suspiciously like amusement. No doubt at what he considered to be the childishness of her claim, she realised.

It was the spur Darcy needed to carry out her threat, lifting her leg back before kicking forward with all the impotent rage that burned inside her, the pointed toe of her shoe making painful contact with Logan's shin bone.

She knew it was painful—because of the way Logan cried out in surprise at the agony shooting up his leg!

But it had the desired effect; he let go of her wrist, to move his hand instinctively to his hurting shin.

'Goodbye, Logan,' Darcy told him with a pert smile of satisfaction, before turning on her heel and walking out through the restaurant, totally unconcerned with the curious looks that were being directed towards her, the confrontation not having passed unnoticed. Which wasn't surprising, when Logan had actually yelled out his pain!

Her feelings of defiant satisfaction lasted until she got outside. They even lasted while she flagged down a taxi and got inside. It was only when the driver asked her where she wanted to go that her feelings of self-satisfied anger deflated.

Because, as of this morning, when she had told her father she was moving out of their home, she had nowhere *to* go...

CHAPTER FIVE

'SHE hates my guts!' Logan informed Fergus, his cousin having arrived at his office a few minutes ago. Logan hadn't returned from the restaurant very long ago himself.

Fergus stayed perfectly relaxed as he sat opposite Logan. 'I see you handled the situation with your usual tact and diplomacy,' he drawled mockingly.

Logan scowled as he remembered Darcy's earlier fury. In truth, he hadn't had a chance to be either tactful or diplomatic—how could he have been when Darcy had already been well aware of exactly who he was when she'd joined him for lunch?

He had thought he'd had time to tell her the truth himself, but it should have occurred to him that her father, or someone else, might just drop that little bit of information into a conversation before the two of them had met today! No wonder Darcy had seemed different when she'd arrived at the restaurant!

He glowered across at Fergus. 'I didn't get a chance to handle anything—her father must have already told her I was Margaret Fraser's son!'

'Poor Logan.' Fergus grinned, shaking his head.

'You don't know the half of it,' he retorted.

'No—but I'm hoping you'll tell me,' his cousin returned expectantly.

Because Logan needed to talk to someone, because, for once, he wasn't sure what to do next, where Darcy was concerned—or if, indeed, he should do anything!—he told Fergus exactly what had transpired at the restaurant earlier.

'And then she kicked me!' he concluded slightly incredulously several minutes later.

Incredulous—because he hadn't really thought she would carry out her threat. One thing he had definitely learned from this third meeting with Darcy—never underestimate her!

Logan was so lost in thought that for a couple of minutes he didn't even notice the twitching of Fergus's mouth, his cousin's Herculean effort not to actually laugh. A fight he finally lost, bursting into loud laughter. At Logan's expense.

'She really kicked you?' Fergus sobered enough to choke out. 'In the middle of the restaurant?'

'Actually it was in the middle of my shin,' Logan replied succinctly. 'And, yes, she kicked me; I have the bruise to prove it!' Once out of the restaurant, sitting alone in the back of the taxi, he had had a chance to look at his leg; a purple bruise was already forming there.

'Can I have a lo— No, perhaps not,' Fergus amended as he saw Logan's mutinous look. 'I think I like the sound of your Darcy,' he murmured appreciatively.

'She isn't *my* Darcy,' Logan rasped, not even sure she would ever talk to him ever again.

Which was a pity. He could still remember how good she had felt in his arms when he'd kissed her the evening before—

Forget it, Logan, he instructed himself sternly. There were too many complications attached to being attracted to Darcy Simon. Complications he intended dealing with at the earliest opportunity.

'So what happens now?' Fergus seemed to guess at least some of his thoughts.

Logan pondered awhile. 'A meeting with my mother,' he bit out with obvious reluctance.

His cousin looked surprised. 'Will that do any good?'

'Probably not,' Logan conceded. 'But it might make me feel better. These are good people she's playing around with.' He paused, then went on, 'Daniel Simon was recently widowed; he doesn't need someone like my mother messing up his life.'

'Hmm.' Fergus looked thoughtful. 'I wonder—' He broke off as the door opened after the briefest of knocks.

Talk of the devil—!

Logan's gaze narrowed as his mother walked unannounced into the room, as beautiful as ever in a fitted black suit and vibrant red blouse.

'Karen told me you were closeted in here with Fergus,' she said, closing the door behind her.

Fergus had stood up at his aunt's entrance, glancing across frowningly at Logan's set expression as he made no effort to do likewise. 'I was just on my way to see Brice.' He moved to kiss Logan's mother lightly on the cheek. 'Bye, Aunt Meg. Logan,' he added evenly.

Logan ignored the warning note in his cousin's voice; he had no intention of pulling any verbal punches where his mother was concerned.

'Do stop scowling, Logan,' his mother snapped impatiently once they were alone, a frown marring the creaminess of her brow. 'I know I don't usually call on you here, but I've come to ask you for advice—'

'Ask *me* for advice?' he said incredulously; this wasn't what he had been expecting at all.

Not that he had expected to see his mother here in the first place; if the two of them ever did meet, it was usually by accident and not design. As in the restaurant yesterday evening…

She gave him an irritated look as she sat down in the chair Fergus had so recently vacated, crossing one shapely knee over the other. 'You seem to be on friendly terms with Darcy—'

'Correction, Mother, I *was* on friendly terms with Darcy,' Logan cut in coldly, having physical evidence to prove that friendship was a thing of the past! 'Before she realised I was your son. Or do I mean before she realised you were my mother? Same thing, I suppose,' he ruminated. 'The end result is that Darcy no longer sees me as a friend.' Or anything else. And it was amazing how much more that pained him than the bruise on his leg!

'I see,' his mother said. 'What am I going to do, Logan?' She gave a confused sigh.

Logan couldn't hide his surprise. This was something new; his mother had never asked for his opinion—on anything!—before...

'About what?' he prompted harshly.

'Darcy, of course,' she returned. 'Do try not to be obtuse, Logan,' she admonished. 'I'm sure you are well aware by now of my engagement to Daniel Simon. Darcy's father.'

'I believe someone did mention it to me, yes,' he drawled.

His mother's eyes flashed deeply blue, two wings of angry colour in her cheeks. 'If you ever showed an interest in me or my life, Logan, then I would have told you myself! But as you don't...' She drew in a ragged breath.

'Last night you gave the impression you had no idea who Darcy was,' Logan said questioningly.

'Well, of course the two of us have never met, but I guessed who she was last night,' his mother retorted. 'I was merely trying to avoid a scene in the restaurant. You see, Darcy doesn't like the idea of her father marrying me—'

'I wonder why.' He couldn't resist his taunting reply.

His mother gave him a considering look. 'You know, Logan, you were a lovely little boy, so loving and caring. What happened to change that?'

Logan could see, by the genuine puzzlement on her face, that she really wanted to know. Incredible!

'Life, Mother,' he bit out economically. 'Yours,' he added hardly as she would have spoken.

She shook her head. 'I can't believe that after all these years—Logan, I know I've made mistakes in the past—'

'Mistakes!' Now he did stand up, moving impatiently to the coffee machine that stood on a sidetable, pouring himself a cup of the dark steaming brew. 'Your life has had all the stability of a helter-skelter! And during the early years, after my father died, when I wasn't old enough to have a say in things, you took me along for the ride!' he concluded disgustedly.

His mother's eyes, as she looked up at him, flooded with sudden tears, and she suddenly looked very tiny, and slightly vulnerable. Strange, he had never seen her in quite that light before...

No! His mother was a consummate actress—she had made a living the last thirty years, both on and off screen, with that acting! He must not be taken in and manipulated by the role she apparently saw herself in now.

'I know I was far from the perfect mother to you, Logan, after your father died,' she began huskily. 'But I just missed him so much—'

'I missed him too,' Logan told her coldly.

'I know,' she acknowledged shakily. 'I do know, Logan,' she insisted as he would have protested. 'But it isn't the same. I had lost the man I loved. *I* was lost, seemed to lose all direction in my life. I—I made a mistake when I married again, I know that,' she admitted. 'But I was lonely, and— There's nothing I can do or say now that will take away the past. It's the future we have to look to now.'

Logan looked down at her. This really was a different role for her. His mother had never spoken to him in this way before, never confided in him in this way. And he wasn't quite sure how to deal with it.

'Whose future are we talking about, Mother?' he queried. 'Yours or mine?'

She looked back up at him, her gaze unwavering. 'I love Daniel Simon,' she told him quietly. 'He's the first and only man I have loved since I lost your father. And I would like to marry him.'

Logan shrugged. 'The last I heard, that's exactly what you intend doing!'

She shook her head. 'Not without Darcy's approval.'

His mouth quirked. 'Again, the last I heard—and she didn't exactly use these words, you understand?—there was about as much chance of Darcy giving her blessing to her father marrying you as there is of hell freezing over!'

'I know,' his mother agreed dully.

Logan gave her a probing look, still unsure of her in this mood. Usually his mother gave the impression she was totally in control of her world, and the people in it. Perhaps that was the trouble this time…?

'Dear, dear, Mother, don't tell me that you aren't more than capable of talking Daniel Simon round to your way of thinking?' he taunted. Goodness knew there were very few men who could resist his mother's brand of charm!

'You just don't understand, do you, Logan?' His mother shook her head sadly as she returned his gaze unblinkingly. 'Daniel is all for going ahead with the marriage, and dealing with Darcy's feelings later; I'm the one who won't go ahead with the wedding without his daughter's approval.

It's no way to begin our married life together, and I will not come between father and daughter.'

Now Logan was really puzzled. Could it be, could it really be, that his mother really did love Daniel Simon, that she was putting someone else's happiness above her own...? It would be the first time!

His mother gave a shy smile at his obviously stunned expression. 'Not exactly the way you see me, is it, Logan?' she ventured ruefully. 'Maybe if we had been closer the last twenty years or so—'

'As you are well aware, Mother, I despised Malcolm Slater, the man you chose to marry after my father died, preferred to live with Grandfather rather than with you and him,' he revealed with distaste.

'I despised Malcolm myself by the time we were divorced,' she admitted.

Logan was surprised. 'You did?'

His mother gave a wistful smile. 'I did. Mainly because I lost my son during the five years we were married. Logan, why do you think I feel so strongly about having Darcy's approval to her father marrying me? It's because I know how it feels to lose your child in those circumstances,' she continued firmly. 'I lost you for that very reason, because of the way you felt about Malcolm,' she said emotionally. 'And although it may be too late to do anything to salvage our own relationship, I won't do that to Daniel and Darcy!'

Logan stared at his mother, wondering, just wondering, if he could have been wrong about her all these years...

She looked at him with unwavering blue eyes. 'I need your help, Logan. I need you to help me persuade Darcy that I really do love her father, that I intend making him happy. Will you help me?'

Would he?

Wasn't his mother, a woman he had kept at an emotional distance for more years than he cared to think about, asking him to take on the role Darcy had already cast him in at lunch-time—that of championing his mother?

Did he really want to champion his mother? Could he believe the things she was saying to him?

More to the point, didn't Darcy already hate him enough…?

'Call for you, Darcy,' her grandmother called up the stairs.

A call for her…?

Who from? Apart from her father, no one else knew she had been staying with her maternal grandmother the last couple of days; and her father only knew because her grandmother had thought she ought to tell him.

Again, it was only a temporary arrangement, Darcy having found an apartment to rent that very afternoon. Unfortunately the current tenant wasn't moving out until next week.

She ran down the stairs to pick up the receiver in the hallway. 'Yes?' she prompted warily.

'Darcy,' Logan McKenzie greeted with satisfaction. 'You're a very difficult young lady to track down.'

Darcy had stiffened as soon as she'd recognised his voice, her hand tightly gripping the receiver. 'Why did you bother?' she returned coldly.

'I thought you might be interested to know that I'm in hospital with a broken shin-bone,' he came back mildly.

'You're what?' she gasped, remembering all too vividly the way she had kicked him on the leg at the restaurant two days ago.

'That got your attention anyway.' He chuckled. 'Actually…' he sobered '…I exaggerated slightly.'

'How slightly?' Darcy ventured warily.

'I'm not in hospital. And my shin-bone isn't broken.'

'In other words, it was a total lie!' Darcy came back disgustedly.

'Fabrication,' he corrected smoothly. 'It isn't nice to call someone a liar, Darcy.'

'Logan,' she sighed wearily, 'what do you want?'

'To have dinner with you this evening,' he returned lightly.

She was taken aback at the unexpected invitation. 'Why?'

'You really are the most suspicious young lady!' he opined dryly. 'Why not?'

The reasons for that were too numerous to go into. And some of them were reasons she couldn't possibly tell Logan! As in, she found him too disturbingly attractive. As in, she dared not run the risk of having him kiss her again. As in—

'Oh, come on, Darcy,' he cajoled at her continued silence. 'It's only dinner.'

Only dinner...

But what were the implications behind the invitation? What was it supposed to achieve? Because she had no doubts that under ordinary circumstances—such as his mother not being about to marry her father!—Logan would never have thought of asking her out to dinner! He must already be aware, she had no influence with her father whatsoever!

'Logan, my father is a grown man, an adult, perfectly capable of making his own choices and decisions without any help from me,' she told him decisively.

'Yes?'

'Yes!'

Was he being deliberately difficult? Didn't he realise

how much it hurt her to be at odds with her father like this?

Apart from picking up her things from the house, telling her father where she was staying for the moment, the two of them hadn't spoken to each other for two days. And this man's mother was responsible for the estrangement between the two of them.

'I don't see what your problem is, Darcy,' Logan told her. 'You've got what you wanted, by fair means or foul, so why—?'

'What do you mean?' she cut in.

'My mother has broken off her engagement to your father,' Logan revealed.

'She's done what?' she gasped, suddenly feeling light-headed, so much so that she sat down abruptly on the chair beside the telephone.

'Yes, it's all off,' Logan told her happily. 'My mother broke the engagement last night.'

'Why?' Darcy breathed dazedly.

'Does it matter?' Logan replied. 'It's what you wanted, isn't it?'

She hadn't wanted her father to marry Margaret Fraser, no, but until she knew the reasons for the broken engagement she could feel no satisfaction in its ending. If the couple had simply decided they had made a mistake after all, that was okay, but if it were for any other reason— such as her own objections to it!—then it wasn't okay at all. If Margaret Fraser had been the one to break the engagement, how must her father feel now?

'I must say,' Logan continued at her silence, 'I expected you to be happier about it than this.'

But how could she be—when she knew her father must be totally miserable?

This was awful. A mess. It was a mess *she* had helped create...!

'Then you thought wrong, Logan,' she responded. 'And if you think I'm going out with you this evening to celebrate—'

'I think celebration is far too strong a description of my invitation,' he returned mildly. 'Admittedly, we can no longer drink a toast to the happy couple, but—'

'How can you be so unfeeling?' she interrupted accusingly. 'I have no idea how your mother feels, but my father is probably devastated, and all you can do is—'

'Now just a minute, Darcy,' he put in impatiently. 'You're the one that wanted an end to this engagement, and now that you have it, you—'

'You wanted it as much as I did,' she defended heatedly. 'You were the one who thought my father wasn't good enough for your mother!'

'I don't think I ever said that—'

'But you thought it!' Darcy persisted. 'And now it seems, no doubt with more than a little help from you, that your mother is of the same opinion. How dare you presume—?'

'Stop right there, Darcy,' Logan told her firmly.

'I most certainly will not,' she retorted angrily. 'You made it perfectly obvious that you were not happy about my father marrying your mother—'

'As obvious as you did that you weren't happy about my mother marrying your father. Now we've both got our wish, so what are you complaining about? You've won, Darcy,' he taunted. 'Defeated the dragon. In fact, she's turned tail and run!'

Except Darcy didn't feel as if she had won anything— she felt terrible! Not that she had changed her opinion about the older woman's unsuitability for her father, she had just realised—with blinding clarity!—that she didn't have the right to decide those things for another person, least of all her father.

'I think you're an unfeeling brute,' she told Logan indignantly.

'Because I won't pretend to be upset about all this?' he scorned.

'Because you're a selfish swine!' she returned forcefully.

'Does that mean you won't be having dinner with me this evening?' he queried wryly.

'Not this evening, or ever!' she cried. 'Now, if you'll excuse me, I have to go out.'

'To see your father?'

'Mind your own damned business!' she shouted, before slamming down the telephone receiver.

He was a brute. An unfeeling swine. Didn't he care that his mother was probably as unhappy at the broken engagement as her father no doubt was? Obviously not. He was just glad his mother's engagement to—in his eyes!—a totally unsuitable man was at an end.

Well, they would see about that!

CHAPTER SIX

LOGAN felt like a murderer returning to the scene of the crime!

Not that Chef Simon, with its warm decor, wonderful smells of cooking food, and efficiently friendly staff, was anything like a scene of carnage and destruction. Logan just felt, as he walked through the restaurant doorway, as if he were entering an arena!

Although, admittedly, it was an arena of his own making!

He had no doubt that Darcy really did hate his guts after their telephone conversation earlier. But he had been the way that he had for a reason.

Except he hadn't been able to resist coming here this evening, if only to see if Darcy had been reunited with her father. Which had, after all—although she would never see it that way—been the purpose of his telephone call to her earlier...

'Good evening, Mr McKenzie,' the *maître d'* greeted him warmly. 'How nice to see you again.'

Coming here to eat twice in one week probably did seem a little excessive, Logan accepted, but his curiosity, he inwardly admitted, had got the better of him.

'James,' he said with a nod, after reading the name on the man's lapel. 'My secretary telephoned earlier and booked a table for me. For one,' he added dryly; this eating alone was becoming a habit!

'She certainly did,' the *maître d'* assured him. 'The same table as before, if that's okay with you?'

Why not? He was no more in the mood for company this evening than he had been three days ago!

'Fine.' He smiled. 'And I'll endeavour to get through the whole evening this time, too,' he quipped.

The other man waved away his words of apology. 'Your cousin explained that you had been called away unexpectedly.'

Thank you, Fergus, Logan thought to himself.

'Is Darcy—Miss Simon in this evening?' he casually asked the *maître d'* once he was seated, a menu placed in front of him.

For a brief moment, the other man's cheerful efficiency deserted him, but it was quickly brought under control, although his smile, when it came, still seemed to Logan to be slightly strained. 'She certainly is, Mr McKenzie,' he confirmed. 'Would you like me to tell her—?'

'No! Er—no,' Logan repeated less harshly. 'I merely wondered if she was here tonight, that's all. Thank you,' he added dismissively.

Darcy was here! Hopefully, everything was all right with her world again.

'Can I get you something to drink, Mr McKenzie?' the *maître d'* offered politely.

'Whisky,' he accepted tersely.

'Water and ice?'

Why didn't the man just go away and leave him alone? Logan complained inwardly.

Because now that he was here, seated at this table, he had realised his tactical error!

He could have telephoned and ascertained whether or not Darcy was here this evening; he hadn't had to subject himself to eating here alone…! To eating here at all!

Not that the food wasn't excellent; he just had to get through the whole evening now, with Darcy only feet away in the kitchen, knowing that she wouldn't even give him the time of day if she knew he was in the restaurant. It was not a feeling Logan was familiar with. In the past, he had always been the one to sever any relationship with a woman he had been involved with.

Except he hadn't been involved with Darcy. Not in that sense, anyway...

So what was he doing here? Damned if he knew!

'No water or ice,' he answered the *maître d'*.

This time Logan made sure he knew exactly what he was ordering: a fish starter, and a steak main course!

He had no doubts, when it arrived, that it was delicious too; he just didn't taste a mouthful of it! So conscious was he of Darcy working in the kitchen only a short distance away, that every time the kitchen door swung open he couldn't stop himself casting a furtive glance in that direction.

This was ridiculous!

Why should he feel so uncomfortable? He hadn't done anything other than tell Darcy what was, after all, the truth. Besides, if she was back working here, she had obviously made amends with her father. She should be thanking him!

Except Logan knew that she wasn't, that she thought him an unfeeling, selfish brute. Or words to that effect. Why was it, he wondered ruefully, that the person in the middle of a situation, once things had calmed down slightly, always ended up as the target for both sides? Because his mother was no more enamoured of him at the moment than Darcy obviously was. She—

'What are you doing here?'

So intent had he been on his own thoughts—the penalty for eating alone?—that Logan hadn't even noticed that Darcy had actually come out of the kitchen, that she had been moving from table to table chatting politely with the diners.

Until, that is, she had obviously spotted him sitting alone at the window table!

Logan placed his knife and fork down on his plate before looking up at her. 'It isn't quite what I had in mind when I invited you out to dinner, but it will have to do,' he admitted.

She was wearing the restaurant uniform of a cream blouse, teamed with a black skirt, her hair once more secured at her nape, her face flushed from her exertions in the kitchen.

Or was it anger at seeing him here?

Probably, he acknowledged self-derisively. Well, if she was surprised to see him here, he had been thrown a little himself by having her suddenly appearing beside his table in this way!

'I hope you aren't about to make another scene in your father's restaurant, Darcy,' he taunted mockingly at her continued silence. 'Two in one week just isn't on, you know,' he went on. 'People will start coming here for the ''cabaret'' rather than the food if that's the case!' He looked up at her with assessing blue eyes.

She drew in a sharp breath, seeming to be having difficulty keeping her temper in check.

But obviously also knowing Logan was right about her not making a scene...!

'No, I'm not about to make a scene,' she finally replied. 'I merely asked what you're doing here,' she repeated in measured tones—although her eyes told a different story, flashing that dangerous silver colour.

'I would imagine the same as everyone else,' he said casually, looking about them pointedly to the tables full of chattering diners. 'Eating!'

Her hands clenched at her sides. 'But why here?' she demanded. 'Or did you simply come to gloat?'

'Smile, Darcy,' he advised softly. 'People are beginning to stare.'

'Let them,' she dismissed hardly. 'Contrary to what you and my father both seem to think, I am not a Cheshire cat who smiles on demand!'

Logan looked at her consideringly. 'I would have said, with that copper-coloured hair, that you resemble a fox rather than a cat—Cheshire, or any other kind!'

'Logan—'

'Well, that's promising, at least,' he drawled. 'I was expecting you to call me something much worse than my first name,' he explained as she frowned questioningly.

And it was promising. After the way their telephone conversation had ended earlier, he had winced at some of the things she might say to him when—or if—they ever met again. Logan was pretty okay in those circumstances!

'Do you have a few minutes?' he requested mildly. 'I thought you might like to join me for a glass of wine,' he explained as her sceptical expression deepened.

'Join you—!' She looked ready to explode, bringing her temper back under control with effort. 'Logan,' she finally said evenly, 'if I pick up a glass of wine I am more likely to tip the contents over your head than I am to drink it!'

This was more like the Darcy he knew and— And what? Logan had no idea what. But he did know his evening had suddenly taken on a sparkle, the very air about them seeming to zing with life. One thing he had found about Darcy: she had never bored him.

Which was extraordinary in itself, because in all of his relationships with women so far, intimate or otherwise, he had invariably found himself bored within a few meetings...

'That would be a waste of a good Borolo.' He picked up his glass and toasted her with it before taking a sip of wine. 'This really is an excellent wine—are you sure you wouldn't like to join me for a glass?' He quirked dark brows.

'Absolutely positive,' Darcy assured him between clenched teeth. 'I have to get back to the kitchen. Thanks to you, and your mother, I am absolutely rushed off my feet this evening!' she muttered grimly.

'Well, I can see that the restaurant is busy,' he murmured with a glance round at the full tables. 'But surely that's what you want, isn't it? I don't see how my mother or I are involved?'

'Really?' The sarcasm unmistakable in her tone, Darcy pulled out a chair to sit opposite him at the table. 'Then I'll explain shall I?' She leaned forward, silver gaze steady on his face. 'You obviously advised your mother that she was making a mistake in marrying my father—'

'I—'

'If you will kindly let me finish?' Darcy carefully enunciated each word.

Perhaps he had better; she looked ready to explode. Teasing apart, he really didn't advise another scene in the restaurant so soon after the last one!

'Thank you,' she accepted scathingly at his nod of agreement. 'On your advice, your mother broke her engagement to my father. My father, in the meantime, has decided that he needs a complete break away from everything. Your mother. Me. The restaurant. Everything,' she repeated emotionally. 'And so—'

'Are you telling me that your father isn't in the kitchen?' Logan cut in softly.

'That's exactly what I'm telling you.' Darcy nodded firmly.

'Then who—?' Logan shook his head, his gaze narrowed. 'Are you also saying you're the one that has been producing all the meals this evening?'

She seemed to bristle at his tone, sitting up straighter in her chair. 'Was there something wrong with your meal?'

'No, not in the least,' he assured her a little amazedly.

In fact, the food had been excellent. He just hadn't realised that Darcy could cook like that, thought when she'd said she helped her father out in the kitchen that she probably peeled the vegetables or something. Although perhaps—he dared a glance at Darcy's set features!—he hadn't better actually say that...

The fact that Daniel Simon wasn't actually in the kitchen this evening also explained the *maître d*'s behaviour earlier. Clearly, although James and the rest of the staff were doing their best to make it appear otherwise—and succeeding too, Logan allowed—all was not right in the Chef Simon kitchen this evening!

'I did tell you I had trained as a cook,' Darcy reminded him stiltedly.

Yes, she had, but he had still thought— 'You're very good,' he complimented. 'I had no idea it wasn't your father in the kitchen producing this mouth-watering food.' His scallops had been wonderful, his steak succulent enough to melt in his mouth.

'That's probably because he helped train me,' she explained tersely.

'He did a good job,' Logan said distractedly. 'But where is he now?'

Darcy sat back, eyes having suddenly darkened to smoky grey, her mouth trembling slightly as she spoke. 'I have no idea,' she told him shakily. 'He didn't tell me. And I didn't like to ask.'

Logan stared at her. Twice he opened his mouth to

speak. And twice he closed it again, without having uttered a word.

Another thing that was unusual about Darcy—she had the power to render him speechless!

Why didn't Logan say something? Anything!

The shock of seeing Logan in the restaurant this evening had quickly been superseded by a desire to tell him—again!—exactly what she thought of him, and what he had done to her family, such as it was. Well, she had done that. Only to have Logan simply stare across at her with those enigmatic blue eyes.

This had been the most awful day. That earlier telephone conversation with Logan. Going to see her father. Only to have him tell her that he just had to get away for a few days, and would she take over the cooking at the restaurant while he was away. In the circumstances, what else could she have said to the latter but yes?

Although she had tried to talk to her father about the situation, sure that going away at this time would solve nothing. But he'd remained adamant that was what he was going to do, and nothing Darcy could say would persuade him otherwise.

And so she had agreed, in his absence, to take over the restaurant. But that didn't mean she was at all happy about this situation.

Or the part Logan McKenzie had played in it!

'Well, why don't you say something?' she finally snapped, the tension becoming unbearable.

Logan grimaced. 'I'm not sure I know what to say.'

'That must be a first!' she scorned.

He looked at her reprovingly. 'Insulting me isn't going to help this situation, Darcy,' he admonished.

'Perhaps not—but it makes me feel better!' she told him forcefully.

'I don't doubt that. But it isn't going to bring your father back. From wherever it is he's gone to lick his wounds.'

'Wounds that your mother inflicted on him!' Darcy accused defensively, her cheeks flushed fiery-red now. 'She's the first woman he's really looked at since my mother died, and she's just thrown his love back in his face as if it meant nothing to her!'

Logan gave her a considering look. 'Shouldn't you have thought of that before you threw your ultimatum at him?'

'I didn't—'

'Giving up your job with him here, moving out of the family home, isn't issuing him with an ultimatum: her or me?' Logan reasoned softly.

The flush in her cheeks faded until they were deathly white, her eyes, a dark smoky grey, the only colour left in her face. 'I merely—merely—' She broke off, her bottom lip trembling so badly she couldn't speak any more. 'If you'll excuse me,' she muttered, before getting up and making her way blindly back to the kitchen, relieved when she heard the door swing shut behind her, tears falling hotly down her cheeks now, waving away the concerned gestures of the other staff working in the kitchen.

But she didn't feel quite so relieved when she felt strong arms move about her, pulling her in to the hardness of what she easily recognised as Logan's chest. He had followed her!

'This is becoming too much of a habit,' he said ruefully a few seconds later as a white handkerchief appeared in front of her face.

Darcy took the handkerchief, her sobs subsiding as she mopped up the tears.

She had tried all evening not to think about her father,

and the reason he had gone away, but when Logan had spoken of it just now she had known he was right. Her father hadn't just gone away to escape from his heartbreak at his broken engagement, he had gone away to get away from her too!

And she had taken the easy option and turned her anger at herself round on Logan…

Okay, so he wasn't exactly in favour of the marriage, either, but Darcy doubted very much that he was in a position to order his mother to break her engagement to Darcy's father. No, Margaret Fraser had made that decision all on her own. Much as she hated to admit it, Darcy's aversion to the marriage might just have had something to do with that decision…

'Darcy—Oops!' One of the waitresses stood awkwardly just inside the kitchen, grimacing slightly as she saw Darcy in Logan's arms, and the way the kitchen staff studiously avoided looking at them. 'I'm sorry for interrupting,' the girl said uncomfortably. 'Table number ten liked your creamed spinach so much they wondered if they could have some more,' she explained.

Logan glared across the room at the poor girl. 'Tell table number ten that—'

'No, it's all right, Logan,' Darcy interrupted his angry reply, pulling out of his arms to turn and smile at the waitress. 'Give me a couple of minutes, okay?' she encouraged before turning back to Logan. 'I really do have to get on with this now. I—'

'I'll go back and finish my meal,' Logan told her. 'Then I'll wait and take you home afterwards,' he stated determinedly.

She had to admit, she didn't exactly relish returning to her father's empty house, having moved back there earlier this evening, deciding it would be fairer to her grandmother, now that she was to take over at the restaurant, if she wasn't arriving back at all hours of the day and night. But the alternative of having Logan accompany her home wasn't exactly appealing either!

'This isn't a subject for negotiation, Darcy,' he told her firmly as he obviously saw the doubt in her expression. 'We still have things we need to talk about.'

She hadn't intended negotiating; she had been going to say a very firm no thank you to his suggestion. But one look at his determinedly set features and she knew she would be wasting her time. And time wasn't something she had to waste this evening!

She nodded. 'I should be finished here by about twelve-thirty.'

'Fine,' he accepted briskly before turning on his heel and returning to the main restaurant.

Darcy drew in a deep breath before turning to smile at the four members of staff who helped out in the kitchen each evening. 'The show's over, folks,' she told them. 'And we have a restaurant to run,' she added.

But she couldn't exactly say her mind was on what she was doing for the rest of the evening, conscious of the fact that Logan was waiting to take her home. Her concentration wasn't helped by the fact that, at eleven o'clock, Logan, his meal obviously over, came through to the kitchen, making himself comfortable on a stool at the back of the room.

Everyone else working in the kitchen had already gone home for the evening by this time, Darcy just dealing with late desserts, doing most of the clearing away herself too.

Logan didn't say a word, but Darcy was conscious the whole time of his brooding presence at the back of the room.

'I shouldn't be much longer,' she told him awkwardly,

just after midnight, the last customers gone from the restaurant now, most of the staff too, just the night's takings to deal with.

'Take your time,' he said. 'I'm not going anywhere.'

Except back to her home with her! To talk, he'd said. But what else did they have to say to each other? She was coming to accept they weren't exactly on different sides in this situation—but they certainly weren't on the same side, either!

Much as she wished she didn't, she still remembered the way he had kissed her three days ago.

More to the point, she remembered the way she had kissed him, too!

CHAPTER SEVEN

LOGAN remained deliberately silent during the drive to Darcy's home, appreciating the fact that she was tired from her hectic evening's work. He also didn't like the fact that she looked so exhausted. In fact, he felt more than a little angry towards her father for leaving her in the lurch in this way. It was his restaurant; he had no right just going off like this and leaving everything to Darcy!

'Can I get you a coffee?' she offered once they had reached her home, switching on the lights as she led the way to the kitchen at the back of the house.

'No, you can't,' Logan answered decisively. 'You can sit there—' he suited his actions to his words, gently pushing her down into one of the pine kitchen chairs that stood around the table '—while I make you a cup of coffee. You've waited on people enough already this evening,' he told her as he began to search through the cupboards for the makings of the coffee. 'I had no idea there was so much hard work involved in running a restaurant,' he admitted, as he put the kettle on to boil.

Darcy gave a strained smile. 'Normally there would be two chefs in the kitchen each evening, but it was David's—the other chef—night off, and—'

'With your father's disappearing trick, you were left to carry the whole load,' Logan finished for her.

'Actually, I was going to say—and I didn't feel it was fair to David to ask him to come in and do an extra evening,' Darcy corrected.

'I don't think it fair of your father to just go away and

leave everything to you like this, either,' Logan told her crossly. 'It's a broken engagement, not the end of the world!' He placed a steaming coffee in front of Darcy before sitting down at the table himself to sip at his own cup.

She looked across at him consideringly for several long seconds. 'Have you ever been in love, Logan?'

He sat back, unable to hide his surprise at the intimacy of her question. No one had ever asked him a question as personal as this before, not even Fergus and Brice, and goodness knew, they were as close to him as two brothers!

'Have you?' he finally came back defensively.

Darcy smiled, a less tired smile this time, the respite from the pressures of cooking, and the warming coffee, obviously reviving her slightly. 'Once,' she said. 'But I don't think it counts.'

Logan didn't agree. What sort of man had she once been in love with? Had he loved her in return? And if so, where was he now?

'I was nine,' Darcy told him with a mischievous smile. 'And he was ten.'

She really was starting to feel better if she could tease him in this way, Logan accepted wryly.

But he wasn't; why had it bothered him so much when he'd thought Darcy had been in love with someone else...?

'An older man,' he returned dryly to cover his own confusion.

'Hmm.' She smiled, sipping her coffee. 'But I don't think it's a legitimate basis from which to judge how my father must be feeling at the moment,' she added with a pained grimace.

She might be right; as Logan had never been in love— even at the age of nine or ten!—he really couldn't say.

Although he was still of the opinion that his mother was no great loss to Daniel Simon's life!

He had listened to what his mother had had to say two days ago, and perhaps he even understood her a little better now, but too much had happened, too much time had passed, for him to be able to trust completely the things she had said to him.

Logan shrugged. 'I'm sure he'll get over it,' he said.

Darcy gave him a troubled look. 'I wish I had your confidence. Perhaps if I spoke to your mother—'

'Whatever for?' he burst in incredulously, putting down his coffee-cup. 'The other evening you couldn't even bear to be in the same restaurant as her!'

Darcy pulled a face. 'But maybe I was wrong about her. I've been giving all of this a lot of thought—with my father the way that he is, I thought I had better! And if *he* loves her—'

'You said yourself that he didn't, that he couldn't know how he felt about her after only three weeks of knowing her,' Logan reminded her. He had known his mother for thirty-five years—and even he wasn't sure that he loved her!

Margaret was his mother, yes, and as such he knew he should respect and protect her, but love…? He wasn't sure.

Darcy gave a heavy sigh. 'I thought this broken engagement was what I wanted, but now that it's happened—I just can't bear to see my father so unhappy!'

'Better a brief unhappiness now than a lifetime of it,' Logan assured her.

Darcy tilted her head to one side as she gave him another of those considering looks. 'You really never have been in love, have you?' she stated evenly.

'I simply doubt that it's a basis from which to build a lifetime relationship,' he dismissed hardly.

Darcy gave a start of incredulity. 'What other basis is there?' she gasped.

'I have no idea—I've yet to see a successful relationship!' Logan claimed scornfully.

His mother said her marriage to his father had been happy, but Logan had been too young himself when his father had died to be able to judge the truth of that statement. And Margaret's second marriage had been like a battlefield.

No, he had decided long ago, if he ever took the drastic step himself of getting married—and he couldn't conceive of a situation where he ever might!—then it most certainly wouldn't be because he believed himself in love with a woman. Love made you vulnerable, left you completely exposed to the whims and fancies of the other person. It was not a feeling Logan ever wanted to experience for himself!

A cloud marred Darcy's creamy brow. 'I find that very sad.'

And she did look sad. So much so that Logan found he didn't like being the cause of that sadness. 'Hey,' he chided teasingly. 'We aren't here to discuss how I see love and marriage. It's your father you're concerned about, remember?'

Not the right thing to say, Logan decided as he saw her sadness deepen. But she had been getting too close, asking him questions he would rather not answer.

'I really would like to talk to your mother,' she decided firmly. 'Do you think it could be arranged?' She looked at him with clear grey eyes.

Not by him it couldn't! His mother was definitely not someone he would like Darcy to meet.

'For what purpose?' he probed guardedly.

Darcy looked perplexed. 'To be honest, I have no idea.

It's strange, but somehow I feel the fact that we both love my father gives us a bond of some kind... Can you understand that?' She looked at him questioningly.

Maybe. But— 'Have you forgotten that my mother has broken her engagement to your father?' he reminded her. 'Hardly the act of a woman in love!'

'But that's the whole point. I need to know *why* she broke their engagement,' Darcy persisted. 'If it had anything to do with me—'

'Even if it did, what can you do about it?' Logan insisted, still not sure himself that he believed his mother when she said she wouldn't marry Daniel Simon, the man she professed to love, if it meant damaging his relationship with his daughter. Because if he believed that, he had to believe her regret concerning their own relationship too. And he wasn't sure he could do that... 'My mother is a woman not easily swayed by the needs and wants of others.' He replied.

Logan didn't like the way Darcy was looking at him now, knowing he must have given away too much of his own resentment and bitterness towards his mother.

But after Margaret Fraser had rung him this morning to inform him she had ended her relationship with Daniel Simon, Logan's one thought had been to let Darcy know it was over, too. Darcy had responded predictably by going straight to her father. Daniel Simon was the one who had altered the scenario by going away in the manner that he had. Now Darcy, after expressing deep loathing for his mother, was asking to meet her. Logan wasn't sure he would ever understand women... Correction—most women, he had found, were all too easy to understand; it was his mother and Darcy who were enigmas!

Darcy continued to look at him determinedly. 'Will you

introduce me to your mother, or do I have to find some other way of meeting her?'

'Why can't you just accept that it's over?' Logan demanded. 'And be grateful that it is!'

'Will you?' she persisted stubbornly, totally ignoring his words.

He stood up abruptly. 'No, I will not!' he roared. 'Why can't you just leave the situation alone? My mother will carry on acting, your father will get over his disappointment, and you—'

'*I* won't rest until I've talked to your mother!' Her eyes flashed up at him.

Logan stared down at her frustratedly for several long seconds. She really was the most stubborn—

As stubborn as he was himself...?

Probably, he acknowledged ruefully, his anger starting to fade. If Darcy really was serious about meeting his mother—and it appeared she definitely was!—then wouldn't it be better if he were present when the two met?

Most definitely!

'Okay,' he conceded frustratedly. 'I'll speak to my mother some time tomorrow and see if she's willing to meet you. Will that satisfy you?' It was as far as he was willing to go, so it had better suit her!

Darcy's answer to that was to smile.

At which point Logan felt that sledgehammer hitting his chest, again totally taking his breath away!

'Thank you, Logan,' Darcy said with warm gratitude before standing up. 'Can I get you some more coffee?' she offered politely.

'Coffee...?' he echoed in what sounded like a strangulated voice.

She turned from filling the kettle, brows arched. 'Unless you have to leave now?'

Normally she was very tired when she returned from working in the restaurant, but tonight she was too hyped after the evening's activities to be able to go straight to bed, and would need a couple of cups of coffee and a short read before feeling she would be able to sleep. But obviously Logan hadn't had the same stimulus.

He did look rather grim, however. No doubt because of her determination to meet his mother. But she couldn't help that, felt it was something she needed to do.

Although, in the last few minutes, she had had to do some revising of her earlier opinions concerning Logan's relationship with his mother. She had assumed Logan didn't want her father to marry his mother because he wasn't good enough for her. Logan's comments since arriving back here implied something else completely; he didn't like his mother. Which to Darcy was awful. How could he not like his own mother? And if Logan didn't like her, what chance did *she* have of doing so...?

'Logan?' she prompted worriedly as he still made no effort to answer her. Just stared at her with those dark blue eyes...

He stepped forward, standing only inches away from her now. 'What the hell is it about you?' he muttered angrily.

Darcy gave him a startled look. 'What?'

Logan shook his head self-disgustedly. 'Every time you smile I want to kiss you.'

Her eyes widened even more, and she was too stunned by the admission to step back as he pulled her effortlessly into his arms, anything she might have wanted to say dying in her throat as Logan's mouth claimed hers.

He might feel an urge to kiss her every time she smiled, but every time he did she melted! Her legs became like jelly, the soft contours of her body melded into his much harder ones, her lips parting invitingly as the kiss deepened.

Her hands moved up to grasp the width of his shoulders. Not that she was in danger of falling; Logan was holding her much too tightly against him for that to happen. She just liked the feel of Logan, the hard strength of his body, the caress of his hands against her.

Hands that moved restlessly across her back, and lower spine, before searching out the soft pertness of her breasts, Darcy gasping low in her throat as he sought and found the hardened tips, the caress of his thumbs sending pleasure coursing through her whole body.

Logan broke the kiss, his lips against her throat now, tongue seeking the hollows at its base as he moved aside the material of her blouse, his breath warm against her breasts.

Darcy was burning, yearning, wanted—she wanted this never to stop!

Logan's lips and tongue touched the creamy softness of her breasts, his hands trembling slightly as they moved to unbutton the front of her blouse, peeling the garment aside once he had done so, the clasp of her bra easily dispensed with too.

There was a slight flush in Logan's cheeks as he looked down at her nakedness. 'You are so beautiful!' he groaned achingly, his hands cupping her breasts as his lips moved down to kiss each rosy tip, his tongue moving moistly against the aching hardness.

Darcy felt weak with desire, her body hot and feverish, trembling so badly now she could barely stand up. She wanted this man. Wanted him naked against her, wanted to feel the hard planes of his body, to caress him as he was her.

But the first feel of her fingers moving against his shirt buttons seemed to break the spell for Logan, one of his hands moving to clasp both of hers even as he moved slightly away from her.

Darcy looked up at him, her eyes dark with passion, questioning why he had stopped her.

'This is not a good idea,' he grated, moving sharply away from her, bending to pick up her blouse, not even looking at her as he held the garment out to her.

Darcy grabbed the blouse, consternation washing over her in embarrassed waves.

What was she *doing*?

With her acquiescence, it had taken Logan exactly—she glanced at the clock on the wall—ten minutes—to have half her clothes off.

What on earth must he think of her? A couple of hours ago she had been hurling verbal abuse at him, and yet just now—just now—Oh, dear!

'I think I had better go.' Logan spoke, his expression weary as he ran a hand through the thick darkness of his hair. 'I—I'm sorry, Darcy,' he added tersely.

He was sorry?

Darcy wasn't sure she would ever be able to look him in the face again! Logan had kissed her as she had never been kissed before, caressed her as she had never been caressed before, touched her as she had never been touched before. He had seen her semi-naked, for goodness' sake!

'I really am sorry, Darcy,' he repeated heavily.

Her blouse was back on, the buttons firmly fastened. After that first glance at the grimness of his expression, Darcy found she couldn't look at him, found herself looking anywhere but at Logan.

'Maybe you should just go,' she suggested, staring unseeingly at the tiled floor.

'Yes.'

But he didn't move. Even though she wasn't looking at him, Darcy could still feel his presence in the kitchen, knew that he hadn't gone.

'Please, Logan!' she finally pleaded, not sure how much longer she could remain standing on her feet.

'Yes,' he repeated evenly. 'I—I'll call you tomorrow. Concerning the meeting with my mother,' he explained as Darcy looked up at him in query.

'Of course,' she realised flatly, turning away again. For a moment she had thought he meant something else!

That he wanted to see her again. That the two of them might be able to—

Fool, she berated herself. She and Logan came from different backgrounds, lived in different worlds, had only been thrown together at all because of her father's relationship with his mother; Logan would never have looked at her twice under normal circumstances.

Although, a little inner voice reminded her, neither of them had known of that connection that time in his office…!

She moistened dry lips. 'It might be better if, in future, I didn't smile at you,' she teased huskily in an effort to lighten the tense atmosphere that now existed between them.

A pretty dismal effort it was too, Darcy acknowledged, but she had to make a start somewhere. After all, this man might—just might, if her father and his mother ever sorted out their differences—one day be her stepbrother. Now there was a sobering thought!

'Yes,' Logan agreed quietly. 'I'll call you as soon as I've spoken to my mother.'

She nodded. 'I shall be at the restaurant from eleven o'clock in the morning, preparing for the lunch-time trade.'

Logan shook his head. 'It really is a hell of a life. At this rate, I'll have to make another booking with the Chef Simon outside catering company just so that I can have a private conversation with you!'

In the circumstances, Darcy thought it was probably better if he didn't; their private conversations had a way of turning into something else completely!

'I'm sure my father won't be away for very long,' she told him noncommittally. 'I'll walk you to the door, shall I?' she added pointedly. She really did need some time alone!

'Let's hope he isn't,' Logan answered her question as they walked out into the hallway. 'You already look exhausted!'

Devastated was probably a more apt description, Darcy acknowledged with a sickening lurch in the pit of her stomach. She was having serious problems coming to terms with what had just happened between the two of them, couldn't quite believe it had happened.

And Logan didn't look much happier!

No doubt he was wondering what on earth had possessed him to kiss her at all, let alone make love to her in the way that he had. Despite what he had said during the heat of their lovemaking, she was not beautiful, and never had been. Although her figure wasn't bad, warm and homely probably best described her looks.

It was her smile that had been his undoing, Logan had claimed in his defence. A claim she had joked about earlier. But in future, all teasing apart, she really would try not to smile at him. Unless she wanted to find herself being well and truly kissed by him!

Logan paused in the open doorway. 'Lock the door behind me when I leave,' he advised. 'I can't say I'm exactly happy at the thought of you alone in this big house all night.'

Well, the obvious alternative wasn't acceptable, either!

'Believe it or not, Logan, and despite what you may have thought to the contrary, because I happen to be staying here with my father at the moment—' she resorted to sarcasm to dispel her feelings of awkwardness '—I've actually been taking care of myself for some time now!'

His gaze was scathing as it moved over her face. 'Then, on the evidence I've seen so far, you aren't doing a very good job at it!' he rasped.

Darcy drew in a sharp breath. 'I'm sure a lot of people are interested in your opinions, Logan—but I don't happen to be one of them!'

'Lock the door anyway, hmm?' was his parting shot before he strode over to unlock his car.

Darcy didn't wait long enough to see him open the car door, let alone start the engine and drive away, slamming the front door behind him, being deliberately noisy as she turned the key in the lock.

She leant weakly back against that closed door. How could she have let that happen? she berated herself with a self-disgusted groan. Not only had Logan kissed her— again!—but he had touched her more intimately than any other man ever had, too.

Every time she thought of those intimacies, Logan's hands and lips on her body, she wanted to crawl into a corner and hide! And she didn't even have the effect of *his* smile to claim in her own defence; Logan rarely smiled, and she didn't think she had seen him laugh once.

Possibly because of that unhappiness she had sensed between him and his mother? She simply didn't know.

Just as she didn't know how on earth she was going to face him again tomorrow, this time possibly in the presence of his mother…!

CHAPTER EIGHT

LOGAN was not looking forward to this meeting. But it had nothing to do with his mother being there—and everything to do with Darcy's presence!

Logan had done as she'd asked, and telephoned his mother this morning—at a time he knew she would be up. After years of working in the theatre, mornings were not Margaret's best times. Except that he knew she was filming for a television series at the moment, so her hours were not quite so antisocial; in fact, she sounded quite cheerful when she took Logan's call.

Logan wished he felt as cheerful. But, after a virtually sleepless night, he was feeling tired and bad-tempered. He had laid awake for hours thinking about Darcy Simon, trying to fathom out why it was she affected him in the way she did. It did not help to improve his temper this morning that he simply hadn't been able to come up with an answer!

Blaming his reaction on a smile just wouldn't do. For goodness' sake, it was only a smile!

Darcy was nothing like the women he was usually attracted to: beautiful, self-confident, emotionally independent women. Darcy was only beautiful when she smiled—and that wasn't too often when around him, thank goodness. Her self-confidence could do with a little working on too. As for her emotional independence—he had lost yet another handkerchief to her tears!

So why was it that he couldn't get her out of his mind, that even last night, when he had gone to the restaurant, it had been in an effort to make sure everything was once again right with her world?

Then to cap it all, he had deliberately set himself up for yet another meeting this week with his mother—for Darcy's sake!

He closed his eyes momentarily. A pint-sized girl, with smoky grey eyes, and hair the colour of a fox's fur in the rain filled his mind; a girl, moreover, who had kicked him in the shin, and threatened to throw a glass of wine over his head! Come to think about it, his personal life had been in an uproar from the moment he'd first met her!

No doubt his secretary, Karen, in light of her view that his life lacked surprise and spontaneity, would consider Darcy's unpredictability to be good for him. She would be wrong! He wasn't at all comfortable with the twists and turns things were taking at the moment.

'You're frowning again, Logan,' his mother remarked at his side as he drove them both to the hotel where they were to meet Darcy for afternoon tea, Logan having picked her up from her apartment ten minutes earlier.

'If I am it's because I do not appreciate being dragged into the complexities of your personal life,' he clipped. After years of avoiding his mother's turbulent private life, he was not amused at being thrust into the centre of it in this way.

His mother shrugged. 'You arranged this meeting, Logan, not I.'

'Because Darcy asked me to, and for no other reason.'

'Hmm,' his mother murmured thoughtfully. 'I may have asked you this before, but—just how well do you know Daniel's daughter?'

He gave her a cold glance. 'I don't,' he snapped—at once assaulted with the memory of Darcy in his arms, of the naked softness of her body.

His mother looked puzzled. 'You told me the other day that the two of you are friends.'

'Were,' he corrected. 'And even then that was probably too strong a description of our relationship. Since you came into the equation, an armed truce is probably a better way of describing how Darcy views things between us.'

'Yet you were the one she asked to set up this meeting between the two of us,' his mother said slowly.

'Only because her father didn't stay around long enough to do it himself!' Logan pointed out.

His mother swallowed hard. 'I hurt Daniel very badly when I broke our engagement.'

'Then why did you do it?' Logan exploded.

'What choice did I have, when you refused to help me?' his mother told him bluntly.

Logan's hands tightly gripped the steering wheel. 'Don't turn this around on me—'

'I'm not, Logan.' She sighed, reaching out to lightly touch his arm. 'I'm just pointing out that I did tell you what I intended doing if Darcy couldn't be talked round. Daniel wasn't willing for me to meet her. And you refused to help me...' She paused. 'There seemed no other way.'

'You could have done what you usually do—blast away and not worry who gets mown down in the process,' he said nastily.

His mother looked at him, with a sad expression. 'One day, Logan, I hope that you and I might be able to sit down and talk over the past like the two adults we now are. I said "one day", Logan,' she inserted firmly as he would have made a deriding reply. 'So,' she asked briskly. 'Daniel tells me that Darcy is a level-headed, kind-hearted young lady; what's your opinion?'

Logan was so taken aback by the unexpectedness of the question that, for a few moments, he wasn't able to formulate an answer. Even when he did, it wasn't an answer he could give to his mother! Because he found Darcy tempestuous, not level-headed, and as for kind-hearted—! Anyway, the state of Darcy's heart, kind or otherwise, was something he didn't want to know about!

'My opinion is that you wait until you meet her and judge for yourself,' he replied noncommittally as he drove down to the basement car park of the hotel.

Maybe having his mother around for this meeting with Darcy wasn't such a bad thing after all, he decided, after taking one look at Darcy as she sat in the hotel lounge waiting for them to arrive.

Why had he never thought her beautiful? Today, in a bright red trouser suit—that should have clashed with that vivid red hair, but somehow didn't—teamed with a black blouse, both fitting the slenderness of her body perfectly, and her hair loose and gleaming down to her shoulders, her eyes huge, lashes thick and long, blusher colouring her cheeks, a bright red gloss on her lips, Darcy was absolutely gorgeous!

In comparison, his mother had played down the dark sensuality of her own beauty, wearing a demure grey skirt suit with a black blouse, even her make-up was less pronounced today; she wore only a light blusher on her cheeks, and a pale peach lip-gloss.

Logan had no doubts that both women had made these changes to their appearance in expectation of meeting the other. His mother he didn't give a care about; she played a role so often it was difficult to know with her what was real and what wasn't. But the effect on Logan of this totally different-looking Darcy was one of stunned silence.

Making him fully aware that it wasn't only her smiles that could render him speechless!

Maybe he could just introduce the two women and make

his excuses? Because he wasn't sure he could actually sit here, with his mother on one side of him, and Darcy on the other, looking the way that she did, and behave normally!

But, the introductions over, instead of making his excuses and leaving, he found himself sitting down with the two women, even agreeing to take tea with them when the waiter came over to take their order!

Will-power, Logan, he told himself disgustedly. Quite—wherever was it?

But he very quickly realised as the two women looked warily at each other that it was going to be up to him to break this initial awkward silence.

'Were you busy at lunch-time today?' he asked Darcy conversationally.

She seemed relieved to speak to him, hardly seeming to be able to even look at Margaret. 'Not too bad.'

Logan wasn't altogether sure he believed her; she still looked very tired to him. 'Have you heard from your father?' he asked.

'No,' she answered flatly, shooting his mother a brief look beneath lowered lashes.

Obviously she was wondering if Margaret had heard from Daniel Simon, Logan realised disgustedly. Well, if Darcy wasn't going to ask her, he was!

He looked at his mother with narrowed eyes. 'What about you?' he pressed.

Margaret Fraser took her time answering, crossing one slender leg over the other, before looking up at him with unemotional blue eyes. 'Logan, I— Ah, tea.' She smiled up at the waiter as he began to place tea things on the table in front of them.

The young waiter—predictably!—couldn't take his eyes off Margaret as he went about his duties, obviously wondering if this really could be the beautiful actress Margaret Fraser, but he was too polite to actually ask.

Logan viewed the young man's reaction with a totally jaundiced eye. He had been seeing this reaction to his mother's looks all his life, had found it to be the height of embarrassment when introducing her to schoolfriends, followed by university friends—the fact that she was old enough to be *their* mother making no difference! Old or young, men were always bowled over by the way his mother looked.

Darcy, he could see, looked slightly green as she also noted the young man's response to Margaret Fraser.

'Shall I pour the tea?' his mother offered lightly once they were alone again.

She could damn well answer his question, was what she could do!

'Go ahead,' he told his mother dryly. 'And while you're at it, tell us whether or not you've heard from Daniel.'

Was it his imagination, or did his mother's grasp of the teapot tremble slightly as he repeated the question...?

If it did, she quickly brought it back under control, graciously leaning forward to hand Darcy her cup of tea. But Logan wasn't fooled for a minute; his mother might be a wonderful actress, but he had known her too long to be taken in!

'Well?' he pressed again once she had given him his own cup of tea.

His mother gave Darcy a small smile. 'He was like this as a child, you know,' she remarked. 'Dogged!' She shook her head. 'He had learnt to walk by the time he was nine months old, could talk by the time—'

'Mother!' Logan interrupted her, heated colour on the hardness of his cheeks. 'I'm sure Darcy has absolutely no interest in hearing when I walked, talked, or, indeed, any of those other normal childhood achievements!'

His mother raised dark brows. 'Is it my imagination or are you a trifle tetchy today, Logan?'

A trifle—! One day he really was going to wring her neck for her! 'No, it isn't your imagination, Mother,' he bit out through gritted teeth. 'As I have already explained to you, I do not appreciate being dragged into this mess!'

'Then, my dear Logan,' his mother returned calmly, putting one slender hand on his arm, 'why don't you just leave Darcy and I to it? I'm sure we both appreciate the fact that you're a busy man. I can easily get a taxi back later. I'm sure we can manage without you—can't we, my dear?' She turned to Darcy.

Logan also turned to Darcy. He was only here because of her, and he didn't appreciate being dismissed by his mother as if he were some errand boy who had completed his job! If Darcy now did the same thing—!

Darcy pulled a face. 'I'm sorry, Logan, I really didn't think... Of course you must go. I'm sure you have other things you need to do.'

'Fine.' He slammed his teacup down on the table before standing up. 'I'll leave, then.' Without waiting for further comment from either of them he turned and strode out of the hotel.

To blazes with the pair of them! He had done as Darcy had asked him, his mother had accepted him accompanying her to the hotel, and now he had been dismissed by both of them!

He was so angry he almost forgot he had driven here, that his car was still parked in the basement of the hotel. Which only served to increase his anger; between the two of them, his mother and Darcy were making a complete mess of his ordered life—and him!

*   *   *

Darcy watched Logan leave with a certain amount of dismay, concerned that he had left in a temper, and not exactly relishing the idea of being alone with his mother, either. But, by the same token, she didn't think the two of them would talk frankly with Logan present, which was something they needed to do.

'I shouldn't worry too much about Logan,' his mother cut gently into her thoughts. 'He has a hot temper—which he hates. Logan likes to be in control, you see,' she explained affectionately. 'But a temper is often something beyond our control. However, as I said, don't worry, his temper is hot, but it quickly goes cold again.'

It seemed quite strange to be sitting here discussing Logan with someone who knew him so intimately; not only did Margaret know when he had walked and talked, she had also been the one to care for his every need as a baby. It was hard to envisage a totally helpless Logan…!

'I'm not worried,' she assured Margaret. 'I'm just a bit sad that he seems to be angry with both of us.'

His mother laughed. 'I'm used to it; Logan has been angry with me most of his life, for one reason or another. But I can see how it would be upsetting for you,' she said almost questioningly.

Because she wondered just how close Darcy and Logan were…?

Darcy wished she knew the answer to that herself. Last night— Better to forget last night, she instantly berated herself. But even today, Logan had telephoned his mother and set up this meeting, as Darcy had asked him to, had driven his mother here. That didn't seem like the actions of a man who was completely indifferent to her.

She had even dressed up today, was wearing more make-up than she usually did, in the hope of showing herself in a different light to Logan. Too often he had seen her as a weeping mess, or hot and tired from working in the kitchen; she had wanted to show him that she wasn't always like that. For all the notice he had taken of her chic appearance today she might as well not have bothered!

Darcy gave a dismissive shrug. 'He's been very kind,' she answered Margaret Fraser noncommittally.

'Hmm, most unLoganlike,' his mother offered thoughtfully. 'Oh, don't misunderstand me, Darcy,' she continued. 'I think my son is a pretty wonderful man: kind, caring, considerate, very much the gentleman. It's just that, usually, he tends to hide it very well.'

Darcy couldn't help it; she smiled. It was such an accurate description of the man she had come to know this last week that she couldn't do anything else. Logan was all of the things his mother said he was, and he really didn't like people to realise that.

'That's better.' Margaret smiled back warmly, leaning forward to pick up the plate of delicacies that had arrived with their tea. 'Have a cake, Darcy,' she invited. 'We can both think about our waistlines tomorrow!'

Margaret Fraser didn't look as if she needed to think about hers at all, slender but shapely. But then, neither did Darcy normally—so she took one of the offered cakes, a nice gooey, chocolatey one.

'We couldn't do this in front of Logan,' Margaret continued before biting into the chocolate éclair she had chosen. 'There's simply no way of eating a fresh-cream cake with any degree of ladylike delicacy!' she said, before dabbing with a napkin to remove some of the excess cream from her mouth. 'I love your father very much, you know, Darcy.'

The remark was so unexpected Darcy almost choked over her second bite of chocolate cake!

They had been talking about waistlines and cakes, for goodness' sake; where had that last remark come from?

She looked across at the older woman, finding Margaret looking straight back at her, her gaze steady and direct, all pretence totally gone as that gaze revealed the full extent of her emotions.

This woman really did love her father...

Darcy swallowed hard before moistening her lips. 'Logan asked you a question before he—left,' she began slowly. 'Do you know where my father is?'

Margaret's gaze didn't waver. 'Yes.'

Darcy's breath left her in a relieved sigh. 'Is he okay?'

Again Margaret met her gaze head on. 'Yes.'

Darcy nodded. 'That's all I need to know.'

Margaret smiled slightly. 'Can you imagine Logan accepting my answers as easily?'

'No,' Darcy answered honestly. 'But then, he doesn't have the same interest in my father's welfare that I do.'

'No.' Logan's mother sighed. 'Logan's interest, unfortunately, is much closer to home. I made a bad second marriage,' Margaret enlarged at Darcy's questioning look.

She frowned. 'I don't think—'

'It's relevant, Darcy,' the older woman told her quietly. 'Logan was eleven when his father died, twelve at the time I remarried—not a good age for any boy to be presented with a stepfather!' She looked sad. 'More to the point, he disliked Malcolm intensely. What I wasn't aware of, for some time, was that the dislike worked both ways. My husband Malcolm, without my knowledge, was an absolute brute to Logan. So much so that when he was fourteen, Logan informed me that he hated my husband, and me, and moved to Scotland to live with his grandfather. It took me several more years of being married to Malcolm before I realised exactly why Logan had gone. By which time our own relationship had been irrevocably damaged. He's never forgiven me,' she concluded sadly.

Darcy really didn't think they should be discussing Logan in this way, and yet a part of her wanted to know, wanted to try and fathom what made Logan the man that he was. The things Margaret had told her already answered some of the questions she had about him. His willingness to help her, for one thing; he obviously knew exactly what she was going through at the thought of her father's second marriage.

Except, because of the little time she had spent talking to her, Darcy didn't think she was going to hate Margaret Fraser...

'He was a child still,' Darcy excused Logan's behaviour.

Margaret shook her head in disagreement. 'Adulthood, unfortunately, hasn't changed our relationship. As far as Logan is concerned, I let him down when he needed his mother the most.' She stared Darcy right in the eye. 'Which is precisely why I won't come between you and your father.'

Darcy had already realised that. But she wasn't the child Logan had been at his mother's remarriage; she was twenty-five years old, far too old to have any say in her father's life any more. Besides, now that her initial shock at the idea had dissipated, maturity meant she simply couldn't be that selfish.

'Daniel told me that, if the two of us ever met in the right circumstances, I would like you,' Margaret said hesitantly. 'He was right.'

Darcy drew in a shaky breath. 'He told me the same thing about you,' she admitted gruffly. 'And, again, he was right. When you next speak to him, would you please tell him—?'

'Why don't you tell him yourself?' Margaret suggested

warmly. 'After he telephoned me yesterday I— It was very difficult when Logan called for me earlier. You see—your father is at my apartment, Darcy,' she admitted awkwardly. 'I couldn't bear it when I knew how deeply upset he was, and so I—'

'It's all right, Margaret,' Darcy cut in happily. And it was—she was just relieved to know where her father was. 'Does he know the two of us are meeting this afternoon?'

'I didn't tell him,' Margaret confirmed. 'He would probably have insisted on coming with me if I had, and— Can you imagine Logan's reaction to that?' she said knowingly.

After witnessing the way he behaved towards his mother, and hearing his anger directed towards her father—yes, she could imagine only too well!

'Do you think my father is likely to suffer a heart attack if I arrive back with you now?' she prompted lightly.

'Probably.' Margaret laughed softly. 'But he'll quickly get over that when—' She broke off.

'When…?' Darcy prompted.

Margaret gave a small smile. 'I was being presumptuous, jumping two steps ahead.'

'Because you believed I would give my blessing on your marriage to my father?' Darcy easily guessed. 'That isn't being presumptuous, Margaret; I should never have objected in the first place. Even if you were absolutely awful—which you aren't,' she added hastily.

'I wish you could convince Logan of that,' Margaret told her almost wistfully.

Logan!

It wasn't just a possibility now that he might be her stepbrother—it was a fact!

How on earth was he going to react to knowing that…?

CHAPTER NINE

LOGAN had no idea what he was doing standing outside the entrance of Chef Simon at eleven-thirty in the morning!

When he'd left his mother and Darcy at the hotel yesterday he had been absolutely furious at what he deemed to be their dismissal of him, had had no intention of talking to either of them again in the near future. But as the hours had passed, and he hadn't heard a word from either of them, that anger had changed to a burning curiosity.

Had the two women ended up hating each other, or had they actually come to some sort of truce? He could perfectly well understand if Darcy disliked his mother, but he would find it most unlikely that his mother could have disliked Darcy; apart from the fact she had kicked him in the shin, and threatened to throw wine over him, she was far too nice for anyone to actually dislike!

Apart from the fact—!

Logan stopped that thought. Knowing Darcy had certainly never been dull.

But if the two women hadn't ended up hating each other, they must have reached some sort of agreement over the situation. And Logan wanted to know exactly what that agreement was.

But he wasn't curious enough to put himself through another meeting with his mother. So he had come to the restaurant at a time when he knew it wasn't actually open, but Darcy would be busy in the kitchen preparing for the lunch-time trade.

He could see someone moving about inside the closed

117

restaurant now, although, with the room still unlit, he couldn't actually see who it was.

Oh, well, faint heart, and all that—

No, that wasn't right, he thought darkly. He wasn't here to win Darcy; he just wanted to know what was going on.

His initial knock on the door heralded no response, and so he knocked louder the second time. This time there was the sound of movement inside, the key turning in the lock seconds later, the bolt shifted back, before the door slowly opened.

'I'm sorry, but we don't open until— You!' Daniel Simon's polite smile faded rapidly as he incredulously recognised Logan.

No more incredulously than Logan recognised the other man. He had been expecting to see Darcy, or maybe one of the waitresses; he certainly hadn't expected to see the owner of the restaurant, Darcy's own father, opening the door!

Logan's mouth twisted mockingly. 'You're back, then,' he said derisively.

Daniel Simon raised blond brows. 'Obviously,' he drawled.

'And not before time,' Logan responded harshly. 'Darcy has been run off her feet in your sudden absence,' he added critically.

Daniel Simon's mouth tightened. 'I believe that is between my daughter and myself.'

'I disagree. You—'

'Logan, exactly what is it you want?' the other man interrupted curtly.

He drew in a sharp breath. The last thing he had expected had been to be confronted by Darcy's father. But, nevertheless, he wasn't about to be put off doing what he had come here to do.

'To speak to Darcy,' he told the older man abruptly.

Daniel Simon nodded, opening the door wider so that Logan could enter the strangely quiet restaurant. 'She's in the kitchen,' he supplied shortly. 'Oh, and Logan...?' he said as Logan strode past him on his way to the kitchen.

Logan stopped, turning slowly. 'Yes?' he replied arrogantly.

The chef's expression had softened. 'Don't do or say anything to upset her, hmm?' he suggested, his tone implying Logan would have him to deal with if he did so.

'*Me* upset her—!' Logan exploded. 'I like that! I don't believe I'm the one who only days ago calmly dropped the bombshell of his remarriage on her over the breakfast table. Neither am I the one—'

'Logan, again, that is between Darcy and myself,' Daniel Simon said sharply. 'But while we're on the subject of your mother—'

'We weren't,' Logan told him flatly, his hands clenched at his sides. He was beginning to wish he had never met any of the Simon family!

The other man wasn't about to be put off. 'Yes, we were,' he insisted firmly. 'And isn't it time you gave her a break? Or do you intend to hold it against her for ever that she made a mistake in her second marriage?'

Logan's mouth thinned angrily; how dared his mother discuss him—and his feelings!—with this man? 'What was it you said to me a few moments ago?' he returned icily. 'I believe that is between my mother and myself!' With one last glaring look at the older man Logan continued on his way to the kitchen.

Darcy was standing with her back towards the door when he entered the kitchen, working at one of the tables in the centre of the room. The door closed with a swishing noise behind him alerting her to the presence of another person.

'Could you bring me some eggs from the fridge?' she asked without turning.

There was a large refrigerator against the wall a short distance from the door and, after a brief look inside, Logan was able to locate a box of a dozen eggs, moving to place them down on the table beside Darcy.

'Thanks. I—' She came to an abrupt halt, having looked up and seen Logan standing beside her. 'I'm sorry, I though you were my father...' She gasped, colour instantly brightening her cheeks.

Logan's expression tightened at the mention of her father. 'Hardly,' he said sardonically. 'When did he get back?'

'Last night,' she answered awkwardly. 'I—do you mind if I carry on preparing this?' She indicated some concoction she was constructing in a saucepan. 'Only we need it for lunch, you see, and—'

'Darcy, you're waffling,' he interrupted, glad to see someone else being disconcerted for a change; he had been taken by surprise so many times the last few days, and it wasn't an emotion he was comfortable with.

'Actually...' she smiled slightly '...it's a lemon meringue pie. Not a waffle,' she explained.

'Very funny,' he returned dryly, leaning back against the table. 'You seem happy today?'

After all, the fact that Daniel Simon was back in his restaurant did not mean that everything was back to normal...

'You've seen my father?' She was busy separating eggs now.

Very efficiently, too, Logan noted. 'He was the one who

let me in,' he explained. 'Is he back for good, or just until you can get someone else in to help you?'

Which didn't fool Darcy for a moment, he could see, as she gave him a knowing sideways glance. But *when* was someone going to tell him exactly what was going on?

Darcy picked up a saucepan and placed it on the hot-plate, deftly adding the ingredients she needed. 'Why don't you just ask what you really want to know?' she mused.

Because, after arriving here and finding Daniel Simon back at the restaurant, Logan wasn't a hundred per cent sure he knew what that was any more!

He gave Darcy a considering look. 'And just what might that be?' A wonderful tangy smell of lemons came from inside the saucepan now as the ingredients heated.

Her mouth quirked. 'Did your mother and I manage to get through tea together yesterday without scratching each other's eyes out!'

'Well—did you?' He leant back against one of the kitchen units, arms folded across his chest as he waited for her answer.

Again Darcy gave him a sideways glance. 'I'm happy to report there are no physical injuries,' she finally answered.

Except to his pride, it seemed; his feelings of being a dismissed servant yesterday, when assured by both women that they could manage without him, had not abated!

He nodded abruptly, that same pride precluding him asking for more information on how that meeting between Darcy and his mother had gone. 'And your father?' he pressed. 'Exactly where did he come from?'

'I didn't ask,' Darcy answered quietly, still busily stirring the contents of the saucepan.

'You didn't—! Whyever not?' Logan exclaimed.

Given the same circumstances, it would have been the first thing he would have wanted to know!

She shrugged. 'Because it's none of my business.' Satisfied with the consistency, she put the hot saucepan on a rack to let the contents cool.

Logan didn't agree with her. But one look at her determinedly set features told him it would be useless to pursue the point; Darcy could be as stubborn as him if the occasion merited it.

He drew in a deep breath. 'Okay,' he said tautly. 'Let's try this from another angle. What—?' He broke off as a buzzer sounded behind him.

'Excuse me for a moment, Logan.' Darcy moved deftly around him to open an oven door and take out a dozen or so individual pastry cases. 'Perfect,' she said with satisfaction after checking the pastry.

Logan frowned as he watched her. 'Are all the desserts made on the premises too?'

'Of course.' Darcy gave him a scandalised look. 'Any chef who has pride in his—or her—work wouldn't dream of serving bought desserts.'

Despite the fact that Darcy had chosen to move to a different career, it was rapidly becoming obvious to Logan that she was actually an excellent cook. Coupled with her immense loyalty and warmth of personality, that meant she was going to make some lucky man a wonderful wife one day—

Where on earth had that come from? What did it matter to him what sort of wife Darcy was or was not going to be?

'Could you just excuse me for a few minutes while I put on the electric beater to whisk up these egg-whites?' Darcy didn't even wait for his answer, pushing the switch, the noisy drone of the beater making it impossible to make further conversation.

Not that Logan particularly minded—he was still stunned by the strange direction his thoughts had just taken!

He had come here today simply to put his mind at rest concerning Darcy's meeting yesterday with his mother. Well, he could see that Darcy looked, and sounded, just fine, so he had no further reason to stay.

Except, she hadn't really told him anything...

'There.' The silence in the kitchen was gratifying as Darcy switched off the beater. 'Now, can I get you a cup of coffee?' she invited lightly. 'I can finish the lemon meringues in a few moments,' she explained easily, smiling at him brightly. 'Oops.' She grimaced as she obviously saw the way his expression tightened. 'I forgot I'm not supposed to smile at you!'

Logan could have kicked himself for so plainly reacting to that smile that Darcy couldn't help but notice it. It was time he got himself out of here. And stayed out!

'I'll pass on the coffee, if you don't mind,' he refused coldly. 'I only wanted to confirm that there were no repercussions from your meeting yesterday.' He moved away from the work unit. And Darcy. 'Everything appears to be back to normal,' he pronounced.

In fact, everything was so normal—Daniel Simon back in his restaurant, father and daughter obviously reconciled—that Logan was decidedly in the way.

How he felt it!

Darcy looked at him with dismay now. Without Logan's help in meeting his mother—albeit reluctantly!—the situation between her father and herself could still be termed as one of armed warfare. The least she owed Logan was a cup of coffee. At most, she probably owed him an explanation of exactly what had taken place yesterday after his departure from the hotel. In fact, it would probably be better—for everyone!—if she were the one to tell him that!

'Please stay for coffee, Logan,' she pressed. 'It's already made, I only have to pour it.' She indicated the perculator of coffee being kept hot on one of the worktops.

As she watched him, it was obvious Logan was having an inner battle with himself. No doubt a part of him was still angry with both Darcy and his mother. But the other part of him, the part that had compelled him to come here at all today, really wanted to know what was going on. As his mother had already stated, Logan was not a man who felt comfortable when he wasn't one hundred per cent in charge of a situation, and this one was well out of his hands. More so than he could even imagine!

'Okay. Coffee,' he finally agreed tersely. 'But I can't stay long,' he stated determinedly as she moved to pour the steaming brew into two mugs. 'I have a luncheon appointment at one o'clock.'

In other words, get on with it, Darcy, because I've already wasted enough of my precious time on this ridiculous situation!

Which was probably fair enough, she conceded ruefully. But another part of her couldn't help wondering who his luncheon appointment was with. It wasn't one of the business lunches he occasionally held at his office; she would have seen the booking for that. Which suggested it wasn't a business lunch at all...

So could his one o'clock appointment be with a woman?

After all, Logan might have kissed her—more than once—but those occasions had been spur-of-the-moment things and not the culmination of having spent an evening together. Which meant there might already be a woman in Logan's life...

Somehow Darcy found the thought of that an unpleasant one. As were her thoughts of Logan dining with another woman. Logan spending time with another woman. Logan kissing another woman. Logan in bed with another woman...!

That last vision made her feel physically sick!

Indeed, she was so shaken by it, she had to put the mugs of coffee back on the work surface, her hands shaking so much she was in danger of spilling the hot liquid all over the floor if she attempted to carry them over to the table where Logan sat waiting for her.

When had it happened?

Why had it happened?

Because she had just made the earth-shattering discovery—for her!—that she was in love with Logan McKenzie. The very last man she should ever have fallen in love with...!

What had she once so scathingly said to Logan concerning her father's feelings for Margaret Fraser? How can anyone possibly fall in love in just three weeks; she seemed to have done the same thing herself where Logan was concerned, in only a few days!

Oh, dear, he must never know of it, never even begin to guess how stupid she had be—

'I thought you said this wasn't going to take long?' Logan snarled now at her delay in producing the offered coffee.

Darcy drew in a deep controlling breath before picking up the coffee-mugs and walking over to the table. After all, she might have just made a discovery that was in danger of rocking her whole world, but Logan wasn't aware of it. And he must never be!

She simply couldn't bear it if Logan were ever to realise how she felt about him. From what she already knew of Logan, and his feelings regarding love, he was likely to run a mile if he even half guessed that she was in love with him. In the circumstances, that just wasn't possible...!

'Biscuit?' she offered, not quite able to look at him yet, suddenly shy in the realisation that if she never saw this man again she would be absolutely devastated.

Although again, in the circumstances, that wasn't very likely, either. But to watch him through the years, perhaps even witness him making one of those loveless marriages he had talked about, was surely going to be even more painful than never seeing him again?

Darcy sat down abruptly at the table opposite him. How could she have been so stupid as to fall in love with Logan, of all people?

'Apparently not,' he dryly refused her offer of a biscuit, his gaze mocking now. 'So, what did you think of my mother?'

Attack always seemed to be Logan's own form of defence; perhaps it would be as well if she were to adopt that attitude herself towards him in future.

She straightened, looking unflinchingly into the mockery of those deep blue eyes. 'I thought she was gracious, charming, obviously very beautiful—'

'Let's forget the general—totally unknowledgeable— consensus, shall we?' Logan interrupted harshly. 'What did you think of her?' His gaze was narrowed now.

Darcy hesitated. 'You aren't going to like this...'

His mouth twisted. 'She took you in!' he realised scornfully. 'She gave you the forlorn, poor misunderstood woman act, and you fell for it!' he exclaimed with a disgusted shake of his head.

Darcy bit back her own angry retort with effort. The

two of them ending up in a slanging match, over something of which they had absolutely no control, was ridiculous.

'Not completely,' she assured Logan.

The two women might have eaten cream cakes together like giggling schoolgirls, Darcy might have accepted that Margaret Fraser did genuinely love Darcy's father, but that did not mean she wasn't quite capable of knowing the other woman had her faults, that she was far from perfect. Or did he think that, as his mother, Margaret Fraser should be? It wasn't a very realistic view if he did believe that. Even Darcy, who absolutely worshipped her father, didn't expect him to be infallible.

Logan gave an impatient shake of his head. 'I can't believe you let her fool you,' he said almost angrily.

Darcy leaned forward over the table. 'Logan, what I did or didn't think of your mother is not important,' she told him softly. 'It isn't my opinion that counts,' she reasoned, having come to that conclusion all too painfully herself over the last few days.

He didn't look convinced. 'Don't tell me, your father, even though she's broken their engagement, still thinks she's wonderful!'

'My father,' she began slowly, 'is far from the stupid man you take him to be.' And far from the besotted widower she had believed him to be, too!

She and her father had talked long into the night after Darcy had accompanied Margaret Fraser back to her apartment, and Darcy was utterly sure now that he knew exactly what he was doing, that he loved the other woman in spite of her faults. As the actress obviously loved him in return.

She moistened dry lips, swallowing hard before she began speaking, aware even now that, at almost twelve o'clock, her father should really have returned to the kitchen by now, that he was deliberately allowing her this time alone with Logan. 'Logan, the engagement is very much back on,' she informed him gently. 'In fact, the two of them are going to be married—'

'You can't be serious!' he cut in incredulously.

'Perfectly,' Darcy affirmed.

He gave a disgusted snort. 'That is not a word I ever associate with my mother!'

Darcy sighed, wishing there were some way she could help alleviate the pain he had known in the past that had caused him to feel this way about his mother. But at the same time knowing, as Margaret Fraser did herself, that until Logan was receptive to what she wanted to say to him concerning the past, that she, and Darcy, would be wasting their breath.

'Nevertheless, the two of them are going to be married,' she continued determinedly.

His gaze was glacial now. 'I hope you aren't expecting me to offer them my congratulations?'

She shook her head sadly. 'I think that might be expecting a bit much,' she conceded.

'But no doubt you've given them yours',' he guessed. 'And—don't tell me—you're going to be a bridesmaid!' he scorned.

Darcy drew in a quick breath. 'Logan, has no one ever told you that bitterness is simply a form of self-destruction? That—'

'I believe I have already made my views on your amateur psychology more than plain,' he cut in coldly.

'Oh, yes, Logan, you can be assured you've made your views on several subjects more than plain!' She was becoming angry herself now. 'But it just so happens you aren't a primary player in this particular situation. As I'm not.' Something she had learnt all too painfully over the last couple of days! 'So, like mine, your opinion is not of particular importance to either your mother or my father.'

'In other words, our parents are going to marry each other, with or without our blessing,' Logan acknowledged hardly.

Darcy nodded. 'But they would obviously rather it was with.' She looked at Logan expectantly.

He remained impassive. 'You might feel prepared to play happy families, Darcy,' he told her. 'But I am not.'

She looked across at him with narrowed eyes, her frustration with this situation rapidly rising. 'Meaning?'

'Meaning they will have to get married without my blessing. In fact, as I have no intention of attending the wedding, they will have to get married without my being present at all!'

He was so obstinate, so stubborn, so uncompromising! What was it really going to cost him to be present at his own mother's wedding? Nothing as far as she could see. Unless he considered his own personal pride more important than wishing the older couple well?

Nevertheless, she tried one last time to reach him. 'Logan, you're being unreasonable—'

The loud slamming down of his empty mug interrupted her, Logan's own expression one of fury now. 'I don't see what's in the least unreasonable about it. I certainly wasn't present at my mother's first wedding—'

'You weren't even born!' At least, she presumed he wasn't...?

'Correct,' he confirmed icily. 'But I was very much alive when her second marriage took place, and, as she and Malcolm sneaked off to be married and told the family about it afterwards, I didn't attend that one either. I see absolutely no reason to break the habit of a lifetime!'

Darcy stood up, two spots of angry colour in her otherwise pale cheeks. 'You're not twelve years old now, Logan.'

He remained in his seat. 'No matter how old I was, my answer would still be the same.'

Darcy breathed hard in her frustrated anger towards this man. 'Logan, Meg and my father have asked me to be one of their witnesses at the wedding—'

'How nice for you!'

'They would like it very much if you would agree to be the other one!' she burst out.

'In their dreams!' Logan remained unmoved.

'I—you—'

Logan leant back in his chair, a half-smile curving his lips. 'So now you can report back to both of them that their little ploy in getting you to be the one to ask me didn't work,' he told her contemptuously.

Darcy saw red at that. Neither her father nor Margaret Fraser had so much as suggested she should do that—she had done it because she'd thought Logan might have been less insulting in his answer to her than he would either of them. She had been wrong!

'You are the most unforgiving, pigheaded man I have ever had the misfortune to meet!' Her voice shook with rage, her hands clenched into fists at her sides.

Again, Logan looked unmoved by her outburst. 'And you, my dear Darcy, are the most naively gullible young lady *I* have ever met,' he returned with insulting coolness.

She didn't think, didn't reason, reacted purely on instinct, which told her to pick up the bowl of recently whisked egg-whites—and put it over the top of Logan's head!

Then, as he slowly removed the bowl and placed it carefully back on the table-top, the fluffy egg-whites slowly congealing on his hair and face, Logan's expression through the gooey mess one of stunned surprise, Darcy could only stare at him in horror for what she had just done.

She had done some terrible things to him in the short time she had known him, but Logan was never going to forgive her for this one.

Never!

CHAPTER TEN

'WILL you just get a grip, Fergus? It wasn't in the least bit funny!' Logan glared across the restaurant table—not Chef Simon!—at his cousin, as the other man seemed incapable of stopping his laughter.

'I'm sorry!' Fergus finally gasped. 'I can't help it! I just—my goodness, I bet you looked a sight with all that uncooked egg-white all over you!' Fergus went off into paroxysms of laughter once again.

Logan continued to scowl at the other man. Maybe one day he might be able to see the funny side of this himself—although he wouldn't count on it! But at this particular moment, only an hour or so after it had happened, he still didn't find it in the least funny.

He had stared up at Darcy in complete disbelief at the time, sure he'd been in the middle of one of those unbelievable nightmares one sometimes had. But the slow descent of the gooey white mess down his face had given instant lie to that hope; there was no way he could ever have imagined the cold stickiness of those egg-whites against his skin and hair!

Darcy had looked stunned herself at what she had done, staring down at him in horror. As well she might have done!

Logan wasn't a hundred per cent certain what his immediate intention had been—probably he had been about to wring her pretty little neck! But before he'd been able to do that, he'd heard the kitchen door swing open behind them.

132

'I thought I heard raised voices—good grief!' Daniel Simon gasped as he took in the scene, his gaze disbelieving on Logan's dishevelled appearance. 'What on earth happened?' He looked appalled as he moved further into the room.

Logan turned to the other man with glacial eyes, knowing how utterly ridiculous he must look. And exactly who was responsible for that? 'Your daughter has been proving to me yet again the danger of antagonising an unpredictable redhead,' he drawled hardly, his glacial gaze now taking in Darcy too.

She swallowed hard. 'I just—'

'Save it,' Logan rasped, standing up abruptly. 'It's time I was leaving, anyway—way past!' he added curtly, moving to pick up one of the towels from the rack, wiping off the excess egg-whites before looking straight at Daniel Simon. 'I would appreciate it if you could inform my mother there will be no necessity to send me an invitation to the wedding.'

The older man eyed him warily. 'You'll attend as one of our witnesses?'

Logan gave a scathing snort before throwing down the towel he had been using. 'I won't be attending at all. As I'm sure Darcy will be only too happy to explain to you once I've gone!' He strode forcefully towards the door. 'Besides, going on past—and present!—history,' he stormed, 'Darcy is likely to do something even more outrageous if we meet at the wedding—like stabbing me with a knife at the reception!'

'Logan!'

He turned slowly at the sound of Darcy's anguished cry. 'Yes?' he prompted icily.

She gave a self-conscious grimace. 'I'm sorry.'

'So am I,' Logan returned. 'So am I!' he repeated with pointed feeling.

She didn't try and stop him a second time, for which he was very grateful. Logan just wanted to get home now, before anyone else saw him, and shower off all trace of this sticky mess.

Before meeting Fergus for their one o'clock luncheon appointment.

Unfortunately, he had still been so angry when he'd got to the luncheon restaurant that the events of the morning had just come tumbling out as the two men ate their meal. But far from sympathising with him, Fergus obviously found the whole thing hilarious!

'Oh, come on, Logan, lighten up,' Fergus sobered enough to advise. 'If it had happened to someone else you would be laughing about it too,' he reasoned.

'But it didn't happen to someone else,' Logan grated, still not in a mood to be reasoned with. Darcy Simon had humiliated him for the last time!

His cousin shook his head, still smiling. 'I have to say I wasn't particularly impressed when I met Darcy the other evening. She looked a plain little thing to me,' he opined as Logan looked across at him, brows raised questioningly. 'But further acquaintance might be interesting; there's obviously a lot more to Darcy than initially meets the eye!'

Logan had thought Darcy plain to look at too when he'd first met her, but somehow he did not appreciate hearing his cousin say it. Besides, he didn't see her like that any more; Darcy's inner beauty shone out of those candid grey eyes, and when she smiled—!

Logan shrugged dismissively. 'I'm sure the two of you will have a chance to meet at my mother's wedding.' Although he couldn't say he was exactly enamoured of the idea of his charming, good-looking cousin becoming further acquainted with Darcy... 'I have no doubt you will receive an invitation to the wedding!' he said sarcastically.

He had no doubt that his only other male cousin, Brice, would receive an invitation too. And Brice was even more rakishly attractive than Fergus!

Damn!

Just the thought of the expletive he had first heard Darcy mutter brought the woman herself vividly to mind. As he had last seen her. A look of utter misery on her face, those deep grey eyes dark with despair at what she had just done.

Whereas, in all honesty, Logan couldn't have blamed her if she had laughed at his discomfort, as Fergus was doing now; he must have looked a sight, with that egg-white all over him. In fact, now that he could begin to think about it objectively, the whole situation had bordered on the farcical.

'That's better.' Fergus nodded his approval as Logan began to grin. 'I knew your sense of humour would kick in eventually.'

Logan's smile was rueful. 'What do you do with a woman like Darcy?' he mused.

'I have to admit I've never met one like her,' Fergus agreed. 'She sounds like a one-off to me,' he said admiringly.

Unique, Logan admitted slowly. Totally, outrageously, adorably unique.

'I think you *should* go to the wedding, Logan,' Fergus told him. 'If only to provide the other guests with a side-show they'll never forget!' he added mischievously.

Logan was coming to the same conclusion himself concerning attending the wedding—but not for the reason Fergus stated! He simply didn't like the idea of Brice and Fergus being anywhere near the emotionally vulnerable—or did he mean volatile?—Darcy. The two men were complete charmers, and, once Fergus had informed Brice of Darcy's antics where Logan was concerned, he had no doubt Brice would want to meet her too. Darcy needed protecting from herself!

At least, that was what he told himself as he drove back to his office a couple of hours later, seriously thinking of reconsidering his refusal to be a witness at the wedding. Not that his motives were exactly honourable; they had absolutely nothing to do with his mother's feelings. He simply didn't feel he could leave Darcy to the mercy of the lethal charm of his two cousins.

'Darcy Simon called three times while you were out,' Karen informed him as he entered her office that adjoined his own.

Logan came to an abrupt halt, turning slowly. 'On the telephone?' he prompted casually.

Karen gave him a quizzical look. 'Well, of course on the telephone, Logan; how else could she have called?'

After this morning, he wouldn't put anything past that particular young lady! 'You might be surprised at what Darcy can do,' he drawled. 'So Darcy telephoned?'

'Three times,' Karen confirmed.

'And?' he pressed impatiently when she didn't enlarge on the subject.

'And nothing,' Karen replied. 'The first two calls she just asked to speak to you, ringing off without leaving her name when I told her you were out to lunch. I realised it was the same caller when the third call came in only ten minutes or so ago, and this time I did get her to leave her name.'

Logan frowned. 'Does she want me to call her back?'

'She didn't say,' Karen responded. 'But she sounded a bit—distracted, I thought,' she added helpfully.

'If she calls again, put her through, hmm?' Logan instructed before going through to his own office.

So Darcy had telephoned him three times in the last three hours? No doubt to apologise once again. Well, she could stew on her apology for a bit longer; he had no intention of putting her out of her misery by returning her calls!

Logan had told Darcy his luncheon appointment had been for one o'clock, and at almost four o'clock, the time of her last call, he still hadn't returned to his office. No doubt her earlier suspicion that it wasn't a business luncheon had been a correct one; Logan had probably been meeting the current woman in his life.

Oh, she felt miserable, Darcy acknowledged at just after five o'clock as she cleared away in the kitchen following lunch. Things had been bad enough before between herself and Logan, but she was sure he was never going to forgive her for tipping egg-white all over him.

What on earth had possessed her to do such a thing?

She had asked herself that question a dozen or more times since Logan had left earlier, and she still didn't have an acceptable answer. It simply wasn't good enough that she had been so angry with his pigheaded stubbornness concerning attending their parents' wedding that she hadn't been able to even think straight, had only been able to act. She had no doubt it wasn't an excuse Logan would accept either...!

She had no idea what she was going to say to him when she saw him again, she only knew that she had to apologise to him properly for what she had done to him earlier. Whether or not he would accept that apology was another matter!

What a family they were going to make: mother and son

barely talking, stepson and stepfather not particularly on friendly terms either, and as for stepbrother and stepsister—! What a way for their parents to start a marriage!

'I can't ask whether or not you have a home to go to,' her father teased as he strolled back into the kitchen after checking that the dining-room was ready for this evening, 'because I know you do!'

Of course she did, she just didn't feel like going back there at the moment. Maybe Logan would return her telephone calls once he returned to his office, and if she went home she would miss him. Or maybe he would come back here himself—

And maybe pigs might fly, she told herself with a self-disgusted shake of her head.

'Just forget about it, Darcy,' her father advised after watching the different emotions flickering across the openness of her expression.

She grimaced. 'Do you think Logan has forgotten about it?' she asked miserably.

Her father smiled. 'I doubt that young man ever forgets anything,' he said with feeling. 'Look how long he's kept up his grudge against Meg.'

Logan's feelings over that situation weren't exactly a grudge, Darcy knew. He had been a young boy of twelve when his mother had remarried, an age when he'd been on the very brink of manhood, a time when he had needed his mother's love and understanding. Instead he had been given a stepfather whom he'd hated, and who had loathed him. Given his young age, the resentment Logan felt towards his mother for ever putting him in that position was perfectly understandable.

'I don't think that's quite the same thing, Daddy,' Darcy told her father firmly. 'Admittedly, it was a long time ago, but it's no less painful to Logan for all that.'

Her father raised his hands in a conciliatory gesture. 'Margaret is going to be very upset once she knows he isn't going to attend the wedding. In fact,' he said worriedly, 'she may even decide to call the whole thing off until he will agree to attend.'

Margaret Fraser was perfectly capable of doing that, Darcy knew; the other woman's own love for her son had never changed, no matter how cutting Logan might have been to her over the years. But Darcy also knew that her father couldn't bear that uncertainty a second time where the woman he loved was concerned.

It had been a painful thing for Darcy to realise that her father had fallen in love with another woman only a year after her mother had died, but she had accepted it now, and she was well aware of how much her father loved Meg and needed her as his wife.

Her father was looking thoughtful. 'Maybe Margaret doesn't have to know,' he muttered. 'You and Logan appear to have become friends, so perhaps you could try talking to him again once—'

'Oh, please, Daddy,' Darcy protested. 'Would you still have friendly feelings towards someone who had tipped egg-white all over your head?'

And cried all over him. Three times. Kicked him in the shin. Once. And threatened to throw wine all over him! Again, once...

Her father shrugged. 'That depends on what the provocation had been. In your case, I believe it was quite severe. It would also depend on whether or not I had a sense of humour,' he added critically. 'You're probably right,' he instantly conceded heavily. 'I haven't seen any evidence of a sense of humour in that particular young man, let alone the ability to laugh at himself!'

'The restaurant door was unlocked, so I let myself in,'

the young man in question drawled as he strolled arrogantly into the kitchen. 'I believe you were discussing the
merits—or otherwise—of my sense of humour...?' Logan
said in a dangerously soft voice, looking from one to the
other of them, dark brows raised challengingly.

Was that a pig she had just seen fly past the window?

She might just as well have; the thing she had thought
would never happen, Logan once again seeking her out,
had actually happened—but it couldn't have been at a
more inopportune moment. It took only one glance at
Logan's coldly set features to know that he did not appreciate walking in here to hear himself being discussed between Darcy and her father in this way. In fact, it felt as
if he were emitting shards of ice from the coldness of those
deep blue eyes!

'Lack of it is a better description,' Darcy's father was
the one to scathingly answer the young man. 'It's going
to break your mother's heart when she knows you won't
attend the wedding.'

Logan's mouth twisted. 'You have to be in possession
of a heart in the first place for it to be able to break!'

'No, Daddy!' Darcy just had time to shout before her
father made a lunge at the younger man, moving quickly
to put a restraining hand on his arm before he could actually reach Logan.

Logan, who had remained completely unmoving as the
older man had lunged at him!

Maybe he just didn't believe her father would really
have hit him? Although, after her own behaviour, he
should have known better! Darcy had certainly believed
her father was going to strike the younger man.

Logan eyed Daniel Simon coldly now. 'It's easy to see
where Darcy gets her hot temper,' he said.

'Verbally reasoning with you doesn't seem to make any impression,' her father retorted angrily.

Logan shook his head. 'At least Darcy doesn't leave her marks on me where they can be seen,' he murmured dryly. 'And I very much doubt my mother would appreciate it if one, or both, of us were to arrive at the wedding with a black eye!' he taunted the older man.

Darcy was too busy still reeling at Logan's remark about leaving her marks on him where they couldn't be seen to be able to take in the rest of what he had just said, deliberately not looking at her father as she sensed his sharp interest at the other man's remark. Damn Logan, he made it sound as if she—as if the two of them—

'Do I take it from that remark,' her father began slowly—disbelievingly, 'that you have reconsidered your previous decision not to be present at the wedding...?'

It did sound as if Logan might have done exactly that, Darcy also realised dazedly. Unbelievable as that might seem!

Logan gave an abrupt inclination of his head. 'After further thought, I have decided it would be churlish not to be your second witness,' he bit out with economic harshness.

Darcy's hand slowly dropped from her father's arm as she turned fully to look at Logan. Had he had further thought, or had the woman he'd had his over-three-hour lunch with pointed out—in a less dramatic way than Darcy had earlier—that she thought he ought to reconsider his decision, and attend his own mother's wedding? Somehow Darcy thought the latter was probably nearer the truth. And the realisation, in view of her own recently realised feelings towards Logan, that some other woman had this much influence on him made her feel thoroughly depressed!

'Well?' He was eyeing her closely now.

Darcy stiffened defensively, her own emotions making her far too vulnerable where this man was concerned. 'Well, what?' she challenged. 'Are you expecting congratulations for doing what you should have done in the first place? Because if you are—'

'Darcy!' her father cut in sharply, warningly. 'I think this is very decent of you, Logan.' He held his hand out to the younger man.

Logan shook that hand briefly. 'Just be happy, hmm,' he said gruffly.

'Oh, we will,' Daniel assured him with certainty. 'If the two of you will excuse me, I think I'll just go and tell Meg the good news.'

Neither Darcy nor Logan attempted to stop him. Logan, no doubt because, having made his decision, it was no longer of interest to him what Daniel did about it. And Darcy because—because she was still smarting from the knowledge that there was a woman in Logan's life somewhere who had this much influence over him!

'Well?' he prompted again once they were alone together in the kitchen.

What did he want—a medal? Just for agreeing to do what he shouldn't have refused in the first place? If he did, he was going to be out of luck! She—

'You telephoned my office earlier, Darcy,' he continued softly, his gaze searching on the paleness of her face. 'Three times, I believe,' he added as she made no response.

She had totally forgotten those three telephone calls during the last few amazing minutes! And in light of the fact that there was obviously a woman of importance already in his life, she now felt rather foolish for having made those calls at all. It looked as if she were chasing after him!

She shrugged. 'I just wanted to apologise.'

'Again?'

Darcy looked sheepish. 'You didn't seem very receptive to the one I made earlier.'

He gave a smile. 'My ears were still full of egg-white!'

She winced at this reminder of her earlier behaviour. She just didn't know what came over her whenever Logan was around; she had certainly never behaved in this outrageous way with anyone else!

Had he told his lady-friend about her? About the awful things she had done to him since they'd first met? Oh, goodness, she hoped not! She was miserable enough already at the discovery that Logan obviously already had a romance in his life, without imagining him laughing at her antics as he related her outrageous behaviour to his girlfriend.

'How did lunch go?' Logan enquired. 'I trust the lemon meringues were a popular dessert?'

She nodded awkwardly. 'Once I had whisked up some more egg-whites to make the meringue.'

Logan laughed. 'Well, I hardly thought you were going to scrape up the remains of the first lot and use that!'

She managed a faint smile. 'There wasn't enough of it left to do that!'

He looked about them pointedly at the otherwise deserted restaurant. 'Have you finished here for now? Can I offer you a lift home?'

A lift home didn't in any way cover what she wanted from Logan!

But those wants, she knew, were going to remain unfulfilled. She hadn't stood much of a chance with Logan before, but now that she knew there was someone else in his life—someone he obviously cared about enough to actually listen to!—she knew she was completely wasting her time loving Logan.

She just wished she could convince her aching heart of that!

She sighed. 'No, I don't think so, thank you, Logan,' she refused. 'It's been a long day already, I think I could do with a walk in the fresh air.'

He gave her a searching look, his own expression unreadable. 'Sure?'

She wasn't sure about anything any more—except that she loved this man!

'Sure,' she confirmed huskily, unable to meet that searching gaze. 'I—thank you for changing your mind about the wedding. As you saw, it's made my father very happy.'

Logan grimaced. 'Let's hope it has the same effect on my mother.'

'Oh, it will,' Darcy said with certainty.

Neither of them seemed to know what to say after that, the silence in the kitchen becoming unbearable to Darcy as the seconds slowly ticked by.

'I really am sorry about my behaviour earlier,' she finally burst out. 'I promise that in future—for your own safety!—I'll try to stay well out of your way,' she said miserably, knowing that she probably wouldn't see Logan again now until the wedding next month. Even then, he was likely to bring the woman he had lunched with today as his partner...!

'I don't believe you have to go that far,' Logan replied, smiling ruefully.

Darcy's own smile was bleak. 'I think it might be better.'

'For whom?' he probed sharply.

She turned away, swallowing hard. 'For both of us,' she answered. 'After a bit of a shaky start—all my own fault, I admit—I'm very pleased that my father and Meg are to be married. But that—that doesn't mean we have to be—that the two of us—'

'I see,' Logan said flatly.

Darcy looked at him sharply. Did he see? She sincerely hoped not. It was bad enough that she knew she was in love with him, without Logan realising it too!

But, no, there was no amusement or pity in the harsh scrutiny of his gaze, only cold arrogance.

'I'll see you at the wedding, then,' she told him with forced brightness.

He nodded abruptly. 'It would seem so,' he responded tautly. 'I— Goodbye, Darcy.'

She had barely mumbled a reply to his cold dismissal when she heard the kitchen door swing shut behind him, quickly followed by the slamming of the restaurant door.

Darcy sat down shakily on one of the kitchen stools, her face buried in her hands as the tears began to fall.

Logan must never know—never guess!—that she had made her biggest blunder of their acquaintance, and fallen in love with him!

CHAPTER ELEVEN

LOGAN sipped the champagne from his glass, eyeing the noisy family gathering belligerently. *What* was he doing here?

Stupid question; he knew exactly what he was doing here. His grandfather had been persuaded into holding an engagement party for Meg and Daniel two weeks prior to their wedding. Usually this was the type of family gathering Logan most wanted to avoid, and he would have done so, but for one thing...

But so far that one thing didn't appear to be here!

After ten days of not seeing her, Logan had mistakenly thought Darcy would be one of the guests at his grandfather's castle this weekend, that Daniel's daughter was sure to be invited. Admittedly he had only arrived himself a short time ago, his flight to Aberdeen having been delayed, meaning he had only had time to quickly shower and change before coming downstairs to join the thirty or so guests in the main salon. But they would soon be called in to dinner, and there was definitely no sign of Darcy.

It simply hadn't occurred to him that she wouldn't be at her own father's engagement party. If it had, he wouldn't have bothered to make the journey himself!

'Cheer up, Logan,' his cousin Brice advised dryly as he stood at his side, the two of them making a formidable pair, both darkly handsome, but Brice's eyes green where Logan's were blue. 'It might never happen!'

He wasn't sure what had happened—he only knew that he had missed Darcy the last ten days, had been sure that he would at least see her at his grandfather's this weekend. He wished now he had asked his mother if Darcy were going to be here, and not just trusted that she would be!

He scowled. 'How soon after dinner do you think I'll be able to make my excuses and go to bed?'

Brice grinned at his obvious discomfort. 'I thought you and Aunt Meg had reached some sort of truce the last few weeks?' He raised mocking dark brows.

That might be exaggerating things slightly, although Logan accepted that he and his mother were at least giving the impression that hostilities had been suspended!

Logan put down his empty champagne glass. 'We have,' he confirmed tersely. 'But, as you very well know, I hate these sort of parties, with all the family trying to get on. And usually failing miserably!' He watched his grandfather playing the grand host to family and friends alike. It was all a sham for the latter, of course; the McDonald clan were not known for their family togetherness! 'In fact, I'm surprised to see you here this weekend, too,' he added questioningly.

Brice led a solitary existence, often disappearing off the social scene for months at a time. The fact that he was here this weekend must mean he was either between commissions or looking for inspiration.

Brice eyed him teasingly. 'I'm wondering which one of the single beauties is Darcy,' he prompted interestedly.

Logan stiffened, turning to him swiftly. 'You've been talking to Fergus!'

His cousin gave a gleeful grin. 'Bet your life I have—nothing else but the chance to meet this fiery virago would have induced *me* to come here this weekend!' He looked at the glittering, chattering guests with the same distaste Logan had minutes ago.

Logan retorted resentfully, 'She is not a candidate for one of your brief flings, Brice.'

His cousin raised an innocent expression. 'I didn't for a moment think she was,' he replied. 'I just wanted to meet the young lady who had got the better of my arrogantly self-assured cousin!'

'That arrogance is obviously a family trait,' Logan returned pointedly. 'And I'm afraid you're out of luck—because Darcy isn't here!' He announced this with satisfaction.

'Ah,' Brice said with feeling.

'What do you mean, "ah"?' Logan demanded suspiciously.

'Just, ah,' his cousin responded with feigned innocence.

Logan scowled once more—an expression that was becoming all too familiar with him just recently. But there didn't seem to be much to smile about any more! Oh, his business interests were still successful; they just seemed to have lost their challenge the last couple of weeks. If he was completely honest, he missed having Darcy around to threaten him, kick him, and throw things over him...

· He should be pleased his life had returned to its calm predictability!

But he wasn't.

And he knew he wasn't...

His mouth set grimly. 'I—'

'If you'll excuse me, Logan,' Brice said slowly, distractedly, his gaze fixed somewhere across the crowded room. 'I've just seen someone over there who merits a second look...'

Most of the women here this evening, single or otherwise, were so beautiful they merited a second look in fact, third ones too, most theatrical acquaintances of his mother. It was just that none of them held any interest for Logan.

Although he thanked this particular woman, whoever she was, for distracting his cousin from a subject that was far too personal as far as Logan was concerned!

'Go ahead,' he invited affectionately. 'Which one is she?' he asked interestedly.

'She's disappeared for the moment, but—ah, a Mona Lisa with red hair...' Brice murmured before setting off determinedly across the crowded room.

Logan shook his head as he gazed indulgently after his cousin. If he was the practical, predictable one of the family, then Brice was the artistic, unpredictable one. Fergus came somewhere in between. Which was probably why the three of them always got along so well together—

A Mona Lisa with red hair...?

There was only one woman Logan could think of who could possibly fit that description. Darcy...!

Wasn't he bowled over himself every time she gave that enigmatic smile? Wasn't it a smile he had hungered for the last ten days...?

There were too many people in this room, he decided impatiently as he easily located Brice standing on the far side of the room, but couldn't see the woman his cousin was now in conversation with, Brice's dark head bent solicitously towards her much shorter height.

It had to be Darcy!

She was here, after all. He could hardly wait to—

'Logan, isn't it?' enquired a breathlessly female voice.

He turned sharply, scowling his irritation at being stopped from joining Brice and the woman he was sure now had to be Darcy. A tall blonde his mother had introduced him to earlier now stood at his side, smiling at him engagingly.

At any other time, under any other circumstances, Logan knew he would have responded to the invitation in the actress's smile. But not now. Now when he was sure Darcy was even at this moment being charmed by his oh-so-lethally fascinating cousin.

'Fiona, isn't it?' he acknowledged tersely, his attention still across the room as he tried to catch a glimpse of the woman Brice was talking to.

'Francesca Darwin,' the actress corrected, obviously not too put out that he hadn't remembered her name correctly. 'I play the part of Meg's sister in the television series we're filming at the moment,' she supplied helpfully.

Logan's brows rose. Considering this woman was only aged in her mid-to late-twenties, Make-up must be doing a wonderful job on his mother to make the two women look like sisters!

'Of course,' he replied politely—having had no idea until this moment that his mother's role even involved a sister!

'She's wonderful, isn't she?' Francesca looked admiringly across the room to where Meg was smiling lovingly at her new fiancé as the two of them talked softly together.

The statement didn't actually require an answer—and, in all honesty, Logan didn't have one! He didn't particularly want to be having this conversation at all—would much rather join Brice and Darcy!—let alone hear that this beautiful young woman seemed to have nothing but admiration for his mother.

Daniel Simon, a decent and honourable man, plainly loved Meg. Darcy, straightforward and honest, had come to like her, too. And Francesca, this young woman, who worked with her on a daily basis, had nothing but admiration for her. Could they all be wrong about Meg, and he was right? Or was he the one who was wrong…?

However, it wasn't something he had the time to deal with just now. 'I'm sorry, Miss Darwin—'

'Francesca,' she prompted warmly. 'This castle is something else, isn't it?' she added with an admiring look round, seeming unaware that Logan was trying to make his excuses.

Something else just about described it. Logan had spent his teenage years growing up here, still considered it home, but he easily acknowledged that its splendour was magnificent.

His grandfather, as much as he was able—and with the modern central heating cunningly disguised behind other fixtures!—had filled the thirty or so rooms that comprised this sixteenth century castle with genuine antiques, armour and swords from the Scottish-English wars, huge tapestries adorning the mellow stone walls. The grounds were no less impressive, the deer his grandfather farmed taking up acres of the land, the rest given over to dense forests and streams. There was even a trout lake half a mile or so away.

'It is,' Logan agreed. 'But I really do have to—'

'Logan, I've brought someone over to say hello,' Brice cut in lightly.

Logan didn't even need to turn to know that it was Darcy; even if his senses hadn't already alerted him to the fact, he could smell the perfume he always associated with her.

She looked wonderful! A knee-length shimmering grey dress, the exact colour of her enigmatic eyes, clung lovingly to the perfection of her body, her hair a soft red curtain down to her shoulders, her eyes huge and luminous, soft colour in her cheeks, a scarlet gloss on her lips. She looked good enough to eat, and Logan suddenly found he felt surprisingly hungry!

'Logan,' she greeted huskily.

'Darcy,' he returned gruffly, his dark gaze eating her up—if nothing else could.

She looked slightly slimmer than he remembered, dark smudges beneath her eyes, eyes that appeared deeply shadowed. Despite her well-wishes to her father and his mother, wishes Logan was sure were completely genuine, he could see that Darcy was far from happy.

She was looking enquiringly at Francesca Darwin now, obviously waiting for an introduction. When all Logan wanted to do was carry her upstairs, to the privacy of one of the fifteen bedrooms, and make love to her until he had completely dispelled those shadows from her eyes!

'Francesca,' the actress introduced herself, briefly shaking Darcy's hand. 'And I believe you're—Daniel's daughter?' she asked with friendly interest.

'Yes,' Darcy confirmed stiltedly.

'Poor Darcy has been wandering around lost amongst the turrets and cellars for the last fifteen minutes or so, trying to find her way here from the North Tower.' Brice was the one to explain her late arrival indulgently, a consoling hand at one of her elbows.

Which easily explained why Darcy hadn't been down here when Logan had first arrived. But now that she had arrived, Logan found he wanted to remove Brice's hand from her arm and—

'Why didn't you tell me that your cousin was Brice McAllister?' Darcy said with soft reproval, obviously remembering that painting of Brice's hanging on the wall in Logan's apartment.

He hadn't told her his cousin was the world-renowned painter—because it hadn't occurred to him to do so. The two men had grown up together; he simply never gave it a thought that Brice was McAllister. Just as he never gave Fergus's success as a writer any thought, either. All three men were successful in their chosen field, but to each other they were just cousins and lifelong companions.

But he could see by the reproval in the darkness of Darcy's eyes that explanation would do very little to alleviate the embarrassment she had obviously felt, at their introduction, that Brice was actually the painter of the picture of his grandfather's castle she had so admired at Logan's apartment a couple of weeks ago!

Could he never do anything right where this woman was concerned?

Logan looked wonderful!

Darcy had both dreaded and anticipated seeing him again this weekend. Anticipated, because the last ten days without so much as a sight of him had dragged interminably. Dreaded, because she had been sure the next time she saw him that it would be in the company of the woman who obviously meant so much in his life she was able to influence his decision concerning attending his mother's wedding.

Francesca...

Tall. Blonde. Sexily alluring in a fitted black dress. The other woman was everything that Darcy wasn't. Even the other woman's name was beautiful.

'Is it important?' Logan rasped harshly now.

Was what importa—? 'Well, I did feel rather silly not knowing,' she answered abruptly, realising he was referring to her earlier remark concerning his cousin.

This family were all so talented, so much larger than life. A famous actress. A multimillionaire businessman. A world-renowned painter. Even the grandfather, Hugh McDonald, with his castle, his distinguished good looks so like Logan's own, was intimidating. Darcy felt totally out of her depth in such company.

She had known this weekend in Scotland was going to be difficult, but, for her father and Meg's sake she had known she had to come here. But seeing Logan, his dark good looks a perfect foil for the blonde beauty of the lovely Francesca, she knew it was going to be even harder to get through than she had imagined. Thank goodness Brice McAllister was here on his own too, and inclined to be friendly!

'Don't give it another thought, Darcy,' Brice assured her easily now. 'Just concentrate on thinking over my earlier suggestion, hmm?' he added eagerly.

'You haven't propositioned her already, have you, Brice?' Logan put in hardly.

Darcy gave him a frowning look, heated colour in her cheeks. 'Your cousin has very kindly suggested that he would like to paint me,' she explained carefully, not liking Logan's implication at all. Although she hadn't particularly taken Brice McAllister's suggestion seriously, either, sure he was just being friendly. After all, the man was world-famous. Besides, who would ever want to buy a painting of her, even a McAllister...?

'How wonderful!' the woman Francesca gushed excitedly.

'Really?' Logan raised scornful brows. 'Is that another way of inviting her to your studio to see your etchings?' he taunted his cousin.

Darcy could feel her temper beginning to rise. Something that hadn't happened once in the ten days since she had last seen Logan. What was it about him that made her so angry all the time?

'Hardly,' Brice was the one to answer dryly, smiling down at her reassuringly. 'But if it bothers you that much, Logan, you can always come along to Darcy's sittings...?' he added challengingly.

Darcy looked frowningly up at Brice. Why on earth should it bother Logan what she did? Unless Brice was simply mocking Logan's future role as her stepbrother? Well, he could forget that; she was far too old to welcome the protection of a reluctant stepbrother. Especially when that stepbrother was Logan!

It was obvious from Logan's darkly scowling expression that he did not appreciate his cousin's mockery.

They really were an extraordinarily handsome family, Logan, Fergus, and Brice, although Fergus didn't appear to be present this weekend. But Logan and Brice were enough to cope with at one time!

'I doubt that will be necessary,' Logan rasped. 'You—' He broke off as the dinner gong sounded.

Darcy breathed a sigh of relief. This meeting with Logan was turning out as difficult as she had imagined it might; they obviously had nothing to say to each other. But one look at him had told her that her feelings for him hadn't changed; she was in love with him!

But her relief was shortlived once they reached the dining-room. The volume of guests meant that there was no set seating arrangement at the long dining-table, and once Hugh McDonald and the guests of honour, Meg and Daniel, had been seated, everyone else just found a place for themselves. Darcy found herself seated with Brice McAllister on one side, and Logan on the other, Francesca on Logan's other side. Wonderful!

'How are you?' Logan said softly as the butler moved discreetly about the table filling wine-glasses.

'Very well, thank you,' she answered awkwardly, not quite able to meet his gaze, suddenly shy in the renewed realisation that she still loved him.

It hadn't been easy this last ten days, but at least she had been spared seeing him and knowing she could never have him. Being near him like this, Francesca at his side, was torture for her.

'You?' she asked politely.

'The same,' he replied tersely. 'Are you going to accept Brice's suggestion?'

She shook her head, smiling ruefully. 'He was only being nice.'

Logan's mouth thinned. 'Brice is never nice where his work is concerned.'

She swallowed hard, still slightly overwhelmed by the talented company she found herself in. 'I think in this case he was,' she persisted.

'Do I hear my name being taken in vain?' Brice interrupted interestedly.

Logan glanced across at his cousin, eyes a glacial blue. 'Darcy seems to think you aren't serious about your suggestion of painting her.'

'Oh, but I am,' Brice McAllister instantly assured her. 'Very serious,' he added determinedly. 'In fact, I have a feeling that Darcy's portrait will be the central focus of my next exhibition.'

'But maybe Darcy doesn't want to be painted,' Logan told him. 'Do you?' he said flatly as he turned to her.

It seemed incredible to her that an artist of Brice McAllister's calibre should even consider her a suitable subject for one of his paintings. Flattering too. But as Logan had so rightly pointed out, she wasn't sure she wanted to be on show for thousands of people to sit and look at.

Just as she didn't particularly want to be a subject of contention between the two cousins. She had hoped to remain very low-key this weekend, do her bit for her father, be visually supportive of his future marriage into this family, before fading back into her own world of obscurity.

Brice McAllister's interest in painting her was making that very difficult to do.

'I'm sure it's something that can be discussed another time,' she dismissed lightly. 'I believe your grandfather is about to propose a toast to the engaged couple.' She had realised this with some relief as Hugh McDonald had got to his feet at the head of the table.

As far as Darcy was concerned, the lengthy dinner that followed was not enjoyable. Oh, the food was wonderful, definitely worthy of Chef Simon's standards. It was just the company that made it unbearable for her. Despite what Logan had said about his cousin, Brice was very kind, the two of them had talked amiably together on numerous subjects. It was just Darcy's awareness of Logan talking with Francesca that made it a nightmare for her.

Would the other couple be sharing a bedroom in this vast castle later on this evening? Just the thought of it made Darcy feel physically ill. In fact, it meant she could barely eat any of the delicious food that was put before her.

'Are you on a diet?'

She turned sharply to look at Logan, realising as she did so that he had been watching her as she pushed the strawberries and cream around in her bowl, rather than eating them.

'No.' she grimaced. 'I'm just not hungry.'

He frowned. 'You didn't eat the smoked salmon or the venison, either.'

Her cheeks felt suddenly warm at the realisation that, for all she had thought him totally engrossed in the beautiful Francesca, Logan must have been watching her for some time to be aware of the fact that she hadn't actually eaten much of the food they had been served.

She shrugged. 'I'm just not very hungry.'

'You start your new job soon, don't you?' he enquired.

She was surprised he had remembered that. And, yes, she began work at the kindergarten next week.

'Nervous?' One of his hands moved to cover hers.

She hadn't been—but she was now. What was Logan doing? More to the point, what was Francesca going to think of him touching her in this way?

'You shouldn't be, you know,' Logan continued gently. 'I'm sure the children are going to love you.'

She wished that he did!

She might as well wish for the moon, and Darcy knew that even more than before after today.

She had been overwhelmed earlier this afternoon when she had arrived at the castle with her father and Meg, not even the rugged beauty of the countryside on the drive up from the airport in the hire car having prepared her for the sheer enormity of Meg's family home. The drive up from the road had seemed to take for ever, thousands of deer grazing in the fields, and as for the castle itself...!

Built of a mellow stone that seemed to have a soft orange hue to it, the main building itself was flanked by four huge turrets, genuine cannons from a sixteenth-century ship flanking each side of the main entrance. It was like something out of a fairy tale!

The inside was even more impressive, furnished with genuine antiques, most of them of a warlike nature, admittedly, but then, in earlier centuries Scotland had seen many wars. Mainly with the English!

Hugh McDonald had turned out to look like an older version of Logan, giving Darcy an idea of what Logan would look like in forty years' time—absolutely formidable!

Darcy had been allocated one of the bedrooms in the North Tower, choosing to take Hugh McDonald's suggestion that she rest until dinner-time. Not because she really needed to rest, but to give herself a chance to gather her scattered defences in anticipation of seeing Logan that evening. The story she had given Brice, of getting lost in the vastness of the castle, was a slight exaggeration; she had simply delayed coming downstairs for as long as she possibly could without missing dinner altogether. Delayed seeing Logan with the beautiful Francesca for as long as possible!

But, in truth, it had made no difference to the pain she felt at seeing him with the other woman, of having to accept Francesca's importance in his life.

Darcy gently removed her hand from Logan's grasp. 'I'm looking forward to starting work,' she assured him. For one thing, it would give her something else to think about besides him!

Logan's mouth had tightened at the removal of her hand, his gaze narrowed now. 'Then why aren't you eating?' He frowned. 'Could it be that you're still upset about Daniel and my mother?' he probed.

'No, it couldn't,' she denied instantly, her smile affectionate as she glanced down the table at the engaged couple; there was no doubting her father and Meg's genuine feelings of love for each other. 'They make a wonderful couple, don't they?' she murmured wistfully.

'Wonderful,' Logan confirmed dryly.

She glanced back at him, frowning slightly. 'But you still have your doubts...?'

'It's not really any of my business, is it?'

No, it wasn't. But his feelings towards marriage, any marriage, still dismayed her.

She glanced over to where the beautiful Francesca was in conversation with the man seated to her right. Was she aware of Logan's feelings towards marriage? Darcy sincerely hoped so, otherwise the other woman had a terrible shock coming to her.

Although the thought of Logan married to another woman made Darcy feel faint!

She swallowed hard. 'I—'

'There's dancing in the main salon after dinner,' Logan told her abruptly.

Almost as if he had known she had been about to make her excuses and escape to her bedroom…?

'Darcy has already promised the first dance to me, old chap,' Brice interrupted brightly, taking a firm hold of Darcy's hand. 'But I'm sure she'll save one for you later on in the evening!' he added tauntingly.

Darcy turned to give Brice a quizzical glance—only to have him give her a conspiratorial wink!

Brice McAllister knew, had somehow guessed, that she was in love with Logan!

The question now was—would he tell his cousin?

All thoughts of making a hasty escape to her bedroom fled as she knew she couldn't allow Brice McAllister to do that. She would have to talk to Brice first, beg him if necessary not to tell Logan of her feelings for him. Because Logan's embarrassed pity was something she couldn't bear!

'It all sounds wonderful!' She gave Brice a big, meaningless smile, and saw a mischievous glint in his deep green eyes as he easily received and acknowledged, her message.

'Wonderful,' Logan echoed hardly. 'But I should warn you to watch out for Darcy's feet, Brice,' he mentioned with a glance in Darcy's direction.

'I'm sure she dances divinely,' his cousin complimented smoothly.

'It's the kicks you have to watch out for,' Logan went on.

Darcy knew exactly what he was referring to, angry colour in her cheeks. 'I'm sure Brice would never be ungentlemanly enough to insult me so that I would need to kick him!' she returned swiftly.

'I must say, Logan, I find it hard to believe you could ever be justified in being ungentlemanly to a lovely young lady like Darcy,' Brice McAllister reproved jokingly.

'All too easily, believe me,' Logan returned, his mouth a thin, angry line.

Darcy turned away so that he shouldn't see the sudden tears in her eyes. Anger was the last emotion she wanted to arouse in Logan. But anger towards each other seemed to be all that they had…

CHAPTER TWELVE

'SHE'S absolutely enchanting, Logan,' Brice whispered at his side.

The two men stood in the main salon, several couples dancing in the centre of the room, Darcy and her father one of them. They made a striking couple, Daniel Simon tall and boyishly good-looking, Darcy so tiny, looking beautiful as she laughed at something her father had just said.

'She is.' Logan didn't even bother to pretend not to know who his cousin was referring to. Considering Brice had only recently finished dancing with Darcy himself, it would be slightly ridiculous to even attempt to do so!

Brice glanced at him. 'Then why don't you tell her so?'

'Now why on earth would I want to do that?'

'Because you're in love with her,' Brice stated evenly.

Logan almost choked over the champagne he had just sipped. 'I'm—I'm what?' he finally managed to burst out.

'In love with Darcy,' Brice repeated, his calmness in direct contrast to Logan's choked disbelief. 'I must say, I admire your taste. I always thought, if you ever did fall in love—and for years I've doubted it would ever happen—that it would be with someone completely unsuitable. But Darcy is unpretentious, charming, beautiful, has a great sense of humour—'

'I am not in love with Darcy!' Logan finally recovered enough to protest. 'I always knew that artistic side of you made you something of a romantic, Brice,' he derided. 'But I didn't realise it made you delusional, too!'

His cousin raised reproving brows. 'It doesn't,' he said flatly.

'Then it must be the champagne,' Logan rejoined.

'It isn't the champagne, either,' Brice replied. 'Logan, do you intend being an idiot all your life?'

'I wasn't aware that I had been,' he returned stiffly.

'You will be if you let Darcy go out of your life,' Brice warned him.

'That's hardly likely to happen,' Logan said wryly. 'In two weeks' time her father and my mother will be married. Which will effectively make us stepbrother and stepsister,' he explained at Brice's enquiring look.

Brice looked quizzical. 'And you're happy to settle for that, are you?'

Logan gave a dismissive laugh, shaking his head. 'I have no idea what you're talking about, Brice.'

'No?' Brice gave him a sceptical glance. 'You didn't like it earlier when I was holding Darcy's arm, and you looked ready to strangle me a few minutes ago when I was dancing with her.'

Damn Brice; he was too observant by half. And, no, he hadn't liked Brice being close to Darcy. But to say that he, Logan, was in love with her, was ridiculous. They had known each other only a couple of weeks, and a tempestuous couple of weeks at that. It was simply that he felt protective towards her, nothing else.

'I was merely wondering at what stage of the evening she would kick you,' Logan quipped.

Brice smiled. 'She won't.'

'Oh?' Logan was surprised. 'And what makes you exempt?'

'I only hope it isn't too late when you decide to wake up, Logan,' Brice warned softly.

Logan's eyes narrowed. 'Too late for what, Brice?'

'She's everything I've said, and more, Logan,' Brice said. 'I can assure you, we won't be the only men to see that.'

Logan didn't like discussing Darcy in this way. And he didn't like Brice talking about her at all.

But that didn't mean he was in love with her. She had been totally vulnerable when he'd met her, still was in many ways; he just didn't like to see her hurt.

'Why don't you ask her to dance?' Brice suggested as the music came to an end and Darcy and her father returned to Meg.

Why didn't he?

'Scared, cuz?' Brice asked.

'Reverse psychology—cuz?' Logan returned bitingly. 'I'm now supposed to rush over and ask Darcy to dance just to prove you wrong—right?'

Brice was unconcerned. 'I was merely wondering why you haven't danced with your future stepsister.'

'Probably because my cousin is being such a pain in the neck about it!' Logan rasped.

'And will continue to be so until you ask Darcy to dance,' Brice assured him unrepentantly.

Logan stared at his cousin. 'Why is it so important to you?'

Brice laughed. 'It isn't important to me.'

'You could have fooled me!' Logan exclaimed.

'She dances like a dream, Logan,' Brice encouraged. 'So light in your arms, and yet so sexy at the same time. I— something wrong, Logan?' Brice said innocently as he heard the slight choking noise in Logan's throat. 'Oops, too late, Logan,' Brice informed him as he looked across the salon. 'Grandfather got to her first!'

Logan turned in time to see his grandfather leading a

rather self-conscious Darcy onto the large area that had been cleared in the centre of the room for dancing.

At almost eighty, his hair showing only a slight salting of grey, his grandfather looked extremely handsome in his black evening suit and snowy white shirt, the slimness of his body showing no signs of age as he led Darcy nimbly around the floor in a waltz.

The two of them talked softly as they danced, Logan able to see that Darcy was slowly relaxing, moving more fluidly to the music now, her steps perfectly matched to those of his grandfather.

Logan couldn't help wondering—given the fact that Daniel would be the third husband of Hugh's eldest daughter, a daughter Hugh was extremely proud of but also shocked by on occasion too—exactly what the two could be finding to talk about. Whatever it was, they were obviously enjoying each other's company, laughing together several times before the music stopped and Hugh gallantly guided Darcy back to her father and Meg.

'The old devil probably enjoyed that immensely,' Brice remarked laughingly.

'Probably,' Logan acknowledged dryly. 'I think we're about to learn firsthand just how much,' he added ruefully as their grandfather made his way over to the two of them determinedly.

'What's the matter with you young men?' their grandfather attacked, helping himself to a glass of champagne as a maid passed by them with a laden tray of glasses. 'Put you amongst a lot of pretty women and you cower in a corner like a couple of idiots!' He drank the champagne thirstily.

'I take exception to the ''idiot'' part of that statement.' Brice laughed.

'And we're hardly "cowering" anywhere, Grandfather,' Logan replied.

'You aren't dancing, either.' The elderly man fixed Logan with a gaze as blue as his own. 'In fact, I haven't seen you dance once yet, Logan. What's the matter with you—company a bit too provincial for you?'

'Hardly. The majority of these people are up from London, anyway.'

'Pretty girl, that,' Hugh said appreciatively.

'Darcy?' Brice put in, his expression completely innocent as Logan turned to give him a hard glance.

'Name's a bit odd.' Hugh nodded. 'But the girl's sound enough. I suppose Meg and this Simon chap might make a match of it,' he allowed grudgingly. 'About time one of you settled down and made me a great-grandfather.' He fixed his steely gaze on both his grandsons.

'Oh, please—not you too!' Logan protested, putting his empty glass down forcefully on a side-table. 'If you'll both excuse me?'

'What did I say?' a bewildered Hugh turned to ask of Brice.

Logan didn't stay around long enough to hear Brice's reply, but strode across the room, reaching Darcy's side just ahead of one of the young actors he had been introduced to earlier.

'Dance?' Logan asked tightly.

She had turned to smile at him as he'd approached, but that smile faded as she took in his coldly angry expression. 'Are you sure that's what you want to do?' she said warily.

No, what he really wanted to do—what he wanted to do almost every time he saw Darcy!—was to carry her off somewhere and make love to her. In the circumstances, dancing with her was as close to that as he could get, so a dance it would have to be.

'Perfectly sure,' he confirmed briskly.

She frowned, undecided, obviously unsure of his mood.

With good reason, Logan allowed impatiently. Damn it, he was irritable when he didn't see her, and angry most of the time when he did. He wasn't sure of his own mood at the moment!

'Perhaps you've danced enough for one evening,' he grated. 'Perhaps you would prefer to go outside for a walk, instead?'

And perhaps she wouldn't, he groaned inwardly as he saw the puzzlement on her expressive face. Would he want to go for a walk with someone who looked as frustratedly angry as he felt? Definitely not!

He drew in a deeply controlling breath. 'I'll try that again,' he said sheepishly. 'Darcy, would you care to walk outside for a breath of fresh air?'

She smiled that shy smile at him. 'Thank you, Logan. Yes, I would like that.'

He held out his arm for her to take, giving the hovering young actor a withering glare as they strolled past him, on their way to the French doors that led out onto the terrace scented with the roses his grandfather grew near the castle.

It was a beautiful moonlit evening outside, the noise of the deer close by, and nocturnal animals calling to each other in the distance, the sound of the bullfrogs nearby in the lily-pond.

'What a beautiful place this is,' Darcy murmured dreamily as she looked out over the wall, the castle, and grounds beyond, bathed in moonlight.

It was a light that seemed to reflect off the silver grey of her dress, giving the woman herself an ethereal quality. Logan found himself transfixed by her the moment they were alone outside.

Darcy turned to give him a searching glance. 'What is it?' she breathed. 'Logan...?'

It was purely instinctive, something he had been wanting to do since the last time he had seen her, something he found himself wanting to do every time he saw her!

His arms moved about the slenderness of her waist, moulding her gently against him as his head lowered and his lips found and captured hers.

Perfect pleasure. It was the first time he had felt complete, any peace of mind, any gentleness of spirit, since the last time he had held her like this.

She fitted so perfectly against him, breathed the same air, and—he hoped!—knew the same pleasure at his closeness that he did at hers.

He wanted this never to stop, wanted to carry on kissing her, touching her, holding her—

'No!' She wrenched her mouth from his, pulling away from him, her face stricken in the moonlight. 'We can't do this, Logan,' she told him breathlessly, tears glistening in her eyes.

He was stunned for a moment, had been totally lost in the sheer pleasure of holding her close to him.

'Please let me go, Logan,' she choked, his arms having instinctively tightened like steel bands about her as she attempted to move away. 'Please!' she said again tearfully.

His hold slackened, but he still didn't release her. 'I'm not going to hurt you, Darcy,' he whispered. 'You should know by now, I would never do that.' Even under extreme provocation, all the times she had done something to him that might have resulted in retaliation, he had never so much as taken an angry step in her direction.

She became suddenly still in his arms, deliberately not looking at him. 'Then let me go,' she said woodenly.

'Why?' he groaned. 'We don't have to go back into the

salon. We can get in through one of the side doors, up to my suite of rooms—'

'No!' She wrenched out of his grasp this time, even though Logan knew it must have physically hurt her to do so. 'No, Logan...!' she choked again before turning to let herself back into the salon, the door closing softly behind her.

Logan stood there stunned for several long, dazed minutes. What had he done? What had he said? What...?

He turned sharply as he sensed a movement behind him, his disappointment acute when he saw it was Brice and not Darcy who had come outside to join him.

'Darcy came back in alone, looking nothing like her usual, calm self,' Brice informed him, 'so I thought I had better come outside and make sure she hadn't thrown you in the lily-pond!'

No, she hadn't done that. But in the last few minutes Logan knew she had done something to him much worse than that. Much, much worse than that!

How could he? How could Logan hold her, kiss her, talk of the two of them going up to his rooms together, when all the time the woman in his life, Francesca, was in the salon with all the other engagement party guests?

She had always known Logan was arrogant, a law unto himself, that he didn't believe in love, let alone marriage. But even so, she had never thought he would behave in such a cavalier fashion. In his grandfather's house, too!

What was she to do now? She couldn't stay down here, when Logan might return to the party at any moment, that was for sure. She simply couldn't face him again so soon after what had happened outside on the terrace. But neither did she want to upset her father or Meg by retiring early.

Surprisingly, it was Hugh McDonald who came to her

rescue, standing up to announce it was almost midnight, that he was going to have the last waltz with the most beautiful woman in the room, and then it was time they all went to their beds or their homes.

Although Darcy wasn't so sure she had been rescued at all when his choice of the most beautiful woman in the room turned out to be her, suddenly finding herself swung expertly into his arms as the band began to play!

'Smile, you silly wee lassie,' he murmured gently in her ear as he whirled her around to *The Last Waltz*. 'Never let a McDonald know he's got you down,' he added reprovingly.

Darcy gave him a startled glance. 'A McDonald...? But you—'

'Logan's mother may have married a McKenzie, but he's more of a McDonald than any of them,' Hugh told her with a mischievous twinkle in his eye. 'A bit slow witted where the ladies are concerned, ye ken?' He gave a loud bellow of laughter at her stunned expression. 'My late wife had to hit me over the head with a frying-pan before I realised I was in love with her!'

Darcy laughed softly at the image he projected. 'I think I would like to hear that story some time!'' But she also knew that approach wouldn't work on Logan...

Darcy knew that Hugh meant well with his teasing, but she had already done too many horrific things to Logan to even think about—and all it had succeeded in doing was having him invite her upstairs to his suite of rooms. Hardly a declaration of love!

'Oh, you've tried that, have ye?' Hugh observed thoughtfully as he easily read at least some of her thoughts. 'He always was a fool where women are concerned.' He sighed. 'If I were forty years younger I'd ask ye to marry me myself.'

Darcy laughed again. 'If you were forty years younger, I think I might be tempted to accept!'

Hugh grinned down at her appreciatively as the music came to an end on the stroke of midnight, looking very much like his grandson at that moment. 'You're a refreshing addition to this family, lassie, and no mistake.' He bent down to kiss her warmly on the cheek. 'I look forward to seeing you again soon.'

At the wedding, of course. In two weeks' time. She hadn't been looking forward to it anyway, the way things were between Logan and herself, but after tonight—! Definitely not an occasion for her to look forward to!

Unfortunately, the first person she saw as she turned to leave the dance-floor was Logan, standing just inside the French doors. A glowering Logan, who stared at her with glitteringly angry blue eyes.

He was angry? He wasn't the one who had been propositioned, with his partner for the evening—night?—just on the other side of those doors!

'Isn't my father wonderful?' Meg was the one to distract her attention as she reached out and squeezed Darcy's arm affectionately, thrilled with the success the evening had obviously been.

'Wonderful,' Darcy echoed sincerely, relieved to be able to look away from that accusing blue gaze as she turned to smile at Meg and her father.

'Daniel and I are just going to have a brandy in the library before retiring. Join us,' Meg invited warmly.

Darcy shook her head. 'It's been a wonderful evening, but, like Hugh, I'm rather tired.' She moved to kiss them both warmly on the cheek. 'Why don't you ask Logan?' she suggested. 'He looks in need of a brandy.'

She didn't linger to see whether they took up her suggestion, hurrying from the room, just wanting to get away now, desperately in need of the privacy of her bedroom. It had been a wonderful—awful, ecstatic, heartbreaking!—evening. One she hoped never to repeat.

She hesitated once out in the main hallway, presented with four sets of stairs, one presumably to each tower. Which was the one to the North Tower? That was the question.

'Are you lingering here looking helpless in the hope that Brice might turn up and offer to escort you back to your bedroom?' a hard voice scorned softly so that the other guests moving noisily past them as they left shouldn't overhear the conversation.

Darcy stiffened, steeling herself before turning to face Logan. A stony-faced Logan, his eyes glittering coldly!

What did this man want from her? More to the point, just what did he think she was? Had he really thought her capable of sneaking off with him when his girlfriend was waiting for him downstairs?

She shook her head sadly. 'I'm merely trying to decide which staircase leads to the North Tower,' she told him flatly, too tired to even attempt to deny the other accusation in his question. Brice had been kind to her, nothing more, and she wouldn't insult that kindness by trying to defend either Brice, or herself.

Logan seemed unimpressed. 'Points of the compass, Darcy,' he said tauntingly. 'East,' he pointed to one staircase. 'West.' He pointed to the one opposite. 'South—'

'Okay, Logan, I get the point,' she interrupted wearily. 'Excuse me for not being a boy scout!' Her voice broke slightly on the latter, and she turned quickly away before Logan could see the tears that had welled so quickly in her eyes, logically making her way to the staircase opposite the one that lay to the south.

'Darcy—'

'Logan, I'm so glad I found you; I've been looking for you everywhere!'

Francesca Darwin's voice was easily recognisable to Darcy as she hurried away up the wide staircase, her legs shaking so badly she wasn't sure she was going to make it.

'I've been right here,' Logan answered the other woman hardly.

Darcy managed to get to the top of the stairs before her legs gave way, turning the corner to lean weakly back against the wall, her tears starting to fall now.

She should move, she knew she should, before anyone else came up the stairs and saw her there, but her legs didn't feel capable of moving just yet. Logan hated her! There was simply no mistaking that glitter in his eyes a few minutes ago...

'I simply wanted to say how nice it's been to meet you.' Francesca was talking again now, her voice bubbling with excitement. 'It's been a wonderful evening.'

'I'm glad you enjoyed it,' Logan returned noncommittally.

Darcy was far less composed. What did the other woman mean, it had been nice meeting him...?

'Perhaps we'll meet again,' Francesca suggested.

'Perhaps,' Logan returned with clear impatience.

Darcy didn't stop to listen to any more of the conversation, moving away from the wall to stumble down the corridor to the bedroom she had been allocated on her arrival, switching on the light to close the door thankfully behind her.

She didn't understand. She had thought Francesca Darwin came here with Logan, had seen the two of them together earlier when she'd entered the salon, and had realised this had to be the woman in Logan's life. But from the conversation she had just overheard, obviously she was wrong. And if he hadn't come here with Francesca, then it would seem he hadn't come here with anyone...

So where was the woman in his life?

If there was one, a little voice in her head reasoned. Hadn't she just assumed there had to be one? Logan had been out to lunch with someone that day ten days ago, changed his mind about being a witness at their parents' wedding, and hadn't she, Darcy, decided it had to be because of a woman's influence?

But if not another woman, what—or who!—had changed his mind?

CHAPTER THIRTEEN

WHY didn't this prattling woman just stop talking and go? Logan fumed inwardly as Francesca Darwin carried on gushing. Didn't she realise he just wasn't interested?

The only thing he was interested in was that Darcy had looked upset when she'd left him a few minutes ago, and he knew it was because of his nastiness to her. But he just couldn't seem to help himself.

Because he was in love with her...

Love. He had realised, when she'd walked away from him on the terrace earlier, that he was in love with her, that love for Darcy was the reason all the meaning had gone out of the rest of his life. It was an emotion he had thought he would never feel for any woman.

It terrified the life out of him!

Love was everything he had thought it would be: frightening, debilitating in the knowledge that all of your life's happiness was wrapped up in a single person.

But it was also many other things: exhilarating, a feeling of gladness just in that person's presence, pleasure in every movement, every word spoken, a driving need to protect, but most of all an overwhelming feeling of completeness. For the first time in his life Logan felt whole, as if he had found the other half of himself. Darcy was that other half.

It wasn't something he could choose to feel, or not, was an emotion that existed entirely of its own volition. He had never known a feeling like it, ached with love for her, for just one of those heart-stopping smiles to come his way, wanted to tell Darcy how he felt. But those feelings of terror held him back. Because she didn't love him.

He had known that outside on the terrace too. She had wanted to get away from him, couldn't wait to escape.

What was he going to do now?

'I'll walk you to the door, Francesca.' Brice stepped neatly into the one-sided conversation, shooting Logan a concerned glance before taking a firm grasp of Francesca's arm, chatting to her amiably as they walked away.

'Logan…?'

He turned dazedly to look at his mother. Had she loved his father in the way he now loved Darcy? Did she now love Daniel in the same way? If she did, then he knew the least he owed her was an apology for the way he had treated her. Not just for months, but for years…

Meg smiled at him gently. 'Daniel and I are going to have a brandy in the library; come and join us.' She didn't wait for an answer, slipping her hand into the crook of his arm as the three of them strolled to the privacy of the library.

A fire had been lit in there, giving off a warm glow of heat, but it was a heat that didn't touch Logan. Neither did the glass of brandy that Daniel had pushed into his hand and which Logan sipped distractedly.

Realising he loved Darcy, and that love wasn't returned, was bad enough, but how did he even begin to apologise to a mother he had repeatedly rejected over the years?

She was looking at him concernedly now. 'Logan…?'

His mother had never seen him like this before, was obviously unsure of his mood, shooting worried glances at Daniel as the two of them looked at Logan uncertainly.

They were probably expecting him to say or do something that would spoil their happiness, of the evening, if nothing else. And who could blame them? He had been

an idiot, a selfish idiot. He had no more right, than Darcy
had quickly realised she had, to dictate what these two
people should or shouldn't do with their lives.

His breath left him in a ragged sigh before he placed
his brandy glass down on the table, walking over to hold
out his hand to Daniel. 'I would like to offer you both my
belated, warmest congratulations,' he said quietly.

To the older man's credit he only hesitated for a fraction
of a second before accepting that warm handshake.

Logan turned to his mother. 'I truly hope you'll be very
happy together,' he told her gruffly. 'Mamma,' he added
softly.

His mother's throat moved convulsively as he used the
name he'd had for her when he was a little boy. In the last
twenty-one years he had only ever called her Meg, or the
more condescending, Mother.

Logan reached out and hugged his mother, feeling the
trembling of her body as she cried softly. Time and time
again, he now acknowledged, his mother had reached out
to him over the last twenty-one years, and time and time
again he had repulsed her. But loving Darcy as he now
did, allowing love back into the hardness of his heart, he
knew he had never stopped loving his mother, that he
never could or would.

'You've made me so happy, Logan,' his mother choked,
cradling his face in both her hands as she reached up and
gently kissed him on the cheek.

'Just be happy together, hmm?' he encouraged huskily.

'And you?' His mother looked up at him searchingly.
'Are you happy, Logan?'

'If I'm not, I have only myself to blame,' he replied
ruefully.

He had chosen to live the way that he did, had hardened

his heart to love; there was no one else to blame if he now found himself alone.

'Darcy—'

'Is a beautiful and charming young lady,' Logan cut in on Daniel's tentative remark, steadily meeting the older man's gaze.

Did Daniel know? Had Logan given himself away somehow? Had his feelings for Darcy been so obvious to everyone but himself…? Did Darcy know?

'She's a credit to you, Daniel,' he added flatly, dismayed at the thought of Darcy guessing how he felt about her. Was that the reason she had run away from him…?

Daniel's arm was about Meg's shoulders now. 'I'm not so sure about the time she threw egg-white over you,' he mused affectionately.

Logan shrugged. 'I probably deserved it. At least she's honest in her feelings.'

Something he hadn't been in a long time. And wasn't it about time that he was? Completely honest. No matter what the cost to his personal pride?

He straightened. 'If you don't mind, I think I'll leave the two of you alone now. What a stupid thing to say; of course you don't mind being left alone.' He shook his head at his own ridiculousness. 'Just take care of my mother, Daniel,' he asked.

Daniel's arm tightened about Meg's shoulders. 'Depend on it.'

Strange, but Logan had a feeling as he left the older couple alone together that he could do exactly that. None of them knew what was round the corner for them, as his mother hadn't when his father had died so suddenly, leaving her bereft and vulnerable. As he hadn't when he'd fallen in love with Darcy…

It took him only a few minutes to find out what he wanted to know, before making his way upstairs.

But there was no answer when he knocked on Darcy's bedroom door. She must already be asleep.

What he wanted to say would have to wait until morning. Why not? It had waited thirty-five years, another night wasn't going to kill him! Or, at least, he hoped it wasn't! A sleepless night was probably the least he could expect. He only hoped he didn't lose his nerve overnight!

It was the shock of his life when he rounded the corner at the top of the South Tower stairs and found Darcy walking along the corridor towards him. Not tucked up in bed asleep at all, but still dressed in that clinging grey dress.

And she looked stricken as she looked up and saw him!

If he dared—if he made one rude remark about her being here—

'Darcy,' he greeted lightly. 'Did you get lost, after all?'

He didn't sound rude, or sarcastic…

But that was no guarantee that he wasn't going to be. He—

'Would you like me to show you back to your bedroom?' he offered gently.

Darcy continued to eye him warily. 'Er—actually, I— my father and Meg invited me to join them for a brandy in the library, I couldn't sleep, so I thought I might join them, after all.'

Coward, she instantly berated herself. She could hardly have expected to find the library in the South Tower! But her courage had completely deserted her at coming face to face with Logan unexpectedly like this.

Logan nodded. 'I've just left them. I…think they would probably like to be alone for a while now.'

'Of course.' There was embarrassed colour in her cheeks now. 'How silly of me.'

'How about joining me in the family sitting-room for a brandy, instead?' he suggested. 'I would like to talk to you, anyway,' he elaborated as she was about to refuse.

Darcy's confusion returned a hundredfold. She had felt she owed Logan an explanation for her behaviour on the terrace after realising her misunderstanding concerning Francesca earlier, had bullied herself into going in search of Logan to make that apology this evening, knowing she would never sleep if she didn't. But her relief had been immense when she'd knocked, on what she had found out from one of the maids was his bedroom door, and he hadn't answered. Now she knew it was because he had been downstairs with her father and Meg.

But didn't she still owe him that explanation...?

'Thank you,' she accepted awkwardly, accompanying him down the stairs.

The family sitting-room was much less formal than the rooms she had seen so far, a warm fire burning in the grate, old comfortable furniture, books and magazines lying around, family photographs everywhere. No doubt some of them would be of Logan when he was a boy. Darcy ached to be able to go and look at them.

'Here.' Logan held out a glass of brandy to her.

She took the glass, gingerly sipping the fiery liquid. Dutch courage, she inwardly taunted herself. 'Logan—'

'Let's sit down, hmm.' He indicated the over-stuffed sofa behind them, waiting until she was seated before sitting down next to her.

Instantly throwing Darcy into confusion again. Being near Logan at any time was torture for her, but with him in this strange, unfathomable mood, she found it even more difficult to bear.

He watched the brandy as he swirled it around in his glass. 'I thought you would like to know I've made my peace with my mother,' he told her softly.

'You have?' She breathed emotionally, unbidden tears springing into her eyes. 'Oh, Logan, that's wonderful!' And she meant it. Logan might not appreciate it yet, but it would be better for him too not to have that awkwardness in his life.

'I have.' He nodded, looking up suddenly, his gaze blazing into hers. 'And now I would like to make my peace with you.'

Darcy sat back slightly. 'With me...?' She frowned.

He sighed, nodding again. 'If I frightened or upset you earlier when we were outside—'

'Oh, but you didn't,' she instantly protested. Fear was the last thing she had felt in his arms earlier!

'I didn't?' He looked bemused. 'Well, no matter.' He shrugged. 'I obviously did something wrong. And for that I apologise. The last thing I ever want to do is frighten or upset you.'

Darcy was suddenly aware of the grandfather clock ticking behind them, of the silence in the castle after the noise of the party earlier. She was also aware that whatever came next had to come from her.

'You didn't do either of those things, Logan.' She chewed on her inner lip. 'I—I thought Francesca Darwin was your—I believed she was staying here. At the castle. With you!' The words came tumbling out.

Logan looked back at her uncomprehendingly. 'Why on earth should you have thought that?' he finally said slowly.

Darcy stood up, moving away from him. She couldn't think straight sitting close to him like that! 'She was with you when Brice and I joined you. She sat next to you at dinner. And you changed your mind about being a witness at the wedding after lunch that day!' she continued deter-minedly.

Logan looked as if he was trying to make sense of what she was saying.

'It was obvious that whoever it was you had lunch with ten days ago had helped change your mind,' Darcy went on frustratedly.

'You're right. They did.' He pursed his lips. 'And you believed it had to be a woman?'

'Of course it—you mean it wasn't?' Darcy looked at him uncertainly.

Logan shook his head. 'It was Fergus. Although a woman was indirectly involved in my change of mind,' he admitted.

Darcy sighed heavily. 'I thought so.'

Logan put down his own brandy glass to stand up, only inches away from her again now. 'That woman was you, Darcy,' he told her gruffly.

Her eyes widened. 'Me? But—'

He sighed. 'Fergus and Brice were both going to be at the wedding. They are both incredibly attractive to women, consummate flirts. And you—'

She held her breath, willing him to go on. And when he didn't, 'I what, Logan?' she prompted.

He took a deep breath. 'Darcy, what were you really doing wandering around the South Tower just now?'

'Looking for you,' she admitted. 'I overheard Francesca talking to you as she left, realised what a terrible mistake I had made concerning the two of you. I—needed to tell you that.'

'Why?'

'Because!' she said. 'I what, Logan?' she pushed again.

He seemed to be fighting an inner battle with himself,

finally giving a deep sigh, before smiling at her. 'You are bright, funny, beautiful, charming, sexy—'

'Logan—'

'And so I decided I had to come to the wedding after all, so that one of those two charming bastards didn't walk away with the woman I love!' he finished.

Darcy stared at him, swallowing convulsively, sure she couldn't have heard him correctly. Logan loved her? But he didn't believe in love. He had said so. Hadn't he...?

'Now I really have shocked you,' he realised with pained self-revelation.

She hesitated. 'I'm not shocked. I—you really do love me?' she said uncertainly, her heart threatening to burst inside her chest.

'I really do,' he confirmed. 'I can imagine nothing more wonderful than waking up with you beside me for the rest of my life, having you to talk with, to laugh with, to cry with, if necessary. I wouldn't even mind if you felt the occasional urge to throw egg-white over me.'

Darcy was still staring at him disbelievingly. 'I—did you know that your grandmother hit your grandfather over the head with a frying-pan in an attempt to get him to realise he was in love with her?'

He looked stunned. 'My sweet ladylike grandmother did?'

Darcy nodded. 'Apparently.'

'Did it work? Obviously it did; they were happily married for over fifty years,' he ruefully answered his own question before looking up at her sharply. 'Darcy, are you trying to tell me, in your own inimitable style, that you did those things to me because you love me?'

She laughed breathlessly. 'Not exactly. Oh, not because I don't love you,' she quickly assured him as he looked suddenly ravaged. 'I just didn't realise then that was the reason you made me so angry all the time.'

Logan was the one to look unsure of himself now. Not an emotion Darcy particularly associated with him, admittedly. And not one she particularly like seeing, either.

She took a step towards him, only inches away from him now. 'Logan McKenzie, I am very much in love with you,' she told him shakily.

'Darcy Simon, I am very much in love with you too,' he returned shyly, his hands reaching out to grasp her shoulders. 'Will you marry me?'

She took a deep breath. 'Marriage, Logan? Don't you want to get used to the idea of being in love first?' she attempted to tease, although her voice broke emotionally.

'No,' he said with certainty. 'I don't ever want to get used to this feeling. It's wonderful. Exhilarating.' His hands tightened on her arms as he bent slightly to gently kiss her on the mouth, that kiss quickly deepening into passion.

Darcy had no idea how long they were in each other's arms, kissing, touching, discovering. It was wonderful!

'I think I fell in love with you that very first day,' Logan finally admitted, his forehead resting against hers as the two of them sat close together on the sofa, their arms about each other.

'I don't believe that,' Darcy responded, resting against his chest. 'I cried all over you. And I looked a mess.'

Logan chuckled throatily. 'Your tears are what make you so human, Darcy. As for your smile—it takes my breath away. Will you marry me?'

'Oh, yes,' she breathed ecstatically, unable to imagine anything more wonderful than being with Logan for the rest of their lives.

'Soon?' he urged achingly.

'Very soon,' she acquiesced, knowing she wanted nothing more than to belong with this man for the rest of her life. She chuckled softly. 'I still can't believe this, Logan.' She cuddled into him. 'I promise I'll never kick you or throw egg-white over you again—'

'Don't promise things you can't keep to, my love.' Logan laughed. 'I'm sure I'll occasionally do things that will annoy you, and you'll react instinctively. I love your unpredictability, Darcy. In fact, I'm quite expecting you to present me with twins—possibly even triplets!—one day, as your pièce de résistance!'

What a wonderful thought!

In fact, the future, with Logan, promised to be full of wonderful things...

To Marry McCloud

CAROLE MORTIMER

To
my husband, Peter,
for his love and understanding

CHAPTER ONE

'CELEBRATING?'

Fergus didn't even bother to look up from where he sat slumped in a corner of a noisy nightclub, staring down morosely into his champagne glass, totally removed from the loud music that played and the hundreds of chattering people that surrounded him drinking and smoking, and generally enjoying themselves.

What a stupid question; did he look as if he were celebrating?

'Has no one ever told you that you should never drink alone?'

Damn, the woman was still here! Couldn't she see that alone was exactly what he wanted to be? And how he intended on remaining, he mentally added vehemently.

'Mind if I join you?'

Of course he minded—

Wow…!

The woman's persistence had at least caused him to look up, the angry dismissal that had rapidly been gathering force inside his head coming to a skidding halt.

This woman—girl?—was absolutely beautiful!

Barely five feet tall, she wore an above-knee-length fitted black dress revealing a slenderness, giving the impression she might snap in half at her tiny waist. Her hair was a long curtain down her delicate spine and the dark colour of midnight. Her face was ethereally beautiful, totally dominated by the deepest blue eyes Fergus had ever seen, and edged with thick, smoky black lashes.

5

So she was beautiful, was his next thought. So what? She was also pushy and forward, something he definitely did not need at this moment. If ever!

He leant back in the padded booth where he sat, his appraising gaze deliberately insolent as it moved from her head to her toes, and then back to that delicate china-doll face. He frowned. 'Are you sure you're old enough to be in here?'

She laughed huskily, revealing tiny, even white teeth. 'I can assure you, I'm well over the age of consent,' she told him in a cultured voice.

He wasn't aware he had asked her for anything! Couldn't she see that he wanted to be left alone, that he had been sitting here on his own for well over an hour now, that he had spoken to no one, and no one—wisely!—had spoken to him, either?

'Mind if I join you?' she asked again, indicating the seat in the booth opposite his own.

Yes—he minded! Did this woman have the skin of a rhinoceros? Could she really not see that he just didn't want to even speak to her, let alone anything else?

Obviously not, he decided frustratedly as, not even waiting for his reply, she slid smoothly onto the seat she had previously indicated.

'Look, Miss—'

'Chloe,' she put in smoothly, her blue gaze very direct as she leant her elbows on the table before resting that tiny pointed chin on her linked hands, staring unblinkingly across at him.

'Chloe,' Fergus echoed with an impatient sigh. 'I don't mean to be rude, but—'

'Then don't be,' she advised.

He had a feeling he was going to have to be if he wanted her to leave any time in the near future!

He sighed again. 'This has not been a good day for me, Chloe—'

'Maybe your luck is about to change,' she murmured.

He didn't *want* his luck to change!

He hadn't been looking forward to the wedding today— after all, it was the second one he had attended in a month. First his Aunt Meg had married restaurateur and chef, Daniel Simon, and today—much worse!—his cousin Logan had married Darcy Simon.

Not that Darcy wasn't a lovely girl, and he knew that she and Logan were head over heels in love with each other. It was just—he hadn't realised just how deeply Logan getting married was going to affect him. Since childhood, it had always been the three of them: Logan, their other cousin Brice, and Fergus.

They had grown up in Scotland, gone to university together at Oxford, had all remained single for the last fourteen years, not living in each other's pockets, but certainly enjoying the bachelor life when they had met. They had become known as the Elusive Three. Now there was only himself and Brice left. The Elusive Two just didn't sound the same…!

His mouth twisted wryly. 'I don't think so, Chloe. Thank you for the offer, but—'

'Would you like to dance?' she suggested lightly.

He wasn't even sure he could still stand up, let alone dance! The champagne had been flowing freely at the reception since the wedding ceremony this afternoon at three o'clock, and Fergus had definitely had more than his own fair share of the bubbly liquid.

When the party had begun to break up about eleven o'clock he hadn't felt he'd been ready to go home to his lonely house just then, instructing the taxi driver to bring him here instead. But at least he had had the sense to realise he had better stick to drinking champagne; otherwise he knew he would wake up in the morning wishing his head weren't attached to his shoulders. He still might!

He gave a heavy sigh. 'What I would like, Chloe, is for you—'

'Could I have some mineral water, do you think?'

He looked across at her darkly, wondering if she was ever going to let him get in a full sentence!

She smiled at him, and Fergus found his expression softening slightly. After all, it wasn't her fault he was in a foul mood. A mood that meant the last thing he wanted was to be so obviously approached by a woman he had never even seen before. Beauty notwithstanding!

'It's only a glass of water,' Chloe teased softly.

How right she was; he wasn't capable this evening of providing her—or any other woman, for that matter!—with anything else.

Okay, one glass of bubbly water, he promised himself, and then she would have to go.

He turned to signal the waiter behind the bar to provide him with mineral water and another glass, taking the bottle himself to pour some of the liquid for Chloe.

At least, that was what he intended doing, but at the last moment his hand seemed to have a will of its own, shifting slightly, some of the water spilling onto the table. Hell, just how much had he drunk today?

'Whoops,' Chloe sympathised gently, before placing a tissue over the spilt water. She raised her glass. 'What shall we drink to?' she encouraged brightly.

'Absent friends?' Fergus returned morosely before taking a huge swallow.

Not that he thought Logan would ever stop being his friend, as well as cousin. But he just knew things would never be the same between them now that Logan shared his life with his wife.

The same age, thirty-five, the three cousins had always been more like brothers, offering each other broad shoulders during times of trouble. It was going to take some time to adjust to the fact that Logan now had Darcy as his soul mate...

Chloe was eyeing him teasingly. 'I was always told that champagne should be sipped slowly in order to be properly appreciated.'

Fergus nodded tersely. 'Whoever told you that was correct.' Especially where a vintage champagne like this one was concerned! 'I did try to warn you I'm not very good company,' he glowered.

'So you did.' She appeared completely unperturbed by his taciturn mood. 'Is it anything you would like to talk about?' she encouraged softly.

Not to a woman he didn't know, and didn't want to know, either, thank you very much!

Chloe tilted her head thoughtfully to one side as she looked across at him, her hair taking on a blue-black sheen in the subdued lighting of the crowded nightclub. 'You're Fergus McCloud, aren't you?' she finally recognised appreciatively.

Fergus stiffened defensively. 'Am I?' he returned warily.

Was that the reason she had been so determined to speak to him? If it was, she was wasting her time; he wasn't into literary groupies. Again, beauty notwithstanding!

'Of course you are,' she answered. 'I've read several of your books, seen your photograph on the cover. You're very good,' she added warmly.

'Thanks,' he replied uninterestedly.

Chloe laughed. 'But you aren't impressed,' she easily guessed.

'Not really,' he returned bluntly. 'You see, I've read them too. They're your standard thriller: a bit of mystery, a touch of violence, mixed together with a lot of sex!'

'You've had six books published during the last six years, and each one has reached the number-one spot on the best-seller list,' she corrected softly. 'I would hardly call that "standard".'

Now, in spite of himself, he *was* impressed! But the fact that she knew all that about him only convinced Fergus more that this woman Chloe *was* a literary groupie. Or worse!

He shrugged. 'That just goes to show you that there's no accounting for public taste.'

'My, you are feeling sorry for yourself this evening, aren't you?' Chloe rejoined speculatively.

Yes, he was—so why didn't she just leave him alone to wallow in it?

Getting to know this man had turned out to be much harder than she had imagined it would be, Chloe admitted inwardly.

For weeks she had been desperately searching for a way in which she might 'accidentally' meet Fergus McCloud, finally coming to realise that it was virtually impossible. The fact that he was so successful as a writer meant that he no longer practised as a lawyer, so he didn't have an office to go to. His social life was sporadic, to say the least. The only thing she had been able to come up with, where she'd known he would definitely be in attendance, was his cousin Logan's wedding today; after all, he was the best man! But as Chloe didn't know either the bride or the groom, there was no way she could have gatecrashed!

Feeling thoroughly disheartened about the whole situation, she had accepted an invitation to spend the evening with a group of friends with whom she had been at university, going out to dinner before moving on to a nightclub. This nightclub. Chloe had hardly been able to believe her luck when, standing near the door with her group of friends and preparing to go on to somewhere else, she had actually seen Fergus McCloud coming in. Alone.

For a moment she had panicked, wondering what to do. Here had been her chance at last—and she hadn't known what to do about it! But then she had forced herself to calm down, to think.

The answer had been obvious; she'd made her excuses to her friends, explained she had changed her mind about going on somewhere else, and was going to go home. But, instead, she had followed Fergus McCloud back inside the club, standing at a discreet distance away to watch him while she'd decided what to do next.

He'd appeared to be alone, but she hadn't been sure whether or not someone, a woman, would eventually join him. After an hour, when he had drunk his way through one bottle of champagne, and ordered another one, she had decided that nobody would.

It was perfect, the ideal opportunity for her to at least have a chance to speak to him.

Except he had made it more than plain from the beginning that he didn't want to talk to her.

Well, she wasn't about to give up now!

'How did your cousin's wedding go today?' she enquired conversationally, making no effort to drink the water he had poured for her; it had only been a way for her to delay having him ask her to leave.

Fergus frowned across at her, his good looks not in the least diminished by his scowling expression.

Chloe had known what he looked like, of course, but even so she hadn't quite been prepared for the sheer physical force of the man. He was tall and powerfully built; there was no doubting he looked wonderful in his evening clothes. His dark hair was slightly overlong, his tanned face carved as if hewn from teak. Only his warm chocolate-brown eyes did anything to alleviate the hardness of his features.

Under any other circumstances, Chloe was sure she would find this man excitingly attractive. Under any *other* circumstances...

'I'm not sure I like the fact that you seem quite so knowledgeable about my private life,' he commented hardly.

That remark about his cousin's wedding had been a mistake, Chloe realised belatedly, laughing softly to cover up the gaffe. 'It's hardly a secret that the business entrepreneur Logan McKenzie is your cousin. Or that he was getting married today.' She shrugged.

'No...' Fergus conceded slowly.

But. He didn't say it, but the word was there in his tone, nonetheless.

Chloe drew in a softly controlling breath. She wasn't very good at this sort of thing, never had been. In fact, her behaviour this evening, approaching Fergus McCloud as she had, talking to him, inviting herself to join him, pressing him to provide her with a glass of water, was all totally out of character. Her friends and family would have been shocked if they could have seen and heard her! But she had been taken completely off guard by seeing Fergus arrive at the nightclub so suddenly, and had simply acted on impulse by inviting herself to join him. He certainly didn't look in a mood to introduce himself to her!

'It's the society wedding of the month, Fergus,' she chided him teasingly.

'Hmm.' He grimaced his distaste in recognition of that

fact. 'Well, to answer your question, it went well. Or, as well as any wedding can be expected to,' he amended.

She raised dark brows. 'You don't like weddings?'

Once again he frowned across at her. 'You aren't a reporter, are you?' he prompted suspiciously. 'I'm not going to see my less-than-sober remarks splashed across the front page of a newspaper in the morning, am I?'

Hardly; she was no more enamoured of reporters than he appeared to be. They had already helped ruin her life once...

'No,' she assured him with certainty. 'I was interested, that's all.'

Struggling for a topic of conversation probably more accurately described it, she acknowledged ruefully. This was certainly heavy going.

'Well, as I've already told you, it was fine,' Fergus said abruptly. 'Now, if you'll excuse me?' He put down his glass, sliding over to the end of the seat in preparation of standing up. 'It's time I got myself a taxi home.'

Chloe stared across at him in dismay. He couldn't go! She hadn't even begun to talk to him yet. If he left now, she might never get the chance to talk to him again. This was—

'Oh, hell—!' Fergus McCloud groaned as, having attempted to stand up, he suddenly found himself sitting back down again. He closed his eyes, breathing deeply. 'I don't suppose you would like to do me a favour, would you?' he asked Chloe very carefully, his eyes still closed.

Anything! As long as it meant he wasn't about to just get up and walk away from her. Although, for the moment—thankfully!—he didn't seem able to do that.

'Yes?' Chloe responded breathlessly.

He continued to breathe deeply, looking across at her with those warm brown eyes. 'I seem to find myself temporarily unable to stand up. Actually, I'm drunk!' he amended with forceful self-disgust. 'Legless. Literally! I can't remember the last time I— Yes, I can,' he groaned. 'It was when I graduated from Oxford fourteen years ago. I couldn't get out of bed for two days afterwards!'

Her own graduation from university had only been a couple of years ago and, as she easily recalled, everyone had let themselves relax and had a good time; after three years' hard work, they had needed to.

'What would you like me to do?' she offered.

'Could you help me outside and put me in a taxi?' He grimaced. Obviously he wasn't a man accustomed to asking anyone for help.

She could do better than that, and it would suit her purpose much better. But she would keep that to herself for the moment...

'Of course.' She stood up smoothly, securing the strap of her evening bag on her shoulder before moving lightly round the table. 'Just stand up and lean on me,' she encouraged.

He eyed the slenderness of her frame with obvious scepticism. 'I don't think I had better "lean" too heavily,' he observed. 'Or we'll both fall over!'

He was a good foot taller than Chloe, even in her three-inch heels, and probably weighed twice as much as her too. But she was stronger than she looked, helping him to his feet without too much difficulty, her arm about his waist, his across her shoulders as the two of them began to walk towards the exit.

'This is so embarrassing,' Fergus muttered grimly when they had crossed half the distance to the door without mishap.

Chloe turned to grin up at him unsympathetically. 'Just think of it as practising for your old age!'

He gave a disgusted snort. 'I feel a hundred now!'

He didn't look it. In fact, he looked rather boyish, younger than the thirty-five years she knew him to be, his expression one of dazed disbelief at his own inability, dark hair falling silkily across his brow.

Chloe made no effort to put him into any of the waiting taxis once they were outside. Instead she helped guide him over to the green sports car in the adjoining car park, pressing the remote button on her keys as they approached to release the locks, swinging open the passenger door before helping him inside.

'This isn't a taxi,' Fergus finally realised, looking around him dazedly, the fresh air outside obviously having done nothing to clear his head. In fact, the opposite.

'No, it isn't,' Chloe confirmed as she got in behind the wheel to turn the key in the ignition.

Fergus looked ready to protest, and then thought better of it, leaning his head back weakly against the cream leather seat, his eyes once again closed. 'Whatever,' he accepted dismissively. 'Do I need to tell you my address— or do you know that too?'

Chloe turned sharply to look at him. Had she given herself away so completely?

Fergus opened one eye at her lack of response. 'Well?' he prompted impatiently.

She gave a slight inclination of her head. 'I know that too,' she conceded huskily, accelerating the car out of the car park and into the flow of late night traffic.

'Remind me, some time, to ask you *how* you know,' Fergus murmured drowsily. 'I have a feeling I'm not going to remember too much about this evening when I wake up tomorrow!'

Chloe sincerely hoped that wasn't the case...!

CHAPTER TWO

FERGUS woke slowly, totally disorientated for several long moments as he moved his head gingerly to look around what he recognised as the comfort of his bedroom, his head feeling as if it were full of cotton wool.

How had he got here?

Damned if he knew!

He glanced at the bedside clock. Nine-thirty. He lay back on the pillows, his eyes once again closed.

What day was it?

Logan and Darcy's wedding had been yesterday, he remembered that. So today must be Sunday, he decided. No need to worry about getting up just yet. He didn't have anywhere else to go, no one to see, and Maud, his housekeeper, always had Sundays off. He usually worked all day on a Sunday, grabbing a sandwich to eat if he felt hungry, so there was really no need for Maud to be here—

Then why could he smell coffee?

Champagne delusions? Because coffee was what he most felt in need of? As he had hoped, he didn't have a hangover, but his mouth felt as if it were full of sandpaper. A cup of coffee was very much on the agenda. He—

No, there was no doubt about it, he could definitely smell coffee. Strong, rich, reviving coffee.

But how—?

'Wakey, wakey, Fergus,' chirruped a bright female voice from somewhere over near the bedroom doorway. 'I've brought you up a mug of coffee.'

Fergus frowned, unmoving, eyes still closed, aware that

16

the smell of coffee was much stronger now, but completely uncertain about the plausibility of that first statement. He couldn't possibly be awake. There was a woman in his bedroom.

Not that it was unknown for a woman to be in his bedroom; he had spent some very pleasurable hours with women in this four-poster bed. Just not last night. Not just champagne delusions, then, hallucinations, too!

'Come on, sleepyhead,' that female voice continued teasingly. 'Sit up and drink your coffee.'

Fergus slowly opened his eyes, wincing as he turned his head, half afraid of what he was going to see.

Deep blue eyes. A long cascade of blue-black hair. A slender female body obviously completely naked beneath his casually buttoned white evening shirt, the legs bare beneath its thigh-length.

Not hallucinations; he had to still be asleep. There couldn't possibly be an almost naked woman in his bedroom. He distinctly remembered he had left the wedding reception alone yesterday.

'Coffee.' She put down one of the mugs she carried on the table beside him. 'Black. No sugar,' she encouraged lightly.

Exactly how he took his coffee. But how did she know—?

'What are you doing?' he gasped disbelievingly as she sat down on the bed beside him.

She raised surprised brows, smiling down at him. 'You don't mind if I sit here and drink my coffee with you, do you...? Or that I borrowed your shirt to wear? It's cold downstairs in the kitchen.' She gave a slight shiver before taking a sip from her own steaming mug of coffee.

Fergus stared at her, not sure whether he wanted her to sit with him or not.

She had been roaming around the house, rooting around in the kitchen to find the makings of the coffee, obviously wearing nothing but his shirt! It was just as well it was Maud's day off! His housekeeper was perfectly aware of his bachelor lifestyle, but that didn't mean he had to flaunt it in her face.

Fergus turned away, ostensibly to pick up his own coffee and take a sip, but in actuality it was to give him a few more seconds' thinking space. Except that it didn't. By moving, he had discovered *he* was *completely* naked beneath the bedclothes!

Not that he should have been surprised by the fact, he realised dully. He didn't remember meeting this woman, didn't remember coming home with her, so why should he remember taking his clothes off?

There was, however, one undeniable truth to this situation: this woman—whoever she was—had obviously spent the night here. With him. In this bed. And he didn't remember a thing about that, either!

Not even her name…

How the hell had this happened? Too much champagne on an empty stomach, came the obvious answer.

He remembered leaving the wedding reception. He vaguely recalled going on to the nightclub. After that— nothing!

'"Thank you, Chloe",' she mocked behind him. 'You're welcome, Fergus,' she answered liltingly.

Chloe. Her name was Chloe, he acknowledged with some relief. But he didn't—

Yes, he did. Some of it was coming back to him now. The nightclub. She had come over and spoken to him. Sat with him, even though he had been less than enthusiastic. Had drunk with him. Gone to bed with him…?

Somehow he seemed to have missed something between

drinking the champagne at the nightclub last night and waking up to find her in his bedroom this morning. He didn't remember the two of them going to bed together at all, let alone—let alone—

How the hell did he get himself out of this one? He groaned inwardly. One thing was certain: he was never going to drink champagne—or anything else!—to excess, again.

'Er—Chloe…?' He turned slowly, slightly more awake now, blinking dazedly as he took in this woman's delicate beauty.

She was so tiny. The hands that were cupped about her coffee mug were almost like a child's. Hands that were bare of rings, Fergus noticed with a certain amount of relief; at least he didn't find himself in this predicament with a married woman!

But that it was a predicament, he was in no doubt. How on earth were you supposed to behave towards a woman with whom you had obviously spent the night in bed—a night you didn't remember? An apology didn't seem to exactly fit the bill!

'It's good coffee,' he said inanely instead.

'Thank you,' she accepted warmly, putting her empty mug down. 'I simply can't tell you how wonderful it was to meet you last night, Fergus,' she added a little shyly

It was…?

Personally, he wouldn't have thought himself capable of giving of his best in the condition he had been in last night, but who was he to argue if she—?

Damn it, it wasn't a question of arguing; he simply didn't remember anything of being intimate with this woman the night before, and he could not pretend otherwise. But he could hardly tell her the truth, either, his conscience warned him softly. Not only would that be insensitive, it would be extremely insulting!

'I'm glad,' he answered noncommittally, absently playing with the dark silkiness of her hair as he wondered what to do next. 'Er—did we—?' He broke off as the strident noise of the doorbell ringing resounded through the house.

Someone was at the front door!

Obviously, you idiot, he instantly scorned himself. But who on earth could be calling on him at—nine-forty-five, the bedside clock showed—on a Sunday morning?

There seemed only one way to answer that question. But with the beautiful Chloe dressed in nothing but his shirt, Fergus was loath to get out of bed to go downstairs and answer the door. Maybe if he just lay here and ignored it, whoever it was would go away—

The doorbell rang again. Longer this time.

His caller wasn't going to just go away!

Chloe stood up. 'Shouldn't you go and answer that?' she prompted.

Of course he should. But it could be anybody: his mother, who was in town for the wedding yesterday, or one of the women he had taken out during the last couple of weeks. He could hardly introduce any of them to Chloe when he didn't even know who she was himself!

'Wait here,' he warned as he straightened, sitting up to swing his legs to the floor.

Yep, he was naked, all right. And a quick look round the room told him his dressing gown was in the bathroom where he had left it yesterday morning.

It was stupid to feel in the least self-conscious as he walked to the bathroom to get his robe. And yet he did. This woman might know exactly what he looked like without his clothes on, but *he* didn't *remember* her knowing.

He obviously knew what she looked like without her clothes too, but he didn't remember that, either!

'I won't be long,' he assured her before leaving the bedroom, more relaxed now that he was at least wearing his robe.

What an awful situation. Who was Chloe? Where had she come from? More to the point, what was he going to do with her now...?

'Brice...!' he breathed hoarsely after opening the door and finding his cousin standing there on the doorstep grinning at him cheerfully.

'Fergus,' Brice greeted lightly. 'Nice car.' He turned to look appreciatively at a green sports car parked behind him in the driveway. 'Anyone I know?' Brice raised inquisitive brows.

Fergus stared at the car. He had never seen it before. For that reason alone he knew it had to belong to Chloe.

Well, at least that answered one of the questions that had been plaguing him since he'd woken up earlier and found her standing beside his bed; with a car like that she was unlikely to be someone who expected paying for whatever services she had provided last night!

'Or do I mean, anyone I should *like* to know?' Brice amended teasingly.

No doubt his cousin would be as knocked out by the way Chloe looked as Fergus was himself. But Fergus suddenly found that he didn't like that idea at all.

'What can I do for you, Brice?' he asked briskly.

The other man shrugged. 'Don't you remember that we made an agreement yesterday to play golf today? You said you weren't working today, so I've booked us in for a round at twelve o'clock,' he explained.

Golf. He had made arrangements to play *golf* today?

How on earth could he do that, when Chloe was still

upstairs in his bedroom? When he had to find out exactly what—

'Good morning!' Chloe greeted cheerfully at that moment from directly behind him.

Fergus closed his eyes briefly in a wince. He had been hoping to put Brice off before going back upstairs to talk to Chloe; that way he could have avoided having the two of them meet. Her sudden appearance behind him meant it was going to be impossible.

'And a good morning to you too,' Brice returned lightly, looking past Fergus to smile at Chloe.

Fergus turned slowly, dreading the moment; Chloe had looked enchanting in his shirt, sexy as hell, actually, but, dressed like that, it was also obvious that she must have spent the night here. He and Brice were close, yes, but that didn't mean he wanted his cousin to see Chloe looking like that.

But he needn't have worried—she was completely dressed! The white shirt had gone, a short, slinky black dress in its place, her legs silky in sheer tights, high-heeled shoes on her tiny feet. Her hair was no longer tousled but brushed in a shiny blue-black curtain down the length of her spine, and her face was almost bare of make-up, except for a red lipgloss. But there was no doubt in Fergus's mind that she was the most exquisitely beautiful woman he had ever seen in his life!

She joined the two men at the door, her movements gracefully elegant. 'Aren't you going to introduce us, Fergus?' She looked up at him expectantly.

Introduce her to Brice? Yes, he supposed he better had. It was just that for a moment there her beauty had actually taken his breath away!

He took in a ragged breath, his arm moving lightly about her shoulders as he drew her to his side. 'Chloe, this is my cousin, Brice McAllister. Brice, this is Chloe—' He came to an abrupt halt, looking down at her frowningly. He had no idea what her surname was!

'Fox,' Chloe provided laughingly as she easily read his confusion, holding out her hand to shake Brice's. 'Don't mind Fergus, Brice; too much champagne!' she quipped. 'Now, if you'll both excuse me?' She included both men in the warmth of her gaze. 'I overheard you two say you're off to play golf, and I have an appointment myself at one o'clock. I obviously have to shower and change before then,' she added with a self-derisive grimace at her evening dress.

Obviously, Fergus acknowledged tautly, already wondering who this one o'clock appointment was with. Besides, she couldn't just disappear like this! When was he going to see her again? If at all?

Because suddenly Fergus found that he did want to see her again, very much so. It was very frustrating having this complete blank about their time together last night. He wanted to see her again, needed to see her—if only to have the chance to refresh his memory!

Chloe turned to him, smiling up at him before standing on tiptoe to kiss him lightly on the cheek. 'I'll ring you later, shall I?' she murmured discreetly.

The effect of that kiss on Fergus told him at least some of what must have happened to him last night; his cheek still tingled, and his insides felt as if they were melting.

He had dated some beautiful women in his time, some incredibly sexy ones too, but he could never remember reacting that strongly to a single, almost platonic kiss before. Chloe Fox was pure dynamite!

'Do that,' he confirmed abruptly.

'Nice to have met you, Brice,' she said with a nod before walking over to her car.

Fergus watched her go, admiring the lean grace of her body as she moved, her legs shapely as she swung easily into the low confines of the sports car, giving the two men a brief wave before reversing the car down the driveway and speeding away.

Brice whistled softly at his side. 'She's absolutely beautiful, Fergus,' he opined appreciatively.

She was gorgeous, Fergus mentally agreed. She—

She had just driven out of his life, he realised with a sickening jolt!

He, Fergus McCloud, a man who always ended relationships before they could possibly become serious, had just been given the brush-off. Big time!

Because Chloe Fox wasn't going to call him—she didn't have his telephone number!

Chloe managed to keep up her charade of cheerfulness until she had turned the corner away from Fergus McCloud's home. And then her knees began to shake, quickly followed by her hands, the latter so badly she was having trouble steering the car. So much so that she knew she had to pull the car into the side of the road, or end up crashing into something.

Leaning her head back against the leather upholstery, she closed her eyes as her whole body seemed to be shaking now.

She had forced her company on Fergus McCloud last night with the sole intention of talking to him, had driven him home for the same reason. Having him collapse unconscious on the bed as soon as she'd got him up the stairs had not been part of her plan!

She had stared down at him frustratedly for several long minutes as he'd lain on the bed gently snoring, knowing that if she'd left then, as he had already predicted, along with nearly everything else about last night, he wouldn't remember meeting her, either!

Having got that far, she hadn't been able to allow that to happen. And so she had stayed, curled up uncomfortably in the bedroom chair, while Fergus McCloud had slept the sleep of the untroubled in the huge four-poster bed!

It had seemed like a good idea at the time; now she wasn't so sure... She had aroused his curiosity, of that she was certain—he had obviously been stunned to wake up and see her in his bedroom this morning! But it was his compassion she really wanted. The problem was, she still wasn't sure he was capable of it...

And then his cousin had arrived so precipitously this morning, putting an end to any chance she might have had of talking to Fergus!

She drew in a ragged breath, having finally stopped shaking enough to turn on the ignition and continue the rest of the drive to her home. A home she shared with her parents.

What would Fergus McCloud make of that if he knew? No doubt, on the evidence he had from last night, he thought her a completely free agent, able to come and go as she pleased. She hadn't missed that quick glance he had given the ring finger on her left hand, had easily seen him relax when he'd discovered no wedding band there. But to assume she was answerable to no one just wasn't true.

Although she should be in luck this morning; her parents should have gone to church by now, leaving her free to enter the house undetected.

She parked her car in the driveway beside her mother's car, her father obviously having ferried them to church in his four-wheel drive.

Chloe breathed a sigh of relief, knowing that if her parents saw that she was still wearing the dress she had worn to go out in the previous evening, they would guess immediately that she hadn't been home all night. And the last thing she wanted were any questions concerning her whereabouts previously!

She had reached the bottom of the wide stairway to go up to her bedroom, completely undetected by any of the household staff, when a door suddenly opened behind her.

'Chloe…?'

David. Her brother-in-law, and also her father's assistant. It could have been worse!

She turned to smile at him. 'Don't you have a home to go to?' she joked, knowing that her sister, Penny, and their three children would be waiting for him there. And this was Sunday, after all…

Tall, and sparely built, his blond hair thinning slightly on top, David Latham had been her father's personal assistant for the last fifteen years.

His presence in the house had brought him into close contact with all the family, and twelve years ago he had married Chloe's older sister Penny. Their parents had been thrilled at the match, and absolutely doted on their three grandchildren: Paul, aged ten, named after his grandfather, Diana, aged seven, and five-year-old Josh.

'I just had to stop by and drop off some papers your father needed as soon as he gets back from church.' He held up the papers. 'And shouldn't I be the one asking if you forgot last night that you have a home to go to?' he drawled, eyeing her clothes pointedly. 'I'm pretty sure you aren't going to join your parents at church dressed like that!' he added forthrightly.

'You would be right,' she grimaced.

'Don't look so worried, Chloe.' He laughed softly. 'I was young once, too, you know.'

David obviously assumed she had been on a raucous

night out. And it would be better for everyone if he continued to think that.

'I won't tell my father about you if you don't tell him about me,' she returned lightly, knowing that, right now, given her father's precarious political position, appearances were everything, including those of his son-in-law and assistant, as well as his youngest daughter. 'Now I think I had better go upstairs and shower and change—before anyone else sees me!'

David grinned. 'You look as if a little sleep mightn't come amiss, either.'

He was right, Chloe discovered a few minutes later on looking in the dressing-table mirror in her bedroom. There were dark shadows beneath her eyes, and her cheeks were very pale too.

But it had been a long night. Most of it, she remembered, spent sleeplessly as she'd sat in that chair in Fergus McCloud's bedroom, wondering what sort of man he really was.

Oh, she knew his background. Knew Fergus and his mother had gone to live in his Scottish grandfather's castle after his parents had divorced, that he had gone on to become a lawyer after university, that his career had been put on a back-burner since his rise to stardom as a writer six years ago. But those weren't the things she needed to know about him...

Was he a kind man? A compassionate man? A man who believed in fairness, even at a cost to himself?

Those were the things she needed to know about Fergus McCloud—before she could even begin to ask him for what she really wanted from him.

Contrary to David's advice, she didn't go to bed, lunching at home with her parents, and David, Penny, and the children would join them, as they usually did on a Sunday.

Chloe spent the afternoon with her mother answering letters, and accepting or refusing the numerous social invitations they had received during the week. Where possible they were accepted; her father was about to make a political comeback, and being seen socially was necessary to that campaign.

But thankfully there were only the three of them at home for dinner this evening, meaning they could eat more intimately in their family dining-room, rather than the much larger room they used when they had the numerous guests that were invited to dine here at least once a week.

The meal was superb, as usual, but by the time they had been served and eaten dinner Chloe was definitely feeling the effects of her lack of sleep from the night before, excusing herself as her parents lingered over their coffee and brandy.

'You're looking a little pale this evening, darling.' Her father looked up at Chloe concernedly after she had bent down to kiss him goodnight.

He was tall, handsome, and distinguished-looking, at fifty-five, his dark hair only showing faint tinges of grey at his temples. Chloe absolutely adored her father, would do anything in the world that she could for him. Anything!

He was infinitely kind, his compassion all consuming. He always thought of others before himself. In fact, he had all of the attributes Chloe was hoping to discover in Fergus McCloud!

She felt a heaviness in her chest just at the thought of the other man. He was another one of the reasons she was going to her bedroom earlier than usual. She had been putting off telephoning him all day, partly because she felt a certain apprehension, but also because she hoped it would make him more curious about her when she did eventually make the promised call.

Until she knew Fergus a little better, and could gauge the best way to approach him, she wanted to keep him guessing where she was concerned.

And she had certainly done that this morning! It was probably extremely naïve of her, but it really hadn't occurred to her when she'd made the decision to stay last night that Fergus would believe the two of them had spent the night together in his bed. One look at his face this morning and she had known that was exactly what he had thought!

'I had rather a late night,' she answered her father rue-fully.

'Then an early night today is the ideal thing, darling,' her mother encouraged warmly as Chloe kissed her good-night.

Also in her mid-fifties, her mother was still very beautiful. She was tiny, with dark shoulder-length hair; her face was youthful, almost unlined, and her figure still as slender as when she had been Chloe's age. Her deep blue eyes were always full of warmth and kindness. And never more so than when she looked at her younger daughter.

Penny had already been ten when Chloe had been born, a rather late surprise for all of them. But even as a very young child Chloe had sensed she was all the more precious to them because of that. As her family, and their happiness, were now infinitely precious to her...

'I'll see you both in the morning.' Chloe's smile included them both, that smile fading as soon as she was out in the hallway. Much as she would like to, she really couldn't put off telephoning Fergus McCloud any longer...!

Once in the privacy of her bedroom, she took out her mobile phone and dialled his number—before she could change her mind! If she thought about it too long, she simply wouldn't do it!

She felt her heart sink as the number kept ringing and ringing. It had never occurred to her that he wouldn't be at home when she did decide to ring him!

What—?

'Fergus McCloud,' came the sudden abrupt response as the receiver was finally picked up the other end.

Chloe drew in a controlling breath before answering. 'Have I interrupted something?' she enquired with a husky confidence she was far from feeling. But it wasn't going to help her cause if Fergus knew she had been so nervous about making this call and talking to him that she felt physically sick!

There was a brief silence on the other end of the line, and then, 'Chloe…?'

He sounded uncertain, less sure of himself than he had last night and this morning. Perhaps the waiting game had worked after all…?

'Who else were you expecting?' she came back. 'Or is that a silly question?' After all, he could have a woman— several women!—in his life.

The enquiries she had made about him discreetly the last couple of weeks hadn't uncovered too much concerning that side of Fergus's private life. Although it seemed he hadn't gone to his cousin's wedding yesterday with a companion, otherwise he wouldn't have been on his own last night at the club. Would he…?

'Not at all,' he drawled, sounding more relaxed now. 'Actually, I was in the bath when the phone rang; I had to get out to answer it.'

But he didn't sound too put out by that fact… 'Does that mean you're standing there completely naked even as we talk?' Her tone was deliberately provocative.

Which was far from the way she was actually feeling! Just the thought of it conjured up visions of last night and this morning, of Fergus, in all his naked glory, strolling casually across the bedroom in order to get his robe from the bathroom.

It had taken every ounce of will-power she possessed not to turn away, to act as if she thought nothing of his nudity!

Although, she had to admit, Fergus was well worth looking at. Tall and muscular, his skin lightly tanned, not an ounce of superfluous flesh on his body, he moved with a lithe grace that was almost feline.

'Not exactly,' Fergus answered dryly.

'Oh.' She sounded disappointed.

'I'm sitting down, actually,' he corrected laughingly. 'And I'm getting rather cold too,' he added uncomfortably.

'Mobile phone,' Chloe told him abruptly—in order to stop her thoughts dwelling too long on those memories of his physical attributes.

'I beg your pardon?' he came back in a puzzled voice.

'If you had a mobile phone, you could take it into the bathroom with you,' she explained self-consciously.

'No, I couldn't,' Fergus assured her firmly. 'I hate the damned things. They're an intrusion into man's privacy,' he stated with distaste. 'There's something rather unpleasant about the idea of just anyone being able to invade your bath; I'm rather more choosy than that!'

Chloe clearly remembered from this morning the luxurious bathroom that adjoined his bedroom, the large round sunken bath that dominated the gold and cream room; yes, it was more than big enough for two people to share!

'Just a thought,' she dismissed.

'To what do I owe the honour of this call?' he prompted.

Your unthinking actions are threatening to destroy my father, my family, all over again! she wanted to scream at him.

But she didn't...

'I said I would ring,' she reminded him.

'And do you always do what you say you will?' Fergus commented throatily.

'I find it's usually best to, yes,' Chloe rejoined. 'How did the golf go?' she continued conversationally.

'Brice trounced me,' he answered with obvious disgust. 'What did you do to me last night, woman? I hardly had the strength to hit the wretched golf ball this afternoon!'

She hadn't done anything to him last night! At least, not in the way he meant. By the time she had driven him home, staggered up the stairs with him, got him undressed and into bed, he'd been out cold!

She laughed huskily. 'Poor Fergus,' she returned non-committally.

She knew exactly what interpretation Fergus had put on finding her in his home, his bedroom, this morning. After her initial feelings of shocked dismay at the realisation, she had decided it might suit her purpose better if Fergus were to be a little unsure of himself where she was concerned. But, even so, she was not about to tell him an outright lie…

That would be reducing herself to the same level as the people who had already destroyed her father's career once. And almost destroyed their family too.

Eight years ago her father had been a prominent member of the government, in such a strong position politically that he would probably have become the next leader of his party, and so, in time, the next Prime Minister. But it had all come tumbling down around his ears when one of his aides, a woman, had committed suicide.

Susan Stirling had been aged in her mid-thirties, unmarried, not even in a long-term relationship—and she had been four months pregnant at the time of her death!

The newspapers had gone wild over the story, making a big issue as to who the father of her unborn child could possibly have been. Chloe's father had become the popular choice!

The scandal and speculation had rocked on for days, weeks—her father's official, and private, denials of the affair meaning nothing to the press.

It had been a nightmare; all the family hounded wherever they had gone, and Chloe's life at school had been made miserable as even she had been taunted with her father's so-called indiscretions. But her parents' marriage, thankfully, had survived the furore, her mother's trust in her husband unshakeable. And neither Penny nor Chloe had ever doubted their father's honesty for a moment.

But, finally, the Prime Minister of the time, with another election coming up some time during the following year, had been unwilling to let his government be shaken by such a public scandal, and had regretfully had to ask for her father's resignation.

Her father's place in his constituency had fared no better when the general election had taken place eight months later, her father losing his seat too as his opponent had used the unsolved scandal to his advantage.

Eight years her father had been in the political wilderness. Eight years!

And now, on the very eve of his attempt to restore his career, his campaign for re-election next year already underway, he was being threatened from a completely different source.

Whether he knew it or not, whether he cared or not, that source was Fergus McCloud!

And if it were humanly possible, Chloe intended stopping him!

CHAPTER THREE

'CHLOE...?' Fergus finally prompted when she hadn't responded to the question he had asked her several moments ago. Surely it didn't take this much thought to know whether or not she wanted to have dinner with him! After all, she had been the one to telephone him.

Which was something he wanted to discuss with her over the dinner he had just suggested they have together later this week...

'I'm sorry, Fergus.' She seemed to snap out of some sort of a daze. 'What did you say?'

Maybe she was just tired, too? After all, she couldn't have had much sleep last night, either!

'I asked if you would like to have dinner with me on Friday evening?' Much as Fergus would like to have seen her before then—if only to ask her several pertinent questions!—he had his mother staying in town for the rest of the week, plus he assumed that Chloe probably worked during the week, and the start of the weekend would be more convenient for her, too.

'I would love to. Thank you,' she accepted warmly. 'Where shall we go?'

'Bernardo's?' It was the fashionable restaurant of the moment, the place where anyone who was anyone went to be 'seen'. While Fergus wasn't particularly into such things himself, he thought Chloe was probably still young enough to be.

Not that he had any idea exactly how old she was, but she looked to be in her early twenties. A bit young for him really—but he obviously hadn't seemed to mind that too much last night!

'Could we make it somewhere less…showbiz?' The grimace could be heard in her voice.

'Chloe Fox, you just went up several notches in my estimation!' he announced with satisfaction. 'I hate all that posing too,' he explained ruefully.

'Then why suggest we go there?' She sounded puzzled.

'I thought you might like it,' he answered honestly.

'Thanks—but no, thanks. We could always go to Chef Simon,' she suggested lightly.

'No!' came Fergus's immediate vehement response.

Although he, Logan and Brice had always been close, Fergus preferred to keep the rest of his family very firmly at bay. His Aunt Meg had recently married Daniel Simon, the owner of Chef Simon, and yesterday Logan had married Daniel's daughter, Darcy; the last thing Fergus wanted was to turn up at the restaurant with Chloe and find himself at the centre of family speculation about his own private life!

'Okay,' Chloe didn't question the reason for his protest. 'How about we go to Xander's instead? It's—'

'I know where it is, Chloe,' he interrupted, knowing exactly where the intimately exclusive restaurant was.

He just wasn't absolutely sure he liked the way this young lady kept overriding him and taking charge of things! Domineering women were not his favourite thing. He had his mother as a prime example of how destructive they could be. His father had only been able to take it for ten years before walking out on them both!

'Unless you have somewhere else quiet you would rather go?' Chloe suggested, redeeming herself slightly in Fergus's eyes.

But only slightly. Fergus accepted that she was the most exquisitely beautiful creature he had ever seen in his life, that they had spent the night together—obviously!—but that did not mean he altogether trusted her. She knew too much about him for him to feel confident enough to do that.

'No, Xander's is fine,' he confirmed evenly. 'I'll book a table for eight-thirty, if that's okay?' He was determined to choose the time, if not the place!

'Fine,' she agreed. 'I'll see you on Friday.'

'Er—Chloe?' He stopped her as he sensed she was about to ring off. 'It's customary where I come from for a man to call and collect his date for the evening,' he explained dryly.

'I thought it might be better if we went in my car. Just in case,' she added teasingly. 'I actually don't drink alcohol, you see.'

'Neither do I, to excess. Normally,' Fergus instantly defended; it was impossible to ignore the reference to his inebriated condition of last night, even if the remark had been made jokingly.

'You explained you were depressed about your cousin's wedding,' Chloe sympathised.

Fergus wasn't sure exactly what he had and hadn't said, and done, last night. And it wasn't a feeling he was comfortable with. He was usually so much in control, master of his own destiny, and all that.

'That was the champagne talking,' he dismissed harshly. 'I'm actually very pleased for Logan and Darcy.' And in retrospect he was. Yesterday's churlishness had faded. After all, he and his cousins couldn't have remained the Elusive Three for ever! 'I would also prefer to pick you up and drive you to the restaurant on Friday evening,' he said firmly.

'And I would prefer to meet you there,' she came back just as decisively.

Fergus grimaced his frustration with her stubbornness. Why didn't she want him to call at her home for her on Friday? Did she have something to hide? Someone? Just because she wasn't wearing a wedding ring didn't mean she wasn't in a permanent relationship; not everyone bothered to get married nowadays. Although, if that were the case, her partner must be a pretty weak character to have let her stay out all of last night. *He* certainly wouldn't be as understanding in the same circumstances!

'Please yourself,' he returned flatly. 'Now, if you don't mind, I'm rather cold and wish to return to my bath.'

He was also extremely irritated by this conversation. Something about Chloe Fox—and it wasn't just her seemingly domineering nature!—really annoyed him. They had spent the night together, gone to bed together, and yet he didn't feel that he knew her at all.

Well, on Friday evening he intended changing all that!

At least, he would have done—but Chloe had yet to turn up!

By eight-forty-five, he had been sitting in the restaurant for almost fifteen minutes, and there was still no sign of her. He was starting to feel decidedly uncomfortable!

The secluded corner table was set for two people, so it was obvious he was waiting for someone to join him, and he was starting to receive sympathetic looks from the other diners. When—*if*—Chloe ever did turn up, he was not going to be in the best of moods.

Besides which, he had ordered a bottle of wine while he waited for her, and he knew—to his consternation!—that he had already drunk two glasses of it in his increasing agitation. On an empty stomach too.

But he had been working hard today, and it wasn't unusual, when he worked, that he forgot to eat. Despite Maud's efforts to make sure that he was fed!

In fact, apart from spending some time with his mother before she returned to Scotland following the wedding, he had been working hard on research for his next book all week. It had been a way of diverting his attention while he'd waited for Friday evening to arrive!

Because, hard as he had tried, he hadn't been able to find out a single thing about Chloe Fox!

A few discreet enquiries to his friends and acquaintances hadn't turned up a single person who had ever heard of Chloe Fox. Directory Enquiries had been unable to help him too, when he had no idea of her address; the telephone book was apparently full of Foxes!

It was almost as if Chloe had appeared from out of nowhere. And, apart from that telephone call to him late on Sunday evening, had disappeared as completely.

He—

Wherever Chloe had disappeared to all week, she had now very definitely reappeared!

And, once again, she took his breath away!

If he had thought her exquisitely beautiful on Saturday night and Sunday morning, that was nothing to the way she looked tonight. And Fergus knew he wasn't the only one to think so.

Xander's was a discreetly exclusive restaurant, well accustomed to the rich and the famous coming through its doors. But as Chloe Fox moved gracefully through its crowded midst, the other diners fell silent, stopped eating their delicious food, in order to turn and look at her admiringly.

Her dress was bright scarlet red, Chinese in style, with a small mandarin collar, the silk material fitted to the perfection of her body like a second skin, its above-knee length leaving bare a long expanse of shapely legs. Her hair wasn't loose tonight but pulled back and secured on the back of her head in a neat chignon, the severeness of the style revealing the full extent of her unusual beauty.

Her skin was as delicate as magnolia, liner giving those deep blue eyes a slightly slanted appearance, her lips painted the same scarlet as her dress. She was, undisputably, the most beautiful woman in the room.

Fergus couldn't help feeling a certain satisfaction in knowing she was to be his partner for the evening.

He stood up as she approached their table. 'You look wonderful,' he told her as he pulled her chair back for her to sit down, his senses at once assailed with the delicacy of the perfume she wore.

Fergus had no idea what the perfume was, but he did know that he would never be able to smell it again without thinking of this woman. For good or bad!

'Thank you, Fergus.' She reached up to kiss him lightly on the cheek before sitting down. 'Isn't this a wonderful restaurant?' She looked around them with obvious pleasure.

While Fergus could only look at her!

He was thirty-five years old, had known many beautiful women in those years, quite a lot of them on a very intimate level. But he had never known any woman before who possessed Chloe Fox's sensually mesmerising beauty.

'Sorry I'm a little late.' She smiled at him now, revealing those tiny, even white teeth he remembered from last weekend.

But he couldn't help feeling slightly irritated when she offered no explanation for her tardiness. After all, he had been sitting here for almost twenty minutes, feeling more and more of an idiot as those minutes had passed.

'Would you like a glass of wine?' he offered stiffly.

She smiled ruefully. 'I really don't drink,' she refused with a shake of her head, turning to ask the waiter for some

mineral water. 'Have you had a good week?' she turned
back to enquire of Fergus politely.

His irritation increased. Politeness was fine, in its place,
but between Chloe and himself he found it implied a distance that just shouldn't be there after they had spent the
night together last Saturday.

'Very good,' he confirmed tersely; he had covered a lot
of research towards his next novel this week, should be
ready to start writing very soon. 'How about you?'

'I've kept busy.' She shrugged.

'Doing what?'

'This and that,' she dismissed, those blue eyes dancing
with mirth as she looked across at him beneath lowered
lashes.

Fergus couldn't miss the fact that her mirth was at his
expense! This little minx knew exactly what he was doing—and she was just as determined not to be in the least
helpful!

Fergus drew in a harsh breath. 'Chloe—'

'I'm sorry, Fergus, I shouldn't tease you.' She laughed
huskily, reaching out to touch his hand briefly in apology.
'I'm a fashion designer.'

At last, he knew something about her other than her
name! Not much, admittedly, but it was a start.

'Did you design the dress you're wearing tonight?' he
prompted interestedly.

'Of course,' she dismissed, smiling up at the waiter as
he brought, and poured, her water.

Of course...

In that case, her designs were excellent; the dress looked
wonderful on her, suited her slender delicacy perfectly.

'Who do you work for?' he asked lightly, feeling the ice
was breaking between them at last. In the circumstances, it
shouldn't have been there in the first place!

Chloe sipped her water before answering. 'Myself,' she replied. 'But what about you, are you—?'

'You mean you're a freelance designer?' Fergus cut determinedly over what he guessed was going to be a deliberate change of subject on Chloe's part. Away from herself!

'Not exactly,' she answered noncommittally. 'Shall we look at the menus?' she said with a smile. 'I'm absolutely starving!'

She *was* changing the subject, damn it. Although he couldn't argue with the necessity of choosing their food; he had gone past starving himself and was now onto ravenous!

But if Chloe thought by looking at the menus and choosing their food he was going to let go of the only thing he had actually found out about her so far, then she was mistaken!

Chloe studied him surreptitiously from behind the shield of her menu. He had hidden it well, but she knew he had been absolutely furious when she'd actually arrived here this evening. Not surprising, really; she had been almost twenty minutes late. Deliberately so.

One thing she had learnt about Fergus McCloud in the last few weeks: a simpering sycophant was not going to hold his interest for more than two minutes!

He was a man who had avoided a serious relationship, let alone matrimony, for at least the last fifteen years. Any woman who wanted to hold this man's interest for more than a couple of dates would have to be unusual, to say the least.

Although Chloe wasn't sure, as she saw that tightness about his mouth, the angry glitter in those warm brown eyes, that she hadn't gone too far. The last thing she wanted to happen was for Fergus not to even like her!

Because, strangely enough, she could all too easily like him...

He was interesting. Intelligent. Fun. His good looks unmistakable. And there had been something boyishly attractive, endearingly so, about his protectiveness towards her when his cousin Brice had arrived at the house last Sunday morning and found them there together...

Under any other circumstances, she was sure she would like Fergus McCloud very much indeed.

Again it was 'under other circumstances'...

She put her menu down on the table, smiling across at Fergus as he looked across at her enquiringly. She was right; he had started to feel wary of her. And that wasn't the idea at all!

'Actually, Fergus, I have my own label, sell my clothes to several well-known couturier shops,' she told him brightly.

'Very exclusive,' he guessed.

'Very,' she confirmed.

'And very expensive?' he drawled.

She laughed again softly. 'Of course.'

He relaxed slightly, obviously having just been given the answer to several more questions that he had concerning her; how she afforded her sports car and how she was so obviously at ease in these surroundings, to name but two. However, Chloe easily sensed that there were a lot more questions Fergus wanted answers to than those...

'What's the label called?' he prompted casually, putting his own menu down to give her his full attention.

Her mouth quirked. 'Would you believe, "Foxy"?' Not much help there!

Fergus gave a rueful smile. 'I'd believe,' he acknowledged. 'How come you and I have never met before, Chloe

Fox? That I have never even heard your name mentioned before?'

Because until a year ago she hadn't lived in London all year round, had been at boarding-school in the south of England for years, before going on to university, and then she had spent a year in Paris with one of the top designers there. And in the last year she had been too busy getting her business off the ground to feature too much on the social scene.

There was also the fact that she hadn't been a hundred-per-cent honest concerning her name.

She shrugged. 'Just bad luck, I suppose,' she answered.

Fergus grinned. 'Yours or mine?'

'Both, of course,' Chloe returned. 'It would be very rude of me to say anything else.'

'You don't like to be rude. And you always try to do what you say you will,' Fergus murmured thoughtfully.

This man was making an inventory on what he slowly learnt about her! Not a good development.

'You might also like to know that I like to be fed at least twice a day,' she went on. 'And as I only had time for a quick breakfast this morning, and no lunch...' she added pointedly.

'You would like to eat now.' Fergus nodded, signalling to the waiter that they were ready to order.

Chloe studied him while the waiter noted their choices. Fergus's good looks weren't in doubt. Nor were his wealth or charm. But she would do well to remember not to underestimate his intelligence; Fergus was more than capable of adding two and two together and coming up with the correct answer of four. Maybe not tonight. But it wouldn't take too much probing on his part to discover exactly who the designer 'Foxy' was.

Telling him about that had been a calculated risk, but

one she had deemed necessary in the face of his wariness. She wanted to keep his interest, but she wasn't going to get anywhere with him at all if she made herself too mysterious. And she still had a long way to go with this man if she were to achieve her objective.

'So tell me,' she said conversationally as the two of them enjoyed their starters, melon and strawberries in Chloe's case, and *moules marinière* in Fergus's, 'why didn't you want us to eat at your uncle's restaurant this evening?'

Fergus seemed to almost choke over the mussel he had just spooned into his mouth, looking across at her frowningly.

Chloe eyed him speculatively. 'Sorry—was I mistaken?' But she knew she wasn't, knew Fergus had been horrified at her suggestion that the two of them meet at Chef Simon this evening.

'Not at all,' he replied slowly. 'And the answer is simple, Chloe; I wanted to get to know you without any family distractions.'

There was a word for smooth flattery like this—but Chloe was too ladylike to even think it!

'How nice,' she returned as insincerely.

'I thought so,' Fergus replied. 'I'm sure you'll agree, there's still a lot we don't know about each other?'

What he really meant was there was a lot he still didn't know about her! Although he was obviously hoping to change all that tonight. If Chloe had anything to do with it, he was going to be out of luck!

She smiled across at him. 'What's the saying? "Finding out is half the fun"?'

'Probably,' he acknowledged dryly, not looking in the least convinced of the sentiment.

'I—'

'Chloe! It is Chloe, isn't it...?' the voice added less certainly.

Chloe's air of flirtation immediately deserted her as she looked up and easily recognised the man who had stopped beside their table.

Peter Ambrose!

It wasn't surprising that, having initially believed he recognised her, on closer inspection he was less sure; she had been fifteen years old the last time he'd seen her!

She swallowed hard, deliberately not looking at Fergus now; a previous brief glance his way had told her that he was stunned at the identity of the other man.

Which wasn't surprising! Until three years ago Peter Ambrose had been the British Prime Minister. Even now, he was still the Leader of the Opposition. And he obviously knew Chloe well enough to call her by her first name!

This was something she couldn't possibly have allowed for when she had decided to lay siege to Fergus McCloud!

CHAPTER FOUR

FERGUS once again found himself asking, who *was* Chloe Fox?

She was beautiful, intelligent, had a slightly wicked sense of humour, he was learning, but who *was* she?

'Peter,' she was greeting the other man warmly now as the two shook hands. 'How lovely to see you. Are Jean and the children all well?'

Fergus shook his head dazedly. Chloe also went to fashionable nightclubs, drove an expensive sports car, was a fashion designer with her own label—and she was on first-name terms with the former Prime Minister and his wife!

Peter Ambrose smiled down at her admiringly as he slowly released her hand. Too slowly, in Fergus's opinion!

'Jean is with me this evening.' The other man indicated a table across the room where his wife sat waiting for him. 'And the ''children'' are now aged twenty and twenty-two!' he added wryly.

Chloe laughed softly. 'It's been a while,' she acknowledged.

'Too long,' Peter Ambrose pressed warmly. 'I can't tell you how pleased we are to have Paul back with us,' he continued more seriously.

Paul? Fergus questioned inwardly. Who on earth was Paul? He hated being in the dark like this. It was even more galling when it was with a woman with whom he had apparently been on such intimate terms!

The question that was plaguing him the most was just

how intimate had her relationship with Peter Ambrose once been?

The other man, Fergus knew, was aged in his mid-fifties, had been married to Jean for over thirty of those years. But he was still an attractive man, tall, slim, blond hair flecked with grey; in fact, it was those relative good looks that had helped him succeed in his endeavour to lead his political party.

And he and Chloe Fox obviously knew each other very well!

Fergus felt the stirrings of the same unease he had known last weekend when she'd been so determined to join him; not just who was Chloe Fox—but *what* was she?

'I'm sorry, Fergus, I should have introduced the two of you.' Chloe turned belatedly to include him in their conversation. 'Peter, this is Fergus McCloud. Fergus, this is—'

'I know who he is, Chloe,' he rasped. 'Mr Ambrose.' He had stood up abruptly, briefly shaking the other man's hand.

'McCloud...?' Peter Ambrose repeated with a thoughtful expression. 'Why do I feel I should know that name...?'

Fergus's mouth twisted wryly. 'Probably because I have an appointment to come and see you on Wednesday,' he drawled.

'You do...?' The other man's thoughtful expression deepened. 'Of course you do.' His brow cleared. 'I remember now, you're the writer, aren't you?'

Fergus couldn't believe the coincidence of having bumped into this man this evening. Not that it was his coincidence. It was Chloe whom the other man knew; Peter Ambrose obviously wouldn't have distinguished him from one of the waiters serving on the tables here!

But Fergus still found it strange, after weeks of waiting to see Peter Ambrose, that he had met the man so casually this evening. Because Chloe Fox, a woman who had forced her company on him last Saturday evening, obviously knew Ambrose well. Very well, indeed.

'I am,' he confirmed evenly.

Peter Ambrose nodded. 'I remember my secretary thought you seemed very mysterious concerning your reasons for wanting to talk to me...?'

There was nothing mysterious about it at all, it just wasn't something Fergus intended talking about with anyone but the major players. And Chloe, no matter what her friendship with this man was—or had once been—wasn't one of them.

'I'm sure we really shouldn't keep you from your wife any longer, Peter,' Chloe was the one to put in decisively, looking up at the two men with cool blue eyes.

Peter Ambrose continued to look at Fergus probingly for several long seconds before turning slowly to smile at Chloe once again. 'You're right,' he agreed. 'It's really been lovely to see you again, Chloe. Let's hope I see you again very soon, hmm?' he added gently.

'I hope so,' Chloe replied.

'I'll look forward to seeing you again on Wednesday, Mr McCloud.' Peter Ambrose gave an acknowledging inclination of his head in parting.

Fergus slowly sat back at the table, his gaze narrowed thoughtfully on Chloe. She was a mystery within an enigma, an enigma within a labyrinth of unanswered questions. As a writer he wanted to solve that mystery. As a man, he hadn't got the least idea how he was going to go about it!

He drew in a harsh breath. 'You move in some pretty exalted circles, Chloe,' he ventured speculatively.

She resumed eating her fruit, her outward demeanour one of cool calmness. Outward, because, despite how she might want to appear concerning the unexpected encounter with

Peter Ambrose, Fergus was sure he could detect a slight tremble to her hands.

'Not so exalted; Peter is no longer Prime Minister,' she countered.

'Chloe—'

'I knew his two children rather better than I ever knew Peter or Jean,' Chloe concluded.

Those children who at twenty and twenty-two were no longer children? Somehow Fergus very much doubted that she was telling him the whole truth. Despite the fact that Chloe was breathtakingly lovely, that he found her physically arousing, that he had obviously already spent the night with her, he had no use in his life for lies and deception.

Chloe looked across at him, her gaze unblinkingly compelling. 'You don't believe me, do you?' It was a statement rather than a question.

Fergus was momentarily taken aback by the directness of her attack 'I don't know what to believe,' he finally answered truthfully.

She put her cutlery back on her plate, her food still only half eaten as she looked at him coldly. 'Am I mistaken, or do you have the mistaken idea I've had an affair with Peter Ambrose?'

Fergus winced. Put into words like that, it sounded slightly ludicrous. And yet—because he didn't quite believe her explanation about knowing Ambrose's children—if she hadn't been involved with the other man, how on earth did she know him? Besides, it was noticeable that Jean Ambrose hadn't shared her husband's eagerness to come and say hello...

'You do.' Chloe sighed at his delay in responding. 'Fergus, I may be many things, but ''the other woman'' is not one of them. Do you believe that?' she pressed.

Strangely enough now he did. She had told him very

little about herself, but suddenly he was sure that what she had just told him was the truth. He just found his whole relationship with Chloe—whatever it was!—totally beyond his control. And he wasn't comfortable with that. In the past he had always been the one to call the shots; Chloe, for all she was still extremely young, simply wouldn't allow him to do that.

'I believe you,' he sighed heavily. 'But there's something you aren't telling me, Chloe—'

'There's lots of things I'm not telling you, Fergus,' she admitted with a smile, her tension easing at his assurances. 'I'm sure you have absolutely no interest in hearing how cute my mother thought I was as a baby, what a little brat I was when I first went away to boarding-school, how studious I was at university, what a great time I had in Paris during the year following that. Wouldn't it be terribly boring if we already knew everything about each other?' she reasoned.

Well, of course it would, but that wasn't the point—

If he persisted with this, he would lose her! Fergus knew it as clearly as if she had said the words out loud...

'Apparently my mother thought I was cute as a baby too,' he returned. 'And the three of us, my two cousins and myself, were the bane of my grandfather's estate manager's life when we were growing up in Scotland. I didn't study quite so diligently at university as you apparently did, but I did okay anyway. I enjoyed my years as a lawyer, and I enjoy writing even more. But you're right, we don't need to know everything about each other by the second date.'

'Officially this is our first date,' Chloe corrected dryly.

And it had almost ended with Chloe getting up and walking out on him!

He had sensed it a few minutes ago, knew that she was ready to take flight if he persisted in not believing her. And he had suddenly known that, whoever she was, whatever she was, he didn't want her to go. Chloe Fox intrigued him, bewitched him, and he wasn't going to let her go out of his life until he had unravelled at least some of her mystery.

Chloe watched the expressions as they flitted rapidly across Fergus McCloud's face, sure that he had no idea just how much of his thoughts he was giving away.

It wasn't that he didn't believe her—he just didn't trust her!

Though she couldn't blame him for that, knew he was unsettled by the strangeness of their relationship anyway, that he had been totally thrown when Peter Ambrose had recognised her and come over to their table to talk to her.

That was nothing to the panic she had felt on recognising the other man!

Of all the things that could have happened, accidentally bumping into Peter Ambrose had to be the worst. However, on the other hand, without that accidental meeting she wouldn't have known of Fergus's appointment to see Peter on Wednesday...

Peter would be puzzled as to Fergus's reasons for wanting to see him; perhaps he believed, if he had given it any thought at all, that it was something to do with his political campaign to return his party to power in the general election next year. But Chloe had no such illusions.

She also knew, from listening to the two men, that her time was running out!

'Are you thinking of making a shift into politics next, Fergus?' she asked interestedly as their plates were cleared prior to the main course being served.

He laughed softly, shaking his head. 'Certainly not,' he replied vehemently. 'I like my privacy too much to even contemplate it.'

'But surely there's a certain amount of publicity involved in being an author?'

'Not enough to worry about,' Fergus assured her with satisfaction. 'Besides, do you think my personal life would stand up to the sort of intense public scrutiny that follows every politician?'

She raised dark brows. 'I don't know—would it?'

'No.' Fergus chuckled again. 'I've never been married, so no doubt the press would assume I have to be gay. And when they discover that isn't right, they would then commence speculating about my future marriage to every woman I even look at.' He shook his head again. 'I don't think so, thanks.'

Fergus painted a fairly awful picture for anyone entering public life. But, as Chloe knew all too well, it was also a correct one!

She had been pretty much protected from all of that by her parents during her childhood, but nevertheless she had known of the battering their own private life took on a day-to-day level. It had taken on horrific proportions after the scandal had hit the headlines eight years ago.

Chloe shrugged. 'Sorry. I just assumed, with the meeting you have with Peter Ambrose next week...?'

'Research,' Fergus replied, before sitting back so that their main course could be served.

The interruption couldn't have come at a worse time as far as Chloe was concerned. They were actually approaching the subject she was really interested in now—and their food had to arrive!

She was impatient for the waiter to leave, refusing vegetables or salad with her grilled salmon, although she had to sit by while Fergus was served a little from each of the four vegetable dishes to accompany his rare fillet steak.

'I'm hungry too,' he excused, once they had been left to enjoy their meal.

'You were telling me that you're researching a new book...?' Chloe tried again, picking uninterestedly at the salmon, her appetite having completely deserted her since Peter Ambrose had spoken to them.

Fergus leisurely finished chewing and swallowing a mouthful of steak before answering her. 'I don't believe I said it was for a book,' he replied guardedly.

Chloe gave him a frowning look, knowing he was being deliberately evasive. What else would he, an author, be doing research on if not a book...? Besides, she knew exactly what story he was researching!

'Just say if it's a subject you would prefer not to talk about,' she said lightly.

'It's a subject I would prefer not to talk about,' he repeated evenly. 'I don't mean to be rude, Chloe—'

'You're not making a good job of it, then,' she cut in teasingly, inwardly furious with herself for giving him such an opening for a cop-out, but in truth, she hadn't really thought he would take it! He must be one of the few men she had ever met who didn't enjoy talking about himself!

Fergus sighed. 'Writing, I've found, is a very strange profession. Well, for me it is.' He grimaced. 'I've discovered from experience, that in the interest of keeping the story fresh and alive for me it's best if I never discuss my current work with anyone. Except my agent, of course.' He smiled. 'And even he only gets the barest outline of the plot so that he can sell the idea to the publisher!'

She was already well aware of that!

'Think of it in terms of your most recent designs, Chloe,' he continued slowly. 'I'm sure you don't share those with anyone else, either!'

'That's only because someone might steal the idea—

You don't think that I would steal the plot for your book, do you, Fergus?' she exclaimed. 'I can assure you, I wouldn't have the least idea how to go about even starting to write a book!'

'Do you think it's true that everyone has at least one book inside them waiting to come out, given the right circumstances?' he asked.

She *thought* he was changing the subject—damn him. 'I just told you, I wouldn't even know how to start. That's why I'm so interested in the fact that you do,' she added huskily. 'One thing I do know, Fergus; your next book obviously has a political angle.'

'Maybe,' he returned evasively. 'Tell me, do you have brothers and sisters, Chloe?'

'An older sister,' she confirmed frustratedly; this was like getting blood out of a stone! 'You?' But she already knew that he didn't, had discovered that much about him at least.

'No,' he also confirmed. 'How about your parents? Are they both still alive?'

'I would hope so—they're only in their fifties, Fergus!' she rebuked, her parents, her father in particular, not a subject she wished to discuss with this man. Whatever information Fergus managed to find out about her father certainly would not come from her! 'How about yours?'

'Divorced. But both still alive,' he provided economically, suddenly fixing a compelling brown gaze on her. 'Tell me, Chloe, why are you so guarded about your own private life?'

Inwardly, she stiffened defensively at this sudden breach of good manners. Outwardly, she remained unshaken. She hoped. 'I wasn't aware that I was,' she answered levelly.

Fergus nodded. 'You know, Chloe, I have the distinct impression you're trying to hide something.' He eyed her humorously, but there was a steely edge to his tone.

Chloe forced herself to remain calm, meeting his steady gaze unflinchingly. 'Such as?' she prompted mockingly.

He shrugged. 'Maybe you're married? Or engaged? Or living with someone? Or maybe you're just an axe-murderess in search of a new victim?' he amended mischievously.

But Chloe wasn't fooled for a moment. That last remark had only been added for effect—it was the first three questions he was really interested in having an answer to. Did he really think she would be here with him now if any of those were true…?

'You guessed it—I'm an axe-murderess!' she replied unhelpfully.

Fergus didn't return her smile; instead he looked at her darkly. 'I'm not sure this relationship is going anywhere, Chloe,' he stated softly.

He was right, it wasn't. Not in the direction he wanted, anyway.

'I thought that was the way you liked it?' she returned abruptly.

'It is,' he responded slowly. 'But I find it strange, considering the two of us spent the night together last Saturday, that we don't seem to be making too much progress. In fact, we're behaving as if we're complete strangers to each other.'

He sounded genuinely regretful about that, and Chloe knew that she was the one to blame for that. She was the reason they weren't as relaxed and comfortable with each other as they should be. But how could she possibly be either of those things with Fergus when she knew he intended wreaking havoc in her father's life?

Because she knew exactly what Fergus's current book was going to be about, knew that he intended using the scandal that had wrecked her father's career eight years ago as the main focus of that story.

And the hardback of that book was scheduled to reach the bookshops only weeks prior to her father's bid for re-election!

CHAPTER FIVE

'EXCUSE the pun, Fergus,' Chloe said brightly, 'but you aren't exactly an open book yourself!'

He knew that. He had never been particularly close to any of the women he had been involved with over the years, let alone fallen in love with any of them. He preferred to keep his inner self to himself, never allowed any of his relationships to become too important in his life. In fact, he had been accused, more than once, of being distant and aloof. But he had never before encountered those very same traits in a woman. And a very young woman, at that.

'Touché,' he allowed. 'Do you think two clams like us are ever going to get to know each other?'

She smiled. 'As I've already said, we might have fun trying.'

They might. Fergus just wished that he could remember their being together last Saturday. It might help if he could remember how Chloe had felt in his arms, how her nakedness had felt next to his. Was she a silent lover, or did she give voice to her pleasure? He presumed he *had* given her pleasure; after all, she had been willing to see him again!

Suddenly he knew he had had enough of sitting in this restaurant, of the two of them trying to make polite conversation. He wanted to know Chloe. In the only way it seemed she would let him know her.

'Have you had enough of that?' He indicated the salmon on her plate she had been playing with, but not eating, the last ten minutes or so.

She looked startled. 'Yes...?'

'So have I.' He threw his napkin on the table-top, sig-nalling the waiter to bring him the bill. 'Let's get out of here, hmm?' he prompted impatiently, standing up to move round the table and pull back her chair for her.

Chloe looked confused as she stood up too. 'But I thought you were hungry…?'

'I am.' He grinned down at her wolfishly, knowing his meaning wasn't lost on Chloe as colour suddenly high-lighted her cheeks, giving darkness and depth to those beautiful blue eyes. Good; at least she hadn't become so cynical she couldn't still blush!

He still had no idea how old she was, but he would guess only twenty-three, or -four, at the most. But there was a reserve in her eyes, a wariness in her behaviour, that seemed to imply someone had once hurt her very badly. It was a reserve Fergus wanted to completely erase, if only for the time she was in his arms.

She seemed slightly dazed as he paid the bill, giving Peter and Jean Ambrose a brief wave goodbye before Fergus hustled her out the door.

Fergus had deliberately come by taxi this evening, but Chloe's car was parked only a short distance away, and he folded his long length into the passenger seat once she had unlocked the doors.

'I'd love to know how you got me in here the other night,' he murmured ruefully; his head touched the roof, and his knees were almost under his chin.

'The seat was further back that night. You'll find the controls on the door,' Chloe told him distractedly as she started the engine before pulling the car out into the flow of traffic.

Meaning someone else had sat in this seat during the last week, Fergus realised as he readjusted the seat so that it was more comfortable for him. Someone obviously several inches shorter than him...

Male or female? Fergus found himself wondering—and not liking the idea that it could have been another man. Chloe might be doing everything in her power to prevent him from getting to know her too well, but he found he certainly didn't like the possibility of there being another man in her life!

'Where are we going?' Chloe asked, beside him.

'Your place or mine,' he answered abruptly, still slightly disturbed by the thought of Chloe with another man.

'Yours, then,' she rejoined instantly, taking the turning that would eventually lead to his home.

Reminding Fergus that he still had several things he wanted to ask Miss Chloe Fox; how she had known last weekend where he lived, for one, and how she had known his telephone number so she could ring him on Sunday, for two!

But at the moment he was more interested in the fact that she had once again chosen not to give anything away about where she lived...

He turned to look at her consideringly, abstractly admiring the economy of her movements as she controlled the powerful car. 'Do you actually live in London?'

'Of course,' she confirmed in a puzzled voice.

'Alone?' he prompted softly.

Chloe turned to give him a brief glance before returning her attention to the road. 'No,' she finally answered.

Fergus felt himself tense at the admission. She didn't live alone! Then who—?

'I live with my parents, Fergus,' she informed him quietly. 'Hence the reason it wouldn't be a good idea for the two of us to go there. I take it you aren't into meeting parents?'

Too damned right, he wasn't! Especially the parents of a woman he had only met twice—and didn't really know at all!

'No,' he confirmed dryly. 'You're right, that could have posed a problem.'

She gave a half-smile. 'I thought so.'

Fergus gave her a considering look. 'You seem to know me rather well...?'

'Not at all, Fergus,' she dismissed laughingly. 'I think all men have a parent phobia!'

Unless they had serious intentions, yes. And Fergus had never had those, about any woman.

But he couldn't help wondering what Chloe's parents were like, if she still felt comfortable living with them. Surely that was unusual for a woman of her age; he remembered he hadn't been able to get out of his family home quick enough in order to set up his own bachelor apartment!

Obviously, Chloe came from a close family, then. Another fact about her he could add to the few he already had! Too few, in his opinion. But as she had already pointed out, at least they weren't bored with each other! Somehow Fergus was of the opinion that very few men would ever be bored in Chloe Fox's company!

'Who's Paul—? Careful!' Fergus instantly warned as Chloe veered the car sharply to the right. It would seem he had hit a sensitive nerve with his question...!

'Sorry,' she muttered, the car safely back on course now. 'I thought I saw a cat in the road.'

She had thought no such thing! Her face was slightly flushed, and those beautiful slender hands were tightly gripping the steering wheel; his question about the man Paul had completely unnerved her.

And she had neatly avoided answering it...

'I'm sorry, Fergus,' she said suddenly. 'But I seem to have developed a bit of a headache.'

And he had thought women saved that excuse for when they were married! He really had struck a sensitive nerve...

'Poor Chloe,' he sympathised. 'I'll get you something for it as soon as we get to the house.'

'I think, if you don't mind, that I would rather just call it a night and go home.' She grimaced.

Yes, he did mind! He still knew virtually nothing about this woman, had thought that once they were alone at his home that he would at least be able to hold her, to kiss her. Her decision to end the evening had put paid to that idea.

'Come in and have a cup of coffee first,' he encouraged as she stopped the car in the driveway.

'I really don't think—'

'I don't like the idea of you continuing to drive while you still have a headache,' he interrupted firmly, his gaze compelling. 'It's only a cup of coffee, Chloe,' he derided as she still looked uncertain.

'Okay,' she sighed, switching off the engine. 'Just a coffee.'

Fergus was frowning as he let the two of them into the house.

Unless he was very much mistaken, Chloe was fighting shy of any intimacy occurring between the two of them. Which, considering they had gone to bed together last weekend, was very strange...

Unless she had just decided, on closer acquaintance, that she wasn't attracted to him after all?

Whereas he, in complete contrast, had found that, on closer acquaintance, he wanted and desired Chloe Fox very much!

*　　*　　*

How on earth had she got herself into this situation? More to the point, how did she get herself out of it?

She had been completely stunned when Fergus had decided to leave the restaurant so precipitously, so stunned she hadn't been able to come up with a reason for them to have stayed, it must have been obvious to him that she'd no longer been eating her meal!

As for that question about Paul once they'd been in the car…!

Going back to Fergus's home with him had not been in her plans for the evening. She had intended saying goodnight to him after they'd left the restaurant. Although, she had realised once they'd been outside, ten-thirty had probably been a little early for that!

'Come through to the kitchen,' Fergus invited now. 'It's okay, Chloe,' he encouraged as she hung back reluctantly. 'My housekeeper will already have retired to her own rooms for the evening.'

If he meant to reassure her, he had failed miserably! She would have found it much more comforting to know that there was someone else around. Because it was one thing to act, for Fergus's benefit, as if they had spent the night together last Saturday, something else completely for him to expect that to actually happen again tonight!

She had been involved in relationships in the past, had even thought of marrying one of the men she'd met in Paris last year, but none of those relationships had ever gone beyond what she was comfortable with. She simply wasn't the type who could leap in and out of bed with a succession of men.

But Fergus believed they had already been to bed together once, and he would surely expect for it to happen again tonight…?

She should never have started this; it had been an act of madness on her part. Or desperation!

By the time Fergus had removed the jacket to his dark suit and had thrown it over the back of one of the kitchen chairs, moved economically around the kitchen preparing a pot of coffee, Chloe's headache was no longer a figment of her imagination!

'Here.' Fergus handed her two pills to go with the cup of coffee he had placed in front of her on the kitchen table.

He was being very kind and considerate, Chloe decided. Two of the qualities she had wanted to know he possessed. But did he have the third one; was he willing to make a personal sacrifice for someone else's benefit?

'I must say you do look rather pale.' He frowned down at her now. 'Let's go through to the sitting-room, I can switch the fire on in there and warm you up a little.'

She didn't want warming up, Chloe muttered to herself as she followed him out of the kitchen—she wanted to get out of here! Preferably before—long before!—Fergus could discover that they hadn't made love together last Saturday.

It was a very male sitting-room, all golds and browns, the furniture sturdy, no feminine touches to soften its austerity. But, for all that, the room had the warmth of its owner. Which was added to considerably when Fergus turned on the promised fire, the flames almost looking real as they flickered through the artificial logs.

'That's better,' he said with satisfaction before coming to sit next to her on the sofa.

Bad choice, Chloe instantly realised, but the sofa had been the closest seat to the heat from the fire. She really wasn't very good at this. She couldn't help wondering what Fergus would have to say if he knew just how inexperienced she was!

She was very aware of him sitting close beside her, could

feel the warmth emanating from his body, smell the slight tanginess of his aftershave. He really was a most attractive man, she acknowledged achingly as she looked at him beneath lowered lashes.

He turned to look at her, one hand moving up to smooth the wispy tendrils of hair at her temples. 'Feeling any better?' he prompted huskily.

She felt a sight worse with him close to her like this! Her legs were shaking, her hands were trembling as she still held her cup of coffee, and she couldn't seem to breathe properly, either.

She swallowed hard. 'Not really,' she replied, hoping he couldn't feel how nervous she was.

Fergus frowned some more. 'Perhaps you would feel better if you let this down.' He reached round to the neat chignon of her hair, deftly removing the four clips that kept it in place.

Her hair at once cascaded down in a curtain of midnight, and Fergus's fingers threaded through its silkiness as he helped release it about her shoulders, all the time his gaze locked darkly with hers.

Chloe's scalp tingled—but not from having her hair released. It was the touch of Fergus's hands, the desire so apparent in his mesmerising gaze, that gave her that thrill of sensation.

Oh...!

'You've done that before,' she attempted to tease.

He shook his head. 'Not that I can remember. But then, when I'm around you, I seem to have a problem even remembering my name!'

So did she. Or, at least, the parts of her name she had given him...

She moistened suddenly dry lips. 'Fergus—'

'That's it,' he confirmed lightly. 'My name is Fergus.

And you're Chloe. Beautiful, sexy, desirable Chloe,' he murmured softly before his head lowered and his lips gently took possession of hers.

Chloe's whole body seemed to turn to liquid fire at the first touch of those lips, feeling as if she were melting, being consumed. She had never felt anything like this in her life before!

Fergus sipped from her mouth, tasted, his hands once again in her hair as he held her face up to his kiss, his tongue now moving searchingly over the sensitivity of her lips.

Chloe groaned low in her throat as she capitulated to that sensuality, instinctively reaching up to prolong the pleasure of those burning kisses—and instantly gasped as she felt burning of a completely different kind!

'What the—?' Fergus rasped as he hurriedly shifted away from her to look down dazedly to where Chloe had just tipped coffee over the two of them.

She had completely forgotten she'd still held the half-full coffee-cup in her hand as she'd reached up to touch Fergus!

'I'm so sorry,' she groaned awkwardly, relieved to feel that the coffee was rapidly cooling as it soaked through her dress—and Fergus's trousers.

'Well, that certainly put a dampener on things—literally.' Fergus grimaced as he gently took the cup and saucer from her lap to place them on the table behind them. 'I'll go and get a towel.' He stood up to quickly leave the room.

Chloe closed her eyes briefly once she was alone, leaning her head back against the sofa. She felt utterly, completely, stupid! What sort of moron forgot they were holding a cup of coffee in their hand? More to the point, what sort of moron did *Fergus* think forgot they had a cup of coffee in their hand?

'Here we are.' Fergus arrived back with the towel and, much to Chloe's embarrassment, proceeded to mop the coffee from her dress, the material now clinging to her damply.

Could this get any worse? she asked herself.

'Your dress is ruined, I'm afraid.' Fergus sat back to survey the wet silk when he had dried it as best he could. 'You'll have to take it off,' he added decisively.

It *could* get worse! It just had...!

Chloe hesitated before answering. 'It will soon dry—'

'Don't be ridiculous,' Fergus rejoined easily, standing up to reach out a hand to pull her to her feet. 'You need to slip out of that dress and into a hot shower.'

She didn't intend slipping out of anything—or into anything either, for that matter!

'There's really no need,' she assured him as she stood up. 'It's time I was leaving anyway.'

Fergus looked at her with narrowed eyes. 'I thought you were staying here tonight...?'

She was well aware of what he had thought—it just wasn't going to happen! 'I really do have a headache, Fergus,' she told him decidedly, deliberately not meeting that piercing gaze as she knew he continued to look at her.

And look at her...

He was obviously debating whether or not there were some way he could still persuade her to stay. He was wasting his time!

'Fine,' he finally rasped at her deliberately closed expression. 'I'll walk you to your car, then,' he offered with sharp dismissal.

Chloe didn't need to look at him to know that he was furiously angry. A cold, controlled anger. All the more unnerving because of that.

'Thank you,' she accepted huskily, walking through to the kitchen to collect her bag and keys. 'Perhaps we could have lunch together one day next week?' she suggested as the two of them walked to the door, Fergus a brooding presence behind her.

She had deliberately not mentioned the two of them meet over the weekend. Lunch, during the week, she had decided, with the excuse of returning to work to fall back on, would be infinitely safer than having dinner with him again; she doubted Fergus would expect her to jump into bed with him in the middle of the day!

'Perhaps,' he echoed noncommittally as he stood beside her open car door, Chloe already inside sitting behind the wheel.

But, from the tone of his voice, it wasn't very likely, Chloe realised heavily.

Maybe she should have stayed after all...? Maybe she could still have salvaged the evening, somehow brought the conversation round to the subject of Fergus's next book...?

Although, she had to admit, Fergus didn't look in the mood this evening to be told she had only wanted to know him at all in order to be able to gauge his response to being asked not to write his next book based on the scandal that had resulted in her father's resignation from government eight years ago! But, nevertheless, with the knowledge of Fergus's appointment with Peter Ambrose on Wednesday, Chloe knew she didn't have a lot of time left before the whole thing probably became public, anyway...

'I'll call you, shall I?' she prompted expectantly.

Fergus looked down at her, his expression readable in the light streaming from the open door behind him; his mouth was a thin, angry line, his eyes enigmatically hooded.

'I realise that until now you may have thought otherwise, Chloe—but I really prefer to do my own calling,' he finally bit out scathingly.

She looked up at him with a half-smile. 'You don't have my telephone number.'

'No,' he acknowledged shortly.

And he wasn't interested in knowing it, either, she realised with an inward wince. She really had annoyed him, hadn't she...?

But wasn't he being just a little arrogant too, in assuming that she would spend the night with him?

Arrogant or not, that was what he had thought—and he wasn't at all happy with the fact that she was leaving.

'Fine,' she echoed his own earlier terse dismissal, too shaken at the moment to argue the point. 'Thank you for dinner, Fergus,' she added softly. 'I enjoyed it.'

He raised dark brows over mocking brown eyes. 'You didn't eat it,' he pointed out.

She shrugged. 'I enjoyed what I ate.'

Fergus continued to look down at her, his presence in the open doorway meaning she couldn't actually close the door and drive away.

Why didn't he move? Exactly what was going on behind those enigmatic brown eyes?

Chloe knew she hadn't a hope of even guessing that if Fergus didn't want her to know! And he very definitely didn't!

'How does lunch, one o'clock on Tuesday, at Chef Simon, sound to you?' he finally said harshly.

And very reluctantly, Chloe realised ruefully. In spite of himself, Fergus was still intrigued by her.

In the circumstances, that was more than she could ever have hoped for!

But his suggestion of lunch on Tuesday—at Chef Simon, of all places!—meant she still had chance to talk to him before his appointment with Peter Ambrose on Wednesday. Probably her last chance!

It also, she realised more slowly, meant that Fergus would have the same opportunity to talk to *her* before his meeting with the other man. Fergus might be furious with her at the moment, but he wasn't so angry he hadn't been able to work that out...!

Because she knew that Fergus was puzzled by her friendship with the older man, had seen the unguarded questions in his eyes as he'd watched her in conversation with Peter.

On Tuesday, she decided with a nervously fluttering sensation in the pit of her stomach, all would have to be revealed; she couldn't leave it any longer than that without completely alienating Fergus.

And there was always the chance that she had already done that, anyway...!

CHAPTER SIX

'How is the delectable Chloe?'

Fergus didn't move a muscle as he sat in the window-seat of Brice's studio, and yet as he heard the question concerning Chloe a cold steeliness entered a gaze that had already been distantly preoccupied as he stared sightlessly out of the window.

'Or shouldn't I ask...?' Brice amended slowly as he looked over and obviously saw that steeliness.

Fergus drew in a sharply ragged breath, glancing over at his cousin as he stood putting the finishing touches to the portrait of Darcy he intended giving the newly married couple as a wedding present when they returned from their honeymoon.

Fergus had been here two hours now, sitting in this window-seat as Brice worked, unspeaking, totally absorbed in his own thoughts. And they had been far from pleasant!

'You shouldn't ask,' he confirmed bitterly, turning away to once again stare sightlessly out of the window that faced onto Brice's brightly sunlit garden.

Just what did Chloe think she was doing?

Damn it, he had asked himself that question over and over again the last twenty-four hours, and, with less than an hour to go before he was due to have lunch with Chloe, he was still no nearer finding an answer!

He refused to believe any longer that it could possibly be coincidence that she had spoken to him last Saturday. Or that she had gone to bed with him afterwards. So if it wasn't coincidence, what was it?

'Do you want to talk about it, Fergus?' Brice prompted concernedly as his cousin still watched him through narrowed lids.

Talk about what? What sense could Brice make of the last week that *he* hadn't been able to do?

Chloe had deliberately approached him that Saturday. She'd deliberately gone to bed with him. Despite the fact that he might have thought otherwise, she had lied to him. For what reason?

A word came to mind, but it was such an unpleasant one that Fergus found himself shying away from it.

Blackmail...

He winced as the word forced itself into his consciousness anyway.

'There,' Brice murmured with satisfaction as he stepped back from the canvas he had been working on. 'Come and look, Fergus,' he invited excitedly.

He stood up to stroll over and join Brice, glad of a diversion from his own thoughts. He was dressed completely in black; the black shirt and black denims perfectly reflected the darkness of his mood.

The painting was magnificent, of course, Brice having captured Darcy's unusual beauty perfectly: the deep red of her hair, the luminous grey eyes, the smile that reflected her inner warmth and caring. It was wonderful. There was no doubting Brice had a uniqueness of style that had made him the world-renowned artist he undoubtedly was.

'Logan is going to love it,' Fergus confirmed.

'I hope so,' Brice returned before turning to look consideringly at Fergus. 'Would I be wrong in assuming another of the Elusive Three is about to bite the dust?' he ventured.

Fergus flinched at the suggestion, his gaze hardening once again as he realised exactly what Brice was saying.

'You would be completely wrong in assuming any such thing!' he bit out with barely controlled fury. He wasn't falling in love with Chloe Fox—what he most wanted to do was strangle her!

Brice raised dark brows. 'I would?' he drawled sceptically. 'I don't believe I've ever seen you in this state over a woman before.'

Fergus's gaze flashed darkly. 'What state?'

His cousin shrugged. 'You've been here for hours now, you've barely spoken a word since you arrived, and if anything your mood became even blacker the moment I mentioned Chloe.'

Fergus's mouth twisted. 'And that implies I'm falling in love with her, does it?' he dismissed scathingly.

Brice grinned. 'It certainly implies she's got to you in a way I've never seen any other woman manage to do.'

Oh, Chloe had got to him, all right. But the more he thought about it, the more he was convinced it was by design rather than accident.

No doubt seeing him at the nightclub last Saturday had been pure luck; after all, he hadn't known he was going there himself until he'd actually got there. But what had followed had certainly been orchestrated by Chloe.

After days of puzzling over her hot-and-cold behaviour he had slowly been coming to the conclusion that it was because Chloe was a collector of famous notches on her bedpost. But now he realised differently. And the alternative explanation was no more palatable than the original one had been!

It was what he was going to do about it that was the real problem!

He sighed heavily, shaking his head. 'I have to go, Brice.' He glanced at his wrist-watch; twelve-forty-five. 'I'm having lunch with Chloe in half an hour.' He had been debating most of the morning whether or not he should meet Chloe at all, but now he had decided that fifteen minutes late should be long enough to deflate some of that self-confidence she seemed to have in abundance. It was high time Miss Chloe Fox was the one left guessing!

'Say hello from me.' His cousin nodded.

He gave a humourless smile. 'I'll do that.'

Brice gave him a considering look. 'She's very young, Fergus,' he said.

Old enough, as he knew only too well!

Fergus's gaze narrowed thoughtfully on his cousin. 'What's that supposed to mean?'

Brice shrugged. 'You're obviously angry with her about something.'

He shook his head disgustedly. 'Angry doesn't even begin to describe the way I feel at the moment!' he snapped.

'Exactly.' Brice nodded again.

He looked at his cousin, Brice raising mocking brows in response to that look.

'I'm hardly likely to strangle her at Chef Simon, Brice,' he drawled hardly. 'Far too public!'

Brice grinned ruefully at his attempt at humour. 'It would be a pity to mark that beautiful neck at all,' he opined.

Fergus smiled without humour. It came as no surprise to him that Brice was smitten with the way Chloe looked too; she really was the most incredibly beautiful young woman. The problem was, as he had found out, she was also manipulative and deceitful. Manipulative he could handle, it was her deceit he wasn't happy with.

'I'll bear your advice in mind, Brice,' he replied tersely, turning to leave.

'I liked her,' Brice offered softly from behind him.

Fergus's only response was a stiffening of his shoulders as he continued to walk out of the house. Damn it, he had liked Chloe too! Had. He wasn't completely sure how he felt about her any more!

God, she was so beautiful, was his first thought as he entered Chef Simon thirty minutes later and saw her seated at a table across the room.

Unaware of his critical gaze, she was staring pensively out of the window, obviously waiting for him to arrive, her chin resting on her raised hand, blue eyes troubled, those perfectly curving lips unsmiling as she thought herself unobserved.

She obviously believed he had stood her up!

Strangely, Fergus felt none of the satisfaction at her obvious uncertainty that he had expected to feel. A cold knot of anger seemed to have lodged itself in his chest, allowing room for no other emotion.

The fact that her face lit up with relieved pleasure as she turned and saw him approaching the table did nothing to alleviate that angry knot.

'Chloe,' he greeted tersely before bending to kiss her hard on the lips.

'Fergus...' she responded, lashes blinking over dazed blue eyes as she watched him warily as he sat down opposite her at the table, her tongue moving nervously across the lips he had just so arrogantly kissed.

'What's the matter, Chloe?' he taunted. 'Surely it's perfectly in order for me to kiss you hello? After all, we are lovers, aren't we?'

Her expression showed her confusion at his obvious aggression. Confusion! That was nothing to the emotions storming through him. He no longer wanted to strangle her, he decided; putting her over his knee and giving her a good hiding might afford him much more satisfaction!

* * *

Something was seriously wrong, Chloe realised warily.

Fergus was over fifteen minutes late for their luncheon date, and now that he had arrived he was like a cold, merciless stranger. Dressed all in black, his expression hard and unyielding, he looked like the devil himself!

How on earth could she even begin to talk to him about her father when he was in this mood?

'Fergus!' A tall attractive man whom Chloe easily recognised as Chef Simon himself came over to their table. 'I thought it must be you when I saw the booking.' He smiled warmly at Fergus. 'Good to see you again.' The two men shook hands as Fergus stood up politely.

'How's married life?' Fergus asked the other man conversationally.

Daniel Simon grinned. 'Wonderful!' he assured warmly before glancing enquiringly at Chloe.

The coldness in Fergus's eyes hit her like a blast of ice as he also turned to look at her, causing her to recoil involuntarily. He looked as if he hated her!

Admittedly he hadn't been too happy with her when they'd parted on Friday evening, obviously disappointed that she'd been leaving so suddenly, but he certainly hadn't hated her then. What could have happened in the intervening three days to have caused this change in him...?

Chloe felt a nervous fluttering in the pit of her stomach at the realisation that something *had* changed.

'Daniel, this is Chloe,' Fergus introduced economically. 'Chloe, my uncle, Daniel Simon,' he added less coldly.

'Pleased to meet you.' Daniel Simon shook her hand. 'I hope the two of you will excuse me; I have to get back to the kitchen. I hope you enjoy your meal,' he added hospitably.

Chloe gave the stony-faced Fergus a look beneath shadowy lashes as he resumed his seat opposite her; she had a distinct feeling neither of them were going to enjoy any part of their meal!

She had dressed with extra care herself today, wearing a tailored silk trouser suit the same colour blue as her eyes, her hair loose and silky down the length of her spine. But for all the notice Fergus had taken of the way she looked, she might just as well have worn a sack!

'What's wrong, Fergus?' she asked after several awkward moments of silence, neither of them making any move to look at the menus that lay on the table-top, either.

His eyes were dark as coal as he looked across at her. 'Wrong?' he echoed distantly. 'Why should anything be wrong?'

Chloe felt an apprehensive shiver down the length of her spine. Fergus had never been that easy to talk to, but he was like a stranger today, a cold, unapproachable stranger.

She swallowed hard. 'You seem—different, today...?' she tried again.

His mouth twisted humourlessly. 'Different from what?'

Chloe frowned. 'I'm not sure,' she admitted.

Fergus gave a dismissive shake of his head. 'I have no idea what you're talking about, Chloe. And I'm not sure you do, either,' he added insultingly before picking up the menu. 'Shall we order?' he prompted.

Chloe continued to look at him searchingly, not liking the challenge in those hard brown eyes as Fergus looked straight back at her.

She had known before she'd come here today that this was her last opportunity to talk to Fergus, that once he had seen and spoken to Peter Ambrose tomorrow he would probably know exactly who she was. But with Fergus in this mood, how did she even begin to approach the subject of her father?

'What do you want, Chloe?' Fergus suddenly bit out hardly.

She gave a guilty start at the abruptness of the question coming so soon on top of her troubled thoughts. 'I—I wasn't aware I wanted anything,' she finally answered him awkwardly.

His mouth twisted again. 'I was actually referring to your lunch,' he drawled mockingly, with a pointed look up at the hovering waiter.

'Oh!' Colour darkened her cheeks as she hastily looked down at the menu. 'I'll have gazpacho, followed by the monkfish,' she requested hollowly. 'With a green salad.' She closed the menu with a decisive snap.

'So...' Fergus turned to her once they were alone again '...have you been working this morning?'

Hardly; she had been too nervous about this lunch with Fergus to even begin to concentrate on her designs. Besides, she had the distinct impression Fergus wasn't really interested in what she had been doing this morning...

'Not really,' she responded lightly.

He raised dark brows. 'Did you do anything nice over the weekend?'

She shrugged, becoming more and more convinced that Fergus wasn't really interested in her answers to his polite questions. In fact, she had a strange feeling of foreboding, as if there were a sword hovering above her head!

'Not particularly.' She shrugged once more. 'How about you?' Two could play at this game!

Somehow, for reasons she was as yet unaware of, the tables had been turned; Fergus was no longer the one who was unsure of her, it was the other way around.

'I'm still working on the research for my next book,' he answered.

'The political thriller.' She nodded; at least the conversation was going in the direction she wanted it to. 'Have you started writing it yet?' she added casually, trying not to look too interested in his answer as she turned to break the bread roll on her plate.

'Not yet,' he said. 'I like to do all my research first. Be sure of all my facts.'

'It wouldn't do for someone to sue you for defamation of character,' she attempted to tease—and failed miserably. Her father couldn't sue; the puzzle of the identity of Susan Stirling's lover, and the father of her unborn child, had never been solved.

'I'm a lawyer, Chloe; I know just how far I can go. Are you interested in politics?' Fergus prompted softly.

Chloe's breath caught in her throat. She had been brought up on a diet of politics for breakfast, lunch and tea; how could she not have an interest in them?

'You have your opening now, Chloe,' Fergus persisted. 'But do you have the guts to take it, I wonder?' he added with hard mockery.

She looked sharply across at him, feeling the colour draining from her cheeks as she once again met the hard challenge in those enigmatic brown eyes. Strange, when she had first met him she had thought his eyes were like warm chocolate; today they resembled brown pebbles of ice!

She swallowed hard. 'What do you mean?'

'I don't like guessing games, Chloe. I never have,' he told her coldly. 'And you're demolishing that bread roll into inedible crumbs,' he observed.

Chloe snatched her hand away as she saw she had indeed been shredding the bread to pieces. Without even realising she was doing it. So much for looking uninterested!

'I asked if you're interested in politics, Chloe,' Fergus repeated harshly.

'I—' She tried to speak, but her jaws seemed to be locked together!

He knew! She didn't know how he knew, but she was sure that he did...

Fergus leant over the table, his face only inches away from her own now. 'Come on, Chloe Fox-*Hamilton*, answer the question, damn you!' he bit out between gritted teeth.

Chloe Fox-Hamilton. Yes, he did know!

She moistened dry lips. 'Fergus—'

'I have no idea how you know anything about the plot for my next book,' he ground out evenly. 'Although, I can assure you, I do intend finding that out,' he added warningly. 'But one thing I do know, Miss Fox-*Hamilton*,' he grated insultingly. 'The fact that we've been out together a few times, that you've shared my bed, is not going to affect the writing of that book one iota. Do I make myself clear?' he finished with cold deliberation.

As crystal!

CHAPTER SEVEN

LAST Saturday night, dinner on Friday, all those things Chloe had known about him, to her they had only been a means to an end. Yes, going to bed with him had only been a means to an end!

Maybe in the case of the latter it was his hurt pride that made him feel so angry, but knowing the reason for it didn't lessen the emotion.

Fergus looked across the table at Chloe now with furiously glittering eyes. 'Tell me, Chloe—I'm curious to know—besides seducing me, exactly what was your plan of action?'

She looked startled. 'I didn't—'

'Oh, please.' He held up protesting hands. 'Being Paul Hamilton's daughter, you must have had some plan in mind.'

Her cheeks flushed angrily, eyes flashing deeply blue. 'Don't talk about my father in that derogatory way!'

Yes, he decided consideringly, he could see the likeness between father and daughter now, the same dark hair, the same deep blue eyes, a certain similarity in the facial structure.

Chloe was the daughter of the former Minister Paul Hamilton. That was how she knew Peter Ambrose. How Peter Ambrose knew her. Now that Fergus knew the truth of Chloe's identity, he wasn't sure he wouldn't have preferred his first assumption about their relationship to have been the correct one!

He had been eaten up with the knowledge of Chloe's true identity since learning of it yesterday, hadn't slept, hadn't eaten, going over and over in his mind the events of the last eleven days. And not once had those conclusions actually taken him to the point where he could believe Chloe even liked him, let alone anything else!

If he were honest, that was what really rankled about this situation. Because he liked—*had* liked—Chloe, too much for comfort!

He gave a deep sigh. 'What do you want from me, Chloe?' he asked wearily.

Tears glistened in the deep blue eyes as she looked at him. 'I want you to leave my father alone. Find another plot for your book. Hasn't he suffered enough?' she burst out, choking with emotion.

Fergus forced himself to remember just how deliberately Chloe had entered his life, hardening himself to those tears. 'Susan Stirling's family probably don't think so—'

'My father was not involved with Susan Stirling!' she defended fiercely.

He raised an eyebrow. 'The consensus of opinion seems to think otherwise—'

'I'm not interested in the consensus of opinion!' Chloe cut in, still emotional. 'My father loves my mother, is still *in* love with her,' she added with certainty.

Fergus grimaced. 'All children like to believe that of their own parents.'

Her eyes glittered with anger now instead of tears. 'How would *you* know? Your parents are divorced—I'm sorry!' She gasped, putting a regretful hand up to her mouth. 'I shouldn't have said that.'

'No—you shouldn't,' Fergus acknowledged in a dangerously soft voice. 'Look, Chloe,' he continued more gently. 'I understand that you love your father, and because of that love you believe in his innocence—'

'The admiration and love I feel for my father have nothing to do with it,' she declared determinedly. 'Well...obviously they have something to do with it,' she amended self-consciously at Fergus's derisive snort. 'But the truth of the matter is that he *is* innocent of any involvement with Susan Stirling!' She looked across at Fergus as if daring him to contradict her a second time.

Fergus looked back at her for several long seconds, compassion for her conviction warring inside him with the anger he personally felt towards her for her deliberate duplicity where he was concerned. Admiration, too, he admitted grudgingly, that she was willing to go to such lengths to protect her father.

'Eat your soup,' he finally said stiffly. 'Before it goes cold,' he added at an attempt at humour.

Chloe didn't look any more interested in eating her food than he did, picking up her spoon to stir the chilled soup disconsolately round in the bowl.

Finally she sniffed indelicately. 'I always thought that in this country a man was presumed innocent until proven guilty.' She muttered this gruffly, her head bent as she still stared down at her untouched soup.

'He is,' Fergus confirmed heavily.

Damn it, she *was* crying! He could see the trickle of tears now against the paleness of her cheeks.

She sniffed again. 'Are you aware that my father is going to stand for re-election next year?'

'I am now.'

Chloe did look up now, more, as yet unshed, tears brimming to spilling point against her lashes. 'How—?'

'Peter Ambrose had to bring our appointment forward to yesterday instead of Wednesday,' Fergus told her heavily.

He had felt as if the other man had hit him in the stomach with a sledgehammer when Peter Ambrose had unwittingly revealed that Chloe was Paul Hamilton's daughter, expressing surprise that Fergus and Chloe should seem so close considering Fergus was researching a book based on the scandal in her father's past. In fact, Fergus had been so stunned, he wasn't sure how he had conducted the rest of the interview!

He had been in an angry fury ever since. Everything that had puzzled him about Chloe had added up once he'd had that piece of information: Chloe's persistence last Saturday, the fact that she knew where he lived, his telephone number, even how he took his coffee, for goodness' sake.

Although how she knew about his book in the first place he had yet to find out...?

'Chloe, who told you I was writing this particular book?' he said slowly.

She turned away. 'Isn't it enough that I know?' she dismissed raggedly.

'No,' Fergus answered firmly. 'As yet only a few people, like my agent and the publisher, are aware of even the barest outline of the plot of my next book. And yet you seem to know about it too.' He frowned darkly.

She paused. 'I just know, okay?' she came back with uncharacteristic aggression.

No, it was not okay. Until he had spoken to Peter Ambrose yesterday, only a handful of people had been privileged to know that information, and none of them had been at liberty to discuss it with anyone else. Besides, he couldn't help but be aware that Chloe was deliberately not meeting his gaze...

'Do you really still intend writing the book?' She looked at him intently. 'Even now that you know my father is going to stand for re-election,' she explained impatiently as Fergus raised derisive brows.

His mouth tightened, knowing Chloe wasn't going to like his answer. His whole plot-line hinged on that scandal. Besides—and Chloe wasn't going to like this one little bit!—he was one of the people who did believe her father was guilty of what he was accused...

Besides, that wasn't really what Chloe was asking! 'Don't you mean, now that the two of us have slept together?' he drawled.

She gasped. 'We—I didn't—'

'I told you, Chloe, I don't like games,' he bit out coldly, looking across at her with cool cynicism. Did she really think that he would change his mind about writing the book just because she had been to bed with him? He shook his head. He didn't think Chloe had really given this much thought at all!

Her head was still bowed. 'I just wanted to talk to you.' Her words were barely audible now, her voice husky with emotion. 'Plead with you, if necessary, not to do this to my father,' she added shakily.

'Then why the hell didn't you just use the normal means for meeting someone?' he rasped hardly. 'Such as telephoning and asking for an appointment!'

She looked up at him with emotionally bruised eyes. 'And once I had told you my name was Hamilton, would you have agreed to see me?' she challenged disbelievingly.

No! Yes! Probably... Maybe, he finally conceded. After all, she was close enough to Paul Hamilton to—

What *was* he thinking? Chloe might have gone about this the wrong way, and he was furiously angry at being taken for a fool, but that didn't mean he had to compound the situation by behaving exactly as she had obviously imagined he would!

'Probably out of curiosity,' Chloe acknowledged as she seemed to read the emotions flitting across his face. 'But nothing else,' she concluded.

Fergus found that he didn't like having his reactions and feelings predicted for him in this way. No, he didn't like it at all.

'So you decided to meet me, giving me a not exactly accurate version of your name, manoeuvre me into a compromising situation, and—then what, Chloe?' he demanded scathingly. 'Blackmail? After all, I wouldn't come out of the affair looking too good if it became publicly known that I had actually had a relationship with the daughter of Paul Hamilton, now, would I?'

If anything Chloe's face had gone even paler, the darkness of her brows and lashes standing out starkly against the whiteness of her skin, her eyes deep blue pools of pained emotion.

Fergus felt himself melting inside, hating the fact that he was the one responsible for that pain.

No! He mustn't weaken. Chloe had deliberately manipulated this situation, and she hadn't given a damn about him as a person while she'd been doing it. If he weakened now he would find himself agreeing to anything she asked of him—including scrapping a book he had already done weeks of research on!

'Have you ever met my father?' she asked quietly.

His mouth tightened. 'Not yet.'

'But you intend to do so before you begin writing your book?' she persisted.

'Probably,' he conceded grudgingly. He had no intention of telling Chloe he had an appointment to see her father on Friday morning; he was still angry enough with her to want her to squirm a little longer!

She nodded. 'Then I suppose I'll have to settle for that.'

Fergus's mouth twisted. 'The implication there being that once I've met him I'll know I'm wrong about him?' he taunted.

Her head went back proudly. 'Yes.'

Fergus shook his head again. 'I think you're being more than a little over-optimistic there, Chloe.'

'And *I* think we'll just have to wait and see,' she said stubbornly.

'You went too far in going to bed with me, Chloe,' he

rasped harshly. 'Besides which,' he went on, 'as I'm sure you are all too well aware, I have absolutely no memory of the incident. So if you intend going to the newspapers with this, I—'

'You really do believe I was going to blackmail you?' Chloe gasped disbelievingly.

Fergus looked at her coolly. 'What else?'

Chloe was breathing deeply, two bright spots of angry colour on her cheeks now. 'For the record, Mr McCloud—'

'Whose record?' he cut in with mocking disdain.

'Anyone who cares to listen!' She had raised her voice now so that the people dining on the surrounding tables could hear what she was saying. 'For the record, Mr McCloud,' she repeated slowly and clearly, 'I did not share your bed last Saturday, I spent the night—the whole night!—sitting in your bedroom chair.'

Fergus didn't move, feeling as if he were glued to his seat, only his gaze flicking reluctantly around the room. But it was enough to show him they had the attention of all the other diners in the room now, even the *maître d'* and the waitresses stopping in their work to turn and look at them.

He winced. 'Chloe,' he began softly.

'I did not share your bed, Mr McCloud,' she continued with determination. 'And even if I had chosen to do so, you had drunk so much champagne you were totally incapable of my being able to accuse you of doing anything other than sleeping. Have I made myself clear enough?' she challenged scornfully.

More than clear, he would have said! 'I'm not sure the people in the kitchen heard you,' he said sardonically, as he knew himself the object of every gaze in the restaurant.

Chloe gave a scathingly pointed glance in the direction of the kitchen as she stood up, Daniel and a couple of his assistants having appeared in the open doorway. 'Obviously they did,' she snapped. 'If you'll excuse me...' She gave him a sharply dismissive nod before turning to walk across the room, her head held high.

God, she was magnificent, Fergus acknowledged admiringly as he watched her go. Absolutely magnificent. She looked like some exotic princess as she strode confidently through the room, her shoulders back proudly, her head held high, that gloriously long dark hair cascading down to her waist.

'Come through to the kitchen.' Daniel spoke gently at Fergus's side as the restaurant door closed behind Chloe, a soft buzz of conversation immediately starting to fill the room.

Fergus stood up, feeling almost disorientated, allowing the older man to take his arm and lead him into the aromatic warmth of the restaurant kitchen.

'What is it about my restaurant, and you Scottish cousins?' Daniel shook his head ruefully once the door had closed behind them. 'Still, let's look on the bright side,' he added with amused derision. 'At least Chloe didn't tip the bowl of gazpacho over your head before she left!'

Fergus wasn't so fazed by Chloe's dramatic departure that he didn't realise Daniel was referring to his daughter Darcy's relationship with Fergus's cousin Logan. Logan had seemed to spend most of that courtship removing one substance or another from himself, or his clothing, that Darcy had either thrown over him deliberately, or accidentally.

'We didn't go to bed together, Daniel,' he told the other man with vehemence.

The older man's mouth quirked. 'I think we can all safely assume that,' he confirmed dryly.

'Exactly,' Fergus murmured with satisfaction.

And the fact that they hadn't, that Chloe had announced

it in the middle of a crowded restaurant, didn't dismay him as it should have done. In fact, he couldn't have felt happier!

What had she just done?

Chloe dropped thankfully into the back seat of the taxi she had just flagged down to take her home, having scrambled hastily inside as soon as it had stopped, sure she could still feel Fergus's hot and angry breath on the back of her neck.

But a quick glance out of the window showed her that he hadn't followed her, after all. Not that she would have blamed him if he had; she had just announced in front of at least forty people that he had been incapable of making love to her the other Saturday night!

What on earth had possessed her to do such a thing?

The answer to that was simple enough, she acknowledged heavily. She had been goaded into it by Fergus's claim that she intended blackmailing him into silence with the fact that they had been to bed together.

She cringed just at the memory of all those shocked faces as she'd loudly announced that the two of them hadn't slept together at all.

Oh, she had made a mess of this. A complete and utter mess.

Instead of arousing Fergus's sympathy and understanding where her father was concerned, she had only succeeded in arousing his anger and scorn—towards her! Worst of all, Fergus seemed more determined than ever to go ahead and write his book.

And some time—in the very near future!—she was going to have to break the news of that to her parents. It wasn't something she looked forward to at all!

Although there was no opportunity to do that over the next few days. Her father and mother were away visiting the constituency her father intended contesting, and it was hardly the sort of thing she could break to them during one of their brief nightly telephone conversations to check that she was all right!

When her parents returned on Thursday evening, they both looked so tired Chloe didn't have the heart to even broach the subject. And Friday was her sister's and David's wedding anniversary, the five of them due to go out to dinner to celebrate, so that was out too. Hopefully some opportunity would present itself over the weekend.

Chloe knew she simply couldn't leave it any longer than that; if Peter Ambrose hadn't spoken to her father yet, he very soon would do. But it would be better coming from Chloe first. If only so that she could explain her own acquaintance with Fergus!

Although quite how she went about doing that she wasn't sure, either!

She had heard nothing from Fergus. Not that she had expected to after that fiasco in the restaurant, but, even so, she knew that where he was concerned no news was not good news!

Which was why, when she came downstairs on Friday morning, on her way out to buy a gift she could give to Penny and David that evening, she was totally stunned, after giving a cursory glance inside the small reception room off the main hallway, to see Fergus sitting in there!

She gasped, her cheeks paling as she hastily entered the room, pulling the door closed behind her. 'What are you doing here?' she snapped accusingly. As if she really needed to ask!

Fergus looked perfectly relaxed as he glanced up at her. 'Taking your advice, of course; meeting your father,' he said casually, lounged in one of the armchairs, formally dressed today in a dark suit and blue shirt with matching tie.

Her cheeks coloured bright red as she remembered the

occasion when she had given that advice. What had Fergus done that day after she'd left the restaurant? Had he carried on eating his meal? Or had he decided it was time to leave too? Somehow she thought it would have been the latter!

She had dreaded the possibility of their next meeting, still cringed whenever she thought of her behaviour in the restaurant; but she certainly hadn't ever expected they would meet again at her parents' home.

'You're still going ahead with it, then,' she realised dully.

Fergus slowly stood up, his height instantly dominating the room, the intensity of his guarded expression giving lie to his previously relaxed pose. 'I'm here to meet your father,' he repeated unhelpfully.

But, then, why should he feel disposed to be helpful? The last time the two of them had met she had publicly embarrassed him!

'His assistant, David, has just gone to tell him I'm here,' Fergus elaborated.

'Fergus.' Chloe looked up at him with pleading eyes, reaching out to put a hand on the rigid hardness of his arm. 'Please don't let the animosity you must have towards me influence how you ultimately feel towards my father.'

Brown eyes narrowed as he looked down at her. 'Are you going out?' He looked pointedly at the jacket she had recently put on over her tee shirt and jeans.

'I was…' she confirmed slowly, not sure that she should do so now that Fergus was here to see her father. Besides, she hadn't missed the fact that Fergus hadn't answered her question… 'Why?' she prompted warily.

Fergus shrugged. 'No reason. I had just thought that perhaps the two of us could have lunch together once I've finished talking to your father.'

He had just thought—! 'I very much doubt that we will

want to! Besides, do you really think that's a good idea—after last time?' she came back swiftly.

He gave a smile. 'I wouldn't advise you to try that dramatic exit a second time,' he drawled. 'Obviously there were no reporters present at Chef Simon on Tuesday, but you may not be so lucky next time,' he pointed out.

She had lived in dread, the last couple of days, of one of the gossip columns mentioning the incident at Chef Simon on Tuesday, but, as Fergus said, she had been lucky.

She drew in a ragged breath. 'I'm really sorry about Tuesday. I just—you—'

'Just leave it at the apology, hmm, Chloe,' he silenced softly, lifting a hand to gently stroke the creaminess of her cheek. 'As far as I can see, we were both out of order. And Daniel has assured me it did business no harm whatsoever; it seems most people lingered over coffee and liqueurs in order to talk about the incident!'

Chloe could believe that; it had been rather a spectacular show! 'I must say, you seem to be taking it rather well,' she said uncertainly.

He shrugged again. 'I think my reputation as a lover may have taken a bit of a knock, but what the hell? You—'

'Mr McCloud, I'm so sorry to have kept you—Chloe...?' Her father looked at her questioningly as, having entered the room to meet Fergus, he found Chloe in there talking with the other man. 'I didn't know the two of you knew each other...?' he added with light enquiry.

Chloe gave an awkward glance in Fergus's direction before turning back to her father. 'I—'

'Oh, Chloe and I are old friends,' Fergus put in firmly, calmly meeting the stunned look she turned on him. 'In fact I was just inviting her out to lunch,' he added.

Chloe was confused. Exactly what was Fergus up to? They most definitely were not old friends; nearly two weeks of acquaintance made them far from that! And if the positions were reversed, if Fergus had done to her what she'd done to him at the restaurant on Tuesday, she certainly wouldn't be inviting him out to lunch a second time!

She gave him a narrow-eyed look before beaming up at her father. 'Unfortunately I was having to refuse, because I really do have to get into town to do some shopping,' she explained gracefully.

'Then it looks as if it will have to be dinner instead,' Fergus accepted, unperturbed.

Angry colour—at his arrogance—flared in her cheeks.

'It would seem you're going to be unlucky for the second time today, Mr McCloud,' her father was the one to answer him laughingly. 'We have a family celebration this evening. My eldest daughter's twelfth wedding anniversary,' he explained at Fergus's questioning glance. 'Although I suppose there's no reason,' he continued thoughtfully, 'if you don't mind sharing my beautiful daughter with the rest of her family, why you can't join us. If you would care to?'

Chloe gasped her horror of the suggestion. But one glance at Fergus, at the mocking humour in his eyes as he easily met her horrified glance, and she knew he was going to accept the invitation!

How could he?

How *dared* he!

CHAPTER EIGHT

FERGUS had guessed, from her glaring look in his direction, that Chloe expected him to refuse the invitation. That, in itself, was enough to make him want to accept!

'I'll leave the two of you to discuss it,' Paul Hamilton told them tactfully as he sensed their indecision. He turned to smile at Fergus. 'Chloe will bring you through to my study when you've finished talking.'

Fergus watched with observing eyes as the older man left the room. Paul Hamilton looked exactly like the numerous photographs Fergus had of him. But those photographs hadn't been able to project the candidness of his gaze, or the warm pride in his voice as he talked of his beautiful daughter...

'You have to refuse,' that beautiful daughter was now telling Fergus in an angry hiss. 'You couldn't be so hypocritical as to accept!' she added disgustedly.

The high colour in her cheeks suited her, Fergus decided abstractly, adding to her beauty, and giving depth to the angry blue sparkle of her eyes.

He hadn't been sure whether or not he would see Chloe here today, but he had certainly hoped that he would. For one thing it had saved him the humiliation of telephoning her and having her refuse to take his call! And for another, he had just wanted to see her again...

She looked very young today in the casual denims and tee shirt, the sophisticated fashion designer nowhere in sight. In fact, she looked wonderful. But then, she always did...

93

'Don't be ridiculous, Chloe,' he answered her sternly. 'You already believe I'm hard and uncaring, so why not add hypocrite to that list?'

'Because—because you just can't!' she told him frustratedly, looking as if she would like to stamp her foot in protest, but considered it too unladylike.

Fergus held back a smile. 'Of course I can. Your father just invited me.' He held up his hands.

Chloe glared up at him. 'My father could regret that invitation, once the two of you have talked this morning!'

'He might,' Fergus agreed unconcernedly. 'But I'm sure he's too polite to withdraw the invitation once it has been accepted. And I do mean to accept.'

'I can't believe this!' Chloe turned away, walking over to stare out the window, although Fergus was pretty sure she wasn't actually looking at the neatly arranged garden and lawns outside. 'You're even more of an unprincipled bastard than I thought you were.' She shook her head disbelievingly.

Fergus's mouth tightened at the deliberate insult. But what he had to remember was that it *was* deliberate; Chloe was hoping to anger him into refusing her father's dinner invitation.

'"Sticks and stones…"' he murmured tauntingly.

She turned back in turn. 'That's not all I would like to throw at you at the moment!'

He could see that; her hands were clenched into fists at her sides, her whole body tense with that frustrated fury.

And what Fergus most wanted to do at this moment was take her in his arms and kiss her!

But he didn't doubt, if he even attempted to do that, she really would hit him!

He gave her a casual smile. 'No doubt I can get the details for this evening from your father later—'

'Fergus, I really can't allow you to come out to dinner with my family,' she cut in determinedly. 'I shall have to tell my father—'

'Tell him what?' Fergus challenged. 'Exactly what do you intend telling your father about our friendship, Chloe? Are you going to tell him how you deliberately approached me two weeks ago?' he continued as she would have interrupted. 'That you spent that night at my home?' Fergus paused for a moment. 'Somehow I think not, Chloe,' he murmured as she visibly paled.

'I— You— I hate you!' Her eyes glittered with the emotion.

'I'm told there's a very thin line between hate and love,' he offered.

Although inwardly he wasn't quite so unshaken by the outburst. He didn't want Chloe to hate him. He wasn't sure what he wanted from her yet, but it certainly wasn't hate.

'I can assure you, that's a line I'll never cross!' She marched past him to the door, wrenching it open before turning to glare at him. 'You are, without doubt, the most despicable man I have ever met!'

God, she was so young. So tiny. So vulnerable. So much so that Fergus wanted to wrap her up in his arms and stop anything ever hurting her again.

What stopped him doing exactly that was that he might have a little trouble, when he went to see her father in a few minutes, explaining the obviously fresh scratch marks down his face!

'I'll see you this evening, Chloe,' he said instead.

Her mouth tightened. 'Perhaps I'll have a headache and not make the dinner tonight; I can definitely feel one coming on!'

Fergus raised mocking brows. 'Another one? I don't think you would do that to your sister and brother-in-law.'

Her shoulders slumped dejectedly. 'You're right, I wouldn't,' she conceded heavily, her eyes huge pools of pained disillusion as she looked up at him. 'One thing I do wish, Fergus McCloud—I wish that I had never met you,' she told him dully.

That barb definitely went home, and it took all Fergus's iron self-control not to go after her as she walked down the hallway, quietly letting herself out of the house before closing the door firmly behind her.

A nerve pulsed erratically in the hardness of Fergus's firmly set jaw as he watched her leave. He almost preferred her more dramatic departure of Tuesday lunchtime—at least then she hadn't actually told him she hated him!

But there was no doubting that her abrupt departure now left him in a bit of a predicament; he had absolutely no idea where Paul Hamilton's study was, and he certainly couldn't go wandering around the house looking for it, either!

'Can I help you? You're looking rather lost.'

Fergus had turned sharply at the sound of that husky female voice, feeling a jolt in his chest as he found himself looking at Chloe as she would be in thirty years or so. Tiny. Dark-haired. Delicately beautiful. Only fine lines beside the eyes and mouth to show for those extra thirty years of laughter and tears.

He knew who the woman was, of course. Diana, Chloe's mother.

'Mrs Hamilton,' he greeted politely. 'I'm supposed to be in your husband's study, and I'm afraid I got rather lost.' There was no point in explaining Chloe had just walked out and left him to fend for himself.

Diana laughed sympathetically. 'This house can be a bit confusing,' she allowed. 'Come with me,' she invited warmly, turning to lead the way down the carpeted hallway.

Fergus went—with the distinct feeling that not too many men would feel inclined to refuse such an invitation from this beautifully gracious woman!

He had seen photographs of her too, years ago in the newspapers, when her husband had been a big political figure, and more recently in his own research file, but none of those had prepared him for the open warmth and obvious beauty of the woman herself.

'Ah, Mr McCloud.' Paul Hamilton stood up at his entrance to his study, the smile he directed at his wife full of affection. 'Could you ask Mrs Harmon to send in some coffee for us, darling?' he requested.

'Of course,' Diana agreed smoothly. 'Nice to have met you, Mr McCloud.' She gave him a smile in parting, closing the door softly behind her.

'Please, do sit down.' Fergus's host indicated the chair opposite his at the huge mahogany desk. 'I didn't mention to Diana that she might see you again later this evening.' He smiled. 'Just in case you and Chloe didn't manage to sort things out to your mutual satisfaction.'

Fergus shrugged ruefully; he had sorted things out to his own satisfaction, even if it wasn't to Chloe's. 'I would love to join you all for dinner—as long as you're sure I'm not intruding?'

'Not at all,' Paul Hamilton assured him. 'Six is always a much rounder number than five.'

The fact that it had originally been five pleased Fergus immensely; at least it proved Chloe didn't already have anyone important enough in her life to have invited to this family celebration.

Although, having now met both Paul Hamilton and his wife, Diana, Fergus had to admit he felt the beginnings of unease in the pit of his stomach. Mainly, he could at least admit to himself, because he was starting to question whether or not Paul could possibly have ever been unfaithful to such a warmly beautiful woman as Diana undoubtedly was...

He dared, Chloe acknowledged disgustedly, glaring furiously across the room at Fergus as he was shown into the sitting-room later that evening, the family all gathered in there to have a glass of champagne prior to leaving for the restaurant.

She had no idea how Fergus's interview with her father had gone, had only seen her father for a few minutes on her return from shopping. But he hadn't seemed particularly disturbed.

Although Chloe couldn't say she'd felt the same way once he had told her that Fergus would be meeting them here at eight o'clock this evening!

'For goodness' sake, smile,' Fergus told her, having crossed to her side, a glass of champagne already in his hand, looking very handsome and distinguished in his black dinner suit. 'Your family will think you don't want me here,' he warned.

Chloe looked up at him with wary eyes, making no effort to hide her hostility. 'I don't,' she snapped.

Fergus laughed softly. 'Let's try not to spoil this evening for your sister and her husband,' he responded, before bending to kiss her lightly on the cheek. 'Window-dressing,' he explained before she could flinch away.

Her eyes sparkled angrily. 'Don't try and use me to get to my father or my family,' she grated.

His gaze hardened. 'I didn't mean that sort of window-dressing, Chloe,' he rasped, drawing a steadying breath before turning to look at the others gathered in the room. 'Don't you think you should introduce me to your sister and her husband?'

'No,' she answered flatly.

She didn't think he should be here at all. That was the whole problem. And if he couldn't see that—

'Chloe,' he began, slowly turning back to face her, 'if you recall I asked to have dinner with *you* this evening; your family's involvement is purely incidental.'

'Really?' she derided scornfully.

'Really,' he echoed hardly, his hand that wasn't holding the champagne glass reaching out to firmly grasp her forearm as he turned her to face him. 'I don't work that way, Chloe. And you can believe that or not, it's your choice.'

She was so angry with him at the moment that she couldn't even think straight, let alone make any choices!

He had no right to be here, socially mixing with her family as if he were a close friend of hers. That was what hurt the most; no matter what he might try to claim to the contrary, Fergus was merely using her.

'I choose not,' she told him coldly, bending to put down her empty champagne glass on the nearby coffee-table.

Fergus eyed the glass with raised brows. 'I thought you didn't drink…?'

Her mouth thinned humourlessly. 'For some strange reason, this evening I feel in need of it! In fact,' she bit out caustically, 'I think I'll have a refill!' She picked up her glass and crossed the room to where her father was just refilling Penny's glass.

Older than Chloe by ten years, Penny was more like their father, tall and elegant, her dark hair boyishly short, three pregnancies having done little to diminish the slenderness of her body.

'Twelve years, Pen,' Chloe teased, making a decided effort to shake off her anger towards Fergus; after all, this was Penny and David's evening. 'You'll be getting your long-service medal soon!'

Penny laughed, shooting an affectionate smile at her husband as he strolled over to chat to Fergus. 'And when can we expect to hear wedding bells from you...?' her sister prompted pointedly.

It took great effort to keep the smile on her own lips. Damn Fergus. Didn't he realise his presence here tonight would cause speculation amongst her family? Or did he just not care? That was probably closer to the truth!

'I'm not sure I'm the marrying kind,' Chloe replied with a noncommittal shrug.

'We all say that—usually just before we fall flat on our face in love!' her sister said knowingly.

'Not this girl,' Chloe assured with certainty, deciding it was high time—despite the fact that she had no real wish to spend time with Fergus herself!—that she interrupted his conversation with David. Or who knew what family confidences David might reveal without meaning to? 'If you'll excuse me...' she said before strolling over to join the two men.

David turned to give her a cheerful smile. 'I had no idea you knew such a famous writer, Chloe,' he reproved lightly, the teasing lift of his brows seeming to ask if Fergus could possibly be the reason she had crept into the house last Saturday morning still wearing her evening dress from the night before.

Or was that just Chloe's imagination? Her own guilty conscience at work?

'A girl has to have some secrets from her family,' she countered brightly.

'But I'm not a secret any longer,' Fergus put in.

Chloe started visibly as she felt his arm drape lightly about her shoulders. Proprietorially. A pure act of possession.

Forget it, Fergus McCloud, Chloe fumed inwardly. One dinner, and then he was out of her life. For good!

'Isn't it time we were all moving on to the restaurant?' she suggested, using the act of putting her glass down on the table to escape that arm about her shoulders, easily meeting the challenge in his dark brown eyes as she looked up and found Fergus looking at her with amusement.

Challenge away, Fergus; her own gaze shot the message back at him. His time for calling the shots came to an end the moment this evening did!

'I think it's been decided that the two of us will travel in my car, and the others will go in your father's car,' Fergus told her with obvious satisfaction.

Decided by whom? She didn't remember being party to such a conversation. She—

'Is that okay with you, Chloe?' David was the one to ask her politely, seeming to have picked up a little on her mood.

'Absolutely fine,' she assured him airily—it would give her a chance to tell Fergus exactly what she would and wouldn't accept about his presence here this evening. Having him lay claim to her in such an obvious way was definitely unacceptable.

She was totally unprepared, once they all got outside, for the fact that Fergus's car was a dark-grey-coloured replica of her own!

'Odd, isn't it?' Fergus observed as he pressed the button to unlock the doors.

Chloe instantly damped down her surprise, shrugging dismissively as she got into the passenger seat. 'Not particularly,' she said as he got in beside her. 'It just proves that on certain subjects you have good judgement!'

Fergus chuckled softly. 'But only on certain subjects, hmm,' he acknowledged wryly.

Chloe didn't even qualify the statement with an answer,

sitting silently at his side as he manoeuvred the car to follow behind her father's to the restaurant.

But that wasn't to say she wasn't completely aware of
Fergus. Much more so than she wanted to be. And more
so than she wanted to admit!

Why him? The very last man she should find herself
attracted to!

Because she *was* attracted to him. Half the anger she had
directed at him already tonight had been because the moment he'd walked into the sitting-room she had been aware
of him. It had been as if all her nerve endings had suddenly
come tinglingly alive, each and every one of them finely
attuned to Fergus McCloud.

'What are you thinking about?' Fergus suddenly asked.

Chloe instantly tensed, wondering if her expression could
possibly have given away any of her disturbed thoughts.
She certainly hoped not!

'I was wondering what poison would be the least de-
tectable when given in food,' she answered with saccharine
sweetness.

Fergus chuckled. 'I don't think I've told you yet how
beautiful you look tonight,' he said admiringly.

'In this particular case, Fergus, flattery will get you nowhere!' she told him tautly.

But she couldn't help feeling pleased that her effort to
look good this evening had obviously paid off. Her figure-
hugging, knee-length silk dress was the colour of pale
milky coffee, perfectly complementing the tan she had ac-
quired earlier in the summer, her long hair looking almost
black against the light-coloured material, her make-up kept
to a glowing minimum, peach-coloured gloss enhancing her
lips

'I'm not trying to ''get'' anywhere, Chloe,' Fergus told
her wearily. 'Could we not just agree to drop hostilities for

this evening—all coming from your side, I might add!—
and enjoy a nice dinner with your family?'

No, they could not! She daredn't let down her guard
when around Fergus McCloud. And not just because of
what he was trying to do to her father...

She was very much afraid she had fallen in love with
the enemy!

CHAPTER NINE

'I'M NOT the enemy, Chloe,' Fergus told her grimly, very aware that she certainly regarded him as such. 'In fact,' he continued carefully, 'I would like to talk to you later. Alone. I have a proposal to put to you.'

She gave him a startled look. 'A what?'

Fergus smiled humourlessly at her obvious shock. 'Not that sort of proposal, Chloe,' he corrected. 'A suggestion. An idea I have that might help both of us,' he enlarged.

Chloe looked scathing now. 'Why do I have the feeling I'm not going to like this idea?'

'Probably because at the moment you don't particularly like anything about me?'

'I wouldn't have clarified that remark with at the moment,' she told him flatly, turning to uncooperatively look out of the side window.

Fergus couldn't help but smile at her candidness. Although…come to think of it, what she had said wasn't that funny, he realised. Did she really not like him at all? In the circumstances, he couldn't exactly say he blamed her, but that didn't make the fact any more palatable.

'Your father doesn't share your dislike of me,' he pointed out.

'No,' Chloe acknowledged guardedly. 'Why is that?'

'Probably because when I told him I was researching a political thriller, I omitted to mention the subject of Susan Stirling,' Fergus admitted grimly.

Chloe turned to him searchingly, looking totally nonplussed by his statement. 'I don't understand,' she finally responded.

Neither did he. Not completely. Oh, he had been shaken slightly earlier in the week by Chloe's complete belief in her father's innocence, but he had also known that, in the circumstances, her loyalty was understandable.

But meeting Paul Hamilton today, listening for over an hour to what he was sure was the man's complete candidness in answer to his questions, Fergus hadn't felt able to broach the subject of the scandal that had brought the other man's political career to a halt eight years ago. Especially when Paul was so obviously thrilled with his decision to re-enter the political arena.

Fergus knew that his wife, Diana's, likeness to Chloe could also have had something to do with his reluctance to alienate the other man...

'I'm reserving judgement, okay,' he rejoined impatiently.

But he could feel Chloe's gaze was still on him, as if she might read something else from his expression. She wouldn't. Before concentrating full time on writing, he had been a practising lawyer for over five years, had learnt only too well how to mask his inner emotions.

Besides, he wasn't a hundred-per-cent certain what his emotions were at the moment. On one level he was angry with himself for chickening out during his meeting with Paul Hamilton this morning. But, on another level, he knew that if he hadn't made that last-minute decision, he certainly wouldn't be here with Chloe now.

Finally she drew in a long breath. 'How big of you,' she said contemptuously, obviously not impressed.

He couldn't help that; at the moment it was as far as he was willing to go on that particular subject. 'I thought so,' he acknowledged dryly. 'The important thing is, are you willing to do the same?' He quirked dark brows as he kept his gaze on the road ahead.

'Concerning what?' she returned guardedly.

'Concerning dinner, of course. As far as your family are aware, I'm only here this evening as your partner. Can we leave it at that for the moment?'

'That really depends on you—doesn't it?' she countered.

He sighed deeply. 'I'm hardly likely to ask any embarrassing questions in front of your mother!' There was no way he could deliberately hurt the graciously lovely Diana!

'I suppose that's something to be grateful for!' Chloe exclaimed disgustedly.

Fergus gave up trying to reason with her, concentrating on following Paul Hamilton's car to the restaurant. He was satisfied that, for the moment, Chloe wasn't going to give away his ulterior motive for seeing her father this morning; if she had been going to do that, then she already would have done it!

It didn't need too much time spent in their company to see the Hamiltons were a close family, Fergus realised once he was seated with them at the table and they had ordered their meal. There was a playful warmth amongst them all that spoke of affectionate familiarity.

Fergus had shared a happy camaraderie with his two cousins as he'd grown up in Scotland after his parents' divorce, and his grandfather had shown them all a taciturn affection. But there had never been any of the teasing and laughter over their meals that the Hamiltons obviously enjoyed together.

If this evening was doing nothing else, it was showing him exactly why Chloe had tried to intercede with him on her father's behalf. Even if her method had been more than a little lacking in judgement!

'My husband tells me you're in the middle of writing a

political thriller, Mr McCloud?' Mrs Hamilton prompted interestedly.

He didn't even need to glance Chloe's way to know of her tension as she obviously overheard the question. Damn it, didn't she believe him when he told her he was here for no other reason than to have dinner with her? Obviously not, he accepted irritably, after the briefest of glimpses at her rigidly set expression.

He turned to smile at Diana. 'Please call me Fergus,' he invited smoothly. 'And in the middle of writing is a slight exaggeration; I'm still heavily into the research,' he admitted.

'Do you have to do much of that?' Diana asked interestedly.

Fergus found himself relaxing totally as he talked to Chloe's mother. There was no doubting that Diana made a good politician's wife; she had a way of putting one at one's ease, while at the same time showing genuine interest in what was being said.

'For goodness' sake,' Chloe hissed at him ten minutes later, having exhausted, for the moment, her own conversation with David Lantham, who sat on her other side. 'My mother was only being polite,' she snapped once she had Fergus's full attention. 'You didn't have to give her a step-by-step account of your research process!' Her eyes flashed deeply blue.

Fergus looked at her searchingly for several long seconds, head tilted on one side, unrelenting in that reproachful gaze until he saw the uncomfortable colour that entered her cheeks.

'That's better,' he murmured with satisfaction. 'What would you rather I talked to your mother about?' he taunted, aware that the others seated at the table were deep in a political conversation.

Chloe glared at him now. 'I would rather you didn't talk to her at all!'

'Not very practical, in the circumstances,' he drawled. 'Besides, I like your mother, and there's no way I could be rude to her.'

'I— You— Oh, eat your prawns!' Chloe muttered with obvious frustration, putting down her fork as she gave up any attempt to eat any more of the whitebait she had ordered as her own starter.

Fergus reached out and lightly covered one of her hands with his own. 'Just relax, Chloe,' he advised gently. 'I'm not here tonight as Fergus McCloud, writer.'

'Then what are you here as?' she scorned.

'Fergus McCloud, lover?' He raised mocking dark brows.

The colour deepened in her cheeks even as she drew in an angry breath. 'I've already told you that we didn't—'

'Wishful thinking on my part?' he cut in. 'For the future,' he added huskily.

That had the power of totally silencing her, Fergus noted with satisfaction, her mouth opening and shutting like a goldfish's in a bowl. Although it also had the effect of Chloe snatching her hand from beneath his, and hiding both hands under the table. Which didn't please him at all...

He chuckled. 'You really are incredibly sweet, Chloe,' he told her warmly.

'You make me sound as if I'm ten years old!' she came back disgruntledly.

Fergus smiled. 'Sometimes you behave as if you were. But not too often,' he amended as she would have retorted again. 'I think the next few weeks could be rather fun...' he said enigmatically.

Whatever did he mean by that remark...?

And that other one—wishful thinking for the future...!

If he thought she was going to go on seeing him, while at the same time he made every effort to gather information that was going to disgrace her father, then he was in for a nasty surprise!

Surely Fergus couldn't be that insensitive?

He was obviously slightly bemused by the teasing and cajoling that went on amongst her family, and she believed him when he said he liked her mother. But none of that changed the fact that he intended writing a book that would throw the Hamiltons into turmoil all over again.

Perhaps he was *that* insensitive, after all...

She was also slightly bemused herself by that proposal he had mentioned in the car on the way here. If it had anything to do with the two of them continuing to see each other, then he could just forget it. There was absolutely no way she could agree to do that.

Although it wouldn't necessarily be because she didn't want to...

That alive feeling she had experienced earlier this evening when he'd arrived had continued to stay with her, so much so that she was aware of every movement he made, every word that he said. Her hand still tingled from where he had touched it minutes ago!

In truth, her chagrin at his lengthy conversation with her mother wasn't completely because she thought he was being duplicitous; she had jealously resented every smile, every word, he had directed at Diana.

Was this what being in love with someone was like? Feeling jealous of your own mother because the man you loved could talk more easily with her than he could with you? Or was it just that she knew Fergus didn't return that love...?

What good would it do her, would it do either of them,

if he did fall in love with her? Nothing could change the fact that he had the power to destroy her family. Something she could never, ever forgive him for.

'You're looking very serious all of a sudden.' Fergus looked at her searchingly now. 'What are you thinking about?'

The same thing she had thought about constantly for the last two weeks—him!

Chloe gave him a scathing glance. 'My thoughts—thank goodness!—have always been completely my own!'

He nodded consideringly. 'I've never really thought about it before, but it can't have been easy growing up in your father's political spotlight.'

She stiffened resentfully. 'I thought you weren't going to discuss that this evening,' she reminded him.

'I never said I wouldn't talk about you.' He sighed impatiently.

Chloe smiled humourlessly. 'I'm my father's daughter.'

Fergus gave a sardonic smile back. 'You're a damn sight more than that!'

She quirked dark brows. 'Am I?' she prompted. Not sure that she was. To him, at least.

His eyes narrowed. 'Do you know what I really want to do at this moment...?'

Chloe eyed him warily, not sure she wanted to know the answer to that. 'Smack my backside,' she guessed slowly.

'I've thought about it,' he admitted with a grin. 'But my grandfather brought us all up, Logan, Brice, and myself, to treat women with a certain respect,' he explained. 'I think that rules out smacking their bottoms!'

She grinned. 'Your grandfather sounds like a very sensible man to me.'

Fergus returned her grin. 'Actually, he's an old devil. But I don't doubt that he would like you. No, Chloe, what

I really want to do right now is kiss you,' he continued conversationally. 'Preferably until you're senseless. Or, at least, silent!' he added ruefully.

'It's sometimes the only way where women are concerned!' her father was the one to answer Fergus laughingly.

Chloe turned self-consciously to find that all her family were looking at them, her cheeks blushing bright red as she wondered exactly how long they had been listening to the barbed conversation between Fergus and herself. Obviously not long enough for them to have heard her earlier accusations, or they wouldn't all be smiling so indulgently!

'Please, Daddy, Fergus needs no encouragement in being outrageous!' she reproved lightly, doing her best to minimalise the importance of Fergus claiming he wanted to kiss her until she was senseless—or silent. Even if just the thought of it made her tremble with longing!

'Obviously not,' her father responded approvingly.

That approval of Fergus, by all her family, became even more apparent as the evening progressed.

Not that Chloe could exactly blame them. Fergus had an array of amusing stories to entertain them all with, was very charming and attentive to all the Hamilton women—something else his grandfather had no doubt instilled in him. In fact, Fergus was the ideal dinner guest!

'What's wrong now?' Fergus asked wearily as he drove the two of them back to her home at the end of the evening.

Chloe snapped out of the reverie she had fallen into the last few minutes, turning to look at him as she realised she must have been frowning. 'Truthfully?' she returned dully.

'It's always preferable to a lie—no matter how politely it's given,' he confirmed wryly.

She sighed. 'I was wishing you were anyone else but who you really are,' she admitted candidly.

It was Fergus's turn to look serious. 'Explain, please,' he bit out.

She wasn't sure that she could. Not without revealing exactly how emotionally involved she had become with him without really meaning to.

'I actually quite like you, Fergus,' she began cautiously.

'Careful, Chloe,' he taunted. 'Let's not get too effusive!'

She gave him an impatient glance. 'Don't worry—I don't intend to,' she assured him. 'I like you, and under any other circumstances, I might even enjoy your company,' she told him grudgingly. 'But as it is…'

'As I told you earlier, Chloe, I am not the enemy,' he cut in tersely.

'Can't you see that to me that's exactly what you are?' she came back fiercely, her hands tightly clenched.

'I also mentioned earlier that I want to talk to you,' he ground out, his hands gripping the steering wheel. 'Is there anywhere we can go so we can talk privately?'

Chloe thought for a minute. No doubt Penny and David would stay and have a nightcap once they reached her parents' home, which ruled that out. And, as she shared that home with her parents… But going to Fergus's home was just as unacceptable; she would then be totally reliant on Fergus to drive her home after they had talked.

'Drop me off at home so that I can drive over to your house,' she said flatly. 'I presume we can talk privately there?'

'We can…yes,' he replied slowly. 'I only said I would like to kiss you until you're senseless, Chloe; that doesn't mean I'm going to!'

'You won't be given the chance to,' she assured him with certainty.

Fergus shot her a narrow-eyed glance before turning his attention back to the road.

But his anger was a tangible thing, the relaxed atmosphere that had developed over their meal completely dissipated.

However, Chloe couldn't help that. She had to keep this man at arm's length; she had no choice. No matter how much she might wish it were otherwise!

It took her only a couple of minutes, once she reached the house, to say goodnight to her parents, Penny and David, collect her car keys, and set off to join Fergus at his home. Having already said goodnight to her family at the restaurant, Fergus had driven off as soon as Chloe had got out of his car, the angry set to his features telling her he'd still been far from happy about the arrangement.

Tough. This suited her much better, and, where Fergus was concerned, she knew she had to maintain her independence.

The lights were on in the house when she pulled her car up onto the driveway, Fergus answering the door after her first ring, offering no greeting, looking completely unapproachable as he led the way through to the sitting-room.

'Brandy?' he offered tersely, having already poured one for himself before she arrived.

'Not when I'm driving, thank you,' she refused as she steadily met his gaze across the room and sat down in one of the armchairs.

Fergus took a sip of his own brandy, grimacing slightly as the alcohol hit the back of his throat. 'Hear me out first, hmm?' he finally said. 'And don't get defensive at my first comment.'

She raised dark brows. 'Surely that depends on what you have to say?'

He began to pace the room, his height and presence totally dominating.

But Chloe refused to feel intimidated, sensing Fergus's own uncertainty with what he was about to say.

Finally he came to an abrupt halt, turning to face her, his expression grim. 'I know who told you about my book, Chloe.'

Her gaze didn't waver, but she could feel the colour receding from her cheeks. 'How?' she croaked.

His mouth thinned humourlessly. 'Process of elimination,' he explained. 'My agent's talks with the publisher were only verbal, and only with my editor, so that was pretty much a dead end. Which brought me back to the agent himself. Bernie is many things,' he acknowledged dryly, 'but indiscreet is not one of them. He has an assistant and a secretary, the former being female, and as ambitious as Bernie himself. Besides, Stella Whitney does not strike me as a woman who indulges in girlish confidences! Which only left the secretary,' he concluded.

Chloe was barely breathing—how could she, when her heart was in her mouth?

Fergus looked grim. 'I didn't have to dig too deeply to discover that Victoria Pelman, coincidentally, is your cousin. The daughter of your mother's sister.' He looked at Chloe with raised brows.

She swallowed hard, moistening suddenly dry lips. Victoria had been in a terrible state when Chloe had met her for lunch five weeks ago, obviously having needed to tell Chloe something, but at the same time having been aware that it had been a professional confidence she shouldn't have shared. With anyone. Family loyalty had— fortunately for Chloe!—won out.

'What do you mean to do with that information?' she prompted Fergus hollowly.

'What do you think I should do with it?'

Chloe grimaced. What she would really like was for him

to just forget he had ever found out about it. But she doubted that was about to happen.

'Victoria acted in good faith,' she defended.

'It isn't her motivation that's in question,' Fergus rasped.

Chloe stood up, now feeling at too much of a disadvantage as she sat in the armchair. 'If it had been you, or one of your cousins, who had discovered something that could hurt someone in your family, what would you have expected them to do about it?' she challenged.

'Exactly the same as Victoria did,' he acknowledged heavily. 'But, unfortunately, that doesn't really solve this present dilemma for me—does it?'

No, she could see that, Chloe accepted. But she and Victoria were the same age, had grown up together. During their childhood years the two girls had spent almost as much time in each other's homes as they had their own.

Of course, their lives had taken separate paths as they'd reached adulthood, but the two women were no less close because of that. Victoria might love her job as secretary to Bernard Crosby. It was just that she loved her family more.

Chloe drew in a shaky breath. 'I ask you again, what do you mean to do with that information?'

She had tried so hard to keep Victoria's involvement out of this situation, had hoped—futilely!—that Fergus would be so caught up in the fact that Chloe knew so much about him and his proposed book that he wouldn't actually question how she knew.

Fergus's gaze was narrowed on the paleness of her face, his mouth twisting hardly as he seemed to guess at least some of her thoughts. 'I'm sure you and your cousin have had a great time discussing my private life—'

'We didn't—well...not in the way you're implying,' Chloe amended awkwardly.

'I think knowing a detail like how I take my coffee

comes under the heading of my private life,' he drawled. 'Don't you?'

'Don't be ridiculous,' Chloe snapped to cover her own discomfort. 'Apparently Victoria has made you coffee at least a dozen times during your appointments with your agent.'

'Probably,' Fergus conceded. 'But my address and telephone number definitely come under the heading of privileged information!'

Chloe winced at the justified attack. 'I didn't use either of them; until after I had actually met you at the nightclub,' she replied.

'To your credit, no, you didn't,' he agreed wearily.

Nevertheless, Chloe didn't take any comfort from the admission, sensing Fergus was far from finished. 'How long have you known?'

'A couple of days.'

But he had waited until now to confront her with it. There was also the fact that he had arrived for his appointment with her father this morning with the intention of inviting her out to lunch with him today...

'What do you want, Fergus?' she asked tonelessly.

His head went back. 'What makes you think I want anything?'

She smiled without humour. 'The fact that I stopped believing in Father Christmas and the Tooth Fairy years ago!'

The last thing she wanted to do was endanger Victoria's job with Bernard Crosby. And if Fergus's own family loyalty was anything like her own, and she thought it probably was, then he was going to know that about her too.

'Your idea, Fergus?' she prompted hardly, referring to his remark at the beginning of the evening, even more sure now that she wasn't going to like this idea.

'I want you to help me with the research for my book,' he stated evenly.

Chloe stared at him. He couldn't be serious!

But she could see by his unwavering gaze, his unsmiling mouth, the inflexibility of his jaw, that he was. Deadly serious!

CHAPTER TEN

CHLOE, Fergus realised in the split second before her hand slowly began to rise from her side, was going to hit him!

He reached out and easily grasped the wrist of that threatening hand. 'I don't think so, Chloe,' he warned.

She struggled in that grasp, her face suffused with angry colour. 'You bastard!' she gasped. 'You scheming—'

'*I'm* scheming?' he echoed incredulously.

'—blackmailing—'

'Stop right there, Chloe,' he bit out harshly, his hand tightening on her wrist. 'Before you say something we're both going to regret!'

She glared up at him, breathing hard. '*I* won't regret it!'

'I don't know what context you've put on my idea—although, from your reaction, I can guess!' he rasped disgustedly. 'But I am most definitely not suggesting an exchange, my silence about Victoria's involvement for information on your father and Susan Stirling.' He was angry himself now. Furiously so. 'If I were the type of man to want something in exchange for my silence, you can be assured I would be likely to ask something from you of a much more intimate nature than that!'

Chloe became suddenly still, her only movement now the quick rise and fall of her breasts as she breathed deeply in her agitation, the colour slowly draining from her cheeks. She looked, Fergus acknowledged achingly, absolutely beautiful!

She swallowed hard. 'I think asking me to betray my

own father is quite intimate enough!' she exclaimed distastefully.

'I don't want you to betray your father, damn it,' Fergus snapped impatiently. 'Hell, Chloe, you certainly aren't making this easy for me.' He shook his head frustratedly.

She glared up at him, her face only inches away from his own. 'And I never will,' she assured him determinedly.

This wasn't the time. Fergus knew it wasn't. It could only make the situation between them worse than it already was. But for the moment, her perfume invading his senses, her warm closeness totally arousing, he just couldn't stop himself. He bent his head and kissed her.

For stunned seconds she stood completely still, but as he released her wrist, his arms moving about the slenderness of her waist, she was galvanised into action.

But as she tried to wrench her mouth from his Fergus moved one of his hands behind her head, resisting the movement, the struggles of her body against his, as he moulded her against him, doing nothing to lessen his sudden desire for her.

She tasted so good as he sipped and tasted her mouth, felt so right in his arms, his own body alive with wanting her.

All evening he had sat and watched her as she'd talked and laughed with her family, wishing she could be that relaxed and happy with him, but inwardly knowing that all he could have was this. Chloe might try to deny that she responded to him, but he knew differently; on this level the two of them were in complete accord.

And, for this moment, this was all there was...

Chloe was no longer fighting him, her mouth moving hungrily against his, her fingers threaded in the dark thickness of his hair, the softness of her breasts pressing against the hardness of his chest.

Fergus knew that he wanted her. Wanted desperately to make love to her. To lay her down on the carpeted floor and lose himself completely in the scented softness of her body.

But if he did that now he knew he would be no better than she had accused him of being. Worse, that he would lose her for ever.

It wasn't easy dragging his mouth from hers, in fact it was probably the hardest thing he had ever had to do in his life. But he did it nonetheless, his hands moving so that he now cradled her heated cheeks. If they didn't, he might have allowed himself to touch the softness of her breasts—and then he wouldn't have been *able* to stop!

'I want you to work with me, Chloe,' he told her gruffly. 'Not against your father, but *for* him,' he continued firmly as she would have spoken.

Her gaze was slightly unfocused as she blinked up at him. 'I don't understand,' she murmured huskily.

Fergus drew in a sharp breath. 'I told you, I'm reserving judgement,' he reminded softly. 'You maintain your father wasn't involved with Susan Stirling—'

'He wasn't,' she cut in.

'Or the father of her child,' Fergus continued determinedly. 'But someone was. Obviously,' he added dryly. 'If we can find out who that someone was—'

'We?' Chloe echoed scathingly.

Fergus's hands dropped from her face as he moved abruptly away from her; he couldn't think straight when he was that close to Chloe. 'I'm willing to make a deal with you, Chloe,' he said sharply. 'If, in the course of our research, we discover that there was another man, then I'll hold up my hands and admit I was wrong, okay?'

She stared at him with hard blue eyes. 'And if we don't discover "another man"?' she prompted scornfully. 'After all, why should we? The police did their own investigation after Susan's death, and they couldn't find any involvement at all. Which fuelled the rumours even more,' she added bitterly.

Fergus was well aware of that. But, hard as he had tried, he couldn't think of any other way round this problem. If they could find this other man, maybe Chloe would stop hating him...

His eyes narrowed. 'You called her Susan... Did you know her?'

Chloe turned away. 'Of course I knew her. She worked for my father. Eight years ago she was at the house practically all the time.'

Somehow that fact had never occurred to Fergus. There were a lot of things about this situation that had never occurred to him! In fact, he was beginning to wish he had never involved himself with that scandal eight years ago.

Although, if he hadn't, he would probably never have met Chloe at all...

He gave Chloe a considering look. 'What did you think of her?'

Chloe turned back angrily. 'I was fifteen years old; what do you think I thought of her?'

'Most fifteen-year-old girls nowadays seem very—um—probably ''worldly'' is the best word to use,' he grimaced thoughtfully.

'Well, I wasn't,' Chloe snapped. 'I was away at boarding-school most of the time, anyway. Susan just seemed—she was over thirty—she just seemed old to me!'

Fergus smiled grimly. Probably in the same way he, at thirty-five, now seemed old to her! 'But you must have formed some impression of her, surely?' he persisted doggedly.

'Okay,' she sighed her impatience. 'Susan was beautiful.

Very beautiful, in fact. Is that what you wanted to hear?'
Her eyes sparkled deeply blue.

Not particularly. As with Chloe's parents, he also already
knew what Susan Stirling looked like. He was more interested in what sort of person she had been.

'You didn't answer my question, Fergus,' Chloe bit out
tautly. 'What happens if you can't find another man for
Susan to have been involved with?'

That was something he hoped wouldn't happen! It would
totally ruin his storyline if they did find another man, but
Fergus knew that would now be preferable to him to having
Chloe learn that she had been wrong about her father all
along…!

'We would be working on the basis that there is another
man.'

Chloe shook her head. 'There is no we, Fergus,' she said
hardly. 'I don't intend helping you to hammer any more
nails in my father's political coffin.'

'I'm not trying to do that,' he came back frustratedly.
'Damn it, I'm trying to help your father, not harm him!'
And, at the same time, he hoped to spend some time with
Chloe, help her to see that he really wasn't the bad guy.

'I can't help you, Fergus,' she told him flatly.

She really was the most stubborn—! 'What about
Victoria? Your cousin,' he reminded her.

Her mouth turned down humourlessly. 'I know who she
is, Fergus.' She sighed again heavily. 'I don't know. All I
do know is that I can't help you.'

'Won't, Chloe,' Fergus responded tautly. 'In this case,
there's a vast difference between can't and won't. The truth
of the matter is, you don't trust me, do you, Chloe?' His
gaze was concentrated on the paleness of her face.

She returned that gaze for several long seconds, finally
looking away. 'I have very little reason to trust you—'

'You've given me even less reason to trust *you*,' he cut in. 'But doesn't the fact that I'm offering to work alongside you in this show that I'm willing to do just that?'

'It shows you're willing to let me help you to continue to deceive my family into trusting you—'

'Damn it, I don't remember even mentioning your family!' His eyes blazed furiously.

'You don't need to; how else do you intend finding out the truth? No, Fergus, if I were interested in having anyone as Dr Watson to my Sherlock Holmes, you can be assured you would not be in the running!'

'Wrong billing there, Chloe; *I* would be Sherlock Holmes,' he contradicted with hard derision.

She smiled sadly. 'You see, we wouldn't even be able to agree on that—'

'We don't *have* to agree to discover the truth!' Fergus pushed determinedly. '"The truth shall make you free",' he quoted.

Chloe's smile was tremulous now. 'And some truth has to be taken on blind faith. The sort of faith I have in my father,' she added huskily.

Fergus couldn't argue with that. In fact, it was that faith, as well as the meeting with Paul Hamilton himself, that made him question his own earlier conviction that this had just been another case of a politician arrogantly breaking the unwritten rules of moral decency that his job as a public administrator insisted upon.

'Wouldn't it be better, for your father's re-entry into politics, if the whole situation had been cleared up, put away, and forgotten?' Fergus tried another approach.

'It would be better if the situation were left where it's been the last eight years—put away,' Chloe told him fiercely.

'But not forgotten,' Fergus pointed out softly.

'My answer is still no, Fergus,' she said firmly. 'I'm sorry, but that's the way it has to be.'

'It isn't the way it has to be. It's the way you've decided it should be.' He paused momentarily. 'Look, Chloe, I can either do this with you or without you. I would have preferred to do it with you.'

Her eyes widened. 'You're going to continue with your research, regardless?'

Fergus didn't particularly care for the distaste he could easily read in her expression. But he knew they had come too far along this route for him to be able to stop now.

He could agree right now not to write the book, but at the same time he knew, if he wanted to continue to see Chloe, that, unresolved, it would always be between them. An unmentioned shadow. And, above all else, no matter how she might try to fight it, he knew that he intended to continue seeing Chloe!

'I have no choice, Chloe,' he told her gently.

Her expression conveyed her disgust. 'You have a choice, Fergus—you're just not taking it! I should have known what sort of man you were that first night I met you!' Her eyes were glacially blue as they raked over him scornfully.

His hands clenched at his sides at her deliberately insulting tone, forcing himself to remember that was exactly what it was—deliberate. Chloe was determined to totally alienate him. But, perversely, that very determination gave him some sort of hope for the future. A future that might include Chloe...

'Oh, but you did know what sort of man I am, Chloe,' he murmured. 'Victoria told you—remember?'

Colour heightened her cheeks. 'I think I had better leave, Fergus,' she said stiffly. 'I don't think we have anything further to say to each other.'

He was silent, knowing that wasn't the case where he was concerned. But Chloe was probably right for the moment; she was too angry and upset right now to really listen to what he had to say.

'I'll walk you to the door,' he offered politely.

'Making sure I leave this time?' she taunted as she preceded him out of the room.

He didn't need any reminder of the night she had spent here without his knowledge—he had been kicking himself over it for the last two weeks!

'I would rather that you weren't leaving at all,' he assured her gruffly. 'But I accept that isn't even a possibility.' He smiled ruefully as she gave him a mocking glance.

'Goodbye, Fergus,' Chloe returned a bitter-sweet smile before getting into her car.

He felt his heart sink at the finality of her words. 'Good-*night*, Chloe,' he said with emphasis. 'I'm sure I'll be seeing you again very soon.'

She didn't exactly look thrilled at the prospect, Fergus acknowledged as she drove away. But, hopefully, the next time he saw her, he would have better news to give her...

'How long have you known Fergus McCloud?'

Chloe frowned at David as she looked up from the design she had been working on for the last hour. 'Sorry?' She delayed answering him, instantly on the defensive at the mention of Fergus's name.

She had lived in dread the last three days, since dinner on Friday night, of one of her family questioning her about her supposed friendship with Fergus. Her parents had been understandingly quiet on the subject, perhaps suspecting a serious romance, and not wanting to pry until she was ready to talk about it herself. She hadn't seen or spoken to Penny since Friday—but, from David's interest now, her sister and her husband had obviously discussed the subject of herself and Fergus!

'I asked how long have you known Fergus McCloud?' David repeated.

She put down her pencil, smiling at her brother-in-law as he came fully into the room at the top of the house that had been converted into a studio for her, several overhead windows installed to give her better light to work in. 'A few weeks,' she replied casually. 'So you can tell Penny not to shop for a wedding outfit just yet!' she added with a lightness she was far from feeling.

The last three days had not been easy ones, part of her dreading any mention of Fergus by her family, the other half of her wondering what Fergus was doing, how much deeper he had gone with his research. And wondering if she should have been quite so vehement in her refusal to help him. Perhaps it would have been better to know what Fergus was doing rather than sit here in absolute darkness waiting for the axe to fall!

David didn't return her smile. 'In your father's absence, I've just taken a telephone call from the advisor to the Leader of the Opposition,' he said, concern in his tone. 'He had something of a personal nature that he thought your father should know about. Something Peter Ambrose felt your father should be made aware of without going through any official channels.'

Chloe felt a tight knot in her chest. 'Yes...?' she prompted, really only to give herself time to think.

Any mention of her father, Fergus McCloud, and Peter Ambrose in the same conversation could only mean one thing!

David looked grave. 'I don't want to hurt you, Chloe, but— Fergus McCloud wasn't exactly truthful when he came to see your father here last week. He forgot to mention that the political thriller he's thinking of writing is loosely based on the Susan Stirling scandal!' he revealed.

Chloe drew in a sharp breath; David certainly wasn't pulling any punches on this one! 'On what he believes to be the Susan Stirling scandal,' she corrected firmly. 'We all know that isn't what really happened.'

'Do we?' David retorted. 'Hell, Chloe—why on earth didn't you tell any of us what he was up to?' he groaned exasperatedly. 'Why did you let me find out from another source like this? More to the point, don't you realise that Fergus McCloud has been using you to get to your father?'

That wasn't strictly true; she doubted Fergus would have bothered getting to know her at all if she hadn't forced her company on him. But she wasn't about to tell David that; he was clearly annoyed with her enough already.

She stood up impatiently, feeling like a little girl being chastised by the headmaster. 'Of course I realise that,' she snapped back angrily. 'Why do you imagine I'm no longer seeing him?' Her eyes blazed across at him.

David rubbed a hand across his furrowed brow. 'How long have you known what he's up to? Apparently Peter saw you out to dinner with him some time ago.'

'Just over a week ago, actually,' she amended with irritation. 'And it's irrelevant how long I've known about the book.' She didn't intend bringing Victoria into this any more than she had to; it was bad enough that Fergus knew of her involvement! 'Fergus intends writing it.'

'There must be legal moves we can—'

'Fergus is a lawyer, David,' she told him solemnly. 'He knows exactly how far he can go on that narrow line between fact and fiction without ending up in court defending a libel suit.' As he had already assured her! 'The real problem, as I see it, is which one of us is going to break the news to my father?'

It was something she had been putting off doing herself, loath to burst her father's bubble of happiness at the thought of re-entering politics. Oh, he had continued to be successful at business the last eight years, but politics was what he was really good at. But now that Peter Ambrose had unofficially issued a warning to her father, all idea of resurrecting her father's political career might have to be forgotten…

Damn Fergus McCloud, she thought, and not for the first time.

'I'll tell him,' David said grimly. 'Although he will probably want to talk to you afterwards,' he warned.

She expected that. Although she still had no idea what she was going to say…

'You say you've stopped seeing Fergus?' David said slowly.

'Most definitely,' she assured him.

'Are you sure that's a good idea…?' her brother-in-law commented thoughtfully.

Chloe shook her head impatiently. 'Make your mind up, David! In one breath you're berating me for having anything to do with the man, and in the next you're suggesting— Exactly what are you suggesting, David?' she asked warily.

'I don't know!' He ran an agitated hand through his thinning hair. 'I've been totally thrown by all of this. I can't think straight. I thought it was all over, that the past was dead and buried—'

'Along with Susan Stirling?' Chloe put in huskily.

David gave her a stunned look. 'That's a hell of a thing to say…'

She shrugged apologetically. 'You seemed to express some doubt earlier about my father's personal involvement with Susan.' She hadn't missed that earlier question mark when she'd asserted that they all knew the truth. 'Do you know something we don't?'

David gave her a sharp look. 'What do you mean?'

'Exactly what I said.' Chloe sighed, a sick feeling seeming to have settled in the pit of her stomach. 'You and Daddy have always been close, perhaps he confided in you when he couldn't confide in anyone else in the family—'

'Chloe, your father was not—absolutely not—involved with Susan Stirling,' David told her.

She heaved a sigh of relief. 'Nevertheless, he will have to be told about Fergus's book.'

'But maybe not yet,' David said. 'I would like to talk to Fergus myself before either of us say anything to your father.'

'He won't listen to you any more than he would listen to me,' she warned.

'Maybe not,' David accepted ruefully. 'But I still feel I have to try. Your father is a damned good politician, and he's already sacrificed enough to this mess.'

She was well aware of that, the whole family were. And she admired David for at least wanting to plead her father's case. She just knew he was wasting his time.

But Fergus had offered them one way out... At least, he had offered it to her...

'Could you just leave it for a few days, David?' she said at last. 'I would like to have one last try at reasoning with Fergus myself before anyone else gets involved,' she explained at David's frowning look.

'And what do I tell Peter Ambrose in the meantime?' David demanded.

'That the situation is under control?' she suggested, hoping that might be the case once she had pleaded her father's case just once more with Fergus.

But very much afraid that it wouldn't be...

CHAPTER ELEVEN

THE ringing doorbell was not a welcome interruption to Fergus's solitary dinner. Not that he was particularly enjoying the wonderful steak and kidney pudding Maud had prepared for him; he hadn't tasted a single mouthful he had eaten so far. He simply wasn't in the mood for company.

It had not been a good weekend after his unsatisfactory parting from Chloe on Friday evening, and the week itself was getting progressively worse.

He groaned as the doorbell rang again, knowing that with his car still parked in the driveway rather than put away in the garage, as it should be, it must be obvious to the caller that he was definitely at home.

In any other circumstances, he would have been thrilled to find Chloe standing on the doorstep, but, with the information he had so recently obtained, she was the very last person he wanted to see!

Not that she didn't look absolutely lovely, because she did, the simply designed black dress she wore a perfect foil for her long dark hair and creamy skin.

She smiled up at him. 'Are you still angry with me, or are you going to invite me in?' she prompted hopefully.

He opened the door wider so that she could come in. He wasn't in the least angry with her, hadn't been angry with her on Friday evening either. But knowing what he now knew, he wasn't sure what to say to her...

'We both look as if we're in mourning,' she said once they were in the sitting-room; Fergus was also dressed completely in black: black denims and a black shirt.

Fergus was mentally apologising to Maud for her wasted dinner, even if Chloe's visit turned out to be a short one, he felt even less like eating now.

'What can I do for you, Chloe?' he asked soberly.

She moistened her lips with the tip of her tongue, clearly not as self-possessed as she wanted to appear. 'A cup of coffee would be nice,' she suggested brightly. 'Do you mind if I sit down?'

'Help yourself,' he invited, watching broodingly as she did so, crossing one shapely knee over the other, her legs lightly tanned.

Stop it, Fergus, he instantly instructed himself sternly. He was in enough of a dilemma as it was, without feeling this aching desire for Chloe.

'I wasn't actually offering you refreshment in my earlier question,' he told her dryly. 'But I'm quite happy to get you a cup of coffee.' And then she would have to go, he decided firmly as he went out to the kitchen. He had a lot of thinking to do, and he certainly couldn't do it with Chloe around!

He moved economically around the room preparing the pot of coffee, wondering why Chloe was here—wondering what on earth he could possibly find to say to her!

'I seem to have interrupted your dinner,' Chloe said apologetically from behind him. 'I didn't mean to startle you,' she continued as she saw the way he had jumped when she'd first spoken. 'Please don't let your meal get cold.' She indicated the meat pudding and vegetables that were slowly congealing on the plate that sat on the kitchen table.

'I wasn't enjoying it anyway,' he dismissed, picking up the tray with the coffee things on. 'Let's go back into the other room, shall we?'

Chloe eyed him searchingly once they were back in the

sitting-room, the coffee poured. 'Is there something wrong, Fergus?'

Everything! Almost everything. Damn it, he wished— and not for the first time—that he had never started this!

He sat down in the armchair opposite hers. 'Not particularly,' he avoided. 'Why are you here, Chloe?' He was deliberately more specific this time.

'Well...I could say I just called in to see you,' she parried. 'Or that I was just passing. Or that—'

'I believe I've already told you that I much prefer the truth to fabrication,' he cut in.

'So you did,' she returned easily. 'Maybe I should have telephoned first.' She chewed worriedly on her bottom lip.

Fergus wished she wouldn't do that! Because he would like to be the one doing it; nibbling, tasting, savouring the allure of those pouting, very kissable lips!

'You're here now,' he replied, hoping none of his inner hunger—and not for food!—showed in his expression.

She drew in a deep breath. 'Peter Ambrose has contacted my father—not officially,' she added hastily, 'concerning the proposed storyline of your book.'

Once again Fergus wished he had never even contemplated writing that particular book. Because now, in light of the new information he had received, Chloe was going to be hurt no matter what he did. Which meant she would only hate him all the more!

He sighed. 'Yes?' After his own conversation with Peter Ambrose last week, he was only surprised the other man had waited this long.

Chloe put down her coffee-cup, her hand shaking slightly. 'It isn't too late to stop all this, Fergus.' She looked across at him pleadingly.

Oh, yes, it was. Far, far too late. Because it was out of his hands now, like a tiny snowball rolling from the top of a mountain, growing bigger and bigger as it gained momentum.

He sat forward in his own chair, desperately searching for the right thing to say. 'Chloe,' he began hesitantly, 'can't you talk to your father? Perhaps try to persuade him that going back into politics is not the right thing for him to do?' Now, or ever, if Fergus's information was correct!

Her eyes widened. 'Because you want to write a book?' she questioned incredulously.

'No—'

'Don't you think you're being more than a little selfish?' she accused. 'You're a writer, you must have dozens of storylines floating around inside your head—

'I appreciate your confidence in my imaginative capabilities, Chloe,' he interrupted her. 'But I'm afraid that—'

'This is the story you want to write!' she finished, standing up agitatedly. 'Fergus, I'm pleading with you, begging, if necessary; please, please stop this.' Her eyes were full of as yet unshed tears.

He wished he could agree to do that, wished it were within his power to do so. But he had received a visit from someone this afternoon who had made that impossible...!

'Chloe, your father must have known, when he made his decision to go back into politics, that—my book apart—the past was sure to be thrown up at him again,' he tried reasoning.

'The past, yes.' She nodded. 'He's ready for that. After all, he has always maintained his innocence. But, can't you see, your book will sensationalise the whole thing? I'll do anything, Fergus,' she continued chokingly. 'Anything at all, as long as you agree not to write this book!'

Fergus felt sick, knowing that within twenty-four hours, forty-eight at the most, Chloe was going to hate him with a vengeance. And when she thought back to what she had just offered him, she was going to hate him all the more.

His gaze ran slowly up, and then equally slowly down, the slender length of her body, keeping his expression deliberately insolent even as Chloe blushed painfully. Better to hurt her now than later.

'You seem to rate your physical attributes rather highly, my dear,' he finally drawled.

Her pain obviously warred with the anger she also felt as she fought for control of her temper—and lost. 'You—'

'No more name-calling, Chloe,' Fergus advised mockingly, standing up himself now, having come to a decision during the last couple of minutes, one that required Chloe to leave. Now. 'I really don't think we have anything further to say to each other—do you?' He quirked dark brows.

Her cheeks lost all their colour at his deliberate snub. 'I can't think why I ever thought that appealing to the nice side of your nature would work—you obviously don't have one!' she exclaimed, grabbing up her car keys from the coffee-table. 'I don't know how you can sleep at night!' she finished disgustedly.

Just recently he hadn't been—and it had nothing to do with the guilty conscience Chloe was implying he should have. Just thinking of Chloe was enough to give him sleepless nights!

'As you already know, I have very little trouble doing exactly that,' he reminded her of the night she had spent in his bedroom. A night he hadn't been able to get out of his mind!

He had innocently slept that night away, completely unaware of the fact that Chloe had shared the room with him. Something he was sure, despite her recent offer, would never happen again.

'Now, if you wouldn't mind?' He glanced at his wrist-

watch; only seven-thirty. He had plenty of time. He hoped!
'I have an appointment this evening.' At least, he hoped to
have, after a brief telephone call.

After this visit of desperation by Chloe, he now knew he
couldn't just sit here and do nothing. Even if he failed to
stop that rolling snowball, he knew he had to at least try
to find someone else who could. If it hadn't already crashed
at the bottom of the mountain!

Chloe's mouth turned down scathingly. 'I'm sorry to
have wasted your time,' she gritted through her teeth,
marching over to the door.

'It was your time you were wasting,' he taunted softly.

'Obviously!' She turned briefly to glare at him, eyes
sparkling deeply blue.

Fergus kept up his nonchalant pose for as long as it took
Chloe to stride angrily out of the house, get into her car,
and drive away. After which his shoulders slumped like a
deflated balloon.

He shook his head determinedly. This wouldn't do. He
had things to do. Places to go. Someone to see.

But first he had to make that telephone call...

Why was it that Fergus always made her so angry she forgot all her good intentions, all her persuasive tactics, as
soon as she saw him?

And that she ended up in tears every time she left him!

Those hot rivulets of frustration and disillusionment were
running down her cheeks as she drove away from his house,
uncontrollable tears, as she knew she had once again failed
to convince Fergus of the damage his book would do to
her family.

Not only had she failed, she had totally humiliated herself by offering herself and being so callously rejected!

She would have to tell David tomorrow morning that

they had no choice now; her father had to be told about what was going on. It would be so much worse if he were to learn of it from another source.

But the thought of going home, of sitting down to dinner with her parents, with that knowledge burning inside her, was not a pleasant one. Besides, after this most recent conversation with Fergus, she was positive she wouldn't be able to eat a thing...

The lights blazed welcomingly in Penny and David's house as Chloe parked her car in the driveway, and while Josh would probably have already gone to bed, eight-year-old Diana, and ten-year-old Paul would still be up. She was very fond of her niece and nephews, and at this moment their innocence seemed very appealing. Much more so than trying to get through an evening of normality with her parents!

'Hello, darling,' Penny greeted warmly as Chloe let herself into the kitchen. 'Just in time to help me bath this horror.' She ruffled the dark hair of her youngest son. 'I'm a bit behind this evening,' she cheerfully explained the fact that Josh was still up, after all. 'David had to pop out unexpectedly.'

Chloe couldn't say she exactly minded that David wasn't here; the fact that he knew what she knew, and that Penny obviously didn't, could have made her visit a little awkward.

'I would love to help with the bath,' she agreed with a smile, already feeling the tension starting to ease out of her.

Penny was such a natural mother, Chloe thought admiringly as her sister organised Diana and Paul into doing their homework before taking Josh upstairs for his bath. Her sister took responsibility for the children's car journeys to school, their horse-riding lessons, swimming, and teas with and for friends. The fact that David very often wasn't there to help her with them didn't stop her from taking it all in her stride, rarely becoming cross or impatient.

The balm of this warm and happy household was exactly what Chloe needed after her last conversation with Fergus.

'And how is the gorgeous Fergus?' Penny asked as she helped Josh undress for his bath, seeming to have picked up on at least some of Chloe's thoughts.

'He isn't,' Chloe answered with finality. 'Gorgeous, or otherwise,' she added.

Her sister showed her disappointment at this news. 'I thought he seemed rather nice.'

Chloe looked unconcerned. 'A bit too arrogant and domineering for my taste.'

'That's a shame,' Penny sympathised.

'Who's Fergus?' Josh asked guilelessly as he played with the bubbles in his bath.

Penny chuckled. 'I forgot little people have big ears,' she said apologetically to Chloe. 'He's just a friend of Aunty Chloe's, darling,' she told her youngest son as she began to shampoo his hair.

Friend hardly accurately described Fergus—at any time during their acquaintance!

'Aunty Chloe has a boyfriend,' Josh announced to his older brother and sister when they returned to the kitchen after his bath. 'His name's Fergus,' he elaborated knowingly.

And Chloe had just been thinking how adorable he looked with his hair still slightly damp, and dressed in a pair of pyjamas that sported a popular cartoon character on the front!

'Are you going to marry him, Aunty Chloe?' Diana asked excitedly; her dearest wish—and she stated it often!—was to be a bridesmaid.

Marry Fergus? She would as soon throw herself into a

cage of lions! At least their attack would be swift as well as deadly...

''Fraid not, poppet,' she disappointed her niece. 'Kiss what you think is a prince nowadays and they turn into a frog!'

Diana giggled, her attention instantly diverted—as it was meant to be!—onto which bedtime story Chloe was going to read to her tonight. Diana was old enough to read to herself when she went to bed, but she occasionally liked to be indulged by having someone to read to her. And Aunty Chloe was usually only too happy to oblige.

'Is that really true?' Penny prompted half an hour later, all the children now in their bedrooms, the two women enjoying a cup of tea together in the tidy sitting-room. 'About the prince turning into a frog?' she reminded her sister laughingly as Chloe looked confused.

'I'm afraid so,' Chloe admitted. 'I think I'll just stick with my career—it's completely trustworthy, and it doesn't answer back!'

Penny made a face. 'I'm glad I'm not still out there looking for a soul mate. It seems to have become more complicated since my debutante days!' She stretched tiredly.

'Why don't you take advantage of the kids being in bed, and David's absence, and go and have a nice soak in the bath?' Chloe suggested, having seen her sister's tiredness. 'I should be getting back, anyway.' Even if the mere thought of it brought back that heavy feeling in her chest.

'I think I will.' Penny smiled in anticipation of an hour or so's relaxation. 'Thanks for helping with the kids. Give my love to Mummy and Daddy.'

Chloe didn't hurry her drive home, still not in any rush to get there. But by arriving home late she should have missed dinner, which was something; at least she wouldn't have to go through the motions of eating now, for her parents' sake.

Although her tension returned in full force, her face paling, her hands tightly grasping the steering wheel, when she reached her parents' home and saw, as well as David's blue car parked in the driveway, the now familiar dark grey sports car was also parked there.

What on earth was Fergus doing here?

As if she really needed to ask…!

Although it was now obvious to where David had been called out so unexpectedly!

It was why that concerned Chloe…

She hastily parked her own car beside Fergus's before hurrying into the house. She had left Fergus an hour and a half ago, was probably already too late to stop him doing whatever damage he had come here to do.

'Hello, darling,' her mother greeted as Chloe hurried into the sitting-room, putting down the magazine she had been flicking through to smile at her youngest daughter. 'I wondered where you had got to. Dinner has been delayed slightly, I'm afraid, your father has some sort of business meeting going on,' she explained unconcernedly.

Chloe knew exactly who that business meeting was with!

The room was empty except for her mother, which meant Fergus had to be ensconced in the study with her father and David. Discussing what? Did her father know everything now? And if he did, what would he decide to do about it?

Damn Fergus!

'Has Fergus been here long?' she enquired conversationally, resisting her first instinct—which was to march down the hallway to her father's study and demand to know exactly what Fergus thought he was doing.

'Of course, you must have seen his car in the driveway,'

her mother realised. 'An hour or so. I thought at first that he had come here to see you, but he asked to see your father. You don't suppose he's formally asking for your hand in marriage, do you?' her mother teased mischievously. 'What fun!'

Chloe was sure that marriage, to her or anyone else, was the last thing on Fergus's mind at the moment! Or any other moment...

'I very much doubt it,' she answered wryly. 'I see David is here too,' she ventured.

'He arrived a few minutes after Fergus,' her mother responded. 'I must say, it's all very mysterious.'

Not to Chloe it wasn't. Although she couldn't say anything to her mother; she had already been through enough over this eight years ago.

And so the two women sat together in the sitting-room, making light conversation, the minutes seeming to tick by very slowly to Chloe as she waited for the three men to emerge from the study. It was at times like this that she wished she did drink!

It was almost half an hour later when she heard the men's voices out in the hallway, breaking off her conversation with her mother to stand up and hurry from the room.

Grim didn't even begin to describe the expressions on their faces, David leading the way, Fergus after him, and her father following behind; David's face was white with tension, Fergus's expression becoming arrogantly distant as he saw her standing in the hallway.

But it was her father who concerned her the most; he suddenly looked ten years older, his face grey with unhappiness, a defeated droop to his shoulders, moving with none of the energetic drive that he usually did.

Her angrily accusing gaze returned to Fergus as he drew

level with her in the hallway, knowing that, for the second
time in the last few days, she wanted to hit him.

'Don't say a word,' he warned, even as he reached out
and took a firm hold of her upper arm. 'Walk me to my
car,' he ground out.

It wasn't a request, and Chloe didn't take kindly to being
ordered about by this particular man. But her efforts to
release herself from his grip only succeeded in bruising her
arm.

'Now,' Fergus added through gritted teeth.

Chloe shot him a fiercely angry look before turning on
her heel and marching towards the front door, dragging
Fergus along with her, his hold still firm on her arm.

'Well, I hope you're satisfied!' She turned on him furiously once they were outside the closed front door, glaring
up at him, easily able to see him in the light over the door.

'Not particularly.' He shook his head, eyes a dull brown,
his mouth a grim line.

'Then why did you do it?' Her voice broke emotionally.
'Oh, never mind—we both know why. What is my father
going to do now?'

Fergus moved his shoulders slightly. 'I think you had
better ask him that. Don't you?'

'I'll never forgive you for this, Fergus,' Chloe told him
chokingly, fighting back the threatening tears. 'Never!'

'I didn't suppose you would,' he acknowledged dully.

'I hope your book is a complete failure,' she added child-
ishly, knowing that it wouldn't be, that Fergus's name on
it alone would make it a success. 'It deserves to be, at
least!'

Fergus looked sad. 'Do any of us ever really get what
we deserve?'

'You certainly should,' Chloe told him with dislike. 'I
never want to see you again!'

'I didn't suppose you would,' he repeated flatly. 'But maybe one day—'

'Never,' she asserted vehemently.

'Then there's nothing more to be said, is there?' He unlocked his car. 'When you're less angry with me, and more in control where your father is concerned, I suggest you talk to him. I'm not sure how much he'll tell you. But talk to him anyway, hmm?'

Of course she would talk to her father; she didn't need Fergus McCloud to tell her what to do!

'Goodbye, Chloe,' Fergus said huskily, seeming to hesitate when it actually came to getting into his car and driving away.

'Goodbye, Fergus,' she returned crisply, feeling no such hesitation where her own feelings towards him were concerned.

She despised him utterly for the way he was intentionally, selfishly, hurting her father. Obviously writing his book meant more to him than anything else.

She hated him for treating her so callously earlier this evening, her pleadings, in light of this immediate visit to her father, so obviously meaning nothing to him.

But as he finally got into his car, reversing out the driveway before driving off, Chloe knew there was another emotion she felt towards him. Despite everything, *in* spite of everything, she knew her love for Fergus was unchanged by any of those things.

And she felt as if her heart were breaking!

CHAPTER TWELVE

'YOU know, laddie, as I see it there are two solutions to your problem.'

Fergus looked irritatedly across at his grandfather as the two of them enjoyed a pre-lunch whisky at Fergus's home, his grandfather having travelled down to London the previous day on one of his monthly visits. At least…his grandfather was obviously enjoying his whisky; Fergus hadn't enjoyed anything in over a week now.

'Problem?' he frowned.

His grandfather nodded, a distinguished-looking man of almost eighty, his face unlined, his body still slimly fit, only the whiteness of his hair, and the wisdom in his gaze, an indication of his age. 'You can either marry the lassie, Fergus, or forget about her. And, if you don't mind my saying so, you don't seem to be having too much luck doing the latter!'

Fergus frowned across at the elderly man. 'What lass—er, girl?' he said finally. Guardedly…

His grandfather sighed. 'As you know, I had dinner with Brice last night—'

'And my dear cousin told you about Chloe,' Fergus guessed. This was the last time he allowed Brice to even know of one of his relationships, let alone actually meet the woman in question. Although, in truth, what he had had with Chloe—briefly!—couldn't even begin to be described as a relationship.

'Chloe… Is that her name? Pretty,' his grandfather said appreciatively. 'Although nowhere near as pretty as the las-

143

sie herself, from what Brice said.' He raised questioning brows.

Pretty didn't even begin to describe Chloe... 'She's beautiful,' Fergus acknowledged dully.

'And...?' his grandfather prompted.

'And nothing!' Fergus stood up forcefully, his expression grim. 'Chloe is beautiful, charming, has a great sense of humour—'

'Married?'

'Certainly not!' Fergus snapped, glaring indignantly at his grandfather. The fact that he hadn't been too sure himself on that point initially wasn't something his grandfather needed to know. 'Although she might as well be,' he added heavily. 'She's just as out of reach!' To him, at least!

'Brice seemed under the impression she had spent the night here at least once...?' his grandfather prompted mildly.

He drew in an angry breath. 'Brice has a big mouth,' he bit out caustically.

'Actually, I think he's as worried about you as I am,' his grandfather rebuked mildly.

Fergus's family may not be as normal as Chloe's, with its parents and siblings, was, but nevertheless the three cousins and their grandfather were close, with each of them caring for the other. Fergus knew he deserved the rebuke, no matter how mildly it was given.

'There's really no need for you to be,' he reassured the old man.

Although the last ten days, since he had last seen Chloe, had been the longest Fergus had ever known. He couldn't eat, couldn't sleep, and he certainly couldn't work. All he could think about was what was Chloe doing now? Had her father spoken to her, confided in her? And if he had, how much more did Chloe hate him...?

'I think you should allow me to be the judge of that, Fergus,' his grandfather told him firmly, standing up to re-fill their whisky glasses. 'Tell me about her,' he said gently.

Fergus's mouth twisted wryly. 'I thought I just did.'

His grandfather shook his head impatiently. 'Who is she? What does she do? Why is she out of reach?'

Fergus knew that it was this last question that intrigued his grandfather the most—which was probably why he chose to answer the first two! 'Her name is Chloe Fox-Hamilton. She's a dress designer,' he provided economically.

'Fox-Hamilton...' his grandfather repeated slowly. 'Any relation to the politician?' His gaze had narrowed speculatively.

'Ex-politician,' Fergus corrected abruptly. 'She's his daughter,' he added defensively, aware that his grandfather probably knew about the scandal eight years ago too.

'A bad business, that,' his grandfather murmured in confirmation that he did indeed remember it. 'So she's Willie Fox-Hamilton's granddaughter, eh?' he mused interestedly.

Fergus looked at him in surprise. 'You know Chloe's grandfather?'

'I knew her father too,' his grandfather confirmed. 'Oh, not for many years now.' He smiled at Fergus's stunned expression. 'As a young boy, Paul used to accompany his father on shoots at the estate.' He frowned. 'Probably a bit before your time,' he recalled. 'I remember now that the lad dropped the double-barrelled part of his name when he went into politics. Willie Fox-Hamilton's granddaughter, aye,' he said again, this time with a definite sparkle of interest in faded blue eyes. 'If the lassie is anything like her grandfather, then I'm not surprised you're having trouble with her!'

He wasn't having trouble with her—he had just hurt her

so badly she never wanted to see him again! 'I—' He broke off what he had been about to say in Chloe's defence as Maud entered the room after a brief knock, turning to look at her questioningly.

'Miss Fox-Hamilton is here to see you, Mr Fergus,' his housekeeper informed him politely.

He had left instructions with Maud last week that if Chloe should telephone, or—unbelievable as it might seem!—actually call on him in person, that, no matter what he was doing, where he was, Maud was to let him know immediately.

But he hadn't thought it would ever happen...

'Out of reach, aye, lad?' his grandfather commented dryly, looking across at him questioningly.

Fergus could feel the colour tinge his hard cheekbones. 'I—'

'Please don't bother to say you aren't at home, Fergus,' Chloe stopped him sarcastically as she walked into the room, if not unannounced, as yet uninvited, her eyes widening slightly as she saw Fergus wasn't alone. 'I hope I'm not interrupting anything?'

'Not at all, lassie,' Fergus's grandfather was the one to answer her.

Which was probably as well; Fergus was still too stunned by Chloe's unexpected appearance at his home to be able to speak!

He drank in the sight of her, his gaze narrowing, his mouth thinning, as he saw that the last ten days hadn't been kind to her, either. She had always been slender, but now she was so delicately thin she looked as if she might break, her denims very loose on her hips, the blue silk blouse looking at least a size too big. And her face, while still beautiful, had a gaunt look to it, her cheeks very pale, dark shadows beneath the deep, haunting blue of her eyes.

Fergus's own cheeks paled even more as he knew he had helped do this to her...

'In the absence of my grandson remembering his manners...' His grandfather was again the one to speak to cover the awkward silence that had fallen since Maud had quietly left the room, closing the door behind her. 'Hugh McDonald.' He held his hand out to Chloe.

'Grandson...' Chloe repeated uncomfortably even as she shook that hand, grimacing slightly as she turned to look at Fergus. 'Perhaps I should come back another time,' she said reluctantly.

'No! Er—no.' Fergus at last regained his voice, inwardly panicking at the thought of her leaving without at least having told him why she was here at all. 'I'm sure my grandfather won't mind if we delay our lunch for a short time while the two of us go through to my study and talk privately...?' He raised dark brows at his grandfather.

'Not at all,' the elderly man confirmed lightly. 'Unless Miss Fox-Hamilton would care to join us...?' He smiled enquiringly at Chloe.

'Er—no. No, thank you,' she refused awkwardly, two bright spots of colour in her cheeks now. 'I just wanted to have a few words with Fergus, and then I really must go.'

That sounded ominous, and from the too-innocent expression on his grandfather's face as he glanced across at Fergus, it was obvious that he had picked up on it too!

'Nice to have met you—Chloe, isn't it...?' his grandfather said warmly.

'Er—yes,' she confirmed, again giving Fergus a frowning look. 'Nice to have met you too, Mr McDonald.'

'Somehow I doubt that.' The elderly man chuckled wryly at her politeness. 'Would you give my regards to your father?' Hugh continued.

Fergus closed his eyes briefly as he saw the accusing

look Chloe directed at him. Of all the things his grandfather could have said...

It was obvious from the anger now burning in Chloe's cheeks that she had sensed some sort of hidden sarcasm in his grandfather's words.

'Chloe...!' Fergus reached out a placating hand towards her.

'So much for classified information!' She spat the words at him scathingly, her head going back proudly. 'Well, since you seem to have told the whole world exactly what you intend doing to my family with the publication of your damned book, I see absolutely no point in us going to your study so we can talk privately!' She was breathing hard in her agitation. 'I thought you were many things, Fergus, but vindictive wasn't one of them!'

His mouth thinned at her insulting tone. 'I'm not—'

'Not vindictive?' she cut in hardly, her face animatedly beautiful in her anger. 'My father has decided to retire from public life completely and take my mother off to live in Majorca, David is to take control of all my father's business dealings here. But once the house is sold, I will no longer have a home in London to go to, so I've decided to move to Paris—'

'To Paris...?' Fergus echoed dazedly. 'When?'

'The sooner the better!' Chloe snapped. 'I just thought you might like to know! Oh, not about me,' she dismissed scornfully as Fergus still looked stunned by the things she had just told him. 'About my whole family, but my father in particular,' she bit out with distaste. 'You've won, Fergus.'

He shook his head. Chloe was leaving London. She was going to live in Paris.

'It wasn't a battle, Chloe,' he told her raggedly.

'Of course it was,' she scoffed. 'The famous Fergus McCloud versus the infamous Paul Hamilton!'

'Have you spoken to your father as I asked you to…?'

She shook her head. 'He refuses to discuss the situation. Even with my mother,' she added emotionally, her gaze hardening once again as she recognised that emotion. 'He's made his decision. And that's the way it's going to be.'

The way it shouldn't be, Fergus knew frustratedly. But what else could he have done? What could he do now? What could he have done ten days ago, when he'd discovered the truth, that would put the situation right? Even if he told Chloe that truth, in the face of Paul Hamilton's intransigence it would solve nothing. And her family, though it was already shattered enough, was slowly unravelling.

'There, Fergus.' She gave a humourless smile. 'I've told you what you must have been burning to know, so now I can leave.' She turned sharply on her heel and did exactly that.

'Well, don't just stand there like a great gork, laddie,' his grandfather rasped. 'Go after her!'

And do what? Say what? He had made an agreement with Paul Hamilton ten days ago, an agreement that meant, without the other man's permission, he couldn't tell Chloe anything—and the other man flatly refused to give that permission.

'She's Willie Fox-Hamilton's granddaughter, all right,' Hugh opined appreciatively. 'And Brice was quite right, she is beautiful. If I were forty years younger I'd go after her myself—'

'Well, you're not!' Fergus retorted furiously, fighting an inner battle with himself.

He wanted to go after Chloe, of course he did. But he knew, as he had known ten days ago, that ultimately he could change nothing. Paul Hamilton, in making his decision to move to Majorca, had obviously made his choice. It was a choice that only Paul had the right to make...

'Are ye a man or a wee mousie, laddie?' His grandfather's Scottish accent became more pronounced with his increasing anger at Fergus's lack of response. 'Or is it that you're what the lassie just said you were...?' He looked at Fergus disapprovingly.

Fergus's gaze blazed across the room at the elderly man. 'Grandfather, don't interfere in something you know absolutely nothing about!' he snapped coldly.

His grandfather's gaze flashed back the same angry message. 'I admit I have absolutely no idea what all that was about just now, but what I do know is I wouldn't let a lassie like Chloe walk out of my house, my life, in the state that wee lassie just did!' he challenged.

Chloe wasn't just walking out of his house, his life, she was leaving England too. To go and live in Paris. The home of fashion. Soon to be Chloe's home, too...

Chloe was shaking so badly when she left the house that for a few moments she didn't even have the strength to walk the short distance to her car. Instead she leant weakly against the wall outside, willing the world to stop tilting on a dangerous angle.

She had needed to see Fergus one last time, needed— never mind what she needed! It had been a mistake. The last of many she had made where Fergus McCloud was concerned.

'Chloe...!' Suddenly Fergus was standing there beside her, his hand like a vice about the top of her arm. 'Please don't cry, Chloe!' he pleaded raggedly.

She instantly blinked back the tears she hadn't even realised were falling. 'I'm not crying. I—I have an insect in my eye,' she excused lamely.

She had done nothing *but* cry the last ten days, her emotions towards Fergus see-sawing drastically between anger and despair. On the one hand she was so angry with him she wanted to spit at him, and on the other she loved him so much she just wanted to launch herself into his arms and beg him to put everything back as it had been before she'd known about the book he intended writing. But at the same time still keeping Fergus in her life...

'Let's go for a walk,' he muttered grimly, that vice-like grip remaining on her arm as he turned her towards the park gates across the road from his house.

Of course, they couldn't go back into his house, Chloe realised numbly; his grandfather was there. What on earth must Hugh McDonald think of her outburst just now?

Not that it really mattered; she doubted she would ever see the elderly man again!

'Let's sit here,' Fergus suggested as they reached a park bench that faced towards a pond.

Chloe sat, glad to feel the support of the bench beneath her, her legs feeling slightly shaky now. But she didn't remember when she had last eaten, let alone slept, so was it any wonder she felt so awful?

It was so peaceful sitting here, the sound of traffic outside the park muted by the trees and bushes that surrounded them, couples walking along together arm in arm, mothers with young children feeding the ducks that glided so smoothly over the surface of the pond.

Hard to believe, when surrounded by such serene normality, that her own world was falling apart!

Fergus sat grimly at her side, leaning forward on the bench, the atmosphere in the park not seeming to be having the same calming influence on him.

Chloe studied him surreptitiously from beneath lowered lashes. He looked so good to her, so tall and strong, so sure of himself, so—so Fergus!

He shook his head. 'I don't know what to say, Chloe.'

Her mouth quirked. 'There doesn't seem to be a lot either of us can say,' she replied dully.

Fergus turned to look at her where she sat back on the bench. 'No—I mean, I really don't know what to say to you. There's so much I could say, but—damn it!' he exclaimed angrily. 'I can't!'

Chloe sighed heavily. 'Don't worry about it, Fergus—'

'Of course I worry about it!' he snapped, his hands clenched into fists. 'You look bloody awful,' he rasped frustratedly.

'Thanks!'

'I'm only stating a fact, Chloe,' he carried on. 'Can't your father and mother see what this is doing to you?'

'I think they have other things on their minds other than how I look.'

Her father was grimly going through the process of preparing his business affairs for David to take over, as well as putting the house up for sale, in preparation for the move to Majorca. Her mother was trying to remain cheerful, outwardly at least, by calmly going through the process of supporting him in his decision.

It was all like a nightmare to Chloe!

Fergus shook his head. 'Then they damn well shouldn't have! You're their daughter, too, and— Your father is really going to just up stakes and move to Majorca?' he queried disbelievingly.

Chloe nodded. 'We have a villa there. He's just decided it's the right time for him to retire.'

'Rubbish!' Fergus cried. 'It's time for him to fight damn it.'

Chloe eyed him humorously. 'Do you always swear this much when you're angry or upset?'

'Angry *and* upset,' he corrected. 'And damn is pretty mild considering how deeply I'm feeling both those emotions at the moment!'

Chloe had no idea why he should be feeling either, and, in truth, she felt too weary to find out why.

'Damn is Darcy's favourite swear word,' Fergus mused distractedly.

'She's your cousin Logan's wife,' Chloe remembered, wondering what significance the other woman had on this conversation, knowing that she probably didn't, that it was simply a case of she and Fergus having nothing else to say to each other! 'Are they back from their honeymoon now?'

'Last weekend,' he confirmed. 'And they're obviously idyllically happy,' he added sardonically.

Fergus obviously still hadn't quite got over his feelings of loss where his cousin was concerned...

He looked at his feet. 'I never meant to hurt anyone, you know, Chloe.'

She put a consoling hand on his arm. 'If Logan and Darcy are that happy together I doubt they've even noticed you aren't exactly over the moon at their marriage,' she assured him.

Fergus turned to her. 'I'm not talking about Logan and Darcy,' he dismissed impatiently. 'I'm over that stupidity, have been for weeks. I was referring to your family when I said I never meant to hurt anyone,' he corrected harshly.

She sighed. 'It was always a time bomb waiting to go off.' She had accepted that much herself now. With the Susan Stirling situation unsolved, any move her father made politically was always bound to cause a certain amount of controversy.

What was happening now, her parents' move to Majorca,

the breaking-up of the family home, while not being exactly pleasant, had perhaps always been inevitable. She had come to that much of a conclusion over the last ten days!

Fergus turned to her fully, his gaze intense as he looked at her. 'I tried to tell you earlier—when you thought I was going to deny being vindictive. I've decided not to write the book, after all.'

Chloe's eyes widened. 'Why ever not?'

His gaze no longer met hers. 'I—My heart is no longer in it. Besides, as you said...' his mouth twisted self-derisively '...I'm a writer, I have a lot of other plot-lines in my head that I can use, without hurting anyone in the process.'

Now he decided not to write the book, now—when it could do no good whatsoever. The damage had already been done, and for Chloe and her family nothing was ever going to be the same again.

'I'm glad, Fergus.' She squeezed his arm in gratitude before removing her hand. Although she could still feel the strength of him beneath her fingertips, the aching need to— No! It was over. All of it was over. 'Would you please pass on my apologies to your grandfather for my behaviour just now? He must think I'm incredibly rude!'

Fergus gave the ghost of a smile. 'Actually his last comment to me was if he were forty years younger he would be chasing after you himself!'

'Did he?' Chloe smiled herself now, even if it was tinged with sadness. Fergus would never chase after her...

'He did,' Fergus responded. 'You really are going to live in Paris?'

'I really am,' Chloe confirmed lightly. 'I made a lot of contacts when I lived there for a year, and now that I've established my own label... I've had the offer of doing a collection for next spring. Now seems as good a time as any to take up that offer,' she added ruefully.

It hadn't been an easy decision to make, but, with all that was going on around her, Chloe had decided this was probably a good time for her to set up her own household. And Paris was a good place for her to make a start.

Besides, if she were in Paris, intensely involved with her work, she might just be able to put Fergus from her mind for more than a few minutes at a time!

'How long do you intend staying there?' Fergus asked huskily.

She had no idea; all she could think about at the moment was getting away from England. From Fergus…

'I may decide to stay permanently,' she replied.

'Permanently!' he echoed incredulously.

'I told you there will be no family home here for me to come back to. Oh, no doubt I'll come back from time to time to visit Penny, David, and the children. But other than that I'll have no reason to come back.' No reason at all, except the man she loved lived here… 'If you're ever in Paris, why don't you look me up?' she felt compelled to add, unable to bear the thought of never seeing Fergus again. 'I'll be in the phone book.'

'Under Fox or Hamilton?' he rejoined gruffly.

She smiled sheepishly at his unmistakable reference to her initial subterfuge as regards her name. How long ago had that been now? Three weeks? Four? It seemed like a lifetime ago, so much had happened.

'Both,' she answered him firmly. 'Keep an eye out for the Foxy label, too, Fergus; I intend to make it one of the most well known in women's fashion!'

He gave her a considering look. 'I think you'll probably do just that,' he said.

'I hope so!' She stood up decisively. 'Now, I think I've

kept you from your grandfather, and delayed your lunch together, quite long enough,' she announced briskly.

Fergus stood up more slowly. 'I can't believe your father is just giving up like this—'

'He isn't giving up!' Chloe defended angrily, her earlier calm completely erased. 'Someone held a loaded gun up to his head—he's just trying to move out of the way before they pull the trigger!'

'You mean me?' Fergus queried.

'Of course I mean you!' she confirmed impatiently. 'Who else could it have been?'

'But-I'm-not-writing-the-book!' he enunciated clearly.

'This time.' Chloe steadily met his gaze.

His expression darkened. 'At any time!'

She shrugged. 'You'll have to take that up with my father. But I don't think it will make any difference. His mind seems to be pretty well made up.'

'Then it will just have to be unmade,' Fergus ground out through his teeth.

'It's too late, Fergus,' she told him huskily.

She had known she had to see Fergus this one last time. Not through any wish to try to put things right; she knew it was too late for that. But she had just needed to see him, to commit his face, the way he talked, the way he moved, to memory. But other than that, it was as she had said: too late...

'We'll see about that,' Fergus said grimly.

'Just leave it, Fergus.' She put a beseeching hand on his arm. 'Before anyone else gets hurt.'

He gave her a sharply searching look, before looking quickly away again. 'I'll call you—if I'm ever in Paris.'

She looked at him for several minutes, knowing that this really was goodbye. After all the times she had told him she never wanted to see him again, he was now the one saying goodbye to her...!

'Do that,' she finally said before turning to slowly walk away, knowing that her heart really was breaking.

CHAPTER THIRTEEN

'WELL, laddie, it seems to me you've got yourself into a merry old tangle,' Fergus's grandfather pronounced. The two of them were lingering over brandies after their meal. A meal Fergus had neither eaten nor enjoyed.

'I can assure you, there's nothing merry about it,' Fergus answered dully.

He had returned to the house, eventually, more out of consideration for his grandfather than a real wish to be here. Over lunch the elderly man had dragged the whole sorry story from him.

Fergus couldn't say he wasn't glad to share it with someone, but his grandfather's condemnation was all he needed on top of his own feelings of guilt.

'And you say Chloe has no idea of the truth?' His grandfather looked serious.

'None,' Fergus confirmed heavily. 'And before you say it—I have no intention of telling her what really happened, either!' He looked at his grandfather unblinkingly. 'I made a promise to Paul Hamilton over a week ago that the truth would go no further than the four walls of his study.'

'You've just told me, laddie,' his grandfather pointed out dryly.

'Only in the terms of a confessional,' Fergus maintained; he and his two cousins had always been able to talk to their grandfather when they hadn't been able to confide in anyone else, especially parents, knowing that what they told him would go no further.

'So you intend keeping this promise to Paul Hamilton,'

his grandfather realised impatiently. 'I know I brought you all up, you, Logan and Brice—despite the men your mothers may have married!—to be McDonalds. Men of your word. But there's a time and a place for it—and this is neither the time nor the place!'

Fergus shook his head. 'I disagree—I think this is exactly the time and the place.' Even though it meant he was losing Chloe.

Not that she had ever been his to lose...

But without this tangled mess, without his proposed book, without her father, without— There were too many withouts, he realised heavily. Chloe had never been his, and now she never would be.

'And what about Chloe?' his grandfather persisted.

'You heard her as well as I did, Grandfather; she's going to live in Paris,' Fergus muttered before taking a large swallow from his glass of brandy.

'And you're just going to let her do that?' the older man queried.

'I'm just going to let her do that,' Fergus confirmed.

His grandfather sighed frustratedly. 'I admit I brought you all up to be men of your word, but I didn't think I had brought any of you up to be idiots as well!'

Fergus's smile lacked humour. 'Chloe would not thank me for telling her the truth.' It certainly wouldn't bring her running into his arms!

So much for his claim 'the truth shall make you free'; in his particular case, the truth had put him in a prison. A prison of silence...

'Don't you think she should be the one to be the judge of that?' his grandfather asked.

'Probably,' he conceded. 'But I don't have the right to—'

'The way I see it, you have every right,' the older man cut in.

Fergus raised dark brows. 'And just how do you work that out, Grandfather?'

'Because you love her!' the elderly man told him.

Fergus sat back abruptly, staring across at his grandfather in stunned disbelief.

Did he love Chloe?

The ache in his chest, the black bottomless void that had appeared in his life at the mere thought of her move to Paris, seemed to say that he did...

Fergus stood up abruptly, walking over to the window, staring slightlessly outside.

He loved Chloe...

He *loved* Chloe...?

He loved *Chloe*!

How long had he been in love with her? He didn't know. But he did love her. Was in love with her. Loved everything about her, from the top of her beautiful head to the end of her delicate toes. He even loved the temper she had displayed from time to time!

But, most of all, he loved the loyalty she had shown to her father, in the past, but especially these last few weeks. Her herculean efforts on the other man's behalf to ensure that no book was written that could upset her father's return to politics. The way she maintained her father's innocence even in the face of her father's own refusal to defend himself.

What wouldn't he give to have Chloe love him in that same, unquestioning, all-forgiving way!

'Well, Fergus?' his grandfather prompted softly from across the dining-room.

Fergus drew in a deeply controlling breath before turning to face the other man. 'Well, what?' His manner was deliberately obtuse. 'This isn't a fairy tale, Grandfather, this is real life, and in real life the prince doesn't always get the princess!'

'Not when he's a pigheaded idiot, he doesn't, no!' his grandfather conceded disgustedly, standing up himself now. 'I can see that there's no reasoning with you, lad, so if you'll excuse me? I promised Darcy and Logan I would go over and see them this afternoon.'

In truth, Fergus was glad of the respite, needed time with his own thoughts. If only to come to terms with loving Chloe!

Strange, but he had never thought he would ever fall in love. Not that he had deliberately set out not to; his parents' divorce, and his subsequent move to Scotland to live with his grandfather, hadn't put him off falling in love. In fact, his childhood and teenage years in Scotland couldn't have been more idyllic! It was just, as the years had passed, with only brief relationships in his life, and none of them based on love, he had thought it would never happen to him.

But now it had. And with Chloe Fox-Hamilton, of all women. The one woman who had every reason to hate him.

He was under no illusions. While he didn't agree that he had held a loaded gun to Paul Hamilton's head, he did realise he had been the catalyst to all that had happened the last three weeks.

But that was something, he knew, Chloe could never forgive him for...

Perhaps in time—?

No, he accepted. Time wouldn't take away the sting of the destruction he had unwittingly caused in her father's life—as well as her own!

But what was his own life going to be like, loving Chloe, and knowing she would never be his?

He had to try, one last time, to speak to Paul Hamilton,

to make the other man see reason, to ask him once again to fight this thing. He had to!

Because Fergus really wasn't sure he could live the rest of his life knowing he loved Chloe but could never tell her so...!

Mrs Hamilton answered his call herself. Fergus would recognise that politely honed voice anywhere—it was just like Chloe's, only more mature.

'I'm afraid Paul is in a business meeting at the moment, Mr McCloud,' Diana said apologetically once Fergus had introduced himself and asked to speak to the other man. 'He seems to do nothing else at the moment,' she added wistfully. 'Could I get him to call you— Just a moment, Mr McCloud, I think I hear my husband now,' she said briskly, silence at her end of the line for several moments.

Fergus tapped his fingers impatiently on the desktop in front of him as he waited for Diana to come back on the line. Perhaps he shouldn't have bothered to telephone first. Perhaps he should have just gone over to the house—because there was always the possibility that Paul would refuse to see him.

But there had always been the chance that, having gone to the house completely unexpectedly, he might have accidentally bumped into Chloe. And, after lunchtime, he wasn't sure either of them were up to that!

'Sorry about that, Mr McCloud,' Diana came back on the line. 'My husband wonders if you would care to join us for dinner this evening?'

Fergus was stunned by the invitation. Not that he and Paul Hamilton had parted on bad terms, but he certainly hadn't expected the other man would ever want to sit down to dinner with him again!

'It's by way of being a farewell dinner,' Diana continued at his silence. 'One of several we're giving to say goodbye to family and friends. You see, Paul and I are moving to Majorca next month.'

He already knew that. But obviously, from her warm tone, Diana still had no idea of his own part in the necessity for their move...

Dinner with family and friends was not exactly what he had had in mind when it came to talking to Paul Hamilton again. But it did have the advantage of his being able to see Chloe again. And maybe, just maybe, the fact that her parents had invited him to dinner might help her to see that they at least held no grudge against him...

'I would like that very much, thank you,' he accepted; his grandfather would just have to forgive him for being a less than attentive host!

'Eight for eight-thirty, then,' Diana told him lightly before ringing off.

Fergus slowly put down his own receiver. The decision made, he was now full of indecision, totally unsure how Chloe would react to his being a dinner guest of her parents this evening.

The two of them had said goodbye earlier today, and he had no reason to feel she would be in the least pleased to see him again, as a dinner guest of her parents, or otherwise.

But maybe he was just worrying unnecessarily.

Maybe Chloe wouldn't even be there this evening!

Chloe was not looking forward to the dinner party tonight. Oh, she realised that her parents felt a need to say goodbye to friends before their permanent move to Majorca, but wouldn't it have been better to have just thrown one big party and got it over with in one go, rather than a series of small dinner parties like the one this evening?

Obviously her parents didn't think so, had decided they

could cope with their parting if it were done in small stages. Chloe was willing to support them in whatever they decided to do. Which was why, even though a dinner party was the last thing she felt in the mood for, she was determined to be there for them.

Penny and David, showing the same family loyalty, were already downstairs when Chloe entered the sitting-room shortly before eight o'clock. Penny looked pale, but seemed as determined as Chloe to make all this as pleasant for their parents as possible.

Chloe was a little surprised when, shortly after eight o'clock, the first of the dinner guests were shown in. Peter and Jean Ambrose! She had known there were to be eight of them sitting down to dinner, but had no idea who the four guests were to be.

Obviously this particular dinner party was going to be worse than she had imagined it would be. She knew that her father hadn't yet informed the Leader of the Opposition of his decision to quit not only politics but Britain too; obviously all that was going to change tonight.

Chloe winced in her sister's direction, Penny giving a heavy shake of her head before she turned to look over to where their parents were now greeting the other couple.

Their father looked so handsome in the black evening clothes, their mother as lovely as ever in a dress Chloe had designed for her, its style fitted, the blue the same colour as Diana's eyes.

'Mr McCloud,' the butler announced a few minutes later.

Chloe gasped, her hand tightened around her glass of mineral water, her face draining of all colour as she saw that it was indeed Fergus who now entered the room. Fergus as she remembered him from that first night: arrogantly self-assured, tall, and very handsome in his evening clothes.

What was he doing here? He hadn't mentioned he was dining with her parents when she'd seen him earlier today. What—?

'And Mr McDonald,' the butler announced before Chloe had even had a chance to recover from her first shock of the evening.

Her gaze moved sharply from Fergus to the doorway behind him. Hugh McDonald, Fergus's grandfather, stood there. And any idea Chloe might have had that his call was unexpected was instantly dispelled as she took in his distinguished appearance in black evening suit and snowy white shirt.

It was bad enough that Fergus was here, but what on earth was his grandfather doing here, too?

Perhaps, as his grandfather was obviously staying with Fergus at the moment, that was why he'd been invited too. She was sure Fergus would have had no difficulty in finding a female partner for the evening if he had wanted one!

She turned accusing eyes on Fergus, only to see that he looked as stunned by Hugh McDonald's appearance as she felt; he *hadn't* known his grandfather was going to be here, either.

He didn't look pleased to see him!

Chloe strolled over to where the two men, having said their hellos to her parents, were now in a muted, but obviously heated, conversation.

'—for visiting Darcy and Logan today! I don't know what you're up to, Grandfather,' Fergus was telling the older man angrily as Chloe approached them. 'But it had better not have anything to do with our conversation this afternoon.'

Hugh McDonald looked completely unperturbed by his grandson's less than welcoming behaviour, turning to smile at Chloe as she joined them. 'May I say, my dear, you look absolutely stunning this evening,' he told her admiringly. 'I did tell you I knew your father,' he added, his eyes twinkling mischievously.

'So you did,' she replied. 'And thank you,' Chloe accepted the compliment, her dress a soft, muted gold, above-knee length, sleeveless, and with a scooped neckline that showed the creamy swell of her breasts. 'You're looking rather distinguished yourself,' she returned the compliment with a lightness she was far from feeling.

What on earth were Fergus and his grandfather doing here? Hugh McDonald had given every impression earlier today that he was acquainted with her father, although Chloe could never remember meeting him before. And as for Fergus—! She would have thought he was the last person her father would want to see just now!

The elderly man grinned at her roguishly. 'The McDonald men have always aged well.' He looked pointedly at Fergus.

A grim-faced Fergus, who hadn't so much as looked at her yet, let alone spoken to her!

'But Fergus is a McCloud,' she returned with saccharine sweetness, turning to look challengingly at Fergus.

He finally returned her gaze, mockery in those dark brown eyes. 'As my grandfather would no doubt be only too happy to tell you, I'm a McCloud in name only!'

Despite their argument a few minutes ago, there was obviously a deep affection between the two men. In fact, they were more like father and son.

'Come and meet my sister and her husband,' she suggested lightly to Hugh McDonald as she draped her arm through his. 'You too, Fergus, if you would like to?' She arched dark brows at him.

'I've already met them, thanks,' he said dismissively. 'I think I'll just go and get reacquainted with Peter Ambrose instead.' He turned sharply on his heel to stroll across the room and join Peter Ambrose and his wife.

Hugh McDonald chuckled as he stood beside Chloe. 'You'll have to excuse Fergus, I'm afraid, my dear.' He gave a rueful shake of his silvery head. 'He never was any good at sharing the things that matter to him,' he added enigmatically.

At least, it was enigmatic to Chloe; she had absolutely no idea what Hugh McDonald was talking about. What she did know was that Fergus was behaving extremely rudely this evening. More so than usual!

'Come and say hello to Penny and David,' she invited again, smoothly making the introductions seconds later, slightly relieved when David took the lead in the conversation with the older man, having apparently spent a lot of his school holidays as a child fishing in different parts of Scotland.

The respite gave Chloe chance to look at Fergus unobserved. He was chatting quite naturally with Peter and Jean Ambrose and her parents, showing none of the bad-tempered rudeness of a few minutes ago. She didn't think she would ever be able to fathom out exactly what Fergus—

She wouldn't have chance to fathom out the workings of Fergus McCloud's mind! She would shortly be moving to Paris, and Fergus, well, who knew what—or who!—Fergus would be moving on to?

At least…she had thought she was unobserved in looking longingly at Fergus!

Hugh McDonald, while smoothly keeping up his conversation with David, was actually looking at her, one silver brow raised in mute enquiry.

Chloe felt her cheeks colour with embarrassment as she hastily looked away from that searching gaze.

Not that she fared any better at dinner; for reasons best known to herself, her mother had seated Chloe between Fergus and his grandfather! Hugh McDonald was charming enough, but Fergus barely spoke a word to her.

In fact, apart from the elderly Scot, who kept the conversation flowing, everyone else at the table seemed as subdued as Chloe.

'How do you think the general election will go next year?' Hugh McDonald addressed his remark, quite naturally, to the Leader of the Opposition.

'I—' Peter broke off his reply to look at Penny, who had just dropped her knife on the floor, the eight of them having reached the main course of their meal.

'Sorry,' Penny muttered before bending to pick up the knife.

Chloe shot her sister a sympathetic grimace as she straightened; obviously the strain of the evening was getting to her too. Which wasn't surprising. Penny was as aware as she was that their father hadn't yet spoken to Peter Ambrose about his future political plans—or lack of them.

'You were saying?' Hugh McDonald prompted Peter Ambrose.

'Since when have you been interested in English politics, Grandfather?' Fergus cut in hardly, the darkness of his eyes, to Chloe's frowning gaze, seeming to flash a warning to the older man.

Hugh grinned wolfishly. 'Since they started leaving us alone to run our own country!' he answered controversially.

Peter Ambrose chuckled. 'A Scotsman through and through, eh?'

'It's the most beautiful place on God's green earth,' Hugh McDonald confirmed decisively. 'So, what are your predictions for the next election?'

Peter smiled. 'We're going to win, of course.'

'Of course.' Hugh chuckled. 'And what post do you have in mind in your future government for our friend here?' He looked across at Chloe's father admiringly.

Peter Ambrose looked taken aback by the directness of the question.

As well he might. Not too many people had actually been aware of the fact that Chloe's father was contemplating going back into the political arena. And even fewer people knew he had since decided not to!

She looked at Hugh McDonald with shrewd eyes. Just how much did he know about this situation!? Whatever he knew, it didn't take two guesses to know exactly who it was who had told him!

Chloe turned accusing eyes on Fergus, his shrug of resignation telling her that he had no more hope than she did of diverting his grandfather from this potentially explosive conversation.

'Do something,' she ground out in a hushed voice.

'Other than tying him up and gagging him, you mean?' Fergus returned as angrily.

'Just gagging him will do,' she whispered, her eyes flashing deeply blue.

Fergus gave an impatient sigh. 'I—'

'What are you two lovebirds whispering about so cosily?' his grandfather enquired teasingly.

Fergus's expression was grim as he looked across Chloe to his grandfather. 'Hardly lovebirds, Grandfather,' he dismissed icily. 'And could it not just be that we find politics dull table conversation?'

Chloe gasped at the comment, knowing that Fergus, while trying to defuse this potentially dangerous conversation, had probably just insulted half the people seated at the table as a consequence!

Silver brows rose over shrewd blue eyes. 'I find that hard

to believe in Chloe's case,' Hugh returned. 'I'm sure she's as eager as we all are to see her father returned to his rightful place in the political arena.'

'You see, Paul, I told you you've been worrying far too much about what people will have to say at your return.' Peter Ambrose smiled his approval of Hugh McDonald's remark. 'People do have very short memories.'

'But selective ones,' Chloe's father replied, his face now white with strain. 'And, in view of that—'

'No, Daddy, I can't let you do this!'

Chloe looked across at Penny in stunned surprise at her sudden outburst. Her sister had been unusually subdued all evening, but now she looked positively ill, her face grey, her eyes swimming with tears as she stood up to face them all.

'I've kept quiet until now, Daddy,' Penny spoke directly to their father now. 'I've tried to respect the decision you made eight years ago,' she continued emotionally. 'But I can't let you make any more sacrifices on my behalf.'

Their mother reached out a soothing hand towards her. 'Penny, darling—'

'Or you either, Mummy.' Penny shook her head decisively. 'Or Chloe,' she added enigmatically before taking in a shaky breath and looking around the dining-table at them all. 'It's time the truth was told. All of it.' She was looking at David now. 'Isn't it…?' she prompted him.

Chloe had absolutely no idea what was going on. But as she looked around the table, at her parents, the Ambroses, Hugh McDonald, Fergus, all their expressions full of sympathy, rather than her own puzzlement, as they looked at Penny, Chloe knew that she was the only one here who didn't…

And for the first time she also became aware that Fergus was tightly gripping one of her hands in his!

CHAPTER FOURTEEN

FERGUS tightened his grip on Chloe's hand as he sensed she was about to remove it.

This situation had arisen so quickly it had spiralled out of his control. If he could do nothing else for Chloe, he could at least be here for her. Even if she didn't want him to be!

'David?' Penny pressed her husband again, her expression full of tenderness, but at the same time resigned.

Fergus couldn't help wishing it hadn't come to this, and he shot his grandfather a reproving look, knowing that in this case Hugh *had* been the catalyst to this situation. He had obviously decided to take matters into his own hands this afternoon, the visit to Logan just a ruse—and, dearly as Fergus had always loved and admired his grandfather, at this particular moment he felt like strangling him!

Paul Hamilton stood up. 'I really don't want you to do this, Penny.' He crossed to his eldest daughter's side. 'There's really no need, darling,' he assured her as he took her in his arms.

Penny gazed at him unflinchingly, almost the same height as her father in her high-heeled shoes. 'David and I discussed it before coming out this evening, Daddy,' she said softly. 'We've decided, for everyone's sake, that it would be better if we just made a clean sweep of things.' She looked at the other dinner guests. 'And, as everyone with any relevance to this situation is here this evening—'

'I don't think my grandfather and I come under that category,' Fergus interjected.

Chloe, he noted achingly, still looked totally bewildered. In a few moments she was going to be well and truly stunned; he had been more than a little thrown by the truth himself!

Penny gave him a wistful smile. 'Oh, I think you do, Fergus,' she said knowingly. 'And as for your grandfather—he was the one who helped me to see this afternoon when he came to see me that this madness had to stop, that, painful as the truth might be, it has to be better than pushing it to the back of my mind and hoping the thing will just go away!' Her voice broke emotionally over those last words.

'Penny...!' David was instantly on his feet, crossing to his wife's side to take her hand in his. 'Don't do this to yourself,' he pleaded gruffly. 'I'm the one who was to blame—'

'Nonsense,' Penny put in strongly. 'If I hadn't had an affair—'

'Your husband is right, Penny,' Fergus's grandfather was—surprisingly—the one to interrupt this time. 'You have no need to do this. Everyone here—with the exception of Chloe...' he turned to smile at her apologetically '...is aware of what happened eight years ago. There's no need to keep beating yourself with the same stick,' he told Penny gently. 'You and David had a few problems eight years ago, they unfortunately, ultimately, with Peter's agreement, led to your father's resignation from politics. It's only the last factor that is of any importance now,' he assured her firmly.

Fergus could feel Chloe's tension as she sat at his side, her hand tightly gripping his now. Although Fergus was sure she was completely unaware of how tightly she was clinging to him; she would never willingly have shown such shocked dismay—to anyone!—as the truth finally dawned on her.

Because David Latham, Penny's husband, Chloe's brother-in-law, had been Susan Stirling's lover eight years ago...

Fergus had been stunned himself ten days ago when David Latham had come to see him, admitting the true circumstances to him, adding that he had decided to go to the press himself and tell them everything, no matter what the personal cost might be, as a way of clearing Paul of any wrongdoing eight years ago.

This was the snowball running down the hill, getting bigger and bigger, and totally out of control!

Paul had known exactly what had taken place eight years ago, had discussed it with Peter Ambrose, and taken the blame to save his eldest daughter any more unhappiness.

Eight years ago David and Penny had been going through a difficult time in their marriage. Penny had admitted to David that she had briefly, stupidly, become involved with another man. David had gone—again very briefly—off the rails himself at the admission.

As well he might, Fergus had inwardly acknowledged. In the same circumstances, Fergus knew he was capable of doing the same. That any man was.

Unfortunately, David's brief affair with Susan Stirling had resulted in the other woman, once he had ended the affair, becoming totally obsessed with him. She'd followed him everywhere, telephoned him at home, threatened to tell Penny about them.

By this time David and Penny had managed to work out their problems, had had a second child on the way, and David had known Susan Stirling couldn't be allowed to do that, had told her that their affair was definitely over, that he would never leave Penny, that he loved his wife. That was when Susan Stirling had told him she was expecting their child.

'You knew about this!' Chloe turned accusingly to Fergus now.

He swallowed hard, knowing she had a right to be angry with him. But what else could he have done ten days ago but respect David Latham's confidence?

After thinking about David's confession for a while, and following on from Chloe's visit to him that same day, he had actually managed to put a stop to the other man going to the press with the story, by going to see Paul Hamilton and telling him of the younger man's intention. But he had done so at the price of promised silence on his own part. To everyone. And that included Chloe.

'Yes, I knew,' he confirmed quietly.

Chloe snorted. 'All this time…!'

In real time, ten days wasn't so long. But to Fergus it seemed more like a lifetime he had been keeping the truth from Chloe. And he could see by the accusation in her face that it had seemed much longer to Chloe too.

'Your father acted in good faith eight years ago, did what he had to to protect his eldest daughter, her husband, and their children from the publicity that would have ensued if the truth were known. In the circumstances, would you have expected me to do any less?' He looked at her searchingly.

She snatched her hand away from his before standing up. 'You should have told me, Pen,' she told her older sister gently as she moved to her side. 'I'm not a child, you know,' she rebuked.

Penny reached out to grasp her hand. 'Eight years ago you were,' she reasoned. 'Besides, I had to respect Daddy's judgement, after all that he had done for us.' She looked lovingly at the man who had sacrificed so much for her sake eight years ago.

'I would do it all again,' Paul assured her gruffly.

'But don't you see, man, there's no need for anyone to make any more sacrifices?' Fergus's grandfather was the one to cut impatiently into the conversation. 'What really happened eight years ago is only relevant to six people in this room—for the moment I'm excluding Fergus and myself,' he added with an apologetic glance in Fergus's direction.

A glance Fergus acknowledged with a rueful shake of his head; his grandfather never had been able to resist playing God occasionally. But in this particular case he seemed to have excelled himself!

'Five of you have always known the truth.' Hugh included the Leader of the Opposition and his wife in his glance now. 'And it's provided no barrier to Paul's decision to re-enter politics. What I'm really trying to say, Paul—'

'And, as usual, taking his time about it,' Fergus couldn't resist putting in dryly.

His grandfather shot him a dark glance. 'As it appears to be your proposed book that started all this, laddie, I would keep quiet if I were you!'

Fergus gave a smile of acceptance at his grandfather's words. There was no doubting it had been the synopsis of his next book that had set this particular snowball in motion. 'For the last time,' he grated, standing up impatiently himself now, 'I am not writing the damned book!'

'Exactly,' Hugh confirmed with satisfaction. 'So, effectively, apart from the odd negative comment, there will be no recurrence of the publicity you received eight years ago. And as such, there will be no barrier to your going back into politics, Paul. Because at this point in time, nothing has actually changed from when you initially made your decision several months ago.' He turned triumphantly to the other man.

Fergus wasn't absolutely sure he agreed with that last sentiment; Chloe's feelings towards him had definitely changed. She hadn't been over-enamoured of him before tonight, but a few minutes ago she had looked at him with open loathing!

'Peter has always known the truth,' Hugh continued, 'and he wants you back in his future government. Your wife, eldest daughter, and her husband have always known the truth too. As I see it, it's only Chloe who has to reassess her way of thinking. Isn't it, my dear...?' he prompted gently.

Fergus looked at Chloe too, his heart aching at the paleness of her face, her eyes deeply blue with inner pain.

'Reassess her way of thinking...'

At the moment, she couldn't think at all, felt as if she had been hit over the head with a sledgehammer!

Oh, she had always known her father wasn't guilty of what he had been accused eight years ago, had never wavered in that opinion for even a moment. But that it could have been David who had been Susan Stirling's lover had never even occurred to her...

However, these things happened in marriages sometimes, people did make mistakes, and she had no doubt that her sister and David were extremely happy together now, and had been so for many years, that the two of them loved each other deeply, as they did their children.

One thing was very clear to her, however... 'Mr McDonald is right, Daddy—'

'Hugh,' the elderly Scot put in softly.

She gave him a grateful smile. 'Hugh is completely right, Daddy,' she corrected. 'You have no reason to move to

Majorca, certainly not to tell Peter that you've changed your mind about standing for parliament—'

'He most certainly does not,' Peter Ambrose was the one to put in strongly. 'And I wouldn't accept such a decision, either,' he added firmly. 'I need you, Paul.'

Her father looked pleased by these words of confidence. 'I don't want to be a liability—'

'You won't be,' Peter assured him with certainty. 'Hugh is quite right—I do have a place in mind for you in my proposed government.' He gave the elderly man a rueful smile for his insight. 'One that may involve a change of address,' he elaborated meaningfully.

'Well, now that's all settled, I think it's time Fergus and Chloe—'

'Really, Grandfather,' Fergus interrupted, 'don't you think you've interfered enough for one day?' He glared across at his grandfather.

'Not at all.' The elderly man was completely unperturbed by that glaring look. 'I'll have you know, I only interfered at all for your sake,' he stated enigmatically.

Chloe listened to the exchange between the two men in complete puzzlement. Oh, she agreed with Hugh; her father should not recant on his decision to go back into politics. There was absolutely no reason for him to do so. But where did she and Fergus come into that...?

More to the point, there was no Fergus and Chloe...!

'Somehow I find that hard to believe,' Fergus snapped angrily. 'And maybe if you had asked me first—'

'I did,' Hugh came back completely unrepentantly. 'But I have a wish to see my great-grandchildren before I'm in my grave—not have you bring them along to visit me afterwards!'

Chloe was completely lost now. In truth, she was still so stunned by this evening's revelations, she couldn't think straight, let alone make sense of Fergus's conversation with his grandfather.

There were a few things she had no doubts about, though—David's secret had remained exactly that for eight years, and should continue to do so. It would serve no purpose for it ever to be otherwise. Also her father must continue with his initial plan to stand for parliament.

She would move to Paris within the next few weeks…

'Grandfather, you really are an interfering old—'

'Now then, lad,' Hugh cut off Fergus's outburst. 'Remember we're in company,' he admonished. 'If you don't ask her, I will,' he declared tauntingly, before turning to Chloe's father. 'Paul, do you have a garden in which Fergus can walk with your daughter?'

Her father looked as dazed by the conversation as Chloe did. And of course they had a garden, but besides the fact she had no wish to walk in it at the moment, she didn't think Fergus had, either!

'Of course we do,' her mother was the one to answer warmly. 'Penny, darling, show Fergus the way out into the garden. Chloe, go with him,' she directed with unusual firmness.

It was the fact that it was so unusual for her mother to be so firm that Chloe went. At least, that was what she told herself…

Fergus had no such excuse, but he followed Chloe and Penny out into the hallway, too.

Penny turned and hugged her. 'I really am sorry that this has made things so difficult for you and Fergus,' she told Chloe emotionally. 'I really had no idea it was this serious between the two of you until Hugh told me… I don't think Mummy and Daddy did, either, until Hugh called to see them this afternoon, or Daddy would never have allowed it to have gone this far; he loves you equally as much as he loves me,' she said with certainty, squeezing Chloe's arm reassuringly before going back to join the other dinner guests.

Chloe was left standing in the hallway with Fergus, not quite knowing what to do next. At the moment she felt so embarrassed, first by what his grandfather had said, and now Penny, that she couldn't even look at him!

'My grandfather may be the interfering old goat I was going to accuse him of being just now,' Fergus spoke gruffly at her side. 'But his heart is in the right place. Whereas mine...' He paused. 'My heart is completely in your tender hands, Chloe Fox-Hamilton!'

Now she did look up at him, her eyes wide, feeling the colour fade and then rush back into her cheeks as she did so.

Because Fergus was looking at her with such love in his eyes she couldn't breathe...!

He reached out to gently clasp the top of her arm. 'Let's go and find that garden, hmm?' he suggested huskily.

Chloe led the way like an automaton. Had Fergus really just told her that his heart was hers...?

The perfume from the flowers outside was heady and strong, enough to make the senses reel. Except Chloe's were already reeling. Fergus loved her!

She found that incredible to believe. Still couldn't actually believe it.

'Chloe...?' Fergus was looking down at her uncertainly in the moonlight.

She moistened suddenly dry lips. 'I haven't been very nice to you the last couple of weeks,' she said inadequately.

He laughed softly. 'I'm not sure you've ever been that,' he acknowledged ruefully. 'But I live in hope.'

She swallowed hard. 'Is it true?'

'About David?' He frowned. 'I'm afraid so. But you

mustn't blame him for the misconceptions over the identity of Susan Stirling's lover. He wanted to make a clean breast of it eight years ago and your father wouldn't let him, was determined to protect Penny and the children. And your father can be a very stubborn man—'

'No, not about David,' she corrected. 'I'm sure that's true. As I'm equally sure David and Penny now have one of the strongest marriages I know—apart from my parents, of course. But I—I was asking if it were true that you— that I—'

'That I love you?' Fergus finished gently. 'Oh, yes, Chloe, that's true.'

Her breath caught—and held—in her throat as she looked up at him. Fergus was looking at her with such all-consuming love in his face that she couldn't doubt how he felt about her.

Could it be, could it possibly be, after these past weeks of misunderstanding and pain, that everything was going to turn out all right after all...?

'I tried so hard to make everything all right again for you,' Fergus confessed 'But all I ever seemed to succeed in doing was hurting you more. But I really did try, Chloe. Please believe me.'

She did believe him, didn't need him to tell her any more about that. The past was well and truly gone; it was the future that mattered. A future with Fergus...?

'Fergus, I love you,' she spoke breathlessly.

'You do?' He looked as stunned as she must have done a few minutes ago when he'd told her his heart was hers.

She laughed softly, elated happiness starting to build up inside her. 'I do.'

'Enough to marry me?'

'Only if you're sure that's what you want.' Her expression betrayed her own uncertainty with this suggestion.

Loving her was one thing, marrying her was something else entirely...

He reached out to wrap his arms about the slenderness of her waist. 'If you really do love me, then I wouldn't settle for anything less,' he assured her.

Chloe felt her heart leap in her chest. 'Oh, I really do love you,' she told him.

His arms tightened about her. 'Then—Chloe Fox-Hamilton, will you do me the honour of becoming my wife?'

Chloe slid her arms about his waist, resting her head against his chest, able to hear the erratic beating of his heart as he waited for her answer. 'I would love to,' she answered him emotionally.

The next moment she found herself swept off her feet as Fergus lifted her into his arms and carried her over to the wooden bench that stood in one corner of the garden, sitting down with her safely on his knees before his mouth claimed hers.

All the misunderstandings, all the pain, all the unhappiness, of the last few weeks, were swept away in the total honesty of their kisses. They were unable to get enough of each other, Chloe's fingers entwined in Fergus's hair as she kissed him with all the love that burnt inside her for him.

Their faces were flushed, eyes shining brightly, when they at last broke the kiss to simply gaze at each other.

Fergus reached up a hand to gently touch one of her flushed cheeks. 'I can hardly believe you're going to be my wife,' he murmured huskily.

Chloe smiled at him a little shyly, still overwhelmed by the love between them. 'Especially as a wife was the last thing you had on your mind only a few weeks ago!'

It had happened so quickly, this love between them, had taken them both by surprise. But even now, only a few minutes into knowing they loved each other, Chloe also knew she never wanted to be without Fergus in her life. She hoped he felt the same way...

Fergus's arms tightened about her. 'If I'm completely honest—and in future, I intend being completely that where you're concerned,' he stated forcefully, 'I think marriage has been on my mind from the moment I woke up on that Sunday morning and found you standing beside my bed!' he admitted. 'And I've never deliberately gone out of my way to avoid marriage—until now I've just never met the one woman I know I simply can't live without.'

'Oh, Fergus...!' she groaned ecstatically as she buried her face in the warmth of his throat. 'That's exactly what I wanted to hear!'

His arms tightened about her. 'I love you very much, Chloe, and I intend telling you so every day of our lives together,' he promised.

Chloe hadn't known such all-consuming happiness existed until this moment, knew now exactly why her father and mother, and Penny and David, had fought so hard to keep their marriage alive and healthy. Love like this was simply too precious to ever give up.

Fergus looked at her quizzically. 'Exactly when do we move to Paris?'

Her eyes widened in surprise. 'We? But—'

'You don't think I'm letting you go without me, do you?' Fergus raised dark brows. 'All those romantic Parisians paying court to you?' He shook his head firmly. 'I don't think so. Besides, I'm an author, I can write anywhere. Paris sounds as good a place as any.'

Chloe couldn't believe he was really willing to do this for her... 'It will only be for a few months...'

'An extended honeymoon.' Fergus nodded with satisfaction. 'I can hardly wait! You do realise, after all his machinations, that we'll probably have to name our first child after my grandfather,' he added teasingly. 'Hugh McCloud.' He grimaced.

'Let's hope it's a girl.' Chloe giggled happily. She didn't care what they called their first child, the fact that it would be a product of the love they shared would be enough.

Fergus became serious again. 'Marry me soon,' he urged gruffly. 'Very soon.'

'Yes, please,' she accepted ecstatically.

He smiled at her warmly. 'Do you think we ought to go in now and put them all out of their misery?' he teased.

Chloe sobered briefly. 'I think there has been quite enough misery this last few weeks.'

'Then it's time for some celebrating instead,' Fergus decided firmly, sliding her gently off his knee as he stood up, but still retaining a hold of one of her hands. 'Let's go and open up some champagne—and invite everyone to a wedding!' he announced with satisfaction.

A sentiment Chloe was only too happy to agree with!

CHAPTER FIFTEEN

'OH, FERGUS, isn't this just wonderful?' Chloe exclaimed happily at his side. 'I'm so happy I want to cry,' she added emotionally.

'Hormones, my love,' Fergus drawled indulgently, although he knew it wasn't just Chloe's two-month pregnancy that made her so weepy; today really was a wonderful day for them all.

But especially for Chloe's father. Yesterday he and his political party had achieved a landslide victory in the general election, and today Peter Ambrose had asked Paul to be Chancellor of the Exchequer.

The party had started a couple of hours ago at the home of Chloe's parents, and looked like going on well into the evening and night, all the family here, including Fergus's, and many other people from the world of business and politics.

He and Chloe had been married for six months now, had returned from Chloe's successful Paris show only last month, and Fergus knew they had been the happiest six months of his life. Now, with Chloe's pregnancy confirmed only this morning, that happiness was totally overwhelming.

'I love you, Chloe,' he told her huskily.

'And I love you,' she returned as emotionally.

Fergus knew it was all he wanted. All he would ever want.

*   *   *

'When shall we tell them our news?' Chloe looked up excitedly at her husband, her breath catching in her throat just to know that the two of them were so happy together.

'Whenever you like,' Fergus replied indulgently. 'Personally, I want to shout it to the whole world!'

That was exactly how she felt, and she never ceased to be amazed that this wonderful man loved her as deeply as she loved him.

'At least we won't have to call him Hugh now.' She grinned with a wistful look across the room at Darcy and Logan as they cooed over their newborn son, Daniel Hugh.

'He may be a she,' Fergus returned teasingly. 'But I know what you mean.'

He usually did. That was the strange—and wonderful!— thing about marriage; the two of them were totally attuned to each other's thoughts and feelings.

'Poor Brice,' Chloe murmured as she looked across the room to where her cousin-in-law stood alone in one of the bay windows, surveying the party through remote green eyes. 'He needs someone in his life too,' she explained at Fergus's questioning look.

Fergus chuckled, shaking his head derisively. 'Brice is perfectly capable of finding someone if he wants to.'

'But he may not know he wants to,' Chloe reasoned.

Fergus laughed softly as he turned her in the circle of his arms. 'Never mind what Brice does or doesn't want,' he said. 'How soon do you think we can leave?' His eyes darkened to chocolate-brown. 'I have a burning desire to make love to my wife!'

Chloe knew that same desire, and after six months of marriage she knew that she always would.

She and Fergus had a love that would last for ever...

To Marry McAllister

CAROLE MORTIMER

CHAPTER ONE

'MCALLISTER, isn't it?'

Brice tensed resentfully at this intrusion into his solitude. If one could be solitary in the midst of a party to celebrate a political victory!

Ordinary he wouldn't have been at this party, but the youngest daughter of the newest Member of Parliament had married his cousin, Fergus, six months ago, and so all the family had been invited to Paul Hamilton's house today to join in the celebrations at his re-election. It would have seemed churlish for Brice to have refused.

But he didn't particularly care for being addressed by just his surname—it reminded him all too forcefully of his schooldays. Although it was the man's tone of voice that irritated him the most: arrogance bordering on condescension!

He turned slowly, finding himself face to face with a man he knew he had never met before. Tall, blond hair silvered at the temples, probably aged in his mid-fifties, the hard handsomeness of the man's face was totally in keeping with that arrogance Brice had already guessed at.

'Brice McAllister, yes,' he corrected the other man coolly.

'Richard Latham.' The other man thrust out his hand in greeting.

Richard Latham... Somehow Brice knew he recognised the name, if not the man...

He shook the other man's hand briefly, deliberately not continuing the conversation. Never the most sociable of men, Brice considered he had done his bit today towards

5

family relations, was only waiting for a lull in the proceedings so that he could take his leave.

'You have absolutely no idea who I am, do you?' The other man sounded amused at the idea rather than irritated.

Brice may not know *who* the other man was, but he did know *what* he was—the persistent type!

Latham, he had said his name was. The same surname as Paul Hamilton's other son-in-law, his own cousin Fergus's brother-in-law, which meant he was probably some sort of relative of the Hamilton family. But somehow Brice had a feeling that wasn't what the other man meant.

He held back his sigh of impatience. It was almost seven o'clock now; he had been looking forward to being able to excuse himself shortly, on the pretext of having another appointment this evening. But now he would have to extricate himself from this unwanted conversation first.

'I'm afraid not,' he returned without apology; being accosted at a social gathering by a complete stranger wasn't altogether unknown to him, but it certainly wasn't something he enjoyed.

Although, he accepted, being an artist of some repute, that he had to show a certain social face. This man, with his unmistakable arrogance, just seemed to have set his teeth on edge from the start.

Richard Latham raised blond brows at the bluntness of the admission. 'My secretary has contacted you twice during the last month, concerning a portrait of my fiancée I would like to commission from you.'

He was *that* Richard Latham! Multimillionaire, jet-setting businessman, the other man's business interests ranging worldwide, his personal relationships with some of the world's most beautiful women making newspaper headlines almost as much as his successful business ventures. Although Brice had no idea who the 'fiancée' he had just mentioned could be.

He shook his head. 'As I explained in my letter, in reply

to your secretary's first enquiry, I'm afraid I don't do portraits,' he drawled politely. And he hadn't felt the least inclination to explain that all over again in reply to the second letter he had received from this man's secretary only a week later.

'Not true,' Richard Latham came back abruptly, blue eyes narrowed assessingly on Brice's deliberately impassive expression. 'I've seen the rather magnificent one you did of Darcy McKenzie.'

Brice smiled slightly. 'Darcy happens to be my cousin-in-law. She is married to my cousin Logan.'

'And?' Richard Latham rasped frowningly.

Brice shrugged. 'It was a one-off. A wedding gift.'

The other man gave an arrogant inclination of his head. 'This is a gift too—to myself.'

And he was obviously a man, Brice acknowledged ruefully, who wasn't used to hearing the word no—from anyone!

Well, Brice couldn't help that, he simply did not paint portraits, had no inclination to paint a flattering likeness of the rich and the pampered, just so that they could hang it on one of the walls of their elegant homes and claim it was a 'McAllister'.

'I really am sorry—' he began—only to come to an abrupt halt as the room suddenly fell silent, all attention on the woman who now stood in the doorway.

Sabina.

Brice had seen photographs the last few years of the world's most famous model—he would have to have been blind not to have done. Hardly a day passed when she wasn't photographed appearing in some fashion show or other, at a party, or public event. But none of those photographs had prepared Brice for the sheer perfection of her beauty, the creaminess of her skin against the short, shimmering silver dress she wore, her legs extremely long and shapely, her eyes a luminous blue, long hair the colour of ripe wheat reaching almost to her slender waist.

She wore absolutely no jewellery, but then she didn't need to; it would merely be gilding the lily.

His attention returned to her eyes. Luminous, yes, with a black ring encircling the sky-blue of the iris. But there was something else there he picked up on as she looked about the room. A certain apprehension. Almost fear...?

Then a shutter came down over those amazing blue eyes, the emotion masked almost as quickly as Brice's trained eye had recognised it, her smile confident now as she looked across the room in his direction.

'Excuse me while I greet my fiancée,' Richard Latham murmured mockingly before leaving Brice's side to stride forcefully across the room to kiss Sabina warmly on the cheek, his arm moving possessively about her slender shoulders even as she smiled at him.

Brice realised as he watched the two of them that he had been wrong about the jewellery; on the third finger of Sabina's left hand gleamed a huge heart-shaped diamond.

Sabina was the fiancée Richard Latham had referred to? The fiancée he wanted Brice to paint a portrait of...?

The one woman in the world, now that he had seen her in the flesh, that Brice knew he simply had to paint!

Oh, not because of her beauty, spectacular though it might be. No, it was that quickly masked emotion that intrigued Brice, that momentary glimpse of fear and vulnerability, that made Sabina more than just a beautiful woman.

It was an emotion he wanted to explore, if only on canvas...

'Sorry I'm a little late.' Sabina smiled warmly at Richard. 'I'm afraid Andrew was being extremely difficult over fittings today.' She grimaced as she lightly dismissed one of the top fashion designers of the day. Andrew might be at the top, but he had a volatile temper to go with it, which made him hell to work for.

'You're here now, that's all that matters,' Richard assured her lightly as he turned back into the room.

Sabina's tension left her. How nice it was to have someone in her life who was never difficult over the demands of her career. In fact, it was the opposite where Richard was concerned; her famous face as she stood at his side was all that he wanted from her.

And, thankfully, the conversation seemed to have resumed in the room again now. Even after seven years as a top model, Sabina didn't think she would ever get used to the way people stopped to stare at her wherever she went, had had to build up a veneer over the years to cover up the dismay she often felt at the effect her looks had on people.

The only place she seemed to get away from being recognised was when she went to one of her favourite hamburger restaurants. No one ever believed, with her willowy slenderness, that it could possibly be the model Sabina, dressed in denims and casual top, her hair hidden under a baseball cap, sitting there eating a hamburger with French fries! But, sceptical as some reporters were, claiming she lived on lettuce leaves and water to maintain her slender figure, she was actually one of those lucky people who could eat anything and never put on weight.

Although, she acknowledged a little sadly, she hadn't dared to make one of those impromptu visits to eat one of her favourite foods for some time now. Six months, in fact…

'I have someone I want you to meet, Sabina,' Richard told her smoothly now. 'And someone I want to meet you,' he added with a certain amount of satisfaction.

Sabina looked at him enquiringly, but could read nothing from his expression as he guided her across the room to meet the man she had seen him talking to when she'd arrived.

The other man was tall, even taller than Richard's six feet two inches, probably aged in his mid-thirties, dressed casually in blue denims teamed with a white tee shirt and black jacket, with over-long dark hair, and a face of austere handsomeness. But it was the green eyes in that face that caught and held Sabina's attention, eyes of such perception they seemed to see right into the soul.

Sabina felt the return of her earlier apprehension run down the length of her spine; she didn't want anyone, least of all this austere stranger, looking into her soul!

'Brice, I would like you to meet my fiancée, Sabina. Sabina, this is Brice McAllister,' Richard introduced lightly.

But again, unless Sabina was mistaken, Richard's voice contained that element of satisfaction as he made the introductions.

She knew Richard was proud of the way she looked, but at this moment he seemed more so than usual.

She looked curiously at the other man. Brice McAllister. Should she know—? The artist! Brice McAllister, she knew, was one of the most sought-after artists in the world today. But that still didn't explain Richard's attitude towards the other man...

'Mr McAllister,' she greeted coolly.

'Sabina.' He nodded abruptly. 'Do you have a surname?' he added mockingly.

'Smith,' she supplied dryly. 'But not many people know that. My mother's more exotic choice of a first name was an effort to make up for the lack of imagination in my surname.' And she, Sabina realised with a frown, was talking merely for the sake of it. And to a man who instinctively made her uneasy.

But she couldn't seem to help it when those deep green eyes were looking at her so intently...

'You're Sabina. It's enough,' Richard put in with a certain amount of arrogance.

Did Richard sense it too, that deep intensity coming from that unblinking, emerald-green gaze?

Sabina felt that shiver once again down the length of her spine, moving slightly closer to Richard as she did so.

'I promise not to tell a soul,' Brice McAllister drawled playfully in answer to her earlier remark.

Although somehow it didn't sound playful coming from this man. Neither was the mention of the 'soul' to Sabina—when she was sure this man could see straight into hers!

What would he see? she wondered. Warmth and kindness, she hoped. Humour and laughter, too. Loyalty and honour. Apprehension and fear—

No! She was careful to keep those emotions under lock and key. Although that wasn't so easy to achieve when she was alone. Which was why she very rarely allowed herself to be alone with her thoughts any more...

'Your fiancée and I were just discussing the possibility of my painting your portrait,' Brice McAllister bit out evenly.

Sabina gave a perplexed frown as she turned to look at Richard. He hadn't mentioned anything about having her portrait painted. And she already knew, from the little time she had spent in Brice McAllister's brooding company, that he was the last man she wanted to spend time with!

'I'm afraid Brice has just ruined my surprise.' Richard laughed dismissively, giving her shoulders a warm squeeze before turning to look challengingly at the younger man. 'You've decided you would like to paint Sabina's portrait after all?' he drawled mockingly.

Sabina looked at Brice McAllister, too, gathering from Richard's comment that the question of painting her portrait hadn't been as cut and dried as the artist had just implied it was...

If not, why had he changed his mind?

If he had...

Brice McAllister shrugged unconcernedly. 'It's a possibility,' he replied noncommittally. 'I would need to do a few preliminary sketches before making any definite decision.' He grimaced. 'But I should warn you now, I don't do chocolate-box likenesses of people.'

The implication being that she had a chocolate-box beauty! Not exactly the most charming man she had ever met, Sabina acknowledged ruefully, although he was at least honest.

But maybe that was what he meant about not doing 'chocolate-box' likenesses of people, Sabina realised with a faint stirring of unease; he liked to capture what was inside the person as well as a physical likeness. Maybe her instinct had been right after all and he really could see into her soul...?

'A "warts and all" man,' Richard realised dryly. 'Well, as you can clearly see, Sabina doesn't have a single blemish.' He looked at her proudly.

Sabina looked at Brice McAllister, only to look quickly away again as she saw the open derision in his expression at Richard's obviously possessive praise. But the intensity of the artist's attention on her didn't seem to allow him to see Richard's possession for exactly what it was: simply pride in ownership of an object of beauty.

'I think you could be slightly biased, Richard,' she told him huskily. 'And I'm sure we must have taken up enough of Mr McAllister's time for one evening...' she added pointedly, wanting to get away from the intensity of that probing green gaze.

She didn't like Brice McAllister, she decided. Something about the way he looked at her made her feel uncomfortable. And the sooner she and Richard distanced themselves from him, the better she would like it.

'If I could just have your address and telephone number...' Brice McAllister drawled questioningly. 'Perhaps I can ring you, and we can sort out a time convenient to both of us for those sketches?'

Sabina swallowed hard, very reluctant for Brice McAllister to know any more about her than he already did.

'That's easy, they're the same as mine,' Richard informed Brice mockingly even as he took one of his personal cards from his wallet and handed it to the other man. 'If neither Sabina nor I are at home when you call, my housekeeper can always take a message,' he added lightly.

Sabina could feel the increased intensity of that dark green gaze now as Brice McAllister digested the knowledge of her living at Richard's Mayfair home with him. His mouth had thinned disapprovingly, those green eyes cool as his gaze raked over her assessingly.

Sabina challengingly withstood the derision now obvious in Brice McAllister's expression as he looked at her, although she had no control over the heated colour that had entered her cheeks.

Damn him, who did he think he was to stand there and make judgements about her behaviour? She was twenty-five years old, for goodness' sake, quite old enough to make her own choices and decisions. Without being answerable to anyone but herself. And she was quite happy with her living arrangements, thank you!

If a little defensive...?

Maybe. But Brice McAllister didn't know of the understanding she and Richard had come to when they'd become engaged several months ago, could have no idea that engagement was only a front, that their engagement was based on liking, not love. A protective shield for her from the fear she had lived with the last six months, in exchange for that object of beauty—herself!—that Richard wanted so badly in his life. And, strangely enough, she had realised over the last few months, that was all he wanted from her...

No doubt to a third person their arrangement would seem odd in the extreme, but it suited them. And it was certainly none of this man's business!

'I'll call you,' Brice McAllister drawled derisively, putting Richard's card in the breast pocket of his jacket before giving a dismissive nod of his head. Leaving them, he strolled over to join a couple sitting in the corner of the room cooing over a very young baby.

'Brice's cousin, Logan McKenzie, and his lovely wife Darcy,' Richard murmured softly at her side.

Sabina didn't care who the other couple were, or what relationship they had to the arrogant Brice McAllister; she was just glad to have him gone. She could breathe easily again now!

In truth, she hadn't even realised she had been holding her breath until he'd left them, and then she had been forced to take in a huge gulp of air—or expire!

One thing she did know—she had no intention of being at home if Brice McAllister should choose to telephone her.

And, in the meantime, she intended doing everything she could to persuade Richard into changing his mind about wanting Brice McAllister to paint her...

CHAPTER TWO

'BUT I'm afraid Miss Sabina isn't at home,' Richard Latham's housekeeper informed him for what had to be the half-dozenth time in a week.

Actually, Brice knew exactly how many times he had telephoned and been informed 'Miss Sabina isn't at home'. It was the fifth time, and his temper was verging on breaking-point. Mainly, he knew, because he was sure he was being given the run-around by the beautiful Sabina.

He had known by the expression on her face at Paul Hamilton's house the previous week, when told that Richard wanted Brice to paint her portrait, that Sabina didn't share that desire.

Which, if he were honest, only made Brice all the more determined to do it.

'Thanks for your help,' Brice answered the housekeeper distractedly, wondering where he went from here. Telephoning to make an appointment to sketch Sabina obviously wasn't working!

'I'll tell Miss Sabina you rang,' the woman informed him before ringing off.

A lot of good that would do him, Brice acknowledged impatiently as he replaced his own receiver. She had probably been informed of those other four calls he had made too—and, despite the fact that he had left his own telephone number, Sabina hadn't returned any of them.

'I would stay away from my Uncle Richard, if I were you,' David Latham had informed him ruefully at the party last week once the other man and Sabina had left. 'He's a collector of priceless items—and he considers Sabina part of that collection. He also brings a whole new meaning to

15

the phrase ''black-sheep of the family'',' David had added with a grimace.

Richard Latham wasn't the one Brice was interested in. Although, as he was quickly learning, there seemed to be no other avenue to reach the beautiful Sabina...

For such an obviously public figure, she was actually quite reclusive, was never seen anywhere without the attentive Richard, or one of his employees, at her side.

Brice knew, because he had even attended a charity fashion show the previous weekend with his cousin Fergus, and his designer wife, Chloe, at which he'd known Sabina had been making an appearance. Only to have come up against the brick wall of what had appeared to be a bodyguard when he'd tried to go backstage after the show to talk to Sabina.

She hadn't joined the champagne reception after the show either, and discreet enquiries had told Brice that Sabina had been whisked away in a private car immediately after her turn on the catwalk had been over.

Sabina brought a whole new meaning to the word elusive—and, quite frankly, Brice had had enough.

He was also pretty sure that Richard Latham would have no idea Sabina had been avoiding his calls; the other man had been so determined to have Brice paint Sabina.

It wasn't too far to drive to Richard Latham's Mayfair home, the single car in the driveway, a sporty Mercedes, telling him that someone was at home. At this particular moment it didn't matter whether it was Richard Latham or Sabina—he intended getting that promised appointment from one of them!

He didn't know why, but he had been slightly surprised the previous week when Richard Latham had informed him that he and Sabina shared a home—and presumably a bed? There was something untouchable about Sabina, an aloofness that held her apart from everyone around her. Obviously that didn't include Richard Latham!

'Yes?'

Brice had been so lost in thought that he hadn't been aware of the door being opened to his ring on the bell, the elderly woman now looking up at him enquiringly obviously the housekeeper he had spoken to on the telephone over the last week.

'I would like to see Sabina,' Brice stated determinedly.

The woman raised dark brows. 'Do you have an appointment?'

If he did, then he would have no reason to be here!

Brice bit back his anger with effort. After all, it wasn't this woman he was angry with. 'Could you just tell Sabina that Mr McAllister would like to see her?' he rasped curtly.

'McAllister?' the woman repeated with a frown, giving a backward glance into the hallway behind her. 'But aren't you—?'

'The man who has telephoned half a dozen times this last week to speak to Sabina? Yes, I am,' Brice confirmed impatiently. 'Now could you please tell Sabina that I'm here?' He knew he wasn't being very polite, that it wasn't this woman's fault Sabina was giving him the brush-off, but at the moment he was just in too foul a mood to be fobbed off any longer.

Because he was utterly convinced, after that slightly furtive glance back into the house by the housekeeper, that the sporty Mercedes in the driveway belonged to Sabina, that she had been at home earlier when he'd telephoned, as she was at home now. She was just choosing not to take his calls.

'But—'

'It's all right, Mrs Clark,' Sabina assured smoothly as the door opened wider and she suddenly appeared beside the housekeeper in the doorway. 'Would you like to come through to the sitting-room, Mr McAllister?' she invited coolly.

He nodded abruptly, afraid to speak for the moment—

he might just say something he would later regret. Strange, he had never thought he had much of a temper, but this last week of having Sabina avoid him had certainly tried his patience.

She looked different again today, was wearing faded denims and a white cropped tee shirt, her long hair secured in a single braid down her spine, her face appearing bare of make-up. Brice had no idea how old she was, but at the moment she looked about eighteen!

'You'll have to excuse me, I'm afraid.' She indicated her casual appearance with a grimace as she turned to face him once the two of them were alone in the sitting-room. 'I've just got back from the gym.'

Brice raised dark, sceptical brows. 'Just?'

She met his gaze unflinchingly. 'Can I offer you some tea?'

'No, thanks,' he refused dryly. 'I've telephoned you several times this last week,' he added hardly.

Her gaze shifted slightly, no longer quite meeting his. 'Have you?' she returned uninterestedly.

Damn it, this really shouldn't be this difficult. Richard Latham was the one who had come to him with this commission—Brice hadn't even wanted to do it.

Until he'd seen Sabina...

'You know damn well I have,' he snapped impatiently.

She shrugged. 'I've been so busy this week. A trip to Paris. Several shows here. A photographic session with—'

'I'm not interested in what you've been doing, Sabina— only in why you've been avoiding my calls,' he rasped harshly.

'I've just told you—'

'Nothing,' he bit out tersely. 'Even if you haven't been here—' of which he was highly sceptical '—I'm sure the efficient Mrs Clark has informed you of each and every one of my telephone calls.'

'Perhaps,' Sabina conceded noncommittally. 'Are you sure I can't offer you any tea?'

'I'm absolutely positive,' he bit out between clenched teeth. A neat whisky would go down very well at the moment, but as it was only four o'clock in the afternoon he would give that a miss too for the moment. But the coolness of this woman was enough to drive any man to drink! 'Now, about that appointment—'

'Please, do sit down,' she invited lightly.

'Thanks—I would rather stand,' he grated harshly, this woman's aloofness doing nothing to alleviate his temper.

Sabina shrugged off his refusal before sitting down in one of the armchairs. 'Strange, but I was under the impression you were an artist of some repute?' she murmured dryly.

Brice eyed her guardedly. 'I am.'

'Really?' she mused derisively. 'And do you usually go chasing after commissions in this way?'

She was meaning to be insulting—and she was succeeding, Brice feeling the tide of anger that swept over him.

But at the same time he questioned why she was trying to antagonise him into refusing to paint her portrait before walking out of here. Because he knew that was exactly what she was trying to do.

He drew in a deeply controlling breath. 'Perhaps I will have that cup of tea, after all,' he drawled, before making himself comfortable in the armchair opposite hers.

But his gaze didn't leave the cool beauty of her face, meaning he missed none of the dismay at his words that she wasn't quick enough to mask. And Brice knew, despite having invited him to have tea in the first place, that Sabina actually wanted him out of here as quickly as possible.

Because Richard Latham might return at any moment and put paid to any effort on her part to elude having Brice paint her portrait...?

'I'm not in any hurry.' He made himself more comfortable in the armchair.

'Fine,' Sabina bit out in clipped tones, standing up gracefully. 'I'll just go and speak to Mrs Clark.'

And also take time to compose herself, Brice easily guessed. He knew he wasn't mistaken now, was absolutely sure that Sabina had no intention of letting him paint her portrait.

Why? What was it about him that she didn't like? Although Brice was sure it wasn't actually dislike he had seen in her eyes in that brief unguarded moment. It had been something approaching the fear he had sensed when he'd first seen her a week ago...

Sabina didn't go straight to the kitchen, running up the stairs to her bedroom first to splash cold water on her heated cheeks.

It had never occurred to her, when she'd refused to take any of Brice's telephone calls this last week, that he would actually come here!

But now she realised that perhaps it should have done; there was a ruthless determination about Brice McAllister that clearly stated he did not like to be thwarted. And never being available for his calls would definitely fall into that category in his eyes. Sabina now realised her mistake, knew that she should have taken one of his calls, if only to put him off coming here in person.

Well, it was too late now. Richard should be back within the hour, which meant she would have to hurry Brice McAllister through his tea, put up all sorts of obstacles to any immediate appointment to go to his studio, and then continue to cancel them thereafter.

Because she was even more convinced by this second meeting with him that she did not want Brice McAllister to paint her. She knew that he was every bit as good an artist as he had been proclaimed, and she also knew the reason that he was so good; Brice McAllister was exactly what she had thought him to be last week. He was a soul-searcher.

Those green eyes saw beyond the layers of social façade, past the protective barriers, straight into the soul, and deep into the real emotions that made a person exactly what they were, and what had made them that way. What had changed her from being happily sociable into a woman who now put up a protective barrier she was determined no one would penetrate?

'Tea will be through in a moment,' she announced lightly a few minutes later when she rejoined him in the sitting-room. 'Richard tells me that you have painted a rather magnificent portrait of your cousin's wife, Darcy McKenzie?' she prompted politely as she sat down.

He nodded abruptly. 'So I've been told.'

Sabina gave a bright, meaningless smile. 'I think he's hoping you will do as magnificent a one of me.'

Brice McAllister looked across at her with narrowed eyes. 'And what do you hope, Sabina?' he drawled.

He didn't really need to ask her that. Sabina was sure he already knew exactly what she hoped—that he wouldn't paint her at all, that he would just go away, and leave her with her barrier intact...

'The same thing, of course,' she returned smoothly, meeting that continuous probing gaze with a completely blank one of her own.

'Of course,' Brice finally echoed dryly. 'I—'

'Ah, tea.' Sabina turned to smile at Mrs Clark as she came into the room, the tray she carried, as Sabina had instructed the housekeeper a few minutes ago, containing just the tea; she did not intend offering Brice McAllister cake as well and delaying his departure by even a few minutes!

'No sugar for me, thanks,' Brice McAllister murmured

as the housekeeper left the room and Sabina sat forward to pour milk and tea into the cups.

'Sweet enough already' didn't quite apply to this man, Sabina acknowledged wryly. Tough, determined, slightly arrogant, very insightful, but Brice McAllister was definitely not 'sweet'!

'You seem quite at home here,' he drawled mockingly.

Despite being caught slightly off guard by the abruptness of the statement, Sabina managed to continue to calmly pour her own tea into the cup. 'Why shouldn't I? It is my home,' she returned coolly, once again sensing that disapproval of the fact that she lived here with Richard.

Which was slightly old-fashioned coming from a man who was probably only aged in his mid-thirties. Or perhaps it was the age difference between herself and Richard that Brice McAllister disapproved of...?

'So when are you free to sit for some sketches for me?' he prompted suddenly.

She shook her head regretfully as she sat back to drink her tea. 'I have a very busy schedule for the next few months—'

'I'm sure you must have an hour free somewhere,' he challenged, his mouth twisted derisively.

An hour, yes, possibly even the odd day here and there. But she didn't wish to give any of that time to Brice McAllister.

'Possibly,' she dismissed. 'But even I deserve some time off for rest and relaxation.'

'Sitting in a chair while I sketch you is not exactly going to tire you,' he returned dryly.

No—but trying to keep that blank wall in her eyes for an hour or so, shutting his probing gaze out of her inner self, definitely would!

She shrugged. 'I'm afraid I don't have my diary available at the moment, but as soon as I do I'll check it over and give you a call,' she added dismissively, having noted that his teacup was now empty.

He raised dark brows, making no effort to stand up in preparation of leaving. 'Tomorrow is Saturday—surely you aren't busy all over the weekend too?'

Sabina held in her frustrated anger with effort. This man wasn't just determined, he was dogged!

He was also, she was slowly coming to realise, all the more intent on doing those sketches because he sensed her own reluctance not to have him do them.

She shook her head with feigned regret. 'I'm afraid Richard and I are away this weekend,' she was able to tell him with complete honesty. And some satisfaction, she admitted inwardly.

At least, she was allowed to feel that way for a few very brief moments—because she then became aware of the sound of Richard's car outside in the driveway!

Usually she was more than pleased to see him, feeling safer when he was around, but today her heart sank at the realisation that he was home. Because Richard, she knew, despite gentle hints from her this last week that she really didn't want her portrait painted, was very determined that it would be done. And he was equally determined that the artist of that portrait would be Brice McAllister.

'Pity,' Brice drawled, obviously not in the least convinced by her excuse.

He also wasn't yet aware that Richard had arrived home, and Sabina schooled her features into one of cool politeness so that Brice McAllister shouldn't see how dismayed she felt at having the two men meet again. Something she had desperately been trying to avoid!

Brice sighed. 'I wonder—'

'Sabina? Are you—?' Richard had come straight into the sitting-room on entering the house, coming to an abrupt halt as he saw Sabina wasn't alone, his gaze narrowing as he took in Brice McAllister's presence in the room, the used cups on the low table clearly stating that he had been here for some time.

'Richard!' Sabina stood up immediately to cross the room to her fiancé's side, linking her arm warmly with his as she smiled at him. 'Mr McAllister called round for tea,' she dismissed with a lightness she was far from feeling.

Brice hadn't exactly 'called around for tea', that had been merely incidental; he had really come here in order to corner her into making a definite appointment for those sketches!

Sabina looked across at him now, wondering exactly what he was going to say to Richard about his reason for being here.

Would he tell Richard of his five unacknowledged telephone calls this past week? Yes, she did know exactly how many times he had telephoned, had instructed the loyal Mrs Clark to repeatedly tell him she wasn't at home!

Would he now tell Richard of her evasive tactics?

She gave an inward groan just at the thought of it, having no doubts that Richard would not be pleased that she had deliberately been avoiding Brice McAllister this last week. Richard would also, once they were alone, want to know the reason for it. She could hardly tell him that she had done it because she didn't want Brice McAllister looking into her soul…!

'I called round in person to apologise for not getting in touch with either of you this last week.' Brice McAllister was speaking smoothly now. 'I've been rather busy, I'm afraid. But that's still no excuse for my tardiness.' He grimaced.

Sabina could only stare across at him disbelievingly. He had been rather busy…? His tardiness…? He was the one apologising…? When she had been the one who—

'That's quite all right,' Richard accepted lightly, the tension relaxing from his body at the other man's explanation.

'Is everything sorted out now?' He looked at the two of them enquiringly.

Sabina looked at Brice for guidance on this one, still stunned by the way he had smoothed over the situation with a few brief—if totally inaccurate—words.

Had they sorted everything out now?

More to the point, why had Brice McAllister lied just now? Only she could benefit from such a misconception— and, as she was only too well aware, she had done nothing in their acquaintance so far to merit such gallantry. As Brice, up to that point, had done nothing to show he was capable of such an emotion!

He looked at her enquiringly. 'I believe so,' he drawled pointedly.

That was why he had lied—so that she had no choice but to make a firm appointment to go and see him. But, in the circumstances, it was probably the least that she owed him...

'Richard, I was just explaining to Mr McAllister—'

'Brice,' he put in dryly.

'To Brice,' she corrected after a slightly irritated glance in his direction; she did not want to be on a first-name basis with this man, intended keeping him very firmly at arm's length. Further, if she could manage it! 'That I have the afternoon free on Tuesday,' she admitted reluctantly.

'And I was just complimenting Sabina on having such a good memory,' Brice McAllister drawled. 'I always have to consult my diary before making appointments,' he added pointedly, that green gaze mocking her.

Sabina shot him a glaring look. Damn him, how dared he mock her when he knew she couldn't defend herself? Probably for exactly that reason! After all, there had to be some recompense for letting her off the hook so nobly!

'Three o'clock on Tuesday afternoon, then.' He nodded abruptly, obviously tiring of the game he was playing, anxious to be gone now as he took a card out of the pocket of his jacket.

Much as he had obviously enjoyed the game, damn him, Sabina inwardly acknowledged frustratedly. But what choice did she have now…?

'Fine,' she agreed abruptly, taking the card with his address printed on it, wishing she could somehow misplace it before next Tuesday. But at the same time knowing it would do her no good even if she did; that appointment might as well be set in stone as far as Richard was concerned!

Richard nodded. 'I have a meeting that afternoon, I'm afraid, Sabina, but I'll have Clive accompany you,' he assured her smilingly.

'Clive?' Brice McAllister repeated slowly. 'I have to tell you now, unlike Sabina, I do not like an audience while I work,' he bit out harshly.

Richard laughed dismissively. 'Clive is completely unobtrusive, I can assure you. But if it bothers you,' he added cajolingly as the other man still scowled, 'he can wait outside in the car.'

Brice nodded abruptly. 'It bothers me.'

No more than it *bothered* Sabina to think of spending that hour alone with him at his studio!

CHAPTER THREE

'WHAT do you know about the model Sabina?'

'Aha!' Chloe said with satisfaction as she put down her knife and fork to look across the luncheon table to Brice. 'I told Fergus, after you accompanied us to the fashion show last Saturday that there was something going on. So much for inviting me out to lunch to cheer me up while Fergus is away in Manchester at a book-signing!' she added teasingly.

Brice loved his cousin's wife dearly, looked on her as the younger sister he had never had, but sometimes...!

'There's nothing ''going on'', Chloe,' he told her dryly. 'I'm going to paint the woman. I just thought I should know something about her before I did.'

'Oh.' Chloe couldn't hide her disappointment at this explanation.

Brice gave a rueful shake of his head at her deflated expression. 'Just because you and Fergus are rapturously happy together—even more so since you knew about the expected baby—does not mean everyone else around you has to be in love too!'

'But wouldn't it be nice if you were?' Chloe came back undaunted.

'She's an engaged woman, Chloe,' he dismissed with amusement.

'But they don't seem in any hurry to get married,' she replied instantly. 'And Richard Latham is so much older than Sabina...'

Brice was all too well aware of that already...

'Nice' wasn't exactly how he would have described the

27

possibility of his falling in love. But he knew that his two cousins, Logan and Fergus, had found true love in the last year, and that they—and their wives!—would like nothing better than for Brice to join them in their obviously happy state. The only problem that he could see was that he hadn't yet found the woman that he could fall in love with!

The model Sabina certainly wasn't her. She was beautiful, yes. And from their meeting last Friday he knew that she was also completely natural and unaffected. He was also intrigued by her, found her engagement to a man so much her senior slightly odd, as he found the way she had the equivalent to a 'minder' accompany her wherever she went; because he had no doubt that the man Clive who would be driving her to his studio this afternoon was exactly that, no matter what guise he might otherwise be appearing under.

What Brice really wanted to know was, in view of David Latham's view of his uncle, was Sabina being protected on Richard's behalf, as a collector of priceless objects, or for some other reason...?

Which was why he had wondered, with Chloe being a fashion designer herself, with her own connections in the design and model world, if she knew anything about Sabina that might answer some of his questions for him. But the last thing he wanted was for Chloe to think he had a personal interest in Sabina!

'How is Fergus's latest book doing?' He decided to change the subject for a while; they could always come back to Sabina later.

'Number one in the hardback best-seller list after only two weeks,' Chloe told him with obvious pride. 'Have you read it?'

'Not yet.' He resumed eating his meal, knowing that he had successfully diverted Chloe's attention from possible wedding bells on his behalf. 'It's set in the fashion-designer world, isn't it?'

It was the perfect way to distract Chloe from the subject of Sabina, and for the next fifteen minutes they talked of Fergus's successful new book, then went on to discuss Chloe's father's return to politics, and now the government.

Anything but the beautiful model Sabina!

Because, as he'd talked to Chloe about everything else under the sun but Sabina, Brice had come to the realisation that his interest in her was personal!

She was deliberately cool and aloof, put up a barrier between herself and others—with the obvious exception of Richard Latham. And yet at the same time there was a vulnerability about her that seemed to be completely inexplicable.

Sabina was the world's top model, very beautiful, very much in demand, and very highly paid. Her earnings had to equal those of the highest paid actress in Hollywood. Which meant she had the money to be and do whatever she pleased. And yet...

It was that 'and yet' that intrigued Brice, that had him thinking about Sabina even when he wasn't aware he was doing it. He was becoming obsessed with her, he realised.

But this afternoon he hoped to go some way to solving the enigma that was Sabina Smith!

'Thanks for lunch, Brice.' Chloe reached up to kiss him on the cheek as they parted outside the restaurant. 'And good luck with Sabina this afternoon,' she added mischievously.

Brice gave a rueful shake of his head as he drove back to his home; he had no doubts that by this evening the whole family would know he had questioned Chloe concerning Sabina!

He arrived back at the house in plenty of time for their

three o'clock appointment. But three o'clock came and went, with no sign of Sabina.

She wasn't coming, damn it. After four days' wait, after all that anticipation, she wasn't coming!

Brice could feel the anger starting to build up inside him, having no doubt that Sabina had done this deliberately. He—

The doorbell rang.

It was three twenty-five, there had been no call to say she would be arriving late, but nevertheless Brice knew it was her. He schooled his features into showing none of his previous anger; that was probably what she expected, so she wouldn't get it!

'I'm so sorry I'm late,' Sabina was apologising profusely even as his housekeeper showed her into the studio a few minutes later. 'I had a photographic session for a magazine this morning, and, although they promised me faithfully that I would be finished by two o'clock, it ran over, and I—'

'You're here now,' Brice firmly cut into her lengthy explanation. Because he was sure, even from their brief acquaintance, that Sabina was not the effusive type, that she would never use half a dozen words when one would do. Which probably meant she was making this up as she went along! 'Have you had lunch?'

She blinked at this sudden change of subject. 'No...'

'Then can I offer you a sandwich or something?' He looked enquiringly at his housekeeper even as he made the offer.

'No, really,' Sabina refused before Mrs Potter could answer. 'I'll have something later,' she dismissed.

'Tea or coffee, then?' Brice offered smoothly.

God, she looked beautiful today, the clinging blue Lycra tee shirt, the same colour as her eyes, clinging in all the right places, as did the body-hugging black trousers she wore with it, her hair loose again today, a shining gold curtain down the length of her spine. Brice's fingers itched to take up paper and pencil and begin his sketches.

Sabina looked set to refuse again, and then obviously thought better of it. 'A coffee would be very nice, thank you.' She smiled warmly at the housekeeper.

'And how about Clive?' Brice couldn't resist asking, sure that the 'chauffeur' was even now sitting outside waiting to drive Sabina back to the home she shared with Richard Latham. As he had no doubt sat outside and waited for Sabina while she'd been in her photographic session this morning! 'Would he like a coffee too, do you think?' he added derisively.

Sabina's gaze narrowed as she looked across at him for several long, silent seconds. 'No, I'm sure Clive will be fine,' she finally answered slowly. 'I hope I'm not putting you to too much trouble,' she added warmly to the housekeeper.

Brice could see, as Mrs Potter left the studio with a smile on her face, that Sabina's apparently guileless charm had obviously worked its magic on her; he had no doubt that there would be more than a cup of coffee on the tray the housekeeper brought back in a few minutes.

'Where do you want me?'

Now there was a leading question if ever he had heard one, Brice acknowledged derisively, sure that most men wouldn't care 'where' with Sabina, as long as they had her!

Brice's outward expression remained impassive. 'The couch, I think,' he answered consideringly. 'To start with. I'm really not sure what I'm going to do with this yet,' he added frowningly. How could he possibly do justice to such a beauty as Sabina's...?

There was no doubting her surface beauty, but there was so much more to her than that, a naturalness that owed nothing to powder and paint, an inner Sabina that he needed to reach too. And he was determined, no matter what barriers she might choose to put up, that he would reach *that* Sabina!

Sabina moved to sit on the couch, the May sun shining in brightly through the windows that made up one complete wall of Brice McAllister's studio. The garden outside was a blaze of spring flowers, and just the sight of that mixture of bright blossoms lightened Sabina's spirit.

'Do you do the gardening yourself?' she asked interestedly.

'Sorry?'

She turned back to look at Brice McAllister, only to find he was already engrossed in the sketch-pad resting on his knee as he sat across the room from her. 'I didn't realise you had already started,' she murmured slightly resentfully, knowing she had been caught off guard as she'd looked out at the beauty of the garden.

'Only roughly,' he dismissed, giving her his full attention now, looking very relaxed in blue denims and a black tee shirt. 'And yes, I look after the garden myself, It's often a welcome relief after being in my studio for hours. Do you garden?'

Her expression became wistful. 'I used to.'

'Before pressures of work made it impossible,' Brice McAllister guessed lightly.

A shutter came down over her eyes. 'Something like that,' she answered noncommittally.

The fact that she no longer gardened had nothing to do with work commitments, and everything to do with the fact that she no longer lived alone in her little cottage. But she was not about to explain that to Brice McAllister.

She was only here at all today under protest, because last Friday she had been given no choice but to agree to the appointment. Part of her knew that she probably also owed Brice a thank-you for not telling Richard how she had been avoiding his phone calls all week. But there was something inside her that wouldn't let her say the words...

'"Something like that"?' Brice repeated softly.

Sabina shifted uncomfortably. 'I'm not sure I'm going to be any good at this; I'm simply not good at sitting still.' She grimaced.

He nodded. 'Stand up and move around if you prefer it; I'm not sure sitting down is the right pose for you anyway,' he added frowningly.

Sabina wondered as she stood up to move restlessly about the room exactly what pose he did think was right for her?

Brice McAllister's studio was a cluttered and yet somehow orderly room, canvases stacked against the walls, paints, pencils, paper, all neatly stored on open shelves, with the minimum amount of furniture; just the chair he sat in, a large, paint-daubed table, and the couch Sabina had been sitting on.

'Here we are.' Mrs Potter came back in with a laden tray, putting it down on the table, sandwiches and a fruit cake also on the tray.

'Thank you,' Sabina told the other woman warmly.

'Help yourself,' Brice McAllister invited dryly once his housekeeper had left the room.

She poured the tea into two cups before helping herself to one of the chicken sandwiches; she hadn't thought she was hungry, but one bite of the delicious sandwich told her that she was.

'Do you often miss out on lunch?' Brice McAllister watched her with brooding eyes.

Sabina shrugged. 'Sometimes. But I usually make up for it later,' she assured him dryly. 'I don't starve myself, if that's what you're thinking; I'm naturally like this.' She indicated the slenderness of her figure.

'And very nice it is too.' He nodded. 'When's the wedding?'

Sabina blinked at the sudden change of subject. 'Sorry...?'

'Richard implied your portrait is a wedding present to himself.' Brice shrugged. 'I was merely wondering how soon I have to finish it,' he added derisively.

She frowned. 'I think you must have misunderstood him.' It had never even been discussed between them that their 'understanding' might lead to marriage...

'No?' He raised dark brows. 'Richard gave me the impression it was imminent.'

'Did he?' she returned evenly, equally sure he must have misunderstood Richard.

'I thought so,' Brice continued determinedly. 'There's rather a large difference in your ages, isn't there?'

Her cheeks flushed resentfully. What business was it of this man if there was an age difference between herself and her fiancé? Absolutely none, came the unqualified answer!

'Spring and autumn,' Brice added derisively.

Her mouth twisted. 'At twenty-five I'm hardly spring— summer would be more appropriate,' she bit out shortly. 'And surely age is irrelevant in this day and age?' she added challengingly.

'Is it?' he returned softly.

Sabina frowned across at him, more disturbed by what he had said than she cared to admit. She and Richard were friends, nothing more; Brice must have misunderstood Richard! Mustn't he...?

'I thought I came here so you could sketch me, Mr McAllister—not question me about my personal life!' she snapped agitatedly.

'The name is Brice,' he told her smoothly.

'I prefer Mr McAllister,' she said tautly. What she really preferred was to keep this man very much at a distance!

He gave an unperturbed shrug. 'Whatever. Could you stand over by the fireplace?' he bit out curtly, once again frowning down at his sketch-pad.

Almost as if that very personal conversation had never taken place, Sabina fumed inwardly as she moved to stand beside the unlit fireplace.

'Yes,' Brice breathed his satisfaction with the pose. 'The clothes are all wrong, of course—not that you don't look lovely in them,' he added as she raised her brows. 'They just aren't right for the way I want to paint you.'

'And what way is that?' Sabina rasped impatiently.

He didn't answer her, frowning across the room at her in between making rapid strokes with his pencil on the pad in front of him.

Sabina remained standing exactly as she was, recognising that transfixed look from some of her photographic sessions; a master was at work, and for the moment she, as a person, did not exist.

Which was fine with her. She was here under protest, and the last thing she wanted was any more personal conversations with Brice McAllister while she was here. Especially of the kind they had just had.

'Will there have to be much of this?' she finally felt compelled to ask him an hour later. The fireplace was really rather nice, but after looking at it for the last hour she definitely knew it didn't hold much scope for the imagination!

Brice looked up at her frowningly, his thoughts obviously still engrossed in his sketching. 'Much of what?'

'These sittings—or, in this case, standings,' she added wryly. 'Will I need to do many of them?'

He put the sketch-pad down on the table beside him, flexing stiff shoulder muscles as he did so.

He really was a very handsome man, Sabina acknowledged grudgingly. Those dark, brooding good looks were almost Byronic, that over-long dark hair giving him a rakishly gypsy appearance. Although Sabina was sure the romantic Byron had never quite had that totally assessing male look in his eyes. Deep green eyes that even now were trying to look past her façade of politeness to the inner Sabina!

'Why?' he finally drawled softly.

She shrugged. 'As I've already explained, I'm—'

'Rather busy,' he finished derisively. 'Yes, you have explained that. Several times, as I recall,' he added mockingly before picking up his cup and drinking the now cold tea in one swallow. 'The question is, why are you so busy?' He looked at her with narrowed eyes. 'As I understand it, you've been one of the top models in the world—if not the top model in the world,' he allowed mockingly, 'for the last five years. Why do you need to keep working at the pace that you do?'

Because work stopped her from thinking, from remembering, meant she was too tired at night to do anything more than fall into bed and go to sleep!

But none of those thoughts betrayed themselves in the calmness of her expression. 'So that I *remain* one of the top models in the world,' she replied dryly.

Brice pursed his mouth. 'And is that important to you?'

Her cheeks became flushed at the mockery in his tone. 'Is it important to you to be one of the world's most sought-after artists?' she returned caustically, deeply resenting the slight condescension towards her career that she sensed in his tone.

Okay, so it didn't need great intelligence to initially become a model, just the right look, and a certain amount of luck, but it certainly took more than those things to remain one. She worked hard at what she did, never gave less than her best, and she deeply resented his implication that it should be otherwise. She had always regarded herself as something of an artist too, in her own way.

'*Touché,*' he allowed dryly. 'I just can't imagine doing what you do, day in and day out.' He shrugged.

Sabina narrowed cornflower-blue eyes on him. 'Are you meaning to be insulting, Mr McAllister, or does it just come naturally?' she said slowly.

He grinned unabashedly. 'A little of both, probably.'

She shook her head, incredulous at his arrogance. 'You just don't care, do you?' she murmured slowly.

He looked puzzled. 'About what?'

'About anything,' she realised in wonder.

How she wished she still had that tolerantly amused outlook to life, that she could laugh at herself as well as other people. But she knew that she didn't. That she never would have again, thanks to—

No, she wouldn't think of that. Couldn't think of that.

'I think it's time I was going,' she decided abruptly, glancing pointedly at the gold watch on her wrist. An engagement present from Richard. That, and his diamond engagement ring, were the only two pieces of jewellery she ever wore.

Brice McAllister was watching her consideringly, head tilted slightly to one side, green gaze narrowed speculatively. 'Why?' he finally challenged.

It was a challenge Sabina easily picked up on. And chose to ignore. 'Because I have somewhere else to go,' she told him determinedly.

'Home to Richard?' he taunted softly, standing up slowly, his sheer size totally dominating the room.

Sabina took a step back, suddenly finding the room op-

pressively small. She also found herself backed up against
the unlit fireplace.

Brice walked slowly towards her, his narrowed gaze not
leaving her face. He stopped about a foot away, that gaze
searching now as he continued to look at her.

For the second time since she had met him Sabina found
she couldn't breathe.

This close to, she could feel the male warmth of him,
could smell the slight tang of the aftershave he wore, could
see every pore and hair on the darkness of his skin. But it
was none of those things that constricted her breathing.
She knew it was his sheer physical closeness that did that.

She swallowed convulsively. 'I really do have to go,'
she told him breathlessly.

Brice looked at her steadily. 'So what's stopping you?'
he prompted huskily.

Her legs, for one thing. They refused to move. In fact,
she felt so weak at the knees they were only just succeeding in supporting her. She felt like a mesmerised rabbit
caught on the road in the glare of car headlights, incapable
of movement, even in the face of such obvious danger.

And Brice McAllister, as she had half guessed on their
very first meeting, been even more convinced of it at their
second, was exactly that—dangerous!

She moistened suddenly dry lips. 'If you would just
move out of my way...?'

He stepped slightly to one side. 'Be my guest,' he invited softly.

Sabina forced her legs to move, quickly, determinedly,
crossing to the door, putting as much distance between
herself and Brice McAllister as was possible in the confines of the studio.

'I'll call you.'

Sabina turned sharply as he spoke, her trembling hand
already on the door-handle. 'Excuse me?'

Brice raised dark brows, his mouth twisted in mocking amusement. 'I said, I'll call you. For your next sitting,' he explained derisively as she still looked totally blank.

Get a grip, Sabina, she ordered herself sternly. What had really happened just now—Brice McAllister had stood what she considered was too close to her? So what? And yet she knew that wasn't really all that had happened, that there had been a frisson of awareness between the two of them that she wished weren't there...

'Perhaps you would do me the courtesy of taking my call this time?' Brice prompted confidently.

Colour darkened her cheeks at his certainty she had no choice but to do exactly that. 'If I happen to be at home,' she bit out harshly.

He shrugged. 'If you aren't, I'm sure that Richard and I can sort out a time between the two of us,' he drawled softly.

Sabina's eyes narrowed. 'Contrary to what you may have assumed otherwise, Mr McAllister—I make my own appointments,' she snapped coldly.

Once again he gave that humourless smile. 'That wasn't my impression at our last meeting.'

Because at the time she had been at the disadvantage of not wanting him to tell Richard she had been avoiding his telephone calls for the past week!

She looked at him consideringly for several long seconds. 'You know, Mr McAllister,' she finally said softly, 'I really don't give a damn what was or wasn't your *impression* at our last meeting,' she told him scornfully. 'In fact, nothing about you is of the least interest to me,' she added scathingly.

He raised dark brows. 'No?'

'No!' she confirmed hardly. 'Goodbye, Mr McAllister.' She wrenched the door open.

'*Au revoir*, surely, Sabina...?' he taunted softly.

Sabina didn't even turn and acknowledge the obvious challenge, striding briskly out of the room, closing the front door softly behind her as she left.

It wasn't until she was safely ensconced in the back seat of the car, Clive driving back to Richard's house, that she allowed free rein to her feelings.

She didn't like the way Brice McAllister looked at her. Didn't like the way he had of talking to her on a very personal level. Didn't like him near her. In fact, she just didn't like him!

And she had no idea how she was going to achieve it, but she had no intention of being alone with Brice in his studio ever again!

CHAPTER FOUR

BRICE cursed himself, for what had to be the hundredth time in a week, for the way he had behaved with Sabina last Tuesday.

He had already seen the fear and apprehension in her eyes at their first meeting, had realised she was inwardly like a startled fawn getting ready for flight, and yet some devil had driven him on to try and get a reaction from her, to taunt and mock her in an effort to get behind the cool façade she liked to present to the world at large.

But all he had succeeded in doing was totally alienating her.

Oh, it hadn't resulted in her refusing to take his calls this time. She had taken all four of them—she had simply come up with a legitimate excuse for every suggestion he'd come up with for a second sitting!

And what had she left him with? She could spare him one hour this morning, but it would have to be at home. Probably with the quietly watchful Richard in attendance!

As he was only at the sketching stage, Brice hadn't been able to come up with a good reason why he shouldn't be the one to go to her home. But that didn't mean he liked it...

Although he had to admit a few minutes later, when he was shown into the sitting-room where Sabina waited—alone—that she was much more relaxed in her own surroundings. In fact, she was the epitome of the gracious hostess, smiling at him politely as she offered him tea or coffee. Both of which he refused.

She looked the part too, in a cream silk blouse and pencil-slim black skirt, the latter finishing just above her knee, her hair gathered up in a neat chignon at the back of her head. Altogether, she looked nothing like the woman Brice wanted to capture on canvas!

'Practising for domesticity?' he drawled mockingly.

He had been determined to be totally professional today, to put Sabina at her ease. But somehow he couldn't help himself; this new Sabina brought back that devil inside him even more strongly than the other one. She was playing a part, adopting a role—and Brice didn't doubt for a moment that it was for his benefit. Only confirming for him that he really had struck a sensitive nerve with his behaviour the previous week!

She smiled across at him coolly. 'You were right last week, Brice—being rude does seem to come naturally to you.'

Which was his cue to apologise. But he couldn't do that, either. Something about this woman made him want to grip her by the shoulders and shake her, to see her laugh, or cry, to show some impulsive emotion. Which would probably result in him being thrown out of here on his ear!

He shrugged. 'Merely being observant,' he dismissed lightly. 'I'm sorry, but your hair has to come down, at least,' he added frowningly, having settled himself down in a chair with his notepad and pencil.

She shook her head. 'I'm afraid I'm going out to lunch immediately after this, and I won't have time to redo my hair,' she refused.

Brice bit back his irritation; she really was only giving him the hour! 'You look as if you're about to meet your bank manager,' he rasped insultingly.

Sabina's gaze didn't waver from his for a moment, although there was, he thought, the briefest flare of anger in those deep blue depths.

'My mother, actually,' she drawled coolly.

Brice raised dark brows. 'Her daughter is the most famous model in the world—and she likes you to look like this?' He couldn't hide his incredulity. And so much for his arrogance in assuming she had dressed in this way as a barrier against him!

Sabina bristled resentfully. 'What's wrong with the way I look?'

It would be easier—and quicker—to say what was right with it. Nothing! Oh, she looked elegant enough, but that hairstyle and those clothes took away all her personality. She certainly had none of the provocative beauty of the model Sabina at this moment.

'My mother has lived in Scotland since my father died, so I only see her a couple of times a year,' she told him defensively. 'She's rather—conventional, in her outlook,' Sabina continued abruptly when he still didn't reply.

Brice's gaze narrowed. 'In what way?'

Sabina shrugged. 'She and my father were very career-minded, both teachers of history at university level. I don't think they ever intended having children, but accidents happen.' Sabina grimaced. 'They were rather older than most parents when I was born, my mother forty-one, my father forty-six. Although I think my father coped with parenthood rather better than my mother did,' she said frowningly. 'But then, I suppose he didn't have to put his own career on hold for five years, until I was old enough to go to school,' she added fairly.

Considering this was the most Sabina had ever spoken to him, Brice could only think she had to be as nervous of this second sitting as he was.

'You must have been rather a shock to them,' Brice said ruefully.

In more ways than one. Suddenly being presented with a very young baby must have been shock enough, but how on earth had her aged parents coped with Sabina's unmistakable beauty? She must have looked like an angel when she was a little girl.

'Yes,' she acknowledged wistfully. 'It was a strange childhood,' she admitted abruptly.

Probably a very lonely one too, Brice realised frowningly. Something he found difficult to contemplate. He had grown up in a young, fun-loving family, and when he hadn't been with his parents he had been in Scotland, with his grandfather, and his two cousins, Logan and Fergus. He had never particularly thought about it before, but his own childhood couldn't have been more perfect.

'Which one of your parents do you take after?' he probed interestedly, going carefully so as not to break the spell; he had a feeling that Sabina rarely spoke of her parents and her childhood, and that to draw her attention to it now would only result in her clamming up again.

Sabina gave the ghost of a smile. 'My father.' That smile faded almost as soon as it appeared. 'He died five years ago,' she added flatly.

And her mother had lived in Scotland since that time.

'I'm sorry.' And he was. Even from the little she had said, it was obvious Sabina had been much closer to her father than her mother.

And perhaps that closeness to her father, and his death five years ago, explained the reason for her engagement now to a man so much her senior?

Sabina shrugged. 'He had been ill with cancer for some time; it was a welcome release for him.' She spoke unemotionally. 'But I've always regretted that he wasn't there to see me get my own degree in history. Oh, yes, Brice—' she smiled at his obviously surprised expression '—I went to university. I haven't always been a full-time model,' she added derisively, for his derogatory remarks about her chosen career the previous week.

And her derision was well deserved, Brice acknowledged inwardly. He had been scathing and rude about her career, without really knowing anything about this woman; no wonder she looked on him as an inconvenient intrusion!

Sabina's humour faded, her expression becoming non-committal once again. 'My mother—obviously—is a great believer in further education for women, believes women should have as many choices in life as they can possibly achieve.' Her mouth twisted ruefully. 'I don't think she's too impressed with the fact that, for the moment, I've chosen modelling.'

'But it is obviously by choice.' Brice shrugged, frowning suddenly. 'And if your mother is so conventional in her outlook, what does she make of your living here with Richard so openly?'

He hadn't even finished saying the words before knowing he had just made a terrible mistake. And the truth of the matter was, he wasn't interested in how Sabina's mother felt about her living arrangements; he wanted to know the answer to this particular question himself.

Because he found the idea of Sabina sharing Richard Latham's house, Richard Latham's bed, completely unacceptable.

Sabina had stood up abruptly as soon as he'd asked the question, blue eyes blazing angrily across the room at him now. 'You're being extremely personal, Mr McAllister!' she snapped, two bright spots of angry colour in her cheeks.

And her anger, Brice realised, wasn't all directed towards him; she had also realised, having been drawn into an unguarded conversation about her parents, that she had actually left herself open to Brice's overfamiliarity. And she was obviously furious with herself because of it.

Brice remained seated. 'Talking of Richard...where is your fiancé today?' he enquired mildly; he really had expected the other man to be here today. If only to keep an eye on one of his 'priceless possessions'!

'He's in New York until tomorrow,' Sabina bit out economically.

'In that case—will you have dinner with me this evening?' Brice heard himself asking.

And then kicked himself. What on earth did he think he was doing? Sabina was an engaged woman. More important, she had given no indication whatsoever that she was in the least interested in spending time in his company. In fact, the opposite seemed true!

Sabina looked as stunned by the invitation as Brice felt at having made it.

The angry colour had faded from her cheeks, leaving them pale as alabaster, her eyes dark and unfathomable as she stared at him uncomprehendingly. Almost as if she didn't believe what she had just heard.

As if to taunt Brice for his audacity, the diamond ring Sabina wore on her left hand winked and shone in the sunlight shining in through the large bay windows. Richard Latham's ring...

Brice held his hands up in apology. 'It was just a thought. A bad one,' he accepted dryly as she continued to stare at him. 'But it was only a dinner invitation, Sabina,' he continued angrily as she stood unmoving across the room. 'Not an improper suggestion!'

She swallowed hard before drawing in a ragged breath. 'I didn't think—' She broke off as a brief knock sounded on the door. 'Come in,' she invited huskily, obviously relieved at the housekeeper's interruption as she turned to smile at the older woman.

Brice's relief was of another kind—the housekeeper had probably just delayed him receiving a verbal slap in the face!

'You asked me to bring the post straight in when it arrived, Miss Sabina.' Mrs Clark held out the silver tray on which she carried at least half a dozen letters.

'Thank you.' Sabina's second smile, as she took the letters, looked rather strained to Brice as he watched her from across the room.

As, indeed, it probably was! Damn it, what did he think he was doing, inviting Sabina out to dinner? She hadn't liked him very much to start with; now she was going to think even less of him!

What on earth had prompted him to make such an invitation? Sabina had gone out of her way to show him she had no desire to be in his company, for any reason, so why put himself in this ridiculous position? Probably because of that complete aversion she made no effort to hide, he accepted ruefully.

Not that he expected every woman he met to fall at his feet; no matter what Sabina might think to the contrary, he really wasn't that arrogant. But he didn't usually have the effect of dislike at first sight, either!

He had had his share of relationships over the years, some of them very enjoyable, some of them not so much fun, but he could never before remember a woman taking an instant dislike to him in the way that Sabina had...

Contrarily, it had only succeeded in making him more interested in Sabina!

The housekeeper having left the room now, Brice stood up abruptly. 'I think we may as well call it a day for now,' he bit out harshly. 'You obviously—' He came to an abrupt halt, Sabina having turned sharply towards him as he spoke, dropping the letters from her hand onto the carpeted floor as a consequence.

Damn it, was he really that much of a monster to her after that stupid dinner invitation that just the sound of his voice now took her back into that 'startled fawn' mode? If so he—

'What is it?' he prompted sharply as Sabina rose slowly from picking up the dropped letters, her face not just white now but a ghastly grey. 'Sabina...?' He moved abruptly to her side, grasping the tops of her arms as his gaze quickly searched the haunting beauty of her face. She looked as if she was about to faint! 'Here, sit down.' He put her down in one of the armchairs before striding over to the tray of drinks on the side and pouring a large amount of brandy into a glass.

'No, thanks,' Sabina refused huskily as she looked up and saw what he was doing. 'I don't think my mother will be too impressed if I turn up for lunch smelling of brandy!' she attempted to tease.

Brice knew the remark for exactly what it was—an attempt to divert his attention from the fact that she looked so awful. It failed!

He frowned down at her, feeling in need himself now of the brandy in the glass he still held. 'Is the idea of dinner with me really so repugnant to you...?' He couldn't believe his invitation had had this much of an effect on her.

'Sorry?' Sabina frowned up at him, obviously confused by the question.

Which led Brice to wonder if it had been his invitation that had brought about this transformation in her.

But if it wasn't his invitation that had caused her to look so ill so suddenly, what—? He looked down at the letters she had just picked up, most of them in her right hand, while her left hand tightly clutched an envelope of pale green. Gripped it so tightly, in fact, that the envelope was crushed in her fingers until the knuckles showed white...!

Brice looked down at her searchingly. She hadn't had time to open any of the letters, and yet just the sight of that pale green envelope had been enough to drain her face of all colour!

'Sabina—'

She stood up abruptly. 'Of course the idea of dinner with you isn't repugnant to me,' she told him with forced lightness, while at the same time totally avoiding his gaze. 'In fact, it sounds a wonderful idea,' she accepted.

That wasn't the impression she had given before the housekeeper had arrived with the mail; in fact Brice was positive Sabina had had every intention of turning down his invitation until that moment.

But for some reason she recognised that particular green envelope, knew who the letter was from without even opening it. And it had disturbed her enough for her to want to accept Brice's dinner invitation...

Curiouser, and curiouser.

'Fine,' he said before she had chance to change her mind. 'I'll call for you at about seven-thirty, if that's okay?'

'Perfect,' she agreed quickly, obviously anxious for him to leave now.

So that she could read the letter in that pale green envelope...?

His mouth twisted ruefully. 'Shall I book the table for three—or will you be giving Clive the evening off?' He certainly didn't relish the idea of sitting down to dinner with Sabina under the other man's watchful gaze, sitting outside the restaurant or otherwise!

Sabina gave him a reproachful glance. 'I'm sure I can manage without Clive for one evening,' she bit out tersely before glancing at her wrist-watch. 'I'm sorry we don't seem to have got very far this morning, Brice, but I'm afraid I have to go now.' Her obvious need for him to leave now became even more intense. 'Otherwise I'll be late for my luncheon appointment.'

'And that would displease your mother,' Brice drawled. 'And we mustn't have that, must we?' he acknowledged derisively.

But he really shouldn't complain, he berated himself as he picked up his things and prepared to leave; he had achieved much more this morning than he had expected to.

Sabina had told him more about her family than he had ever thought she would, her older parents, her conventional mother who now lived in Scotland—which part? he couldn't help wondering, with his own family connections in Scotland—her closeness to her father, his death five years ago.

Yes, he had learnt all of that about her today, and it was so much more than he had expected. But what he really wanted to know was, what was it about the letter she had received that had so upset her...? Because he was more and more convinced that it had been the letter and not him that had brought about that transformation in Sabina. Damn it, she had been so anxious to get rid of him after receiving it that she had even accepted his dinner invitation!

Maybe over dinner this evening—without the watchdog, Clive—he would have a chance to ask her about the letter in the pale green envelope...?

'Call for you, Miss Sabina,' Mrs Clark informed her later that day when Sabina picked up the telephone extension in her bedroom. 'It's Mr Latham,' she added lightly.

Richard...!

'Thank you, Mrs Clark.' Sabina eagerly took the call. After the day she had just had, she was longing to hear the normality of his voice! 'Richard,' she greeted warmly. 'How are you? Is everything okay? There's no delay in your coming home tomorrow, is there?' she added worriedly.

'Hey, one question at a time,' Richard's reassuringly familiar voice teased her indulgently. 'I'm fine. And everything is okay for my return tomorrow. I have a business meeting soon, but I just thought I would give you a call first to see how your week has been.'

Until earlier today it had been fine. She had been so busy that she hadn't really had the time to even think about the fact that Richard was in New York for four days. But that had all changed this morning. And now she just wanted him to come home!

'Fine,' she answered dismissively. 'Very busy work-wise, of course.'

'And what are you doing this evening?' Richard asked interestedly.

Well, so far she had showered, and washed her hair before drying it, had applied her make-up, put on a black sheath dress, and now she was sitting here in her bedroom waiting for Brice McAllister to arrive to take her out to dinner.

But somehow she knew she couldn't tell Richard quite so bluntly that she was going out to dinner with the other man.

She had had every intention of refusing Brice McAllister's dinner invitation, but then Mrs Clark had brought in the post, and thrown Sabina into complete confusion. So much so that, in an effort to get Brice to leave, she had accepted the dinner invitation, after all!

But quite how she told Richard about that she didn't really know...

She winced. 'Actually, I'm seeing Brice McAllister this evening,' she began reluctantly.

'That's good,' Richard told her approvingly. 'How are the sittings coming along? Has the great man come down out of his ivory tower now and realised that you're the most gorgeous creature on two legs and that he just has to paint you?'

'Not exactly,' she answered dryly, at the same time knowing that Richard had completely misunderstood her reason for seeing Brice this evening, that he believed it to be for another sitting.

Not that there was anything wrong with her having dinner with another man; she had done it dozens of times in the course of her modelling career. She just knew that dinner with Brice McAllister didn't quite come into that category...

She drew in a deep breath. 'Actually, Richard—'

'Just a minute, Sabina,' he cut in apologetically. 'I have a call on my other line.'

Sabina waited patiently while he took the other call, but the longer she waited, the more her courage was failing her. She had no doubt that Richard would have no problem with her meeting Brice McAllister for a sitting, but having dinner with the other man—with not a sketch-book or pencil in sight—was something else completely.

She wasn't altogether happy with the arrangement herself, but, having once accepted the dinner invitation, she hadn't felt she could phone Brice McAllister and cancel it. Part of the reason for that, she knew, was that Brice McAllister was sure to know exactly why she had cancelled it. And he seemed to find enough reason to mock her already, without adding to it!

'Sorry about that, Sabina.' Richard came back on the line. 'My business appointment just arrived, so I have to go. I'll call you later this evening if I get a chance, okay?'

No, it wasn't okay! What if Richard telephoned while she was still out and Mrs Clark told him she was out to dinner with the other man? And yet, at the same time, she knew this wasn't the right time to talk to Richard about it, either; he was obviously in a hurry to get to his appointment, meaning she wouldn't be able to explain things to him properly before he had to rush off.

'I was actually thinking of having an early night,' she told him instead. 'But I'll meet you at the airport tomorrow, anyway.' When she would definitely explain about seeing Brice this evening.

'There's no need for you to come all the way out to Heathrow,' Richard assured her lightly. 'Just send Clive with the car.'

As far as Sabina was concerned, there was every need. Besides, the privacy in the back of the car would give her a chance to talk to him on the journey home.

'I'm not doing anything tomorrow, and I would really like the trip out,' she assured him.

'Okay, fine,' Richard answered distractedly. 'I'll see you then,' he added before ringing off.

Wonderful! Not only was she having dinner with a man she would rather not spend time alone with, but she had also just lied to her fiancé about it.

What was it about Brice McAllister that made her so nervous she felt compelled to do such a thing?

Those green eyes that looked directly into her soul, came the instant answer to that question.

Those deceptively sleepy green eyes actually missed nothing, Sabina was sure. He was completely aware of her aversion to sitting for him. Her nervousness about this morning's sitting had resulted in her talking far too much. Ordinarily a very reserved person, she still couldn't believe she had talked to Brice about her family in the way that she had this morning.

She was also sure Brice hadn't missed her reaction this morning to the arrival in the post of that green envelope...

It had been three weeks since she'd last received one, the longest time ever, lulling her into a completely false sense of security, she now realised. Her reaction to receiving one this morning had been all the stronger because of that.

And Brice had seen that response.

Consequently, Sabina had been in a very agitated state by the time she'd met her mother for lunch. So much so that she'd almost missed what was different about this half-yearly visit to London by her mother.

'Have you and Richard set a date for your wedding yet, Sabina?' her mother enquired lightly as they both ate a prawn salad accompanied by a glass of white wine.

Sabina almost choked as she took a sip of that white wine. Why was it that everyone—Brice McAllister, most recently—seemed to be showing an interest in exactly when she and Richard were going to be married?

'Not yet,' she answered noncommittally, not even her mother having any idea of the almost businesslike arrangement of the engagement. 'We aren't in any rush,' she added to take any sting out of her words, watching as her mother carefully replaced her own wineglass on the table after taking a small sip.

Everything about her mother was controlled and careful, from her coiffured blonde head down to her moderately heeled black shoes, the latter worn to complement the black suit and cream blouse she was wearing today.

Sabina loved her mother dearly, had always admired her—she had just never been able to talk to her! Which was one of the reasons these half-yearly lunches together were such a trial. To both of them, Sabina felt sure.

'I only asked because I'm thinking of taking a short holiday early in the autumn, and I wouldn't like it to clash with your wedding,' her mother continued evenly.

'That will make a lovely change.' Sabina nodded approvingly; her mother seemed to lead a very uneventful life at her cottage home in Scotland. 'Are you going anywhere nice?' she added interestedly, relieved to have a neutral topic they could converse on.

'I haven't decided yet,' her mother dismissed with a brief smile. 'I—I'm going with a friend,' she added awkwardly, her gaze suddenly not quite meeting Sabina's. 'We thought perhaps Paris for a few days might be rather fun.'

Sabina frowned across the table at her mother. Fun? It wasn't a word she usually associated with her carefully controlled mother. There was something—

'Do I know this friend?' she prompted lightly, suddenly knowing, from the blush slowly creeping up her mother's cheeks, that she didn't.

Because the 'friend' was male!

Quite why Sabina should feel so shaken at the knowledge, she wasn't sure. Her father had been dead for five years, her mother was only in her mid-sixties, and still a very attractive woman; tiny, her figure slim, shoulder-length blonde hair always neatly styled, the beauty of her face barely lined. But somehow the thought of her mother going away on 'a short holiday', to romantic Paris of all places, with a man other than Sabina's father, threw her into total confusion.

All in all, she decided now as she gave one last check of her appearance in the mirror before going downstairs to wait for Brice McAllister's arrival, this had not been a good day.

And she very much doubted dinner with Brice McAllister was going to make it any better!

CHAPTER FIVE

IT HADN'T needed a mind-reader, when Brice had arrived at the house to pick Sabina up half an hour ago, to know that she wished she were spending her evening in any other way than having dinner with him!

Even now they had arrived at the quietly elegant restaurant, Sabina was anything but relaxed. It was up to Brice to see that she became so. Because she might not have been looking forward to seeing him this evening, but he certainly didn't feel the same way about spending the evening with her!

Sabina intrigued him. Her beauty was mesmerising, very much so in the simple figure-hugging black dress she wore tonight, everyone in the restaurant turning to stare at her admiringly a few minutes ago as the two of them had walked to their table. But it was the woman behind that beauty that interested Brice too, the intelligence behind those deep blue eyes.

Wary blue eyes. Which was why Brice had decided, before coming out this evening, rightly or wrongly, that he wouldn't pursue the subject of her reaction to the arrival of the letter in the green envelope. Not that he intended forgetting about it, but if he pressed Sabina for an explanation this evening he probably wouldn't see her for dust. Also, a part of him knew that she was half expecting him to ask her about it, and, perversely, he had decided not to do so!

'How did your lunch go with your mother?' he asked lightly instead as they perused the menus.

'Fine,' she answered brightly.

But Brice wasn't fooled by that dismissive façade, had

seen the shadow that had entered her eyes at the mention of her mother. He had what he considered a pretty healthy relationship with his own mother—they were good enough friends that he didn't interfere in her life as long as she didn't interfere in his.

But he knew from the little Sabina had told him of her own mother that the two of them didn't have that sort of relationship.

He gave Sabina a considering look. 'Sure?'

She frowned across at him. 'Of course I—' She broke off with a sigh. 'No, not really,' she conceded ruefully, fidgeting with her wineglass. 'It wasn't like our usual lunches together at all.'

Brice put down his menu, already knowing what he was going to choose, having been to this restaurant many times before. 'In what way?'

She shrugged. 'It seems that my mother has a boy-friend,' she disclosed reluctantly. 'Well...not a boyfriend, exactly.' She grimaced at the term. 'But there is a man she intends going on holiday with to Paris in the autumn,' she added frowningly.

'Isn't that good?' But Brice already knew that in Sabina's eyes it wasn't, could hear the underlying strain in her voice. 'She's been on her own for five years, and she must only be in her mid-sixties...?' Sabina was only aged in her mid-twenties, and she had said her mother had been forty-one when Sabina had been born...

'Sixty-six,' Sabina confirmed, giving a self-conscious grimace. 'I'm being selfish, aren't I? I've just never thought of my mother in that way.' She shook her head.

'Obviously this man has,' he said without thinking—and then wished he hadn't when he saw the disconcerted look on Sabina's face. 'I'm sorry, Sabina,' he at once apologised. 'It's just—'

'I know, I know,' she cut in self-derisively, taking a sip of the white wine Brice had chosen for them to enjoy before their meal. 'I really don't know why I'm even bothering to tell you this.' She gave an embarrassed laugh. 'I'm sure you can't be in the least interested.'

Now there she was completely wrong; as Brice was only too aware, everything about this woman interested him! In fact, he couldn't remember being this interested in a woman for years...

'But I am,' he assured her softly.

She shook her head. 'Please forget I ever mentioned it. I'm being silly.'

And Brice knew she was also unhappy with herself for having spoken to him about it!

'What is it you find strange about the situation?' he persisted lightly. 'The fact that your mother may have found a man she obviously enjoys spending time with? Or the fact that it isn't your father?' he added gently, already knowing it was probably the latter.

'Stupid, isn't it?' Sabina murmured self-disgustedly.

'Not in the least,' Brice instantly assured her. 'I don't think you've met my cousin Logan and his wife Darcy...?'

Sabina shook her head, her puzzled expression showing she had no idea where this conversation could possibly be going. 'I believe they were at the Hamilton party the night we first met, but I wasn't introduced to them, no.'

'Well, the two of them fell in love with each other while they were trying to prevent a relationship between Darcy's father and Logan's mother.' And a merry old tangle it had been at the time, as Brice easily recalled.

But he could see he definitely had Sabina's attention now.

'What happened to the father and mother?' she prompted curiously.

Perhaps, he realised too late, making that particular comparison hadn't been such a good idea, after all! 'They were married about a month before Logan and Darcy,' he revealed reluctantly as he realised that was probably the last thing Sabina wanted to hear.

'Oh,' she concluded flatly.

But Brice could see her thoughts were still preoccupied as they ordered their meal. She really didn't diet to keep that wonderful figure, ordering asparagus smothered in butter as a starter, followed by steak in Stilton sauce accompanied by Lyonnaise potatoes as her main course.

'I'll probably have something gooily chocolate as dessert too,' she apologised as she saw him watching her indulgently once the waiter had departed with their order.

Brice wasn't complaining; after years of having dinner with women who chose the items on the menu with the least calories, and then proceeded to only pick at even those when they arrived, it was a refreshing change to be with a woman who obviously enjoyed her food.

'Be my guest,' he invited warmly. 'You're just the sort of customer Daniel loves to cook for,' he assured her.

'You know the chef here?' She took another sip of her white wine.

Brice gave a rueful grimace as he realised he had done it again. 'Would you believe Chef Simon is Darcy's father?'

Sabina laughed huskily. 'I'd believe it.' She smiled. 'He's married to the actress Margaret Fraser, isn't he?'

'My Aunt Meg.' Brice nodded. 'They're very happy together.'

'I said I believe you!' Sabina laughed again, visibly relaxing. 'I wonder who this ''friend'' of my mother's is?' she mused curiously. Obviously having now spoken about it, she was slowly coming to terms with the fact that her mother was involved with someone.

'Why don't you ask her next time you talk to her?' he prompted lightly. 'She would probably appreciate that.'

'Maybe,' Sabina acknowledged noncommittally, not sure she actually wanted to go that far. 'Tell me, when and where do you intend holding your next exhibition?' she abruptly changed the subject, obviously having decided she had told him enough about her private life for one evening.

Well, not in Brice's eyes she hadn't; there were still dozens of things he wanted to know about Sabina Smith! Even if he did accept that some of them would have to wait…

'Richard told me that he attended the exhibition you had two years ago,' she added coolly. 'He said it was very successful.'

Brice didn't doubt that the other man had said that; he just knew that Sabina had really mentioned Richard as a reminder—just in case Brice might have forgotten—that she had a fiancé in her life…

As if he could forget with that damn great rock glittering on her left hand. But that didn't mean he wouldn't like to forget all about Richard Latham. In fact, the more he got to know Sabina, the more he wished the other man would just evaporate into thin air!

This evening wasn't going too badly, Sabina decided with inward relief. Brice McAllister was certainly easy enough to talk to. Too much so, on occasion.

'Mmm, this looks wonderful,' she enthused as her asparagus and Brice's escargot were brought to the table.

'I have no doubt that it will taste as good as it looks.' Brice nodded indulgently. 'Do you—? Oh, no…!' he groaned impatiently.

Sabina looked across at him curiously, only to find he was looking towards the doorway at a couple who had just entered the restaurant. Sabina vaguely recognised the woman as Chloe Fox, the fashion designer 'Foxy', having met her a couple of times, but she had no idea who the man was with her.

Although he looked enough like Brice, very tall, dark,

with an arrogant handsomeness, for Sabina to question the likeness.

'My cousin Fergus, and his wife Chloe,' Brice provided with obvious irritation, his displeasure with the other couple's arrival also obvious, at least, to Sabina. She hoped the other couple, having now seen Brice and walking purposefully towards their table, couldn't see it too!

Brice stood up politely. 'Fergus. Chloe,' he greeted tightly before moving to kiss Chloe lightly on the cheek. 'May I introduce Sabina?' he added with obvious reluctance.

'You certainly may. Although I'm sure we would both have recognised you without the introduction.' Fergus shook Sabina's hand warmly before turning back to this cousin. 'We're not interrupting anything, I hope?' Eyes of chocolate-brown tauntingly met Brice's frosty green ones.

Sabina found she liked the teasing affection Fergus showed towards his cousin. It made Brice McAllister seem much less arrogantly self-assured. Altogether less dangerous...

'Would the two of you care to join us?' she invited the other couple softly, keeping her expression deadpan as she saw the unmistakable look of warning irritation Brice shot in his cousin's direction.

'I'm sure you and Brice would much rather be alone,' Chloe was the one to answer her, but her dark brows were raised over speculative blue eyes as she looked across at Brice.

'Of course we wouldn't,' Sabina replied smoothly. 'It will be much more fun if there are four of us. Brice has very kindly taken pity on me while my fiancé is away on business and brought me out to dinner,' she added pointedly.

'Oh, Brice is well known for his kindness,' Fergus mocked even as he pulled back a chair for his wife to sit down before sitting down himself.

'Well known,' Brice muttered disagreeably as he resumed his own seat at the table.

'Have some wine, Fergus. Don't mind if I do, Brice,' his cousin carried out a conversation with himself as Brice now sat in stony silence, Fergus signalling the waiter to bring over a couple of wineglasses so that he and Chloe might join them in sipping the white wine.

Sabina smiled at his obvious mockery of his cousin, becoming more sure by the second that inviting the other couple to join them had been a good move on her part; Brice didn't seem half as daunting in the company of his cousin and his wife!

'Please don't let your food get cold,' Chloe advised lightly as a waiter discreetly set two more places at the table. 'Fergus and I can look at the menus while the two of you eat,' she added happily.

Sabina watched Brice beneath lowered lashes as she resumed eating her asparagus; anyone looking at him as he hooked the snails out of their shells, before grinding them between those even white teeth, would have thought each and every one of them had done him some personal disservice.

For the first time in their acquaintance Sabina had the feeling that Brice was at something of a disadvantage. It was a pleasant feeling!

Despite the fact that Brice added little to the conversation as the meal progressed, Sabina found she was enjoying herself. Chloe and Fergus were lively conversationalists, with a teasing sense of humour, and their love for each other was in every glance they exchanged. The fact that Brice glowered at the two of them for the next two hours seemed to bother them not one bit.

'I believe we're going to be distantly related,' Chloe observed much later in the evening as the four of them lingered over coffee.

Sabina saw the sharp look of surprise Brice shot his

cousin-in-law. And she had to admit, she was a little puzzled herself. 'I'm sorry...?' she prompted frowningly.

Chloe smiled. 'My older sister is married to your fiancé's nephew,' she explained. 'I'm sure once you're married that must give us some sort of family connection—although for the life of me I can't work out what it is!' she added laughingly.

Neither could Sabina. Especially as there would never be a wedding! But what shocked her the most was that she hadn't given her 'fiancé' a thought for the last two hours. Not one...

'It does sound rather complicated,' she dismissed vaguely before turning to Brice. 'I'm sorry to break up the evening, but I believe it's time I went home.'

His mouth tightened with displeasure; obviously he hadn't liked the fact that they had shared their evening with Fergus and Chloe, but he disliked the idea of her ending the evening even more.

Which was all the more reason to end it!

She had been unwise to come out with him at all this evening, knew he was not a man she could easily spend time with. It had been pure luck—on her part—that his cousin and his wife happened to be here too.

'Maybe we'll get a chance to work together some time soon,' Chloe told Sabina warmly as she and Fergus prepared to leave, the two men in some quiet dispute over who was paying the bill.

'Maybe,' Sabina answered noncommittally, knowing her appointment book was completely full for the next six months. Thank goodness! She already knew that the less she had to do with this dynamic family, the better.

'I was so sorry we didn't get to work together last year, after all,' Chloe added softly. 'But I believe you were ill at the time?'

Sabina gave the other woman a sharp look. What—?

'Harper Manor in November,' Chloe enlarged lightly. 'I was showing a line of evening dresses that weekend.'

Sabina stared at the other woman, clearly remembering now—too late—that she had been scheduled to wear a couple of those dresses at that particular show.

'I hope it was nothing too serious?' Chloe continued concernedly.

Sabina, never particularly big on small talk anyway, found herself completely struck dumb.

This was just too much. First that letter earlier today, and now a reminder of her absence from the catwalk last November. It was just—

'What wasn't too serious?' Brice frowned at the two women, obviously having now come to some sort of agreement with his cousin concerning the bill—as he had insisted initially, he was paying it!

Chloe turned to smile at him. 'I was just reminding Sabina that the two of us should have worked together last year, but she wasn't well.'

Brice looked at Sabina with narrowed eyes. 'What was wrong with you?'

So blunt. So straightforward. So unanswerable!

'Really, Brice,' Chloe spluttered affectionately. 'You can't just demand to know about someone's illness in that way!'

'Why can't I?' He frowned. 'You mentioned Sabina was ill last year. I merely want to know what was wrong with her.' He shrugged, as if he couldn't see what the problem was.

Whereas Sabina could see what it was all too clearly! She simply didn't talk about her absence from modelling at the end of the previous year. And she had no intention of doing so now.

Chloe gave Brice a reproving look, obviously now regretting having mentioned the subject at all. 'Really, Brice, we women have to have some secrets,' she rebuked lightly.

'It was really nothing of great importance,' Sabina dismissed coolly; the last thing she wanted was for Brice to think there was something mysterious about her absence from modelling the previous year! 'Just a touch of flu,' she excused. 'It's been lovely meeting both of you,' she told the other couple sincerely—if nothing else, they had been a very welcome diversion from spending the evening alone with Brice.

Although that was probably being unfair to Chloe and Fergus; the other couple were interesting people in their own right, Chloe a fashion designer of some repute, Fergus an internationally successful author. And at any other time Sabina would have enjoyed talking to them. Just not this evening.

And not now. Now she just wanted to get away from here, back to the house where she felt safe. Away from Brice McAllister.

'Maybe we can do this again some time?' Fergus was the one to answer her smoothly.

'I doubt it—my fiancé arrives back from New York tomorrow.' Her smile was politely apologetic. 'As I told you earlier, Brice was just taking pity on me by taking me out to dinner this evening,' she added firmly.

'That wasn't true, you know,' Brice told her once they were seated in the back of the taxi on their way to the home she shared with Richard. 'What you said back there, about my taking pity on you,' he added hardly. 'Inviting you out to dinner had nothing to do with pity—I wanted to spend the evening with you.'

Sabina suddenly found the confines of the taxi claustrophobic, her breath constricting in her throat. And Brice's closeness to her on the leather seat, his trouser-clad thigh brushing lightly against hers, his arm draped casually across the seat behind her shoulders, did nothing to help alleviate the situation.

He was just too close to her. Too forcefully male. Too magnetically attractive. Just too everything!

She turned to him in the semi-darkness, feeling compelled to say something, anything. 'Brice—'

'Sabina!' he murmured raggedly before his head lowered and his mouth claimed hers.

This shouldn't be happening! She was engaged to Richard. And maybe it was only a business arrangement, an 'understanding', but she still owed him her loyalty. Her gratitude.

As Brice continued to kiss her her body was suffused with a weightless lethargy, like a soaring bird, lifted high by the heated air beneath its wings, all sound stopped, everything but Brice ceasing to exist, only the feel of Brice's lips against hers important.

She couldn't have broken away from him if she had tried.

Not that she did try, pleasure such as she had never known existed coursing through her body, every part of her electrically alive now, her arms moving up about Brice's shoulders, their bodies fused together from chest to thigh as she began to kiss him back.

'That will be eight pounds fifty, guv.'

Sabina felt as if she had had a glass of cold water thrown over her, so instant was the shocked recognition of exactly what she was doing; instead of coolly repulsing Brice McAllister's kisses she had been returning them with equal passion!

She pulled back from the close proximity of him, blue eyes huge in the semi-darkness of the taxi.

Brice stared back at her, his expression unreadable, eyes remote and unfathomable, only the tell-tale passion-induced flush to the rigid hardness of his cheeks to show for the minutes they had just spent lost in each other's arms.

'Sorry to interrupt, love.' The taxi driver turned to speak

apologetically to Sabina. 'But we've been parked outside the house for about five minutes now.'

Outside Richard's house. Her fiancé's house. The house Sabina shared with him.

She drew in a deeply controlling breath. 'That's perfectly all right,' she told the driver smoothly before turning to open the door. 'No, Brice, please don't bother to get out.' To her chagrin her voice was much less controlled as she spoke to him; she was completely unable to look at him, either.

And she might as well have spoken to the door for all the notice Brice took of her!

She had hardly straightened from getting out of the taxi than he was standing beside her, having got out the other side.

'Sabina—'

'Please don't say anything, Brice,' she interrupted much more firmly than she actually felt, her head back proudly now in the darkness as she forced herself to meet his narrowed gaze. 'I very much enjoyed meeting Fergus and Chloe this evening. And thank you for dinner,' she added with a politeness she was far from feeling.

'You don't have to tell me that it will never happen again,' he cut in harshly.

'None of this evening will ever happen again,' she told him in a steely voice. 'Goodnight.' She turned on her heel and walked away, leaving him to get back in the taxi, or not, whatever his choice might be. As long as she escaped his overwhelming presence, she didn't care what he did!

Oh, God...!

Sabina leant weakly back against the solid oak front door once she was safely on the other side of it.

What had she just done?

What had they both just done?

More to the point, how did she explain to Richard, without actually telling him the truth, and totally null-and-voiding their 'arrangement', that she could no longer sit for Brice McAllister?

CHAPTER SIX

'DINNER not to your liking, Mr Brice?' Mrs Potter frowned at him as she cleared away his almost untouched plate of food.

'Dinner was fine, Mrs Potter,' Brice rasped. 'I'm just not hungry.'

He was too damned angry to be hungry. With Sabina. With Richard Latham. With himself.

Most of all with himself.

It had been three days since his dinner with Sabina. Three long, frustrating, lonely days.

Strange, loneliness was something he had never known in his life before, not even when he'd been alone. In fact, solitude to him had always been something to be welcomed, enjoyed, savoured. But all that had changed three days ago. From the moment he'd kissed Sabina.

Something had happened to him as he'd held her in his arms, as his mouth had explored hers, as she'd kissed him back with equal passion. Something he still couldn't put a name to. Something he didn't want to put a name to. All he knew was that he now knew what loneliness was, that his own company was the last thing he wanted.

Because when he was alone all he could think about was Sabina. What was she doing? Who was she with? Had she thought of him at all the last three days?

His mouth tightened frustratedly as he acknowledged that even if Sabina had thought of him it would not have been in any sort of complimentary way. How could it be, when he had abused her trust in him by overstepping the line that should have divided them?

69

God, he disgusted himself, so how could he expect her to feel any differently towards him?

Sabina was engaged to another man!

Much as Brice hated it, much as he might wish it were otherwise, it was undeniably a fact. And Sabina could only despise him for choosing to forget that.

It had been a moment of pure madness on his part, a need, pure and simple, to hold her in his arms and kiss her. And now he would probably never see her again, was sure she would never agree to sit for him again.

Although the fact that Richard Latham hadn't turned up on his doorstep demanding an explanation for Brice's behaviour towards his fiancée seemed to point to her not having told the other man that Brice had kissed her...

So how was she going to explain to Richard Latham her complete aversion to even being in the same room as Brice? Maybe she wouldn't be able to. Maybe—

Hell, he had to get out of here, do something—anything! His thoughts kept going round and round in circles, always coming back to exactly the same spot: his need to see Sabina, and the knowledge that he wasn't able to.

How—?

Mrs Potter entered the room after the briefest of knocks. 'Miss Smith is here to see you, Mr Brice,' she told him warmly.

Miss Smith—? Sabina! Here to see him...?

Mrs Potter gave him a quizzical frown. 'Shall I ask her to come in?' she prompted doubtfully.

'Yes! I mean, no. Oh, hell,' he grated, running a hand through the thick darkness of his hair.

Hair that was already tousled into disarray by his agitated fingers constantly running through it all day. He hadn't shaved the last two days, either. And, he realised as he looked down at the clothes he had on, this morning he seemed to have stepped straight back into the things he had been wearing yesterday, blue denims and black shirt, and they were both badly creased. In fact, Brice decided self-disgustedly, he looked a damned mess!

But with Sabina waiting outside in the hallway, he could hardly go upstairs, shower, shave, and change before inviting her in...

'Yes, please ask her to come in,' he instructed heavily, while at the same time his mind was racing. 'Is she alone, Mrs Potter?' He frowned, wondering if Richard Latham was with her.

'Completely alone,' Sabina coolly answered that particular question herself as she joined Mrs Potter in the doorway.

She looked sensational!

If Brice looked an unkempt mess, Sabina was glossily beautiful, wearing a glittering gold dress the same colour as that long hair cascading down her back and over her shoulders, her eyes luminous blue, lips painted a voluptuous red, long fingernails painted with the same colour varnish, her legs long and silky, delicate feet slipped into three-inch-high gold sandals. To Brice, she had never looked lovelier.

'Thank you, Mrs Potter,' he told his housekeeper harshly.

'Would you like me to bring you anything? Coffee? Tea? Some wine, perhaps?' Mrs Potter offered lightly.

'That's very kind of you—' Sabina bestowed a glowing smile on the older woman '—but I won't be staying long. I only called in on my way somewhere else.'

The last, Brice was sure, was added for his benefit. Completely unnecessarily. The fact that Sabina was here at all was unexpected; he certainly didn't delude himself into thinking she had dressed like this just to come and see him!

'What do you want?' he demanded as soon as the door had closed behind the departing Mrs Potter.

Sabina eyed him coolly. 'You really are the rudest man I've ever met,' she told him calmly.

He raised dark brows mockingly. 'At least I'm consistent.'

'True,' she drawled dismissively. 'I called in—'

'You said that,' he rasped.

'Because I know Richard intends ringing you tomorrow about commissioning the portrait,' she continued firmly. 'I want you to tell him that you can't do it,' she added hardly.

Brice eyed her with mocking amusement. 'And why should I do that?'

Sabina's gaze remained unblinkingly steady on his. 'I'm sure I don't have to explain why.'

No, she didn't have to—but there was no way, after the three days of torment he had just gone through, that he could let her off the hook so easily. Besides, the mask of polite indifference that she was showing him tonight irritated him immensely!

'You're referring to the fact that we kissed each other the other evening?' he challenged.

An angry flush darkened her cheeks. 'Besides being rude, Brice, you obviously have a selective memory,' she snapped. 'You kissed me—'

'Only initially,' he drawled in a bored voice. 'I seem to remember that you kissed me back.' He raised challenging brows.

Sabina drew in an angry breath. 'You-are-not-a-gentleman!' she bit out tautly.

Oh, yes, he was—because if he followed his ungentlemanly instincts right now, he would end up kissing her again; she was absolutely magnificent in her anger!

His mouth twisted derisively. 'And I suppose Latham is?'

She stiffened, her eyes glittering coldly blue. 'Exactly what do you mean by that remark?'

Brice shrugged. 'I don't suppose for a moment that

Latham sleeps in one bedroom of that big house the two of you share, while you sleep virginally in another!' he scorned.

If he had thought her coldly distant before, she now became the ice maiden, every desirable inch of her withdrawn behind an icy barrier Brice knew he could have no hope of penetrating.

'I don't believe that is any of your business, Mr McAllister,' she spat the last out contemptuously. 'I came here this evening hoping to appeal to your better nature—but you obviously don't have one, so—'

'Latham doesn't know about the other evening, does he?' Brice took a calculated guess, more or less sure he was right, but needing to know for certain.

She flushed. 'Richard is aware that I saw you that evening—'

'That isn't what I meant—and you know it!' he rasped.

'Tell me, Brice, can you still walk?' she taunted.

He looked down at his denim-clad legs as he stood across the room from her. 'Obviously,' he drawled.

'Then I think you can take a calculated guess that I haven't told Richard of your—overfamiliarity the other evening,' she drawled mockingly.

Brice smiled without humour. 'What you really mean is that your future husband is nothing but a thug!'

All the time knowing that if Sabina were his fiancée he would feel violent himself just at the thought of any other man kissing her, let alone actually knowing he had done so!

Sabina gave him a disgusted glance. 'You—'

'How's your mother?' Brice abruptly changed the subject, sensing Sabina was about to leave, and knowing a desperate need for her not to do so.

Having her come here at all was completely unexpected; after the other evening, Brice had been certain Sabina would ensure he never saw her alone again. The fact that she had come here like this was evidence of just how much she didn't want Richard Latham to know that, not only had Brice taken her out to dinner the other evening, but that the two of them had ended the evening by kissing each other.

Evidence of how much she loved the other man...?

She looked nonplussed now by his change of topic. 'I haven't spoken to my mother since the day we had lunch together,' Sabina answered warily.

'Putting off the evil moment?' Brice chided softly. 'Is that being completely fair to your mother? After all, from the little you told me, I doubt you were very gracious that day about her proposed holiday plans.'

Her cheeks became flushed once again. 'I really don't think this is any of your business, Brice—'

'Coward,' he murmured softly.

Her eyes widened indignantly. 'Not that it's anything to do with you—but I have every intention of talking to my mother. In my own way. In my own time.'

He nodded grimly. 'And, in the meantime, she can just sit there and stew in her own juice!'

Sabina frowned. 'You know nothing about my mother—'

'I know she cared enough to take the time and trouble to come to London to tell you about her proposed holiday to Paris, with a male friend,' Brice rasped. 'Even though she probably knew exactly how you were going to react,' he added tauntingly.

Sabina was all eyes now, huge blue pools of pained disbelief. Because he was deliberately attacking her, challenging her. But he couldn't help that; the cool Sabina, behind her wall of ice, was not acceptable to him.

Because from the moment she had arrived what he had most wanted to do was kiss her again!

Sabina swallowed hard, giving Brice a quizzical look. He looked different today, and it wasn't just the several days' growth of beard that darkened his jaw, or his rumpled hair and clothes. Those things could easily be explained in an artist of his calibre who became lost in whatever he was working on at the moment.

No, it was something else... She just didn't know what it was!

'And exactly how was that?' she finally breathed huskily.

He shrugged. 'It's okay for you to live with a man old enough to be your father, but heaven help your mother if she tries to find a little happiness of her own in her twilight years,' he rasped scathingly.

She shook her head, smiling without humour, unappreciative of any of his remark, but especially the part about Richard being old enough to be her father. 'I doubt my mother considers she has reached that at only sixty-six!' Her mother came from a long line of octogenarians.

'Exactly,' Brice pounced pointedly. 'Hell, if it were me, I would say good luck to her!'

There were plenty of replies she could have made to such a remark; predominantly that, from the safety of his own parents' obvious longevity of married life, he was hardly in a position to say how he would feel in the same circumstances.

But Sabina had finally realised exactly what Brice was doing—and she wasn't going to give him the satisfaction of being successful. Because, like a small boy, he was trying to pick a fight...

She shook her head. 'I didn't come here to discuss my mother with you, Brice.'

His mouth twisted. 'No—you came here to ask me to tell your fiancé—when he telephones!—that I can't paint you.'

And she could tell, just from looking at his face, that he wasn't going to do that!

'I've obviously wasted my time,' she acknowledged with a sigh before glancing at the slender gold watch on her wrist. 'I really don't have any more time to discuss this with you now, Brice—'

'You mustn't keep Richard waiting,' he taunted hardly. 'And I expect the attentive Clive is sitting outside in the car waiting for you too,' he added scathingly.

'Richard isn't with me this evening,' she dismissed impatiently. 'I'm working.'

She was attending a charity dinner with several other models this evening; Richard away on business again until tomorrow. But Brice was quite right about Clive waiting outside for her in the car. As he would also be waiting to take her home again once the evening was over...

She picked up her evening bag. 'I'm sorry we can't come to some sort of amicable agreement concerning the portrait, Brice,' she told him coolly. 'I really was hoping we could keep this on a friendly level.'

His eyes narrowed to green slits. 'Meaning?'

She shrugged slender shoulders. 'I'm not sure yet,' she answered slowly.

Brice watched her consideringly. 'And I'm not sure I like the sound of that.'

Sabina gave a brief smile. 'But I'm completely sure I don't give a damn how you feel about it!' she told him mildly before turning to leave.

'There's something I would like to know, Sabina.' Brice spoke softly behind her.

Too close behind her, it seemed to Sabina, the warmth of his breath brushing against the bareness of her shoulders.

Reminding her all too vividly of those minutes spent in his arms three days ago.

Remind her? She hadn't been able to put them out of her mind for a moment!

Oh, she had dated several men before meeting Richard

almost a year ago. And they had been pleasant friendships. But none of those relationships had been in the least serious, certainly none of those men causing her pulse to race and her body to turn to liquid fire. And now that she was engaged to Richard—for whatever reason!—was not the time to find herself reacting in that way three days ago, with Brice McAllister, of all people!

But she knew that she had...

She didn't turn to face Brice now, drawing in a steadying breath. 'And what's that, Brice?' she prompted mockingly.

'I'm curious to know what was in that letter you received in the post the other day to have caused you so much obvious distress at the time,'' he probed relentlessly. 'I'm referring to the letter in the green envelope,' he clarified unnecessarily.

Unnecessarily to Sabina, at least. She had known, as soon as he'd mentioned it, exactly which letter he was referring to!

She had become frozen, as if turned to stone, every muscle and sinew in her body locked in place, her breathing seeming to have become caught in her throat, literally able to feel all the blood draining from her face.

'Sabina...?' Brice's hand on her arm gently turned her to face him. 'Sabina!' he groaned worriedly as he saw her obvious physical reaction to his question.

She swallowed hard, trying to speak, but her tongue seemed to be stuck to the roof of her mouth. Her vision was blurring too, Brice's face no longer clear to her. And although she could see Brice's mouth moving, knew he must be saying something to her, the rushing noise in her ears prevented her from hearing him.

And then all she knew was blackness...

CHAPTER SEVEN

SHE looked so damned young with her eyes closed, Brice realised frowningly as he looked down at Sabina, the wariness in those deep blue eyes, that could give her such a look of maturity, hidden now behind closed lids, the thick dark lashes that lay against the delicate magnolia of her cheeks making her appear as vulnerable as a baby.

Brice had managed to catch her before she sank to the carpeted floor, swinging her up into his arms before placing her carefully on the sofa, her hair splayed out on the cushion behind her. Despite what she claimed to the contrary, she was as light as thistledown, and as Brice continued to look down at her, the slenderness of her body, the deep hollows of her cheeks and throat, he was sure she had lost weight in the last few days.

Because of him? Because he had kissed her?

Or was it because of that letter he had just taunted her about?

In view of her reaction just now to his asking her about it, the latter was probably a more accurate guess!

But who could it have been from? What could that letter possibly have contained to have this effect on her, days later?

He could try asking her that, Brice realised grimly, but he very much doubted Sabina would answer!

He frowned down at her as she began to stir, lids blinking open, only to close again as she saw him sitting beside her, looking intently down at her.

'Come on,' Brice mocked. 'It isn't that bad!'

She gave a grimace, as if to say, That's only from where you're looking, before slowly opening her eyes again. She swallowed hard, moistening dry lips. 'Do you think I could have a glass of water?' Her voice was huskily soft, her gaze avoiding meeting his.

'Don't move while I'm gone,' he warned even as he stood up to go out to the kitchen.

As he might have known, Sabina was sitting up on the sofa smoothing down her tousled hair by the time he returned with the water. 'Do you ever do as you're told?' he rasped, watching as she took one sip of the water before putting the glass down on the coffee-table in front of her.

'Rarely,' she grimaced. 'I'm sorry about that. I can't imagine what happened—'

'I can,' Brice said harshly. 'You don't look as if you've eaten a decent meal for days!' And he could tell by the way the colour darkened her cheeks that his guess about that was right. 'Why haven't you been eating?' he demanded to know.

Sabina looked up at him challengingly. 'I don't think my eating habits are any of your concern—'

'You just fainted in my house—so I'm making them my concern!' he bit out grimly. 'Well?' he barked as she made no effort to answer him.

She shook her head, once again glancing at her wrist-watch. 'I really do have to go—'

'I went outside after you fainted and told Clive to cancel your engagement for this evening,' Brice told her softly.

'You did what?' Sabina gasped, her eyes widening disbelievingly.

'I'm sure you heard what I said,' he drawled. 'I also told him you wouldn't be needing him any more this evening.'

Sabina opened her mouth to speak, and then closed it again. Before opening it again. And then closing it yet again.

If the situation weren't so damned serious, Brice would have found her reaction to his arrogance amusing. A speechless Sabina was certainly something to behold. And maybe he had been rather heavy-handed in his behaviour, but if Sabina wasn't prepared to look after herself, then someone else would have to do it for her. But considering Latham was such a watchdog in other ways—

'Where's Richard this evening?' he rasped.

'Away,' she managed to choke out, obviously still stunned by the way he had taken over her evening for her.

'Again?' Brice muttered disgustedly. 'And what does he think you are—a prize exhibit to be taken out and admired whenever he deigns to be at home?' He remembered all too clearly David Latham's opinion of his uncle.

Sabina looked deeply irritated. 'You're being ridiculous. Richard is a very busy man—'

'So am I,' Brice cut in scathingly. 'But I certainly wouldn't leave you on your own to get into this state.'

She glared at him resentfully. 'What state?'

Oh, she looked hauntingly beautiful, there was no doubting that. But she was so thin she looked as if he might snap her in half, and her eyes were like huge dark pools, the hollows of her cheeks only emphasising the shadows beneath those eyes.

Brice shook his head disgustedly. 'You're as skittish as an overbred racehorse—'

'Thank you very much!' she scorned.

'It wasn't meant as a compliment,' he snapped.

'I didn't take it as one,' she snapped right back.

'You—'

'Dinner is served, Mr Brice,' Mrs Potter appeared in the doorway to announce, obviously having knocked but not having been heard.

Not surprising really—when Brice and Sabina were as good as shouting at each other!

Sabina became very still. 'Dinner, Brice?' she questioned softly.

Brice wasn't deceived for a moment by the mildness of

her tone—Sabina was already furious over his having so arrogantly cancelled her plans for the evening; having the nerve to instruct Mrs Potter to serve dinner to them both here as an alternative was obviously going too far as far as she was concerned!

'We both need to eat, Sabina,' he told her dismissively; for some reason his own appetite seemed to have returned to him!

Her eyes flashed her anger at him, but the quick glance she gave in Mrs Potter's direction showed she was too ladylike to actually say to him what she really wanted to in front of his housekeeper.

Thank goodness!

Brice was well aware that his earlier actions had been arrogant in the extreme, but at the time he had been so worried about Sabina that worry had materialised as anger as she'd remained in the faint, so much so that he had marched straight out of the house and rapped out his instruction to Richard Latham's driver-watchdog, not even waiting to see if they were carried out before slamming back into the house.

He had merely compounded that arrogance by asking Mrs Potter, when he'd gone to the kitchen for the glass of water, if she could provide dinner for the two of them!

Brice turned to his housekeeper. 'We'll be through in a few minutes, Mrs Potter,' he assured her dismissively.

'How dare you?' Sabina turned on him as soon as they were alone again, standing up abruptly to glare across at him accusingly. 'How dare you?' she repeated in incredulous anger.

He shrugged. 'I think you need to eat, Sabina—'

'I'm not just talking about dinner, Brice,' she came back heatedly. 'How dare you cancel my plans for the evening? How dare you send Clive away? One kiss doesn't give you those sort of rights, Brice,' she told him scornfully.

After days of tension, Brice could feel himself starting

to relax. Because, despite her denials, he now knew that kiss had meant something to her—she wouldn't have mentioned it otherwise!

Too late for Sabina, he could see that she had just realised that for herself...

He grinned at her unabashedly. 'Ah, Sabina, but what a kiss!'

'You—I—you are incorrigible!' she finally spluttered weakly.

Brice shrugged. 'Part of my charm.'

Sabina eyed him scathingly, but with none of her earlier anger. 'Arrogance is not a virtue, Brice,' she told him derisively.

'Neither is starvation,' he dismissed lightly. 'Shall we go through to dinner?' he invited, dark brows raised challengingly as he held out his arm for her to take.

Sabina returned his gaze frustratedly, obviously fighting some sort of war within herself.

Brice waited for her to come to her decision. Not patiently. But he did wait. He had probably done enough bullying for one evening!

'Okay,' she finally sighed. 'But only as my driver has been dismissed, and my dinner this evening seems to have been cancelled,' she reminded pointedly. 'And under one condition...' she added huskily, her gaze steady on his.

Brice tensed warily. 'Which is?'

She drew in a ragged breath. 'No more questions about my personal correspondence,' she stated evenly.

Brice had thought it might be something like that, and it wasn't a condition he particularly wanted to agree to, especially after her reaction to his questions earlier. But if it meant Sabina stayed and had dinner with him without any more argument...

'Okay,' he agreed, once again filing that piece of information away for a future conversation. Because he had every intention, at some time in the not too distant future, of finding out exactly what had been in that letter.

Sabina made a point of not taking the arm he held out to her as they walked through to the dining-room. But that didn't bother Brice too much, either; now that she had agreed to have dinner with him he had her company for at least another couple of hours, so why push his luck? In any direction!

Brice might think he had won this round, Sabina realised as he saw her seated at the dining table before sitting down opposite her, but she could have told him differently. It merely took less effort to agree to have dinner with him than the alternative of having to call a taxi, sit and wait for it to arrive, and then finding something to eat when she got home.

At least...that was what she told herself.

She was actually very aware now that she had forgotten to eat at all today, feeling slightly shaky and light-headed. As if to prove the point, her stomach gave a hungry growl as Mrs Potter placed a bowl of thick vegetable soup in front of her seconds later.

Sabina looked up and smiled gratefully at the house-keeper. 'I hope I'm not inconveniencing you too much?'

'Not in the least,' the other woman assured her. 'It will be nice to see Mr Brice eat his dinner; he's been completely off his food this last few days,' she reproved her employer lightly before going back to the kitchen.

Sabina made a great show of eating her soup, unable to look at Brice for the moment, having trouble keeping her face straight; she wasn't the only one who hadn't been eating properly just recently.

'Okay, okay,' Brice muttered after several silent minutes had passed, 'so I haven't done justice to Mrs Potter's cooking the last three days, either.' He grimaced self-derisively.

Sabina sobered slightly, not sure that she liked the implication of that statement. It had been three days since she'd last had dinner with Brice. Since he had kissed her...

She had tried not to dwell on thoughts of that kiss the last three days, knowing she shouldn't think of it at all, but finding the memory of it popping back into her head when she least expected—or wanted—it to do so. Which was all the time!

'What a pity—this soup is delicious,' Sabina remarked blandly, unwilling to get into any more discussion about what had happened between them three days ago.

She was engaged to Richard, owed him so much, and the kiss between Brice and herself should never had happened. And the sooner it was forgotten, by both of them, the better she would like it!

'I've been thinking—'

'I really would like you—'

They both broke off, having started talking at the same time.

'You first,' Sabina invited.

'No, you go first,' Brice insisted. 'Despite what you may think to the contrary, I haven't forgotten my manners completely,' he added ruefully.

She shrugged. 'I was merely going to ask if you would reconsider not doing the portrait.' She paused in eating her soup to look at him expectantly.

'No,' he answered uncompromisingly.

Well, that was pretty blunt and to the point! But Brice was being altogether silly about this, must know that it wasn't a good idea for them to spend time alone together.

As they were doing now!

They made a very strange couple too, she realised ruefully; she was dressed to go out for the evening and meet the general public, and Brice, besides being unshaven, looked as if he might have slept in the clothes he was wearing.

'Sorry about this.' He seemed to become aware of at

least some of her thoughts, running a rueful hand over the stubble on his chin. 'I can go up and shave once we've finished our soup, if you would prefer it?' He raised dark brows questioningly.

She actually would have preferred it. But not for the reason he seemed to think. The truth was, Brice looked more piratical than ever with the dark growth of beard on the squareness of his jaw. Altogether too rakishly attractive.

What disconcerted her the most, though, was that Brice once again seemed to have picked up on at least some of her thoughts. Although not all of them, thank goodness!

'Please don't bother on my account, Brice. It's of absolutely no interest to me whether or not you've shaved today,' she told him coolly, aware by the tightening of his mouth that he didn't particularly care for her condescending tone.

'It seems I don't have the monopoly on rudeness,' he rasped harshly.

She sat back, her soup finished, a façade of unconcern firmly in place. 'You haven't told me yet what you were going to say earlier,' she reminded lightly.

Brice's irritated scowl looked as if he would have liked to continue the conversation they were having now, and then he shrugged it off impatiently. 'I'm going up to Scotland for a couple of days next weekend,' he rasped. 'I want you to come with me.'

Sabina stared at him disbelievingly; he couldn't really have just invited her to go to Scotland with him. Could he...?

His mouth twisted derisively as he took in her stunned expression. 'I wasn't suggesting an illicit couple of days away together,' he drawled mockingly. 'I'm going to my grandfather's castle.'

This explanation didn't make the invitation sound any

more innocent to Sabina; after all, he hadn't said his grandfather would actually be at the castle…!

'Exactly what are you suggesting, Brice?' she derided
mockingly.

'I—' He broke off as Mrs Potter returned to take away
their used soup bowls, waiting until the housekeeper had
once again departed before continuing. 'I know exactly
how and where I want to paint you,' he told her with
satisfaction.

'How and where…?' she repeated warily, not liking the
sound of this at all.

'I am not a portrait painter, Sabina,' he dismissed impatiently. 'I told your fiancé that from the beginning,' he
added frowningly.

'But you just insisted you're going to paint me,' she
reminded with a puzzled frown.

'I am going to paint you,' he confirmed enthusiastically.
'The way that you look, it would be a tragedy not to. But
I'm not intending to do some posed portrait of you; if
Latham wants that he can stick a photograph of you up on
the wall,' he added disgustedly. 'No, I want to paint you
in one of the turret rooms of my grandfather's castle, sitting at the open window, with that silken golden hair trailing in the wind—'

'Wearing a diaphanous gown, and little else,' Sabina
concluded derisively. 'The name Rapunzel somehow
comes to mind!' she added tauntingly.

Although that wasn't how she was feeling inside, a nervous fluttering having begun in her stomach just at the
thought of posing for Brice looking like that. What he was
proposing was pure fantasy—and she already knew that,
where Brice McAllister was concerned, she had to keep
their relationship strictly on a feet-on-the-ground basis!

Because, if she didn't, she was very much afraid she
might get caught up in the fantasy!

CHAPTER EIGHT

BRICE could already see the refusal forming on Sabina's lips. And that was something he couldn't allow.

He didn't know how, or when, the idea had first come to him, but he had suddenly known a few minutes ago exactly how he wanted to paint Sabina. That it was the only way he could paint her!

Sabina had been staring at him wordlessly, but now she shook her head. 'I really don't think that was quite what Richard had in mind when he suggested you paint me,' she began mockingly.

'As I recall, he didn't suggest it at all,' Brice rasped impatiently, remembering only too well the other man's arrogant assumption that Brice couldn't possibly turn him down. 'And I really don't give a damn what Latham "had in mind",' he dismissed scathingly. 'If he doesn't like the painting when it's finished, I'll keep the damned thing myself!' he added firmly.

He would probably want to do that anyway, if the painting turned out to be as good as he hoped it would!

Sabina shook her head slowly. 'I really can't come to Scotland with you, Brice—'

'Why the hell not?' he demanded impatiently, fuelled with enthusiasm now that the inspiration had come to him, wanting to get started on the painting as quickly as possible. 'My grandfather will be there, so your virtue will be completely safe,' he assured her dryly.

She blinked. 'Your grandfather will be there?' she repeated doubtfully.

Brice grinned. 'Once I tell him I'm bringing the beautiful model Sabina with me, I'm sure he will,' he confirmed ruefully. 'Grandfather may be in his early eighties, but he still has an eye for a beautiful woman!'

Sabina gave a vague smile at this description of his grandfather, but otherwise continued to look unconvinced.

'Whereabouts in Scotland does your mother live?' Brice tried a different approach, knowing he had to get Sabina's agreement to his idea of the two of them going to Scotland. He just had to!

'My mother?' she repeated dazedly.

'Do try to stay up with the conversation, Sabina,' Brice taunted teasingly. 'I'm suggesting we go to Scotland. Your mother lives in Scotland too.' He deliberately spoke slowly and clearly. 'If it's anywhere near my grandfather's home you could visit her while we're there.'

Sabina shook her head, this conversation obviously running on too swiftly for her liking.

But Brice was always like this when the inspiration hit him. And, despite doing numerous sketches of her, he had been in a complete fog where painting Sabina was concerned; but he could see her at his grandfather's castle now, knew exactly how right she was going to look.

'But I've never—' Sabina broke off what she had been about to say, biting her lip distractedly.

'Never what?' Brice frowned at her. 'Never visited your mother in Scotland?' he realised incredulously. 'How long did you say she's lived there?'

'Five years,' Sabina admitted reluctantly.

'Then it's way past time you did visit her,' Brice told her disgustedly.

Her cheeks flushed resentfully at his obvious rebuke. 'I think any future plans I make to see my mother are—'

'Your concern,' Brice finished derisively. 'Probably they are. But as we're going to be in Scotland, anyway—'

'I haven't agreed to go with you yet,' Sabina protested.

'You'll need to see Chloe early next week too,' he continued frowningly. 'She—'

'Chloe?' Sabina echoed dazedly. 'You mean Chloe Fox?'

'Or Chloe McCloud, whichever you prefer.' He nodded. 'I want her to design and make a dress for you. I know exactly what it has to look like, so Chloe can actually draw the design before seeing you, and then it will just be a case of making it up to your measurements. Am I going too fast for you, Sabina?' he drawled mockingly as she was looking more and more weighed down by the minute with this bombardment of information.

'Too fast!' Sabina repeated agitatedly. 'You—' She broke off as Mrs Potter arrived to serve their main course.

More of the roast chicken that Brice hadn't been able to eat earlier, served with fresh Rosti potatoes and a mixed salad.

'It looks delicious,' Sabina told the housekeeper warmly.

'Thank you, Mrs Potter.' Brice smiled his appreciation at his housekeeper before she left the room. 'You were saying?' he prompted Sabina, even as he put a large serving of the potatoes onto her plate beside the slices of chicken.

'I have no idea how my schedule stands for next week,' she told him determinedly. 'But I very much doubt I have a couple of days free in which to go up to Scotland. Even if I wanted to go,' she added irritably.

'Which you don't,' Brice easily guessed.

'Which I don't,' she echoed forcefully.

'Hmm,' he murmured consideringly. 'You work too hard, you know. Why is that?' he mused lightly. 'You've been at the top for years now, so it certainly can't be because of the money—or can it?' He stopped frowningly.

That letter she had received in the distinctive green envelope; was it possible that someone was blackmailing her? Over what, Brice couldn't even begin to imagine, but it would certainly provide an answer to more than a few questions that had been bothering Brice since the day she had received that letter...!

'Sabina—'

'It isn't the money, Brice,' she told him with certainty. 'I—like to work, to keep busy.' She gave an overbright smile. 'After all, models have a very short shelf-life; I can't expect to be at the top for much longer.'

As an attempt at diverting the conversation, it wasn't bad, Brice conceded. If he were the type of man that was easily diverted. Which he wasn't.

'Good try, Sabina,' he drawled. 'Now what's the real reason?'

Her eyes flashed deeply blue. 'I've just told you,' she snapped. 'Just as I've told you I can't disappear up to Scotland next week on such short notice,' she added impatiently. 'I have work. Commitments.'

Latham, Brice realised. No doubt the other man wouldn't be too happy at the idea of Sabina going off with him for a few days, even if it was so that Brice could paint her. The only way around that Brice could see was to include the other man in the invitation. Which was something Brice was very loath to do...

He wanted Sabina to himself, he realised, even if it were only for two days. He wanted to get to know her, away from London, her work commitments, Latham. Most of all, away from Latham!

He grimaced. 'Perhaps if I explain the situation to your fiancé—'

'Richard will be away in Australia all next week—' Sabina broke off her protest as she realised what she had just said. 'I'm due to join him at the weekend,' she added defensively.

Brice was well aware of the reason for that defence— he had been unable to hide his elation at the news that Richard Latham would be out of the country next week!

'What a pity he won't be able to join us,' Brice said

insincerely. 'But surely there can't be too much of a problem if you delay joining him until Monday,' he reasoned with satisfaction.

Yes! Things couldn't have worked out better if he had planned the whole thing himself!

Sabina gave a sigh. 'You're very persistent, Brice,' she said heavily.

And, with her admission that Latham wouldn't even be in the country next week, she had left herself with no feasible argument against Brice's plan. Except the fact that she obviously didn't want to go to Scotland with him...

Why didn't she?

She had come here at all this evening for the sole reason of persuading Brice into telling Richard Latham he couldn't paint her portrait. Why? Had the kiss they had shared three days ago affected her more than she cared to admit?

If so, as far as Brice was concerned, there was even more reason for them to go to Scotland together. Sabina might be engaged to Richard Latham, but she couldn't possibly go ahead and marry the other man if she was attracted to *him*!

Sabina had little appetite for the food in front of her, too churned up by the fact that she had talked herself into a corner where Brice's idea of going to Scotland was concerned. The trouble was, Brice tied her up in knots, so that what she really meant to say came out all wrong.

She had come here this evening with the sole intention of never seeing Brice again—and instead she found herself with a potential weekend with him in Scotland!

It just wasn't possible.

'I'm sorry, Brice, but I really do have to go now.' She placed her knife and fork on the plate beside the almost untouched food.

'Why?'

She wasn't fooled for a minute by the mildness of his tone, knew by those narrowed green eyes that his mood was far from mild. 'Because I want to,' she told him firmly, pushing back her chair to stand up.

He grimaced, standing up too. 'Mrs Potter will probably hand her notice in after this; it's the second time this evening that the dinner she prepared has gone uneaten!'

Sabina gave a rueful smile. 'I'm sure you're more than capable of handling Mrs Potter's disappointment.' In fact, she was sure that Brice was more than capable of handling most situations!

But she wasn't. And her nerve-endings had taken enough of a battering for one evening. 'Could I use your telephone to call a taxi?' she prompted huskily. As Brice had arbitrarily cancelled all her other plans for this evening, the thought of a long soak in the bath, and then a good night's sleep, was very inviting.

'I'll drive you home—'

''No,' Sabina cut in with quiet firmness. 'I think you've already done enough for me for one evening!'

Her sarcasm wasn't lost on Brice, his mouth tightening angrily at the jibe. Well, she couldn't help that; there was no getting away from the fact that he had cancelled her other plans for this evening. Or that she needed to get away from Brice, not spend more time in the confines of a car with him!

'Fine,' he finally rasped. 'I'll go and call a taxi for you now.' He strode forcefully out of the room.

That wasn't quite what she had said, but by this time Sabina felt too weary to argue with him any further. Besides, the few minutes' respite from Brice's overpowering company gave her a chance to try and ease the tension from her body.

What was it about Brice McAllister that made it so difficult for her to be in his company? Somehow she didn't think she really wanted an answer to that question. In fact, she was sure she didn't!

'The taxi will be here in a few minutes,' Brice informed her abruptly when he came back into the room. 'I'm completely serious about the two of us going to Scotland next weekend, Sabina,' he added firmly.

She knew he was serious—she just didn't want to do it. And if she didn't want to do it, she saw no reason why she should!

'We'll see,' she answered noncommittally; much as she hated to admit it, she knew she would be able to deal much more capably with this situation once she was well away from Brice.

'We most certainly will,' Brice returned determinedly.

The few minutes waiting for the taxi were not the most comfortable Sabina had ever spent, their conversation stilted to say the least, both of them heaving a sigh of relief, Sabina was sure, when the taxi finally arrived.

To her consternation Brice walked outside with her, opening the back door of the taxi for her. Sabina hesitated before getting inside, not quite sure what to say. She couldn't exactly thank him for a pleasant evening—it had been far from that!—but she somehow felt she should say something.

'You don't have to say anything,' Brice advised dryly as he seemed to read her uncertainty. 'A kiss will suffice,' he added softly even as his head lowered and his mouth claimed hers.

Sabina was initially too surprised to resist. And then as the kiss deepened and lengthened she found that she couldn't have moved away even if she had wanted to— her body simply felt too fluid to obey her commands!

Brice moved slightly away from her, one hand cupping the curve of her chin as he looked down intently into her eyes. 'I'll call you,' he told her huskily.

Sabina moved hastily away, her cheeks heated as she

got inside the taxi and closed the door firmly behind her before giving the driver her address, angry with herself as well as with Brice.

She kept her gaze firmly ahead as the car moved away from the pavement, although she was completely aware of Brice standing there watching her until the car turned the corner at the end of the road.

How dared he just kiss her whenever, and wherever, he felt like it? Almost as if he were her fiancé instead of Richard—

Dear Lord—Richard!

What on earth would he say if he knew that Brice McAllister had kissed her, not once, but twice?

She gave a self-disgusted shake of her head. Richard respected the fact that they both had busy careers, that the business relationship of their engagement worked because Richard knew he could trust her, as she trusted him. Okay, so she hadn't initiated either of the kisses between Brice and herself, but she hadn't exactly tried to stop them, either.

Why hadn't she?

That was something she really didn't want to look at too searchingly! Once she could perhaps explain away, but that kiss just now had been completely unacceptable. Not that she had initiated it, but nevertheless it shouldn't have happened.

But she didn't ever intend telling Richard about those kisses. Their own relationship wasn't an intimate one, and it would only create a situation where she was determined there should be none.

To her surprise most of the lights were on downstairs in the house when she arrived home, her relief immense when she entered the house to find Richard in the lounge listening to classical music. Something he seemed to have been doing for some time, if the glass of whisky on the table beside him was anything to go by.

'I wasn't expecting you back until tomorrow.' She smiled at him warmly.

Richard had stood up at her entry, his eyes narrowed now as he looked at her speculatively. 'Obviously not,' he drawled hardly.

Sabina was instantly—guiltily!—aware of the fact that not fifteen minutes ago Brice McAllister had kissed her. Did it somehow show on her face? Were her lips bare of gloss after that kiss? Or was it something else that gave her away...?

Richard turned to pick up his glass of whisky, taking a swallow before speaking. 'Clive returned over an hour ago,' he rasped economically, blond brows raised questioningly.

A Clive who had been arrogantly dismissed for the evening by Brice McAllister...!

She winced at the construction Richard must have put on being told that by the driver. 'I called in to see Brice McAllister on my way out this evening—'

'Yes?' Richard prompted hardly as she paused.

She sighed. 'Could I have a small glass of whisky too, do you think?'

Richard's mouth twisted derisively, even as he moved to pour the drink for her. 'Is what you're going to tell me that bad?' he prompted as he handed her the glass.

Sabina gave him a sharp look, the whisky having warmed her on its way down. 'I don't understand...?'

He shrugged, moving away slightly. 'We've both known from the beginning that our engagement is purely a business arrangement, and you've obviously just spent the evening with McAllister—'

'Hardly the evening, Richard,' she interrupted lightly. 'It's only nine-thirty now. Actually, I called in to see Brice this evening to—to—to—'

'To what, Sabina?' Richard prompted softly.

'To arrange another sitting,' she burst out in what she

knew was a defensive tone. But she couldn't help it; she simply wasn't prepared for answering Richard's probing questions so soon after Brice had kissed her. Because she felt guilty even though she hadn't been the one to initiate that kiss!

'Why not just telephone him?'

Why not, indeed? 'I was passing, anyway.' She shrugged.

'And?' Richard frowned.

'Richard, you're home a day early; let's not waste the evening talking about Brice McAllister,' she dismissed lightly, hugging his arm as she sensed his tension.

'But I don't consider it a waste of the evening,' he came back softly. 'Have you spent other evenings at McAllister's while I've been away?' he prompted lightly.

'Certainly not.' She shook her head frowningly. 'Richard, it was nothing. I didn't want to tell you this—I know how you worry—but I went to Brice McAllister's to arrange a sitting, and I—well, the truth is, I fainted,' she admitted reluctantly.

'You fainted?' he repeated frowningly, grasping her arms to look down at her searchingly. 'What's happened, Sabina? You haven't received any more of those letters?' He scowled darkly.

'No, nothing like that,' she instantly assured him. Although it had been Brice's probing about those letters that had caused her to faint. 'I forgot to eat today, that's all,' she explained with a self-conscious grimace.

'That's all?' Richard echoed reprovingly. 'You silly girl,' he rebuked huskily. 'And I've been sitting here for the last hour with all manner of thoughts going through my mind,' he admitted self-derisively. 'Have you had something to eat now?' he prompted gently.

She nodded. 'Brice insisted on feeding me.' No need to tell Richard that, because of the subject of their conversation, she hadn't been able to eat anything but a bowl of soup!

She had known from the beginning that Richard was possessive, but that possessiveness also made him protective of what he considered his. And these last few months, that was exactly what she had needed...

'Good.' Richard gave her a warm smile. 'I'm sorry if I was less than welcoming a few minutes ago. It's just that you're so beautiful, so absolutely unique—' He shook his head ruefully. 'I should have known better than to doubt you.'

Sabina swallowed hard, knowing that he wasn't altogether wrong to doubt her...

CHAPTER NINE

'WHAT do you mean, you want to bring some girl up here?' his grandfather's voice sounded impatient down the telephone line.

'Exactly that, Grandfather,' Brice replied frowningly.

He had thought it only right, before pursuing the matter with either Sabina or Richard Latham, to ask his grandfather if he minded him bringing a guest with him to Scotland next weekend. He certainly hadn't expected this reaction to his request!

'This isn't a hotel, laddie.' His grandfather's brogue deepened in his agitation. 'I know you boys have never thought so, but I do have a life of my own to live,' he added truculently. 'I don't just sit around here waiting for one of you to honour me with one of your random visits!'

Oops—he really had caught his grandfather on a bad day! And Brice was well aware of how busy the estate in Scotland kept his grandfather, the castle accompanied by several thousand acres of land, some of it given over to the breeding of deer, but the rest of it divided up amongst numerous tenants who lived on the estate. Which, despite the presence of an estate manager, still kept his grandfather very busy.

It was also quite amusing the way his grandfather still referred to Logan, Fergus, and Brice as 'boys'; they were all thirty-six years old, which hardly made them boys!

'Besides,' his grandfather continued before Brice could answer him, 'it's just possible I may have a guest of my own staying next weekend.'

'A guest, Grandfather?' Brice echoed interestedly.

'I do have friends of my own, laddie,' his grandfather rasped.

'Would this guest we're talking about happen to be female?' Brice guessed curiously.

Strange as Brice might find the idea, his grandfather was still a handsome man even though in his early eighties, and he had also been a widower for some years now...

'Don't get cheeky with me, laddie,' his grandfather snapped.

'We are talking about a female guest,' Brice realised slightly incredulously. It was one thing to make the suggestion, another to have it confirmed...!

'We aren't talking about her at all,' his grandfather bit out decisively.

'You aren't the "kiss and tell" type, are you, Grandfather?' Brice drawled mockingly, not altogether sure he was comfortable with the reversal of roles.

'Watch your tongue, boy,' the elderly man came back harshly.

This was a complication Brice had just never envisaged, he had to admit. And he wasn't a hundred per cent sure he knew how to deal with it now that it had happened!

So much for his advice to Sabina to be adult where her mother's relationship was concerned—this was his grandfather, not one of his parents, and he didn't know how to handle it!

'So the answer is no, Grandfather?' he said slowly.

'Now, I didn't say that,' the older man came back dismissively. 'I'm merely trying to point out that my home is not a hotel, somewhere for you to bring the current woman in your life—'

'Sabina isn't the current woman in my life.' More's the pity, Brice could have added regretfully. 'I've accepted a commission to paint her, that's all.' That was all!

His peace of mind had been in turmoil since the other

week when he'd first seen Sabina! And he wasn't sure that painting her was going to get her out of his system, either.

'Sabina?' his grandfather echoed sharply. 'You aren't talking about the model Sabina?'

'The one and only,' Brice confirmed wryly. 'Although I didn't know you kept up with the fashion world, Grandfather,' he added derisively. Although it wouldn't be all that difficult to have seen photographs of Sabina; her face had been adorning the front page of magazines for five years or so now.

'You don't know everything about me, Brice,' the older man scorned.

'Obviously not,' Brice confirmed dryly; he had certainly never heard anything about his grandfather having a woman staying with him before. And he didn't think Logan or Fergus had, either, otherwise they would have been sure to mention it.

'When are you thinking of coming up?' his grandfather prompted thoughtfully.

'I'm not sure. I wanted to confirm it was okay with you before making any definite plans.' And, from the sound of it, it was just as well that he had!

'It's fine with me,' his grandfather assured him lightly.

Brice frowned slightly. His grandfather hadn't sounded as if it were fine with him a few minutes ago...

'Then I'll call you later in the week to confirm a time, if that's okay with you?' he said slowly.

He had an appointment to see Richard Latham in just over an hour's time, would know better then whether or not he was going to be able to take Sabina to Scotland with him. He would have much rather just dealt with Sabina herself, but as Richard Latham was the one commissioning the painting, and—unfortunately!—he was also Sabina's fiancé, Brice had accepted it was Latham he would have to talk to.

Although he was hoping that Sabina would be there too...

It had been two days since she'd left his home so abruptly, two long days when Brice had thought of little else. But he had deliberately left it a couple of days before arranging to meet with Richard Latham; for one, he wanted to give Sabina time to get over being angry with him, for two, he hadn't wanted to look too eager!

Mostly, he admitted self-derisively, it was the latter.

All of his waking moments now, it seemed, were spent in thinking about Sabina, in remembering how she felt in his arms, the taste and feel of her lips against his.

He could never remember being this obsessed with a woman in his life before. A woman who was completely unattainable!

'Fine,' his grandfather answered him. 'But do be sure to let me know what time you're arriving,' he added warningly.

'I'll try not to catch you at an embarrassing moment, Grandfather,' he confirmed dryly, still unsure about how he felt about his grandfather having a 'girlfriend'—although he very much doubted, taking into account his grandfather's age, if that term actually applied in this case! Unless of course—

'I hope you're going to remember your manners, laddie,' his grandfather came back darkly. 'I won't have you making any of your clever remarks to—my friend.'

'I'll be on my best behaviour, Grandfather,' Brice promised frowningly; his grandfather must be serious about this woman if he felt this strongly about his family's behaviour in front of her.

Brice wasn't a hundred per cent certain how he felt about that. His grandparents had both been here for all of them when they'd been younger, his grandfather alone for the last few years; he simply couldn't envisage seeing his grandfather with anyone else but his grandmother.

Although that was probably just selfishness on his part, Brice accepted; after all, his grandfather spent most of his time on his own, the rest of them having their own busy lives to lead, when, as his grandfather had pointed out, weeks would go by without any of them giving a thought to visiting him in Scotland.

'You had better be,' came his grandfather's parting comment.

Brice sat in frowning contemplation for several minutes after the call had ended, only forcing himself to move when he realised he had less than an hour to change and drive over to Richard Latham's house. And, after all, what business was it of his whether or not his grandfather had found someone to spend time with? He was over twenty-one—well over!—a widower, and so at liberty to do with his life exactly what he wanted to do with it.

Time to take note of his own advice to Sabina where her mother was concerned, Brice realised; be happy for his grandfather, not judgmental. After all, it was his grandfather's life.

Brice's disappointment was acute when he was shown into Richard Latham's lounge an hour later and found the other man alone there. No doubt Sabina was working again, Brice acknowledged ruefully. Pity.

Richard Latham was dressed formally in a dark grey suit and white shirt, with a discreetly patterned tie of grey and red, blond hair styled short, only a distinctive sprinkling of grey at his temples.

No doubt the latter added to the other man's attractiveness, Brice acknowledged.

And Richard Latham was a handsome man, he accepted disinterestedly, ruggedly attractive, eyes of deep blue, his tall build still lithely fit despite his fifty-odd years.

But as he looked at Richard, Brice realised he disliked the other man intensely!

On first acquaintance Brice had been deeply irritated by

the other man's arrogance, but, looking at him now, Brice realised his dislike came from a different direction entirely. This man lived with Sabina, spent every day with her—every night! Most of all it was those nights that Brice hated even the thought of, he acknowledged with an inward shudder!

'Sit down,' Richard invited abruptly. 'Can I offer you a drink of some kind?' he offered coolly once Brice had done so. 'Tea? Coffee? Or would you prefer something stronger?' he drawled.

'No, thanks,' Brice refused as coolly, knowing he wouldn't be staying long enough to drink anything. Just being in the same room as this man set his teeth on edge!

The other man looked at him with narrowed blue eyes. 'In that case, what can I do for you?'

Brice's mouth twisted wryly. 'I thought I was the one who was going to do something for you? Paint Sabina's portrait,' he added harshly as the other man continued to look at him with cold enquiry.

'Ah, yes.' Richard nodded slowly, as if just remembering the fact. 'What are your thoughts on that now?'

His antagonism growing by the second, Brice thought he had better just state his case and leave—as quickly as possible!

'I'll do it,' he stated flatly. 'But not here. In Scotland. I—'

'You asked me to let you know when Miss Sabina was awake, Mr Latham.' The housekeeper had entered the room after knocking.

'Thank you, Mrs Clark.' Her employer nodded. 'Tell her I'll be up to see her in a few minutes,' he added dismissively.

'Is Sabina ill?' Brice asked worriedly once the two men were alone. It was two o'clock in the afternoon, for goodness' sake! Much as he didn't want Sabina to be ill, the alternative was totally unacceptable!

Something flickered briefly in the other man's eyes at Brice's obvious concern—irritation? Resentment? Displeasure? It was gone too quickly for Brice to tell.

Although there was no doubting that the smile Richard Latham now gave didn't quite reach the icy depths of those pale blue eyes. 'It's nothing,' he dismissed airily. 'Sabina is—delicate. A little nervy, shall we say?' he drawled softly. 'The slightest—disturbance can be quite debilitating for her, poor love.'

The other man seemed to be choosing his words carefully, and yet at the same time Brice felt Richard was also being quite deliberate. And he didn't agree with the other man that Sabina was delicate, or nervy; she seemed a little tense at times, and he wished she smiled more, but other than that she appeared to him to be a woman quite capable of dealing with anything life chose to throw at her. After all, he had been thrown at her—and she had no problem dealing with him!

'I'm sorry to hear that,' Brice answered noncommittally.

Richard Latham gave a slight inclination of his head. 'Sabina has mentioned your idea of going to Scotland to me...'

Brice tensed. 'And?'

The other man shrugged. 'I see no reason why we shouldn't accept your invitation.'

'We'?

Safe in the knowledge the other man would be out of the country, Brice had made that dismissive remark to Sabina about it being a pity that Richard couldn't join them, but it had only been made because Sabina had told him the other man would be in Australia; he hadn't actually meant the invitation to include the other man. Now it looked as if he might have been taken at his word!

Brice sat tensely on the edge of his chair now; having Richard Latham with them in Scotland was the last thing he wanted! 'Sabina led me to believe that you wouldn't be able to make it?'

'Did she?' the other man returned mildly. 'Change of plans,' he dismissed with satisfaction. 'We would both love to join you in Scotland for the weekend.'

So much for the initial impression the other man had given of not knowing the reason for Brice's visit here today!

He gave the other man a narrow-eyed look, not fooled for a moment by Latham's surface charm and refined manners; Richard Latham was every bit as dangerous as his nephew David had warned Brice he could be.

And Sabina was engaged to marry the man!

'Brice has exquisite taste,' Chloe murmured with satisfaction as she slightly adjusted the sash beneath Sabina's breasts, before standing back to admire her work.

Brice was many things, Sabina would have agreed, but a man of taste would be far from the top of her list. Not that the strapless gold gown he had asked Chloe to design for her to wear for the painting of the portrait wasn't absolutely beautiful, because it was; there was just so much more to Brice than the artist.

She had hardly been able to believe it when Richard had informed her that the two men had arranged for all three of them to go up to Scotland this weekend. She had thought, by telling Richard of Brice's suggestion, that he would deal quickly and negatively with the matter; instead Richard had decided to delay his trip to Australia in order to go with her! And without making a scene out of the whole thing, Sabina had been cornered into going along with the plan.

Which was why she had this fitting with Chloe Fox on the day prior to their departure to Scotland!

She'd had the feeling, since first meeting Brice McAllister, of being swept along by the force of a tidal wave—and it wasn't a feeling she found in the least comfortable!

'Do say you like it,' Chloe encouraged now.

It would be impossible not to compliment the other woman on the gown; the material, as Sabina had mockingly suggested to Brice days earlier, was diaphanous gold, her shoulders left completely bare, the material fitting snugly over her breasts, with that sash beneath emphasising the slenderness of her waist, the rest of the gown a floating gold haze down to her bare feet. Sabina was sure she had never worn anything so beautiful.

'It's lovely.' She squeezed the other woman's arm reassuringly.

'Do you think Brice will like it?' Chloe frowned worriedly.

Sabina bit back her tart retort about not caring whether Brice liked it or not, very aware of the fact that, as well as being a very successful fashion designer, Chloe was also married to Brice's cousin, Fergus.

'He's going to love it,' Brice remarked huskily from behind them.

Sabina swung sharply round at the sound of his voice, the colour first flooding and then as quickly receding from her cheeks at the open admiration in Brice's gaze as he looked at her approvingly.

It was only the gown he was admiring and not her personally, she hastily admonished herself. She must try and remember that. The only problem with doing so was that every time she saw Brice things had a habit of becoming very personal indeed!

'I'm so glad you like it,' Chloe said with obvious relief.

'It's perfect,' Brice reassured her as he stepped further into Chloe's fitting-room, dressed in casual denims and a black fitted tee shirt, the latter showing his muscular arms and chest.

Such a startling contrast to how civilised he had looked in black evening clothes!

'You've had your hair cut,' Chloe realised as she looked at him appreciatively.

He had too, Sabina noticed, the over-long dark hair gone in favour of a much shorter style, almost Roman. Somehow it just succeeded in making him appear more ruggedly attractive than ever!

Brice didn't look pleased at Chloe's observation, putting up a self-conscious hand to the darkness of his hair. 'I thought Bohemian was a little out of date,' he drawled self-derisively.

Chloe laughed softly. 'It suited you! I'll just go and rustle us all up some coffee,' she added lightly before leaving the room.

Sabina was very conscious of being left alone with Brice, not quite able to meet the searching gaze she sensed was turned in her direction.

'I'm not quite sure I know how to take Chloe's last remark,' Brice finally murmured dryly.

Sabina didn't believe that for a moment—he knew exactly how to take Chloe's remark; Chloe obviously adored all of her husband's family, would never insult any of them.

Besides, there was no getting away from the fact that Brice was a magnetically attractive man, no matter whether his hair was long or short.

'I'll just go and change back into my own clothes,' Sabina told him huskily, still having trouble looking at him directly.

'That gown is your "own clothes",' Brice assured her firmly. 'It will go on Latham's bill for the portrait,' he added with amusement as she raised questioning brows.

'Of course.' She nodded abruptly. 'Nevertheless...' She moved towards the cubicle where she had changed earlier, her normal grace of movement seeming to have deserted her as she bumped into a chair on the way in an effort to avoid walking too close to the immovable Brice.

One of his hands snaked out as she passed, his fingers lightly encircling the top of her arm. 'Are you feeling better now?' he prompted huskily, his gaze searching on the paleness of her face.

'Better…?' She frowned, her brow clearing as she realised he was referring to the fact that she had been in bed when he'd called to see Richard the other day. 'Just a slight tummy disorder,' she excused dismissively.

Brice made no effort to release her, standing very close, the warmth of his breath stirring tendrils of hair at her temple. 'Latham seemed to imply it was something else,' he said slowly.

'You must have misunderstood.' She shook her head, her expression deliberately bland. She had actually received another disturbing letter the particular day Brice was referring to—but she had no intention of him ever knowing about that!

Those green eyes were narrowed as Brice continued to look down at her searchingly. 'No, I don't think so,' he finally murmured softly.

Sabina shrugged dismissively, giving an overbright smile. 'So we're off to Scotland tomorrow,' she deliberately changed the subject.

'So *we* are,' Brice confirmed dryly. 'What's wrong— doesn't Latham trust you to be on your own with me in Scotland for two days?' he added scornfully.

She gave him a derisive look. 'I don't think it's me he doesn't trust,' she returned pointedly.

Brice grinned, a wolfish grin of pure devilment. 'He could be right!' he murmured with satisfaction.

Going on past behaviour, she was sure she was right! Although she also knew she couldn't claim to be completely blameless those times she had been in Brice's arms; somehow she just seemed to find herself there!

And Chloe, Sabina suddenly realised, was taking an awfully long time to prepare the coffee...

'Have you telephoned your mother yet?'

Sabina looked up frowningly at the unexpectedness of Brice's question. 'My mother...?'

He gave an impatient sigh. 'We're going to Scotland. Your mother lives there. Or have you forgotten?' he added hardly.

'Of course I haven't forgotten,' she snapped, at the same time shaking off his restraining hand on her arm. 'But my mother and Richard—' She broke off with an annoyed sigh as she realised what she had been about to say. It was simply none of Brice McAllister's business!

'Your mother and Richard...' Brice repeated thoughtfully. 'Your mother doesn't approve of your aged fiancé!' he guessed triumphantly.

Sabina gave him an impatient grimace. 'Richard isn't "aged",' she defended irritably. 'And there's no law that says my mother has to approve of my choice of fiancé. Or, indeed, vice versa,' she added coolly.

'Latham doesn't like your mother, either,' Brice realised derisively. 'Well, I can quite understand your mother's feelings in the matter; after all, the man is only about ten years younger than she is! But I'll reserve judgement as to whether or not he's right about your mother,' he added dryly.

'You'll "reserve judgement"—' Sabina repeated incredulously. 'Brice, you aren't likely to meet my mother. Besides, none of this has anything to do with you,' she snapped impatiently.

'Nothing at all,' he agreed, stepping back, crossing his arms in front of his chest as he did so. 'Tell me,' he mused softly, 'does anyone like your fiancé? Apart from you, of course,' he added scornfully.

She gasped incredulously. 'Brice, you go too far—'

'Not as far as I would like to go, believe me,' he grated harshly.

Sabina did believe him. That was the trouble. Brice was a law unto himself. Heaven knew what this weekend was going to be like!

She had thought, when Richard had decided he would accompany her, that it would at least solve one problem for her concerning this proposed trip to Scotland; Brice wouldn't be able to just kiss her whenever he felt like it with her fiancé around. But with the unmistakable antagonism from Brice directed towards Richard, she wasn't sure Richard's presence wasn't going to just make the weekend even more unbearable.

If that were possible!

The sooner this portrait was completed and she no longer had to see Brice, the better she would like it!

Where on earth was Chloe with that coffee? More to the point, perhaps, had the other woman known Brice would be calling in here today?

'There is just one other thing about this weekend...' Brice said slowly.

Sabina eyed him warily. 'Yes?'

Brice shrugged. 'My grandfather is in his eighties...'

Her tension increased. 'Yes?'

'This is no moral judgement on your lifestyle, I hope you understand?' He grimaced.

No, Sabina didn't understand—yet. But she had a definite feeling she was very shortly going to!

'Go on,' she invited huskily.

'It's quite simple, really,' Brice continued lightly. 'How you and Latham live when you're in London is your business. But when in Rome—or, in this case, Scotland...' He paused.

'Brice, would you just get to the point?' she snapped, having a feeling that Brice was enjoying this. Whatever 'this' was!

'The point is, Sabina,' he bit out succinctly, 'that my grandfather, being elderly, also has some rather old-fashioned views. And the fact that you and Latham live together when you're in London does not mean my grandfather is willing to accommodate that arrangement when you're in his home! Consequently, you and Latham will be given separate bedrooms during your stay in Scotland,' he concluded with satisfaction.

That was the point!

Sabina could feel the colour suffusing her cheeks, swallowing hard before speaking—she didn't want her voice to come out less than assured. Even if she felt less than assured!

'I'm sure that neither Richard nor I will have a problem with that,' she told him coolly.

Brice's expression darkened. 'I don't give a damn how Latham feels about it. It's you I wanted to save from any embarrassment,' he added grimly.

'How thoughtful of you, Brice,' she said dryly—sure that his actions had nothing to do with kindness. He seemed to spend most of his time embarrassing her in one way or another! 'Now, if you'll excuse me,' she added lightly. 'I really should change out of this gown.' She moved away.

'One other thing, Sabina...' Brice called after her.

She stiffened, turning slowly. 'Yes?' she prompted warily.

His eyes glittered, with amusement, or something else, Sabina couldn't tell. As she couldn't tell too much from his bland tone when he finally spoke, either. 'It's a very old castle, centuries old, and while over the years my grandfather has had a lot of the modern conveniences discreetly installed—'

'You mean it now has indoor plumbing?' Sabina taunted. Blonde brows raised mockingly.

'Amongst other things,' Brice confirmed dryly. 'But I

was actually referring to the fact that my grandfather hasn't had too much success solving the problem of creaking doors and floors,' he concluded challengingly.

Creaking doors and floors—?

Sabina's frowning brow cleared, her cheeks filled with angry colour now as she realised exactly what Brice was intimating; he was warning her that any nocturnal wanderings, by Richard or herself, would in all likelihood be heard by the people in bedrooms close by!

Her gazed was steely as she looked across at him. 'I'm sure that Richard and I can manage to sleep alone for two nights,' she snapped, an angry edge to her tone. 'If that's all…?' she prompted coldly, not waiting for his reply before marching determinedly over to the cubicle and closing the door firmly behind her.

How dared he? How dared he!

Moral judgement on her lifestyle, indeed! Brice knew absolutely nothing about her 'lifestyle' when she lived in London.

Absolutely nothing!

Because if he did, he would already have known that she and Richard had never done anything else *but* occupy separate bedrooms…

CHAPTER TEN

BRICE wished, and not for the first time, that he had accepted Richard Latham's offer to drive himself and Sabina up to Scotland independently of Brice. At the time it had seemed simpler to Brice if they all arrived together; for one thing Latham had no idea, once he reached Scotland, of how to actually get to the castle, and for another, Brice had used the excuse to spend as much time in Sabina's company this weekend as possible. But spending time with Sabina in the company of her fiancé was not a pleasant experience.

Not for Brice, anyway. The other couple seemed to feel no such inhibitions, chatting away together quite happily in the back of Brice's car. Almost as if Brice were superfluous. He might just as well have been the damned chauffeur!

'I hope I'm not driving too fast for you?' he rasped, glancing briefly in the driving mirror—only to find Sabina looking back at him with mockingly raised brows. Almost as if she were well aware of how disgruntled he felt. Minx!

'Not at all,' Richard Latham was the one to dismiss. 'We were just saying we hadn't realised how beautiful it is up here.'

'Honeymoon country,' Brice rasped.

'The Prince and Princess of Wales certainly thought so,' Richard Latham acknowledged dismissively.

'But look what happened to their marriage,' Brice couldn't resist returning caustically.

Richard laughed softly. 'I had the Caribbean more in mind for our honeymoon.'

He would, Brice acknowledged irritably, the thought of

113

Sabina spending a honeymoon anywhere with the other man not exactly improving his mood.

Although another glance in the driving mirror lifted his spirits a little when he saw Sabina was looking at her fiancé with more than a little surprise, giving Brice the impression this was the first she had heard about a honeymoon, in the Caribbean or anywhere else.

In which case, Brice acknowledged slowly, that comment about their honeymoon must have been a direct barb aimed at him...

He straightened in his seat a little at the realisation. He had been wary when Latham had changed his plans and decided to come to Scotland with them, but this last exchange seemed to confirm his suspicion that Richard Latham was aware of Brice's personal interest in Sabina...

Great! Now it seemed his every move this weekend, every word he spoke to Sabina, was going to be under scrutiny.

'My grandfather's estate,' he rasped unwelcomingly as he turned the car into the long driveway that led up to the castle.

'It's beautiful,' Sabina murmured wonderingly a few minutes later, having driven up through the huge herds of deer, the castle itself now in sight.

Brice had been used to staying at his grandfather's castle all his life, knew it as his second home, but that didn't mean he didn't still appreciate the haunting beauty of the castle itself, with its mellow stonework, and huge romantic turrets reaching up into the cloudless sky.

'I believe my fiancée fancies herself as a Lady of the Castle,' Richard Latham drawled a few minutes later as they got out of the parked car, Sabina's pleasure obvious by the look of wonder on her face as she looked around her.

Brice eyed the other man coldly. 'I believe my grandfather is already spoken for,' he returned icily before turning to smile at Sabina, her almost childlike pleasure in her surroundings giving him pleasure too.

'Never mind, Sabina.' Richard Latham put his arm about Sabina's shoulders with light possession. 'If you really want a castle, I can always buy you one.'

Almost as if he were indulging a child with a new bicycle, Brice acknowledged frowningly.

This was not going to be an easy weekend to get through, he realised heavily, when everything the other man said and did irritated him almost to the point of violence. How much more pleasant it would have been if he could have brought Sabina here on her own, sharing the unusual serenity of the family home with her, showing her round, walking the grounds with her, going down to the stream where the family fished for salmon.

'This castle has been in my family for centuries,' he told the other man scathingly.

'Brice is right, Richard.' Sabina spoke huskily. 'This sort of beauty can only be inherited, not bought.'

Brice watched as the other man's mouth tightened fractionally, his obviously having taken exception to the conversation. Or, at least, Sabina's part of it...

'I'm not so sure we inherited it originally,' he told them lightly as he led the way up the stone steps to the huge oak front door. 'I believe one of our ancestors claimed it for his own after being involved in a raid where the original owner was killed!'

'The Scots have always loved a fight, haven't they?' Richard Latham said mildly.

Too mildly, as far as Brice was concerned, sure that there had been a double edge to the other man's remark. Well, if the other man thought he was about to give him a fight over Sabina, he was wrong; Sabina was an independent woman of twenty-five, not a possession for two men to fight over as if she were the prize!

'We have been known to dispose of the odd unwanted

Sassenach,' his grandfather was the one to dryly answer the other man as he stood silhouetted in the now open doorway, light streaming out welcomingly from inside the castle.

'Grandfather!' Brice smiled as he moved forward to give his eldest relative the customary hug.

'So you've arrived at last, laddie,' his grandfather rebuked as he stood back. 'Although I might be persuaded into forgiving you for delaying dinner—' his eyes gleamed admiringly as he turned his attention to Sabina '—if you will introduce me to this beautiful young lady,' he added charmingly.

'Sabina,' she huskily introduced herself as she held out her hand, looking beautiful, as Brice's grandfather had just said, in a fitted black dress, her hair gleaming pure gold as it flowed down over her shoulders to her waist. 'And I'm afraid I'm the one you have to blame for our tardiness,' she added with a grimace. 'I had a little trouble deciding what I would need to pack for a weekend in Scotland.'

Brice's grandfather had retained a hold on her hand, tucking it securely into the crook of his arm now as he turned to take her inside. 'I'm sure you always look beautiful whatever you wear,' he told her gallantly.

Brice shot Richard Latham a sideways glance, not altogether sure he liked the look of derision on the other man's face as he watched Hugh walk away with his fiancée. 'Help me carry the luggage in, Latham,' he instructed harshly, opening up the boot of the car, at the same time sure that the other man wasn't accustomed to carrying his own luggage.

A learning experience for him, then, Brice decided hardly. His grandfather employed several household staff, and the castle was run with extreme efficiency by all of them, but that didn't mean Richard Latham could expect a free ride this weekend. No matter what he might be used to!

Brice came to a halt in the doorway of the sitting-room a few minutes later, after delivering the luggage to the bedrooms, as he heard Sabina laughing with his grandfather. It was a huskily girlish sound, completely uninhibited.

'Sorry,' Richard Latham rasped as, given no warning of Brice's sudden stop, he walked straight into his back. 'What's the hold-up, McAllister?' he prompted mockingly.

The 'hold-up' was the complete novelty, to Brice, of hearing Sabina laugh!

It was a wonderful sound, deep and natural, hinting at a slightly wicked sense of humour if allowed free rein. As it was now, Sabina's cheeks flushed, her eyes bright, as she obviously enjoyed her conversation with Brice's grandfather.

'Well, don't just dawdle in the doorway, laddie,' his grandfather instructed lightly as he looked up and saw Brice standing there. 'Make yourself useful and offer our guests a drink.'

Brice was used to his grandfather treating him as if he were still six years old, but he could see that Sabina was enjoying the novelty of it, that smile still lurking about her mouth and eyes as she looked across at him.

Brice felt some of the tension he had known on the journey here ease, suddenly feeling, as he saw how relaxed Sabina was with his grandfather, that it was going to be an okay weekend after all—with or without the presence of Richard Latham!

'What would you like to drink, Sabina?' Brice offered dryly as he moved to the array of drinks that stood on top of a glass cabinet. 'It seems we have white or red wine.' He scrutinised the bottles. 'Gin. Vodka. Or there's whisky, if you would prefer it.'

No doubt, being in Scotland, the men would be drinking

whisky, Sabina acknowledged ruefully, opting for the white wine herself; she had never been particularly keen on strong spirits.

'Isn't this wonderful?' she prompted Richard as he crossed the room to sit down next to her on the sofa.

'Wonderful,' he echoed, with a definite lack of enthusiasm—to Sabina, at least—in his voice.

She gave him a frowning look. Richard couldn't possibly not like this place. It was the most beautiful home she had ever seen, the furniture obviously all antique, suits of armour, swords and helmets, adorning the mellow stone walls. She had even seen a cannon at the bottom of one of the staircases that obviously led up to the turret bedrooms.

Visions of Rapunzel, she had teased Brice last week when he'd made the suggestion of their coming here so he could paint her. But now that she was here Sabina could see exactly why he had found the idea so intriguing. The castle was enchanting, like something out of a fairy story!

'It's very remote here,' Richard remarked as Brice handed him his requested glass of whisky. 'And it must cost you a fortune in heating bills.'

Hugh McDonald's eyes narrowed. 'The remoteness means we aren't bothered too much by nosy sightseers,' he rasped pointedly. 'And if you have to count the cost then you can't afford to live here,' he added dryly.

Richard's practical remark had given the air a certain tension that hadn't been there a couple of minutes ago, Sabina realised regretfully. She was sure Richard hadn't intended any insult, but at the same time she was aware that one had been taken.

'I thought we were to be five for dinner this evening, Grandfather?' Brice remarked lightly as he sat in one of the chairs opposite.

Hugh gave him a steely look. 'My guest will be arriving tomorrow,' he answered abruptly.

'I'm looking forward to it,' Brice returned with relish.

Sabina looked at each of the two men, sensing something in the conversation that neither she nor Richard were aware of. But then, why should they be? Hugh and Brice had a relationship that had existed long before, and was completely separate from, this weekend.

'Could I possibly go upstairs and freshen up before dinner?' She turned to smile at Hugh as she put down her wineglass. 'I feel a little dusty from travelling.'

'You see, Brice, I've been telling you for years to get yourself a decent car,' his grandfather taunted, the teasing obviously a regular thing between the two men; Brice's black Mercedes was obviously a top-of-the-range model, the last word in luxury.

Brice shook his head, standing up. 'I shall treat that remark with the contempt it so obviously deserves,' he dismissed before turning to Sabina. 'I'll take you upstairs and show you your room,' he told her huskily.

She should have realised that Brice would be the one to take her up to her bedroom, Sabina admonished herself as she stood up to follow him. She should have done. But she hadn't.

She had promised herself before leaving London earlier today that she would make every effort to be alone with Brice as little as possible this weekend. And within minutes of their arrival she found herself exactly that!

'Don't be long, Sabina,' Richard told her softly as she reached the doorway. 'I'm sure we've delayed Mr McDonald's dinner enough already this evening.'

'Mr McDonald,' Sabina mused as she followed Brice out into the hallway. Strange, she had found no difficulty in calling the elderly man Hugh from the moment he'd asked her to do so. Except...he hadn't offered Richard the same intimacy.

Just an oversight, she decided. After all, she had been with Hugh the whole time the two men had been taking the luggage upstairs, whereas Richard had only just joined them.

'Mind yourself on the narrowness of the stairs,' Brice warned as she followed him up the stone steps.

It was a timely warning, Sabina having to hold onto the rope on the wall that acted as a banister several times as they negotiated the narrow winding of the staircase.

'After London this is like a different world,' she said almost dazedly, feeling as if she had been picked up and placed in a time warp.

Bruce turned at the top of the stairs to wait for her. 'You'll find the "indoor plumbing" perfectly satisfactory,' he assured her dryly.

Sabina felt the colour in her cheeks as he reminded her of her mockery the day before. Trust Brice to throw that remark back at her! She decided not to qualify the remark with an answer.

Although she did make a mental note to be more careful in future what she did say to Brice. If she could be any more careful than she already was!

Sabina had never seen a circular bedroom before, the luxuriously furnished room Brice showed her into decorated in warm cream and golds.

But it was the narrow windows that intrigued her, and she hurried to each of them in turn to look out at the three-hundred-and-sixty-degree views still visible in the fading light of evening: a forest to one side, a lake to another, walled gardens to another, and the herds of deer grazing to the front of the castle.

'If I lived somewhere like this I would never want to leave,' she breathed wonderingly.

'If you lived here, neither would I,' Brice answered huskily from just behind her.

Far too close behind her, Sabina discovered as she swung round, finding herself almost pressed against his chest, becoming very still, her breathing shallow.

It was as if time were standing still as they looked at each other in the twilight, Brice's face vividly clear to her, his eyes a sparkling emerald-green, the intimacy of his words laying heavily between them.

She should stop this, break the spell—except that was exactly what it felt like, as if she were bewitched, by both Brice and her surroundings.

'I had better rejoin the others,' he finally murmured gruffly.

'Yes,' she confirmed. But she wasn't altogether surprised when he made no effort to do so.

A nerve pulsed in his jaw as he continued to look at her, the very air between them seeming to crackle with an unspoken awareness.

'You really should go down now,' Sabina told him huskily.

He sighed. 'Yes.'

But still he didn't do so, neither moving away nor reaching out to touch her. Just standing there.

He drew in a ragged breath. 'Sabina—'

'Go, Brice,' she cut in softly. 'Please!' she added firmly before he could say anything else.

His mouth tightened. 'Yes.' He nodded abruptly, stepping back. 'I'll see you downstairs in a few minutes,' he added before finally leaving the bedroom.

Sabina didn't move, couldn't move, clasping her hands together in front of her to stop them shaking. What was happening to her?

No—not what was happening to her; what had already happened to her?

She was engaged to marry Richard, had so much to be grateful to him for, knew that she was safe with him. And yet she had just made a discovery that threatened to put all of that in jeopardy.

She had fallen in love with Brice McAllister!

CHAPTER ELEVEN

'FOR goodness' sake relax, Sabina,' Brice rasped impatiently as he looked at her over the top of the canvas he was working on. 'I've already eaten this morning; I'm not about to gobble you up as an after-breakfast treat!' he added disgustedly.

They had been working on the portrait barely half an hour, Sabina standing stiffly across the room from him, wearing the shimmering gold gown, turned slightly away as she looked wistfully out of the window. And not once during that thirty minutes had Sabina been what Brice would have described as relaxed.

When in reality he should be the one who couldn't relax—because when he sat back and glanced across at Sabina it was to see only her head and shoulders, alluringly bare shoulders that conjured up visions in his head of her completely naked.

'I didn't think you were,' she answered him dryly now. 'It's just—I'm a little cold,' she dismissed awkwardly.

A little cold! Brice would have described it as more than that. Since she'd rejoined the three men before going in to dinner the previous evening, Sabina's whole attitude had bordered on the icy, and it had remained that way. Towards him, at least...

He shouldn't have lingered last night having taken her to her bedroom, he acknowledged that; he just hadn't been able to drag himself away. She had just looked so right in that setting, so absolutely perfect; and the realisation had very little to do with painting her in these surroundings!

One positive thing to have come out of her obvious coolness towards him: Richard Latham, basking in the warmth of Sabina's attentions, had become quite convivial company as dinner had progressed, showing a relaxed, charming side of him that Brice, for one, would rather not have seen—it was probably the side of him that Sabina loved!

It certainly hadn't succeeded in encouraging Brice to like Richard Latham any better, and he had seen his grandfather shooting the other man a couple of narrow-eyed glances of speculation during the evening too.

The fact that his grandfather didn't seem to like the other man either had cheered him a little—perhaps his own dislike wasn't so misplaced, after all? But only a little, Brice having wished the evening and night over so that he could once again be alone with Sabina.

But with Sabina still in this coolly remote mood, it wasn't turning out to be much fun!

He stood up abruptly. 'Your heart really isn't in this, is it?' he rasped impatiently. 'Even for Latham's sake,' he added scornfully.

Sabina looked away. 'If I could just have the window closed…?'

'Why not?' He strode across the room and slammed the window shut with barely repressed violence, drawing in a deeply controlling breath before turning back to her, realising that his tension was becoming as acute as her own. 'What is it, Sabina?' he prompted gently.

She took a step back. 'I—you didn't—explain, that the room you wanted to paint me in was your bedroom!' she burst out accusingly, her cheeks bright red, whether with temper or embarrassment Brice wasn't sure.

So that was it! This morning, at least…

Brice shrugged. 'This isn't just my bedroom when I'm here; it's also my studio.' Obviously, with all his canvases and paints about the room.

Although, he supposed—and he had never really thought about it before!—it must seem a little strange with his double bed in the room too... He had never thought of it—because he had never had a woman in his 'studio' here before. For any reason.

His mouth twisted derisively. 'Latham wouldn't like it, hmm?' he scorned.

Sabina's eyes flashed deeply blue. 'I don't like it,' she corrected firmly.

'Why don't you?' he taunted.

She moved sharply across the room to stare out the window that looked towards the lake. 'It's so peaceful here...' she murmured almost to herself.

Brice looked across at her with narrowed eyes. 'You haven't answered my question,' he rasped determinedly.

Sabina glanced back at him, the frown having eased from between her brows as she'd gazed outside. 'Because I don't believe it needs answering,' she told him softly.

He drew in a sharp breath. 'Sabina—'

'Where has your grandfather taken Richard this morning?' she prompted lightly.

To the top of a mountain and pushed him off, for all Brice cared! Although he didn't for a moment think it was something his grandfather would do. Or that it was a reply Sabina would care for.

'I believe they went for a drive round the estate,' he dismissed uninterestedly. 'Don't worry, Sabina, I'm sure you'll see your fiancé again soon,' he added tauntingly.

She shook her head. 'I'm not worried,' she assured him dryly.

Not about that, anyway, Brice acknowledged frowningly. But she was troubled about something...

'Sabina, if you don't tell me what's wrong, how can I help you?' he said gently.

She gave him an incredulous glance. 'I don't remember saying there was anything wrong! Neither do I remember asking for your help!' she added dismissively.

'But you obviously need someone's help,' he bit out impatiently. 'So why not mine?'

Sabina shook her head. 'I have no idea what you're talking about, Brice. And if I should have any worries,' she continued firmly as he would have spoken, 'I have a fiancé, and a mother, I can discuss them with, as necessary.'

And not with the relative stranger who happened to have taken the liberty of kissing her a couple of times, her words clearly implied!

He shrugged. 'I had the distinct impression you don't have that sort of relationship with your mother. Did you call her, by the way, to tell her you're in Scotland for the weekend?'

Sabina's mouth tightened impatiently at this sudden veer in the conversation. 'You're very persistent, Brice,' she snapped.

'Well?' He raised dark, uncompromising brows.

'No, I didn't,' she answered irritably.

'Why the hell not?' he rasped.

She shrugged. 'Scotland is a big place—'

'Where does your mother live?' Brice snapped, his mouth twisting angrily as she named a village only five miles away. 'Sabina—'

'Will you just leave it, Brice?' She moved impatiently, returning to her position across the room. 'I thought we came here so you could paint,' she added pointedly.

'I could always try telephoning her myself; there can't be too many Smiths in this area,' Brice said dryly.

Sabina glared angrily. 'You could always try minding your own business!'

He held up his hands defensively. 'I'm only trying to help, Sabina.'

'And I've just told you I don't need your help,' she returned with displeasure. 'My relationship with my mother is my business, Brice, not yours,' she rasped.

'Or not. As the case may be...' he said softly.

'Oh, this is hopeless!' Sabina threw up her hands in disgust before marching over to the door. 'I need some fresh air,' she bit out tersely. 'We can resume this later,' she added in a tone of voice that brooked no argument.

It was a tone that even Brice knew he would be wise to take note of!

What was the saying, it was always the quiet ones to watch out for...? Sabina, for the most part, was coolly self-possessed, seemingly completely unruffled, but the last few minutes had shown him there was also another side to her; Sabina, if pushed too far, came out fighting!

On balance, Brice decided it was a trait he rather liked...

What a disaster! What an absolute mess, Sabina muttered to herself as she changed out of the gold gown into a pink tee shirt and denims, fully intending to go ahead with her avowal of needing some air.

She straightened from putting on her sandals, breathing deeply. What was she going to do? What could she do?

She was engaged to Richard, a man who had never shown her anything but kindness and concern, and she was in love with Brice, a man who— Who what? A man who had also shown her kindness and concern. In his own way.

But Brice had shown her something else, given her a realisation of her own capacity for passion that, until meeting him, she hadn't known existed.

How could this have happened to her?

Last November she had been deeply upset, her self-confidence in shreds because of what had happened. Richard had already been a friend, she'd occasionally had dinner with, and having seen her obvious distress he had made his suggestion that, for their mutual benefit—Sabina for Richard's protection, Richard because he liked the idea of being seen with the most photographed model in the world—the two of them become engaged, it hadn't taken Sabina too long to decide that she liked the idea, too.

But she hadn't realised when she'd come to that under-standing with Richard that she was capable of loving someone in the way she now loved Brice. If she had thought for a moment she could ever feel this way about another man she would never have accepted Richard's kind offer.

Sabina had gone round and round in her head with these same thoughts as she'd lain in bed the previous evening unable to sleep, wondering what to do next.

One thing she did realise…she had to tell Richard how she felt, knew she could no longer go on being engaged to him, taking advantage of his kindness, sharing his home with him, when she had these feelings, longings, for an-other man.

And she had no idea how to go about telling Richard that!

If she had known, even partially guessed, how this weekend was going to change her life, then she would have run as fast and as far as she could in the other direc-tion.

And being alone with Brice in his bedroom-studio, with her newly discovered feelings towards him, had been ab-solute torture.

She stood up, tired of her own company too now; it was too easy to just sit and think when she was alone.

The gardens, the ones she could see from her bedroom window. She would go there. Anywhere, to get away from Brice!

And maybe, by the time she had taken a leisurely stroll through the gardens, Hugh and Richard would have re-turned from their drive. Although the thought of seeing Richard, with her emotions in such confusion, wasn't par-ticularly appealing, either. Because she knew, instinctively, that he was not going to be pleased with what she had to say to him…

Oh, damn Brice McAllister. She wished she had never met him.

'Going for a walk?'

Sabina turned sharply as, having reached the bottom of the stairs in preparation of escaping, she found herself confronted with Hugh McDonald as he came out of a room at the end of the hallway.

'Richard has borrowed the car to drive to the village and pick up a newspaper,' Hugh supplied the answer to the question Sabina had just been about to ask.

She smiled indulgently. 'He hates it if he misses the business section even for one day.'

Hugh nodded. 'So he said. If you're going for a walk, would you like some company?' he prompted gently.

She would love some company, anything to escape her own tumultuous thoughts. But… 'I'm sure we've already disturbed your routine enough for one day,' she excused.

'Not in the least,' the elderly man dismissed with a smile. 'A man of my age never minds being disturbed by a beautiful woman!'

Sabina laughed, not because she knew she was meant to, but because she genuinely found Hugh's teasing refreshing after the intensity of emotion of the last twelve hours. 'In that case—' she linked her arm in the crook of his '—I would love it if you would accompany me on my walk.'

'Where would you like to go?' Hugh prompted once they were outside in the late May sunshine, blossom on the trees, birds singing amongst their branches.

'I've had a thing about walled gardens ever since I read about one being brought back to life in one of the books I read as a child,' she admitted guilelessly.

Hugh grinned down at her, looking much younger than his eighty-odd years. 'I think I must have read the same book,' he acknowledged conspiratorially. 'Although we don't do as much with those gardens any more,' he added sadly. 'It was my wife who liked to cultivate them, you see.'

Sabina had already realised that he was a widower of some years' standing. 'That's a pity,' she murmured softly.

'Yes,' he acknowledged thoughtfully. 'Actually, Sabina, I'm quite pleased to have this time alone with you.' Hugh looked down at her with quizzical eyes. 'Tell me—from a young female point of view—do you think my family is likely to want to have me committed if I tell them I've fallen in love again, at my age?'

Her eyes widened in alarm at the sudden intimacy of the unexpected question. 'I'm not sure—I don't—erm—'

'Sorry.' Hugh chuckled at her obvious surprise, shaking his head self-derisively, 'I didn't mean to shock you.'

'You didn't,' Sabina assured him, feeling embarrassed now at the stupidity of her own reaction.

'I just wanted someone else's opinion before broaching the subject with any of the family.' Hugh frowned. 'Although I think Brice already has an idea...' He grimaced.

Brice would, Sabina thought irritably, preceding Hugh into the first walled garden as he held the door open for her, instantly enchanted by the profusion of wild flowers whose sight and perfume assailed her senses.

'So what do you think?' Hugh prompted softly.

Her eyes shone with pleasure as she looked around her. 'It's beautiful! Exactly as I would have imagined it—'

'I was actually referring to our earlier conversation,' Hugh corrected dryly.

Which she had no idea how to answer! Hugh, despite being in his eighties, was still an attractive man; so why shouldn't he fall in love, at this age or any other? But, on the other hand, in view of her own reaction to her mother being involved with someone, she could see how Hugh's family might be more than a little surprised by his news...

'I can clearly see men in white coats and bars at the windows in your eyes!' Hugh murmured self-derisively.

'Not at all.' Sabina laughed throatily. 'You've just put me in something of a dilemma, that's all,' she admitted ruefully. 'You see, I've just encountered something—similar, in my own life, where my widowed mother is concerned,' she confided softly.

Hugh looked at her with narrowed eyes. 'And?'

She grimaced. 'I didn't react too well, I'm afraid,' she admitted regretfully.

'Ah.'' Hugh nodded.

'Indeed,' Sabina sighed. 'My only advice to you would be not to take too much notice of initial reactions.'

He raised silver brows. 'Meaning yours wasn't too good where your mother was concerned?' he guessed shrewdly.

She gave a self-conscious laugh. 'Meaning my reaction was pretty awful,' she admitted with regret.

After all, was her mother finding someone else to share the otherwise loneliness of life such a terrible thing? In view of the mess Sabina's own life had become in the last twelve hours, the realisation that she was engaged to one man while finding herself deeply attracted to another one, to the point of knowing herself in love with him, she was inclined to think not.

'Tell me, Sabina,' Hugh began slowly, watching her with thoughtful curiosity. 'What do you think of my grandson?'

Her eyes widened at this next sharp turn in their conversation. 'Which one?' she delayed awkwardly.

Hugh smiled. 'You've met Logan and Fergus, too?'

'Only Fergus. We—' She broke off abruptly; how would it sound to this elderly man if she told him she and Brice had had dinner with the McClouds? 'But I've seen Logan,' she continued slightly breathlessly. 'They look very alike, don't they?' she dismissed lightly.

'They are alike.' Hugh nodded. 'McDonalds, every one. I made sure of that,' he added firmly.

And he was obviously proud of each and every one of them. With good reason; each of the men, besides being extremely attractive, was very successful in his chosen field.

'But you didn't answer my question about Brice, Sabina?' Hugh persisted, his gaze narrowed assessingly.

'I think,' she avoided teasingly, 'that Brice gets his bluntness from his grandfather!'

The elderly man chuckled with pleasure. 'I brought them up to believe that honesty is always the best policy— even if you end up making a few enemies along the way. And talking of honesty,' he began slowly. 'Sabina—'

'Hello, there.' Richard calling to them from the open doorway of the garden interrupted what Hugh had been about to say.

For which Sabina was more than grateful; she hadn't known what she would have said if Hugh had persisted along this line of questions concerning her feelings to-wards Brice! The realisation of her love for Brice was still too new, the whole situation too raw to emotional turmoil, that she didn't want to even think about it just now, let alone talk about Brice!

Although she wasn't sure she felt ready to face Richard at the moment, either...

'Look who I just met outside,' Richard told them lightly as he stepped to one side to reveal someone standing be-hind him in the garden doorway.

Sabina found herself looking at her own mother!

What—?

Sabina looked at her mother frowningly, totally bewil-dered at the suddenness of her appearance here, of all places. If Brice had dared to carry out that threat to tele-phone her mother—

'Joan...' Hugh croaked gruffly.

Sabina turned to look at him, only to find that Hugh looked more than a little uncomfortable himself at this sudden turn of events, embarrassed even, a flush of those ruddy cheeks, anxiety in the deep blue of his eyes.

And then the truth hit Sabina with the force of a blow between the eyes.

Hugh had talked to her of having recently fallen in love.

Her mother had done something similar when they'd met in London for lunch last week.

Hugh McDonald, Brice's grandfather, was the man in her mother's life!

CHAPTER TWELVE

'SABINA, I think you're totally overreacting—'

'I didn't ask for your opinion!' She turned harshly on Brice as he sat on the side of her bed watching as she threw clothes haphazardly into the suitcase beside him. 'In fact, in the circumstances, I think the best thing you can do is not to say a single word on the subject!' She glared at him angrily, eyes glittering deeply blue, her whole body tense with repressed fury.

Some of which, Brice conceded grimly, she was perfectly entitled to feel.

He had arrived downstairs a few minutes ago, just in time to see Sabina come storming through the front doorway, hot wings of temper in the usual paleness of her cheeks.

'What on earth—?'

'Leave her, Brice,' his grandfather had instructed harshly as he'd followed closely behind Sabina.

'But—'

'I said leave her!' his grandfather rasped coldly, both men standing in the hallway watching Sabina before she disappeared round the curve of the stairs.

Brice turned back to his grandfather. 'What on earth is going on?' he demanded to know; Sabina might be in some strange sort of mood with him, but she had seemed to like his grandfather well enough last night. 'What have you done to Sabina?' he prompted accusingly.

Something flickered in his grandfather's gaze, an emotion he quickly masked, although his expression remained grim. 'I haven't *done* anything to her, laddie,' he grated, his accent all the stronger because of his own repressed anger. 'At least—' he frowned '—nothing deliberately designed to hurt or upset her.'

'You seem to have succeeded in doing both,' Brice pointed out tersely, torn between a desire to run after Sabina, and the need to stand here and hear what his grandfather had to say.

His grandfather held up defensive hands. 'It seemed like an act of providence when you told me you were bringing Sabina here this weekend.' He shook his head. 'But, unfortunately, before I had time to explain the situation to her—'

'Go back a step, Grandfather,' Brice cut in evenly. 'What was providential about my bringing Sabina here…?' He frowned his wariness of the possible answer.

Although he couldn't for the life of him think what that answer might be. As far as he was aware Sabina and his grandfather had never met before, so what could the elderly man possibly have needed to explain to her…?

'I think I might better be able to answer that for you,' a calm, female voice remarked from the direction of the doorway.

Brice turned frowningly. A tiny blonde-haired woman stood there, a woman probably aged in her sixties, despite the shoulder-length of her hair, the pretty face and slenderness of her figure. A woman Brice knew he had never seen before.

And yet…

As he looked at her he realised there was something tantalisingly familiar about the deep blue of her eyes, those high cheekbones, and the creaminess of her skin…

Sabina had said she looked like her father, and yet here was clear evidence that wasn't completely true…

Brice drew in a ragged breath. 'I see.'

The woman tilted her head engagingly to one side. 'Do you?'

'I believe so.' Brice nodded slowly, turning back to his grandfather. 'Why didn't you tell me?'

Because it was more than obvious to Brice now that it was Sabina's mother who was his grandfather's 'friend'.

Was it any wonder that Sabina was upset?

His grandfather moved to put a protective arm about the shoulders of the woman Brice only knew as Sabina's mother. 'Joan didn't exactly have a pleasant time of it when she tried to tell Sabina about us the other week,' his grandfather rasped. 'You young people seem to think you have some sort of monopoly when it comes to falling in love!' he added disgustedly.

'Excuse me.' Richard Latham spoke icily from behind the older couple, stepping into the hallway as they moved to one side. 'Is Sabina upstairs?' he prompted curtly.

'She is,' Brice confirmed grimly; he had been wondering where the other man had got to!

Richard Latham nodded abruptly. 'Sabina and I will be leaving shortly. We'll need a taxi to drive us to the nearest airport,' he added arrogantly.

'I'll drive you,' Brice told him coldly.

Richard Latham gave him a scathing glance. 'I don't think so. But if you could see to the ordering of the taxi…?' He gave a dismissive nod before following Sabina up the stairs.

Almost as if he were some sort of hired help. Brice fumed angrily, finding himself wanting to follow the other man up the stairs and punch him squarely in the face!

'Richard doesn't like me, I'm afraid.' Joan Smith spoke ruefully. 'I've been a little too outspoken concerning his suitability as a fiancé for Sabina,' she admitted with a grimace.

'In that case—' Brice turned back to the quietly spoken woman '—I like you very much!' he told her with satisfaction.

Joan laughed huskily, a laugh so like Sabina's, Brice felt an ache in his chest just at the sound of it.

Sabina...

What must she be feeling? More to the point, what must she be thinking?

'I have to go up and talk to Sabina,' he told the older couple distractedly. 'Before Latham has a chance to add his particular brand of poison to the confusion,' he added harshly.

'You're wasting your time, I'm afraid,' her mother told him sadly. 'In the last few months I've watched my beautiful, self-confident daughter turn into someone I hardly recognise.' She shook her head regretfully.

Brice looked at her frowningly, wanting to pursue the subject, but at the same time knowing he had to speak to Sabina. Now.

'Hold that thought,' Brice told Joan forcefully. 'And don't go away before I have a chance to talk to you again,' he urged even as he began to ascend the stone stairs two at a time.

'Joan isn't going anywhere,' his grandfather assured him firmly.

Brice hadn't been sure whether he'd been relieved or disappointed when he'd entered Sabina's bedroom a few minutes later to find her alone; half of him had still been hoping to actually carry out his urge to hit Richard Latham. Although, in the circumstances, that probably wasn't such a good idea at the moment...

'Sabina,' he tried again now, 'is it really so awful that my grandfather and your mother have become—friends?' he concluded awkwardly, having no idea how far the relationship between the older couple had progressed. Although the two of them did intend holidaying in Paris together.

Sabina resumed throwing her clothes into the suitcase. 'I told you I don't want to talk about it!' she snapped.

Brice frowned. 'Is that the way you usually deal with things nowadays—bury your head in the sand and hope they'll go away?' he challenged.

She looked at him with narrowed eyes. '"Nowadays"…?' she repeated warily.

He shrugged. 'Your mother seems to be of the opinion that you've changed since you became engaged to Latham.' Brice saw no harm in trying to get a few answers himself as to the reason for the change in her that Joan had noticed.

'Really?' Sabina dismissed with a shrug. 'I've already told you that my mother and Richard don't like each other.'

Implying her mother was simply prejudiced in her opinion. Except that Brice found he didn't believe that of the woman he had just met downstairs…

He was still amazed at the fact that his grandfather and Sabina's mother had somehow found each other and apparently fallen in love. The chances of that happening had to be incredible.

But was it any more incredible than the way he felt towards Sabina?

Also, it was strange, but with the knowledge that it was Sabina's mother his grandfather was seeing Brice found he no longer felt that instinctive rejection of such a relationship in the older man's life.

Whereas Sabina obviously felt the opposite!

But how much of that was directed towards the unsuitability of his grandfather as a suitor to her mother, and how much was it because it happened to be Brice's grandfather?

'Won't you give them a chance, Sabina?' he prompted gently. 'After all, they're both adults, and—' He broke off as Sabina turned on him fiercely, looking up at him with widened eyes.

'Don't you understand, I can't think about this just now?' she grated emotionally.

Brice studied her more closely. Was that tears he could see in her eyes, building up against the lashes as they threatened to fall?

'Sabina!' He stood up abruptly, reaching out to take her into his arms. 'It will be all right, you'll see,' he told her soothingly as he cradled her head against his shoulder.

It would never be all right again!

How could it be, when she had fallen in love with Brice while engaged to Richard, and now she found her mother was involved with Brice's grandfather? That relationship alone made it impossible for her to distance herself from Brice—or his family!

She had thought last night, once she'd realised her feelings towards Brice, that this situation couldn't get any worse. With her mother's arrival it just had!

'Sabina...?' Brice prompted huskily now as he looked down at her concernedly.

She loved this man, every arrogant, attractive, caring inch of him. What was she going to do?

Brice looked at her searchingly, those emerald-coloured eyes like penetrating jewels. She only hoped he couldn't see what was in her heart!

'Sabina...' he finally groaned throatily, pressing her closer to his chest before his head lowered and his lips claimed hers.

Heaven.

Absolute, complete heaven.

Her arms moved up instinctively about his shoulders as she returned the kiss, senses raging as pleasure coursed through her, her lips parting invitingly beneath his.

Brice accepted that invitation with a low growl in his throat, the kiss instantly deepening as his mouth crushed hers, the warmth of his tongue moving sensually against hers.

Sabina clung to the broad width of his shoulders even as her body curved itself instinctively into the hardness of his, able to feel every muscle and sinew, his own arousal unmistakable.

Her neck arched as Brice's lips moved from hers to trail a blaze of fire down the sensitive column of her throat, his tongue now caressing the deep hollows at its base, one of his hands moving to cup the pertness of her breast against the thin material of her tee shirt.

She gave a gasp of pure pleasure as his thumbtip moved lightly over the hardened tip of her nipple, her legs feeling weak as hot desire swept through her entire body, her panting breath sounding loud in the otherwise quiet of the bedroom.

'Brice...!' she groaned achingly, knowing she wanted more, so much more.

'This is right, Sabina,' he muttered forcefully against the lobe of her ear. 'So very, very right!' His arms tightened painfully about her.

'I—' She broke off abruptly, hearing another noise that she somehow knew—even in her befuddled state of arousal—wasn't made by either Brice or herself.

She quickly pulled back from Brice, pushing against his chest, just managing to free herself from his arms and step away from him as the bedroom door opened, Sabina's sharp glance in that direction showing her that Richard stood there.

Her fiancé!

She felt her cheeks blushing painfully red as she looked guiltily across at the man whose ring nestled on her left hand, wondering if Richard knew, if he guessed, if there was anything about Brice and herself that showed that only seconds ago they had been in each other's arms.

It was impossible to tell anything of Richard's emotions

from his deadpan expression as he looked at them, the blue eyes narrowed speculatively, but not accusingly.

He arched blond brows. 'Are we still leaving?' he drawled interestedly.

'We are.' Sabina gave an abrupt nod of her head, moving to close her suitcase, all the time keeping her gaze averted from Brice as he stood tensely only feet away from her, hands clenched at his sides. If he dared to say anything that would imply—!

'In the circumstances, McAllister, I think it's probably best if we don't go ahead with the portrait, after all,' Richard addressed the other man dryly.

'Circumstances?' Brice echoed harshly.

Richard shrugged. 'Sabina is obviously—upset, by her mother's friendship with your grandfather,' he dismissed derisively.

'Are you?' Brice rasped in her direction.

Sabina slowly raised her head, reluctantly meeting Brice's probing gaze. 'I—I'm not sure how I feel about that at the moment,' she answered honestly, needing time and space to digest the fact before knowing how she felt about it. 'But I do agree with Richard that it would be best if we leave now, that it's better to forget about the portrait, too,' she added firmly.

Brice's mouth thinned angrily. 'Why?'

Because she daredn't be alone in a room with him! Because every time she looked at him she wanted him, shamelessly, unreservedly, completely! Because she loved him!

Because there was no point in the portrait being painted when she was going to end her engagement to Richard...!

She shook her head dismissively. 'As you're well aware, I was never interested in having the portrait done in the first place,' she reminded distantly.

'You only went ahead with it to please your fiancé, is that it?' Brice rasped scornfully.

Sabina's head went back proudly at the open challenge in his words. 'That's it exactly,' she confirmed tersely, a certain defiance in her gaze now as she met Brice's unblinkingly, knowing she was daring him to dispute her words, but unable to do anything about it.

Brice's mouth turned back contemptuously. 'I'm sure there must be many other ways in which you can "please" your fiancé,' he taunted scathingly.

'I'm sure there are,' Sabina returned coldly, not liking the tone in Brice's voice at all.

'Just send me a bill for whatever time and materials you've already used,' Richard told the other man dismissively.

The emerald eyes hardened to angry pebbles of light. 'That won't be necessary,' Brice rasped.

'But I always take care of my debts, Brice,' Richard told him smoothly.

'I said, forget it,' Brice snapped harshly.

Sabina anxiously watched the exchange between the two men. Looking at Brice now, it was hard to believe that only minutes ago they had been in each other's arms, totally lost in their arousal, everyone and everything else forgotten. Brice now looked coldly remote, and she—

Sabina didn't know how she looked, only knew she had to get away from here, away from Brice, away from the spell this place seemed to have cast over her! Back to London where she knew who she was and where she was going.

'If you're ready to leave now, Sabina?' Richard prompted pointedly, obviously bored by his conversation with the other man.

'I'm ready.' She reached out to swing her zipped suitcase onto the floor.

'I'm sure Brice isn't going to be so petty as to let you carry your own suitcase downstairs. Are you, McAllister?'

Richard taunted challengingly as he picked up his own packed suitcase.

'No,' Brice rasped tersely, abruptly relieving Sabina of her burden, his fingers, briefly, icily cold against hers. 'I believe my grandfather is organising that his estate manager will drive you to Aberdeen airport,' he added harshly.

Sabina preceded the two men down the winding staircase, anxious to be gone now. Once she was away from here perhaps she would be able to see her feelings towards Brice for what they were—be able to know if it really was love she felt towards him. Or something else.

Although none of that changed the fact that she had to end her engagement to Richard...

CHAPTER THIRTEEN

IT WAS only Brice's anger that kept him silent as he followed the couple down the stairs, the feeling of complete impotence where Sabina was concerned.

Because if he once started to speak, to protest at Sabina leaving like this, then he knew he wouldn't be able to stop, that everything he wanted to say to her about the rightness of what she was doing would come tumbling out!

How could she leave with Richard Latham after the kisses she had just shared with Brice? And she had responded, he was absolutely sure of it.

But she was still leaving with Latham...

Jeff, the estate manager, was waiting outside with the car, opening the boot so that the luggage could be stowed away.

'No matter what your feelings at the moment, Sabina,' Brice rasped as she would have moved to get into the back of the car, 'I think you should at least say goodbye to your mother. And a thank-you to my grandfather for his hospitality wouldn't go amiss, either,' he added scathingly.

A slight flush had entered her cheeks at the obvious rebuke as she straightened. 'Of course,' she acquiesced abruptly.

'It doesn't need both of you to say thank you,' Brice told Richard as he would have accompanied Sabina back into the castle.

'It's okay, Richard,' Sabina assured as the other man looked at her enquiringly. 'I'll only be a few minutes.' She squeezed his arm reassuringly, much to Brice's displeasure. He couldn't bear the thought of Sabina touching the other man even casually, let alone, let alone—

This was a living hell!

Hell wasn't what all the prophets of doom predicated it was, it wasn't fire and brimstone, an eternal purgatory. Hell was realising you were in love with a woman who was living with another man!

Because he was in love with Sabina, had known it earlier when he hadn't been able to let her leave without holding her one last time.

He didn't know how it had happened, when it had happened, he only knew that he loved everything about her, her beauty, her unaffectedness, her warmth, the huskiness of her voice, the way she moved—her loyalty to a man who didn't deserve to even kiss one of her beautiful feet!

And the thought of never seeing Sabina again gave Brice an ache in his chest that just wouldn't go away...

Hell, he now knew, was loving the unattainable!

'They'll be in my grandfather's private sitting-room,' he told Sabina harshly as she hesitated in the hallway.

She winced at the aggression in his tone. 'Brice, I—' She moistened dry lips. 'I just need a little time to—to adjust, to my mother's—friendship with your grandfather.' She looked at him pleadingly. 'It's been rather a shock,' she added emotionally.

Brice looked at her coldly, knowing that, for the moment, he daredn't look at her any other way; if he did, he wouldn't be able to stop himself from telling her how he felt about her. Which, in the circumstances, was probably the last complication she wanted to hear!

He shook his head. 'You seemed to like my grandfather well enough before you knew of his involvement with your mother,' he reminded harshly.

'I did—do like him,' she amended awkwardly.

'He just isn't your father,' Brice guessed scathingly.

Sabina's eyes flashed deeply blue. 'No, he isn't,' she conceded tersely. 'But—'

'Have you given any thought to how lonely your mother

has been the last five years?' Brice attacked impatiently. 'What it must have been like for her? From the little you've told me about your parents, I would guess that they shared a relationship of emotional and academic equality. Soul mates, in fact,' he rasped. 'I would say your mother has been living only half a life the last five years, feeling as if she's had her right arm amputated!'

Brice already felt like that over Sabina, couldn't even begin to imagine what it must be like to lose a partner after thirty or more years of marriage, to lose Sabina after spending all those years with her at his side.

'Be nice to them, Sabina,' he warned harshly.

Her brows arched derisively. 'Or else what, Brice...?' she challenged softly.

'Or else you'll have me to answer to,' he came back gratingly.

She gave a humourless smile. 'How terrifying,' she returned dismissively.

Brice only just resisted the impulse to reach out and pull her into his arms, taking a step backwards instead. 'It could be,' he assured her grimly before turning to stride forcefully down the hallway to his grandfather's sitting-room.

The older couple were standing close together across the room when Brice and Sabina entered, and if Brice wasn't mistaken there was the trace of tears on Joan's face.

'Take care,' Brice warned Sabina softly.

Her eyes flashed back a warning of her own before she turned to the other couple. 'Richard and I are leaving now.' She spoke huskily. 'I—I just wanted to say goodbye,' she added awkwardly.

Joan squeezed Hugh's arm reassuringly before turning to her daughter. 'I hope my being here hasn't chased you away?' she said gruffly.

'Of course not,' Sabina assured her lightly. 'Richard has to get back to London anyway. He has a few things to do before we fly out to Australia on Monday.'

Brice had forgotten she was going away with the other man, that the trip had been delayed because of coming up here. Obviously nothing that had happened this weekend had affected Sabina's decision to go with Richard...

Joan nodded, obviously used to her daughter's jet-setting lifestyle. 'Call me when you get back, won't you, Sabina?'

Sabina looked mildly surprised by the request, but she nodded anyway. 'Perhaps you and—and Hugh, would like to have dinner when we get back?' she suggested tentatively.

Well, at least she was trying, Brice conceded grudgingly—even if he didn't particularly care for the idea of his grandfather becoming pally with Richard Latham, as Sabina's fiancé!

'That would be lovely, Sabina,' her mother accepted warmly. 'I'm sure we would love to come. Wouldn't we, Hugh?' She turned to him for confirmation.

'Love to,' Hugh confirmed abruptly. 'I'm sorry you have to leave so soon, Sabina,' he added slightly reprovingly. 'I would have liked the chance to get to know you a little better.'

'There's no rush,' Sabina dismissed with a shrug. 'Is there?' she added less certainly.

'Depends how you look at it, I suppose,' Hugh drawled mockingly. 'After all, I'm already well past my allotted three score years and ten!'

Sabina looked at him frowningly, obviously unsure how to take this last remark. Brice knew exactly how he would have taken it—with a complete lack of seriousness. His grandfather was fit and healthy, there was absolutely no reason why he shouldn't live another ten years or more. Especially now that he had someone in his life he was obviously more than a little fond of.

Although Brice doubted, the mood she was in, that Sabina would appreciate hearing that!

'I'll call you when I get back and we'll organise dinner.' Sabina opted for safety. 'Goodbye, Brice,' she added huskily, her gaze not quite meeting his.

'I'll walk you back to the car,' he told her grimly.

She shook her head. 'There's really no need. I know the way. And—we've already said goodbye,' she added firmly.

Brice wasn't in the least happy with this arrangement, would have liked a few more minutes alone with Sabina. But he could see by the strain about her eyes, the paleness of her cheeks, that she had had enough for one day. More than enough, in fact.

He nodded abruptly. 'In that case, have a good flight back.'

'I'm sure we will.' Her smile was so fleeting it barely registered as being one, before she turned and hurried from the room.

As if she were being pursued by something particularly unpleasant, Brice acknowledged impatiently.

He turned sharply to his grandfather. 'Now, if you wouldn't mind formally introducing me to Joan...?' he prompted dryly. 'That way I'm hoping she won't find me too rude when I ask her what happened in Sabina's life a few months ago to bring about the change in her that Joan mentioned earlier!'

Because he was determined to get to the bottom of that mysterious remark. Wanted to know. Needed to know!

'All right?' Richard prompted as Sabina got into the back of the car beside him.

'Fine,' she dismissed abruptly before turning her head to have one last glance at Hugh McDonald's castle home.

It looked beautiful bathed in the May sunshine; serene, calm, a bastion of tranquillity—everything Sabina knew that she wasn't at this moment!

She had left with Richard because, in the circumstances,

she couldn't see that there was any other way. She was totally shaken by the discovery that Hugh McDonald was the man in her mother's life. But she was more shaken still by her response to Brice's kisses a few minutes ago. If Richard hadn't come into the bedroom when he had, she had no idea where it would have all ended.

Which was another reason she had to leave with Richard...

She had no idea if Richard had guessed she had been in Brice's arms only seconds before he'd entered the room, but she did know she couldn't go on with this any more, that she would have to break their engagement. That, in the circumstances, it was the only fair thing to do for Richard...

'That was a bit of a turn-up for the books, wasn't it?' he remarked lightly at her side.

Sabina turned to him blankly. 'What was?'

'Your mother and McDonald,' Richard murmured derisively. 'Still, if she had to find herself an ageing lover, at least he's a rich one!' he added scathingly.

Sabina was very conscious of Hugh McDonald's employee seated only feet away in the front of the car, knew that he must be able to hear their conversation. In fact, from the stiff way he now sat behind the steering wheel, she was sure he had.

Nevertheless, she couldn't let the remark pass by undefended. 'I'm sure Hugh's wealth has nothing to do with my mother's feelings towards him,' she said slightly indignantly.

'No?' Richard raised sceptical brows over cynical blue eyes. 'I wouldn't be too sure of that.' He shrugged uninterestedly.

Sabina would, knew that her mother had never been interested in material wealth. Goodness knew, Sabina had offered to make her mother's life a little easier financially dozens of times, only for her mother to smilingly refuse, claiming that she had enough for what she needed, which was her little cottage in Scotland, and her vast collection of books.

Besides, Hugh had so much more to recommend him than just his obvious wealth, was still handsome in a distinguished way, was highly intelligent, which her mother would appreciate, and, last of all, Hugh was extremely charming. Like his grandson!

But there was no mistaking the slight edge to Richard's tone when he talked of her mother...

She drew in a deep breath. 'Richard—'

'Not here,' he cut in tersely, looking pointedly at the driver of the car.

Now he chose to remember the other man! Not that she was averse to cancelling their talk until they were on their own; she wasn't exactly enjoying this conversation herself.

'We'll talk once we're back in London,' Richard added harshly.

Once they had returned to the home she shared with Richard. Which, she accepted heavily, would also have to change. In fact, everything would have to change once she had explained to Richard that she could no longer keep her side of their bargain.

Although she didn't think it was a good idea to tell him it was because she had realised she was in love with Brice!

Brice...

How her heart ached just at the thought of him, more and more so as the miles between them lengthened. When would she ever see Brice again? She had made her feelings concerning the portrait more than plain, as had Richard, which meant, ironically, that the only link she now had with Brice was through her mother's relationship with Hugh.

Poetic justice for her own unreasonableness the other week when her mother had tried to tell her of the new friendship in her life?

Probably, Sabina conceded heavily as she finally relaxed back in her seat. Something else she knew she would have to put right at the earliest opportunity.

But first she had to sever her engagement to Richard...

Not a pleasant thought, the brief sideways glance she gave in his direction showing her that at the moment he looked grimly unapproachable. This was going to be far from easy!

But, then, why should it be? Richard had been completely honest from the beginning about what he wanted from her in their engagement, and what he would give in return. And he had kept his side of the bargain. Richard hadn't changed; she was the one who had done that. Worse, she had fallen in love with another man. Although, she hoped she wouldn't actually have to tell Richard that part. It was enough that she could no longer continue with their engagement, without involving Brice in its demise.

Especially as Brice had no idea she had fallen in love with him!

And he never would have. It was enough of a folly that she knew she was in love with him, without Brice being embarrassed by the knowledge too. Besides, if her mother's relationship with Hugh became something more permanent, she and Brice were going to be related in some way. In which case, Brice must never know that she had been stupid enough to fall in love with him!

'The sitting-room, I think,' Richard announced grimly hours later when they finally reached the house, marching straight over to the array of drinks and pouring out a large measure of brandy.

It had not been a particularly pleasant journey back to London, Richard not inclined to conversation during the flight or the drive back into the City from the airport. In fact, Sabina felt in need of a brandy herself!

'Could I have one of those?' she prompted huskily.

Richard wordlessly poured a measure of brandy into a

second glass before handing it to her. 'Dutch courage, Sabina?' he finally rasped as he stepped back, his gaze hard as he looked at her through narrowed lids.

He did know about the kisses she had shared with Brice earlier; Sabina was sure of it now as she looked at the hard accusation in Richard's face. Well-deserved accusation, she acknowledged heavily.

'I'm going to save you the trouble of breaking our engagement, Sabina,' Richard continued harshly. 'And break it myself!' he added scathingly. 'I'm sure I made clear to you from the onset what I wanted from you, that I never deal with imperfection!'

Sabina gasped at the look of disgust that accompanied this savagely made insult. 'I've never claimed to be perfect, Richard,' she began softly.

'"Never claimed to be perfect"!' he echoed scornfully. 'You didn't need to claim it—I knew you were. Successful, beautiful, coolly self-composed, untouched,' he added the last forcefully. 'Most of all, untouched! But that's no longer true, is it?' he accused hardly.

She had known Richard was going to be upset when she broke their engagement, but nothing had prepared her for this venomous attack. She had seen Richard angry with other people in the past, but for the main part she had refused to see the callousness with which he could deal with people who had disappointed him. Well, now she had disappointed him—and nothing was going to save her from feeling the sharp edge of that rapier tongue!

She shook her head. 'I don't know what you mean—'

'I mean coming into that bedroom earlier today and finding you still all hot and sweaty from being in Brice McAllister's arms!' Richard cut in icily.

'Hot and sweaty…?' Sabina repeated incredulously. 'Richard, you're being—'

'Crudely honest?' he concluded distastefully. 'Maybe that's because that's exactly what this is.' He shook his head disgustedly. 'I thought you were different, Sabina. I thought, after what happened to you, that you were a person, like me, removed from this physical thrashing about people so often associate with love, that you wanted the things from a relationship that we've had together the last few months: companionship, intelligent conversation, mutual admiration and liking, while at the same time retaining one's personal integrity.' He gave another shake of his head. 'But this weekend—your behaviour with McAllister has shown me that you're just like every other woman!'

Sabina stared at him with complete disbelief for what she was hearing. She had shared this house with Richard for several months now, had thought that she knew him. But the things he was saying to her now told her that she clearly didn't!

'And to think,' he continued disgustedly, 'I was actually thinking of asking you to marry me!' He shook his head.

She had noted his comment about a honeymoon on the drive up to Scotland, remembered several comments Brice had made about Richard's wedding plans. But she had thought they had only been made to give credence to their engagement. She had obviously been wrong...

Sabina moistened dry lips. 'That was never part of our agreement.'

Richard gave her a scathing glance. 'Your behaviour with McAllister has put our "agreement" at an end, Sabina,' he told her coldly. 'In the circumstances, I would appreciate it if you would remove yourself, and your belongings, from my home as quickly as possible.'

Sabina stared at him. He had a right to feel angry, she accepted that, but this was a Richard she had never seen before. A man she didn't want to know, either...

CHAPTER FOURTEEN

'THIS is getting to be quite a habit.' Chloe spoke lightly as she sat beside Brice.

His scowl didn't lighten at the teasingly made remark, his attention all focused on the catwalk in front of him as he waited for the lights to go down and the fashion show to begin.

He had been trying for the last three weeks to see, or at least speak to, Sabina, only succeeding in receiving the proverbial brush-off from Richard Latham's watchdog housekeeper every time he'd telephoned the house; Sabina was either 'away', or 'unavailable'. Brice had a feeling she was only unavailable to him!

And so he had once again resorted to persuading Chloe into letting him accompany her to a fashion show where he knew Sabina was to be the top model on the catwalk.

These last three weeks Brice had felt like a thirsty man in a desert—but his thirst was for sight and sound of Sabina, not water!

'Don't get too used to it,' he told Chloe dryly. 'This really isn't my thing.'

Chloe gave him a knowing look. 'I'm not completely stupid, Brice,' she drawled.

He grinned at his cousin-in-law. 'I never for a moment thought you were!' She would have bored his cousin Fergus in the first week if that were the case, instead of which the two of them were more in love than ever.

'It was rather a surprise for all of us when Hugh announced his intention of getting remarried,' Chloe remarked innocently.

Too innocently, Brice knew. But he had probably been

153

the least surprised of them all when Hugh had telephoned each member of the family last weekend to make his announcement. Yet another reason he needed to speak to Sabina. At least, that was what he told himself...

'To Sabina's mother, of all people,' Chloe continued conversationally.

'So I believe,' he acknowledged dismissively.

He didn't 'believe' it at all—he knew it. And he desperately wanted to know how Sabina had taken the news.

Chloe arched dark brows. 'Fergus tells me you've already met Joan...?'

'Briefly,' he confirmed tersely, having no intention of filling any of his family in on that disaster of a weekend. Not that meeting Joan had been a disaster, far from it, but as for the rest of the weekend...! 'Don't worry, Chloe,' he drawled, 'you'll get your chance next weekend when we're all invited to the formal introduction to our soon-to-be stepgrandmother!'

When was this show going to start? he wondered impatiently. It was scheduled to start at eight-thirty, but it was almost nine o'clock now!

'I'm not worried, Brice,' Chloe assured him dryly. 'I know Hugh well enough to accept he has impeccable taste; I'm sure Joan is lovely. Will Sabina be there next weekend, do you think?'

If Chloe meant to divert him from his scowling contemplating of the catwalk with the suddenness of her question, then she succeeded. Whether or not Sabina intended being at the dinner at a London hotel next weekend was one of the things he had been wondering about himself!

He certainly hoped it was to be the case, and not just for selfish reasons; he had come to like Joan very much over the last few weeks, and he wouldn't like Sabina to do anything that might hurt her mother—and ultimately herself.

'I have no idea,' he dismissed blandly. 'Are these things usually as late starting as this?' he added impatiently.

'Invariably,' Chloe confirmed unconcernedly. 'Don't worry, Brice.' She reached over and squeezed his arm reassuringly. 'I have it on good authority that Sabina is definitely here.'

No doubt with the ever-watchful Clive in attendance! Well, that was just too bad—because he intended seeing Sabina this evening, no matter who might try to stop him.

'I don't—' He broke off as the lights began to dim, the loud music that seemed to accompany all these functions suddenly blasting out over the speakers. 'And about time, too!' he muttered irritably, settling himself more comfortably in his seat as he prepared to see Sabina for the first time in three weeks.

During the next hour model after model came strutting down the catwalk, all of them dramatically beautiful in the designer clothing—and none of them was Sabina!

'She *is* here, Brice,' Chloe assured him again as she sensed his tension rising by the minute.

He scowled darkly. 'Then where the he—' He broke off, half a dozen spotlights suddenly focused on the centre of the stage, the music stopping briefly as the finale of the first half of this fashion show began.

Sabina...!

Beautiful, mysterious, alluring Sabina. She looked exquisite in the sparkling dress of midnight blue, the material shimmering suggestively about the perfect curves of her body as she seemed to glide down the centre catwalk, blonde hair arranged in a fantastic space-age style, the dramatic eye make-up she wore making her eyes appear the same midnight-blue as the glittering dress she wore. She looked to neither left nor right as she came to a halt at the end of the catwalk, but her smile seemed to glow almost as much as that sensually entrancing gown.

Brice was too stunned by her appearance to join in the

enthusiastic applause of the rest of the audience. Sabina had never looked so beautiful to him.

Or so aloof and unattainable!

This was her world, he realised numbly, the world where she was Queen. And he, he suddenly realised, he was chasing that elusive 'end of the rainbow'...

He was paralysed by the realisation, didn't even register the fact that Sabina, after smiling and waving to the enthusiastic audience, had now left the catwalk, the main lights coming back on for the brief interval.

'Do you want to go behind the scenes now?' Chloe asked gently, seeming aware that Brice was totally transfixed.

Even if she had no idea of the reason for it...

'Brice...?' Chloe prompted again after a few seconds when she had received no response.

He pulled himself together with effort, shaking his head self-derisively. 'I'm just fooling myself, aren't I?' he muttered disgustedly. 'This is where Sabina belongs.' Here, and, as Brice was only too painfully aware, in Richard Latham's home.

'I'm not sure I agree with you there.' Chloe shook her head as they joined the other people going outside to stretch their legs before the resumption of the show. 'Most of the models I know, when they aren't actually working, lead a very lonely life. The majority, having reached the fame and fortune they thought they wanted, would give anything for the normality of genuine love and marriage in their lives,' she added softly.

'Sabina already has that,' Brice returned harshly, feeling slightly claustrophobic amongst this glittering, noisy crowd.

Chloe looked thoughtful. 'Do you really think so?' she mused frowningly. 'I've always thought of David's Uncle Richard as rather a cold man.'

Bruce shrugged. 'He's Sabina's choice, not mine,' he rasped.

But even if it meant meeting the other man again—something he had no wish to do!—he knew that for Joan's sake Sabina had to be at the dinner party next week.

He had briefly, while dazzled by Sabina's beauty and success, lost sight of the compelling reason for his being here tonight. Oh, he wanted to see her for himself, but he had told himself the driving force behind his appearance here this evening was to ascertain a promise from Sabina that she would be supportive of her mother next week.

He had told himself that…

But one look at Sabina and he had known he was only fooling himself; if anything, the love he had realised he felt towards her three weeks ago had intensified. To the point where he wasn't sure he could see her without telling her how he felt!

'Maybe it would be better if I just left now,' he acknowledged heavily.

'I don't think—' Chloe broke off what she had been about to say as they were joined by a third person. 'Hello, Annie,' she greeted the young girl warmly. 'It's going well, isn't it?'

'You should see the chaos out the back,' the young girl said with feeling before turning to Brice, giving him a cheeky grin. 'Would you be Mr McAllister?'

'I would,' he confirmed warily, completely baffled by the fact that this girl Annie was looking for him. For one thing, she was dressed casually in jeans and a tee shirt, which meant she certainly wasn't part of this glittering, well-dressed crowd. Also, she had mentioned 'out the back'.

'Then this is for you.'' Annie thrust an envelope into his hand. 'Back to the chaos!' She grimaced before hurrying off, pushing her way unconcernedly through the crowd.

Brice looked down dazedly at the envelope he now held. What on earth—?

'Aren't you going to open it?' Chloe prompted curiously after several minutes of Brice just staring at the envelope. 'Annie is one of the dressers from backstage,' she added helpfully.

Brice had already guessed that much. And as he only knew one person backstage, this letter had to have come from Sabina. So much for his thinking she had been completely unaware of her audience earlier. That was professionalism for you; Sabina, although giving no outward sign of it, had obviously been aware enough to see him sitting out there with Chloe!

But why would Sabina be writing to him? To warn him, having seen him and guessed his intention, not to embarrass himself by trying to see her later this evening when the show was over? Or was it something else? He was almost afraid of the answer to that!

'Just open it and see what she has to say,' Chloe encouraged impatiently as he still hesitated.

Brice gave her a mocking glance. 'Aren't you assuming rather a lot?' he drawled.

'I doubt it,' his cousin-in-law told him dismissively. 'Look, I'll be back in a few minutes. I'm going to the ladies' room for the dozenth time this evening.' She grimaced, the discomforts of early pregnancy already having made themselves felt. 'It will also give you a chance to read your letter in peace,' she urged, squeezing his arm encouragingly before hurrying off.

If Chloe weren't already married to, and deeply in love with, his own cousin, Brice knew he could have fallen in love with her himself at that moment just for her thoughtfulness alone. If, that was, he didn't already love Sabina so deeply!

'If you need to talk to me just show this letter to one

of the security men at the end of the show', Sabina's letter read.

Brice turned the single sheet of paper over just to check there was nothing else written there. There wasn't.

Very helpful! If he needed to talk to her—not that she wanted to talk to him.

Whatever that might mean!

Sabina wasn't sure, looking at the uncompromising expression on Brice's face as he stood in front of the closed door of her tiny changing-room, that this had been a good idea. In fact, the ache in her chest, just at the sight of him, told her that it wasn't.

But she had been completely thrown earlier this evening when she'd seen Brice in the audience seated next to the designer, and his cousin-by-marriage, Chloe Fox—had been sure that he couldn't possibly be here to see the show. Which had to mean he was here to see her. At least, she had thought he was. As she looked at the harshness of his expression now, she wasn't so sure…!

Not that any of that uncertainty showed in her expression as she sat down and turned back to the mirror to start removing the heavy make-up she had needed for the show, looking at his reflection enquiringly. 'What did you think of this evening?'

He grimaced, making no move to come further into the room. 'I have little experience of these things, but it looked okay to me.' He shrugged dismissively.

She couldn't help but smile at the predictability of his reply. 'How have you been, Brice?' she prompted lightly, dressed in her own clothes now, casual fitted denims and a bright red tee shirt, her hair loosely curling down the length of her spine.

'How have I—?' He broke off abruptly, taking a deep, controlling breath. 'I'm sure you didn't invite me back here to indulge in pleasantries,' he rasped.

Sabina calmly continued the ritual of removing her make-up, hoping that Brice wouldn't see the tell-tale shake of her hand just the sight of him produced. 'And I'm equally sure you didn't come here this evening to watch a fashion show,' she returned as scathingly.

'Oh? Then why am I here?' he returned unhelpfully.

Sabina shrugged. 'At a guess, I would say you wanted to see me to make certain that I will be at your grandfather's dinner party next weekend,' she drawled knowingly.

'And will you?' he challenged.

She swallowed down her disappointment as she realised she had been right about Brice's reason for being here this evening. Part of her had hoped—

She should have known better. It had all been a game to Brice, the kisses, the flirtation. A dangerous game admittedly, but a game, nonetheless.

Her eyes flashed angrily as she looked at his reflection in the mirror. 'I'm not sure I particularly like the fact that you believe I could ever hurt my mother by not being there,' she bit out tautly.

He raised dark brows. 'Does that mean you are going?'

She glared at him in the mirror. 'Not that it's any of your business—but, yes, I will be there,' she told him dismissively. 'Was that all?' she challenged, more angry than she cared to admit at his lack of faith in her.

More disappointed than she cared to admit that this was his only reason for wanting to see her.

But what had she expected? That Brice would have missed her as much as she had him the last three weeks? That he had also hungered just for the sight and sound of her? As she had hungered for him…

'No, it is not all!' Brice rasped from behind her.

Very close behind her, she acknowledged a little shakily, Brice having moved swiftly across the room, now standing so close Sabina could feel the heat emanating from his body.

He looked about them impatiently, the room in complete chaos from her hurried changes in the second half of the fashion show. 'Have you finished here now?' he asked. 'Or are you going on to the inevitable party that always seems to follow one of these things?' he added scornfully.

'Parties that I, invariably, choose not to attend,' she reminded dryly.

He nodded abruptly. 'Where's the attentive Clive this evening?' he rasped.

Truthfully, she had no idea. But she wasn't about to tell Brice that... 'Night off,' she dismissed lightly.

'Latham?' he rasped harshly.

'Still in Australia.' As far as she knew.

He gave a mocking inclination of his head. 'In that case, shall we go and have coffee together somewhere?' he suggested huskily.

She looked at him with narrowed eyes. 'What about Chloe?'

Brice shrugged. 'She already left.'

Should she have coffee with him? Her life had changed dramatically during the last three weeks, although Brice could know nothing of that. No one knew. Not even her mother. And, for the moment, Sabina wanted it to remain that way.

But there was no reason, just because she and Brice had coffee together, that he should guess just how different her life was from the last time she had seen him. No reason whatsoever.

'I know what happened to you last November, Sabina.'

The words, for all that they were softly spoken, sliced through the atmosphere like a knife, Sabina turning sharply to look up at Brice. Yes, she could see by the compassion in that emerald-green gaze that he did know.

The last thing she wanted from Brice was his pity— now, or ever!

'So what?' She shrugged dismissively. 'My mother told you, I suppose?' she added disgustedly.

'Only because I asked her,' Brice defended.

'And that makes it okay, does it?' Sabina stood up abruptly, moving sharply away from him, shaking her head disgustedly as she did so.

He shrugged. 'Your mother is a very honest and straightforward woman.'

'And I'm not?' She raised challenging brows.

'I didn't say that—'

'What happened isn't something I ever wanted to become public knowledge,' she snapped impatiently. In fact she had gone to great pains to ensure that it didn't.

'And I'm not the public!' Brice came back harshly. 'In a few weeks' time we'll all be part of the same family!'

Sabina faced him tensely. 'My mother marrying your grandfather does not make us "family",' she scorned dismissively.

His mouth tightened ominously. 'It does in my book.'

'That's your prerogative,' she returned heatedly.

She didn't want to be related to this man. She loved him, ached to be with him all the time. The thought of them occasionally meeting at 'family' get-togethers sounded painful in the extreme. Especially as one day Brice was sure to arrive at one of those get-togethers with the woman he intended marrying!

'Damn it, Sabina, I didn't come here this evening to get into an argument with you in this hell-hole!' Brice rasped, obviously at the end of his own patience too.

This 'hell-hole' was pure luxury compared to some of the conditions the other models had worked in this evening. Although she knew what Brice meant; it was an airless, windowless room, of very small proportions.

She gave the ghost of a smile. 'Where did you intend getting into an argument with me, then?' she returned mockingly. It was what they inevitably seemed to do whenever they met!

Brice didn't return her smile, a nerve pulsing in the rigid line of his jaw. 'Are you going to have coffee with me or not?' he pushed forcefully.

'I—' She broke off her angry refusal. If she said no, the next time she saw Brice would be at the first of those family get-togethers next weekend. 'I am,' she stated firmly instead, having applied a lip gloss as her only make-up now, picking up her jacket in preparation for leaving.

Brice gave an impatient sigh. 'Why couldn't you have just said that in the first place?' He reached out to take a light hold of her arm, as if he expected her to take flight in the other direction as soon as they were out of the room.

Sabina gave him a mocking smile. 'I couldn't make it that easy for you, Brice,' she taunted.

He gave a disgusted shake of his head. 'Believe me, I've never found anything about being around you *easy*, Sabina,' he bit out grimly.

She gave him a searching look, wondering exactly what he meant by that remark. Or maybe she was just looking for something that wasn't there. Wishful thinking.

'Come on, then, Brice.' She walked out into the hallway as he held the door open for her. 'I have my car outside.'

He raised dark brows as they strolled towards the exit. 'That's new, isn't it?'

'Not at all, I've been driving for years,' she told him off-handedly.

'That isn't exactly what I mean,' Brice rasped impatiently.

Sabina had known exactly what he'd meant, knew he was referring to the fact that she was now driving herself again rather than being driven around by other people.

It was the least of the changes that had taken place in her life in the last three weeks...

CHAPTER FIFTEEN

'THERE'S something different about you tonight,' Brice murmured slowly as the two of them sat in the lounge of a leading London hotel, the tray of coffee they had ordered having already been placed on the table in front of Sabina.

Was that a wariness in her gaze as she looked up at him? Or was he imagining it? The look was so fleeting, before it was masked by a polite smile, that he really couldn't be sure...

'Is there?' Sabina dismissed lightly, handing him the cup of black coffee he had asked for before sitting back in her chair to sip her own coffee. 'I'm always a little hyper after a show, so perhaps that's it?' She shrugged.

'Nice car,' he commented lightly on the sporty powder-blue Mercedes she had driven here.

'Thanks,' she dismissed. 'I'm actually enjoying driving in London again,' she added happily.

She had changed, Brice mused frowningly as he registered that smile. That fear he had sensed in her from the first time he had seen her no longer seemed to be there. Although, of course, he now knew the reason it had been there in the first place...

'Your mother really wasn't breaking a confidence by talking to me, you know, Sabina,' he sat forward to tell her huskily. 'She believed—perhaps erroneously—that the two of us are friends,' he added with a self-derisive grimace.

A shutter came down over the previous candidness of Sabina's gaze. 'I'm not the first public figure—and I'm sure I won't be the last, either!—to receive threatening letters and phone calls from someone who doesn't like what I do.' She shrugged dismissively.

Bruce wasn't so easily put off, knew from Joan that there had been more to it than that. 'The man actually broke into your dressing-room at a show one evening and attacked you,' he said huskily, feeling murderous himself at the thought of anyone trying to harm Sabina.

As he had when Joan had first told him what had happened to Sabina to put that fear into her eyes, to turn her into someone almost afraid of her own shadow, into someone that Joan barely recognised any more.

Brice had burned with anger after talking to Joan, had wanted to get hold of the man who had attacked her and— Most of all he had wanted to pick Sabina up, wrap her in the cloak of his protection, and make sure that nothing like that ever happened to her again.

Except Richard Latham had already done that...

He had also been filled with a need to hit the other man because he was the one being allowed to protect Sabina!

Sabina shrugged, still avoiding the directness of Brice's gaze. 'He agreed to be put under psychiatric care for his actions that night,' she stated flatly. 'Which is why it was never taken any further.'

It was also the reason that the incident had never become public knowledge. Oh, Brice could see why Sabina preferred it to be that way. He just couldn't rid himself of the mental image of a female celebrity who had been shot dead in similar circumstances a couple of years ago.

'Look, Brice.' Sabina sat forward agitatedly. 'That's all over now, and—'

'Is it?' he rasped harshly. 'What about the letters you're still receiving?'

He was taking a risk on guessing she was still receiving those threatening letters, but one look at her stricken face and he knew that he had guessed correctly about that distinctive green envelope, the one that had arrived in the post and that she had reacted to so strangely that day he'd called to see her.

His mouth twisted angrily. 'I don't think the *psychiatric care* has been too successful—do you?'

The slenderness of her throat moved convulsively as she swallowed hard. She drew in a harsh breath. 'Brice, I really would rather not discuss this.' She shook her head agitatedly.

'I can understand that,' he acknowledged heavily. 'But the man hasn't stopped, has he? He's obviously just biding his time until he has the chance to get to you again. He—'

'Stop!' Sabina cut in harshly. 'Just stop this, Brice,' she said shakily. 'I— The letters have stopped. I haven't received one for weeks now.' She shook her head.

'At a guess I would say you had received another one the day I called to see you and you were "ill" in bed,' he guessed shrewdly.

Sabina's gaze flickered briefly across his face before being averted once again. 'You're very astute, Brice,' she told him huskily. 'I— That was the last one I received.'

'Four weeks ago.' He nodded. 'How often were you receiving them before that?' His gaze was narrowed questioningly.

She swallowed again. 'Every couple of weeks,' she acknowledged huskily,

'A little early to presume there will be no more, don't you think?' Brice rasped, the anger he felt towards this unknown man making him sound harsh.

Sabina opened her mouth to say something, and then obviously thought better of it, shrugging instead.

'Sabina…?' Brice looked at her questioningly. 'What is it you aren't telling me?' he prompted slowly, more convinced by the moment that there was something.

She forced a bright smile to her lips. 'Goodness, there must be lots of things I'm not telling you, Brice,' she dismissed lightly. 'We don't know each other well enough to share confidences!'

Didn't know—! Brice drew in a sharp breath. He *knew* this woman well enough to know he was in love with her, that he thought of nothing else but her, night and day—how much better did he need to know her?

'Thanks!' he snapped irritatedly.

'You're welcome.' She gave him that mischievous grin again.

Brice gave her a reproving frown. 'You've obviously been very busy the last three weeks.' So busy that she had either been 'out' or 'unavailable' every time he'd telephoned her!

Again he sensed that sudden wariness in her. Not that old fear that he now knew the reason for, just wariness. Why?

'I did tell you weeks ago that my schedule is very heavily booked for the next six months,' she returned noncommittally.

'So you did,' he drawled. 'I haven't been exactly idle the last three weeks myself,' he added dryly.

'Oh?' She gave him a look of polite interest.

A look Brice instantly resented. The last thing he wanted from Sabina was her politeness!

'I've finished the portrait,' he told her abruptly.

She blinked. 'My portrait?'

He gave a mocking inclination of his head. 'None other,' he drawled.

A flush darkened her cheeks. 'But—I—I didn't finish sitting for it,' she said agitatedly. 'Besides, I—you—Richard told you he no longer wanted it,' she concluded awkwardly.

Brice's eyes narrowed angrily. 'Do you think so little of my artistic talent that you believe I'm incapable of painting a subject without having them sit in front of me for hours at a time?' he rasped.

'No! But—' She made a dismissive movement. 'Why bother when you no longer have a—a client, to sell it to?' She gave a perplexed frown. 'I suppose that I could always—'

'It isn't for sale!' Brice cut in harshly.

He had sat and finished Sabina's portrait for his own sake, for the sake of his sanity, it had felt like at times. Painting her image on canvas had been his only way of feeling in the least close to her this last three weeks!

And, even if he did say so himself, it was a wonderful portrait; Sabina painted against the background of that room at his grandfather's castle, a wistfully beautiful Sabina, surrounded by the mystery that was such a part of her.

There was no way that Brice would ever sell it. To anyone. In the circumstances, it was just as well that Latham had changed his mind about wanting it—Brice would have had a difficult time telling the other man that the portrait was not for sale!

Sabina shook her head. 'I don't understand.'

Brice's mouth twisted sardonically. 'Don't you?'

'No.' She looked more puzzled than ever. 'What are you going to do with it?'

'I'm not sure...' he answered slowly. 'I may exhibit it.' Although the thought of letting Sabina's portrait out of his possession for a moment, even to a reputable gallery, told him that he probably wouldn't do that, either. Perhaps he would just hang it in his bedroom—it was the closest he was ever going to get to having Sabina there!

'Let me know if you decide to do that.' Sabina nodded. 'I would love to come along and see it.'

'You can come to my home at any time and do that,' Brice returned harshly.

Sabina gave a tight smile, shaking her head. 'I think I'll wait for the exhibition.'

He shrugged. 'Please yourself,' he bit out tautly.

The atmosphere between them had changed over the last few minutes, Brice realised frowningly, Sabina having lost most of that effervescence he had noticed in her earlier. And he wanted it back!

'Sabina—' He broke off abruptly, becoming very still as he watched her lift her coffee-cup to her lips, totally stunned as he realised there was something else that was different about Sabina this evening. Something he should have noticed earlier, but hadn't.

Her left hand was bare of the huge diamond ring that, to Brice, had clearly represented Richard Latham's possession of her!

Sabina looked at Brice enquiringly, realising as she did so that he was staring transfixed at her left hand. Her bare left hand.

There were several excuses she could have given him for her engagement ring not being there: she never wore it when she was modelling and had forgotten to put it back on after the show; it was at the jeweller's being made smaller—she had lost half a stone in weight the last three weeks, much to the chagrin of the people she worked with, who had had to alter the clothes she modelled—or she could just say she had forgotten to put it on this evening. But none of those excuses would have been the truth...

'Where's your ring?' Brice finally seemed to collect himself enough to ask.

Sabina made a show of looking down at her bare hands. What was Brice going to think if she told him she didn't have the ring because she was no longer engaged? The truth, probably, you idiot, she instantly remonstrated with herself—that she and Richard were no longer together! And that Brice was the reason for that...?

She sat up straighter in her armchair, her gaze very direct as she looked across at Brice. 'I have no idea what

Richard has done with it since I gave it back to him,' she told Brice evenly.

He gave a pained frown. 'You gave Latham back his engagement ring?'

'Yes,' she confirmed shortly. 'I didn't think it was right to keep it as we're no longer engaged,' she added dryly.

'When did you give it back to him?' Brice prompted slowly, very tense now.

If she said, Three weeks ago, the time she and Richard had returned from Scotland, then Brice was going to assume that he had something to do with the engagement being broken—either that Richard had guessed they had been in each other's arms that day, or—worse—that Sabina had broken the engagement because of her realised feelings for Brice. That last reason might be the correct one, but she didn't have to be stripped of all her pride!

Brice leant forward in his chair. 'I've been calling the house the last three weeks to speak to you,' he told her harshly. 'The housekeeper told me you were unavailable!'

Sabina gave a rueful smile. 'I suppose that's technically correct—I haven't lived at the house for several weeks. Look, Brice, it's very late,' she added firmly, bending to pick up her bag, 'and it's been a long evening, so if you'll excuse me—'

'No, I won't excuse you!' he burst in forcefully, his expression grim. 'You can't just get up and leave after telling me you've broken your engagement to Latham!'

'Of course I can,' she told him reasoningly. 'Anyway, the engagement was broken by mutual agreement,' she added hardly. 'It's no big deal, Brice,' she dismissed lightly as Brice still scowled. 'In fact, I've quite enjoyed these last few weeks of freedom,' she added with some surprise.

Something had changed inside her the night her engagement to Richard had ended, a reassertion of her old confident self, her independence, the fear she had lived under for these last months also coming to an end that night. For a very good reason...

Her mouth tightened. 'I like being my own person again, Brice,' she told him dismissively. 'I've moved into my own apartment,' she explained. 'I do what I want, and go where I want.' She shrugged. 'I must admit I had forgotten how good that feels,' she concluded softly.

And she had. After the attack she had lived in dread of something like that happening again, had been only too glad of Richard's offer of protection. She just hadn't realised the price he'd expected her to pay for that protection...

But these last three weeks of standing on her own feet she had regained the confidence she had lost after the attack, had been determined that she had to do that. And she had succeeded. Much better than she had anticipated.

Her apartment had been chosen and paid for, furniture moved in, she had even resumed some of her social life with some of the other models, had decided that she simply couldn't live in fear of the attack being repeated, that she wanted to live the full life she had known before.

She was even—although she doubted Brice would believe it—looking forward to attending her mother's engagement dinner next weekend, was truly pleased for her mother and Hugh.

She had telephoned her mother and arranged to have lunch with her a week ago, and the two of them had talked together in a way that they never had before, had attained a closeness that Sabina cherished. And her mother, Sabina knew, would never repeat any of *that* particular conversation to Brice...!

'I see,' Brice answered her slowly. 'Then there's no point in my asking you to have dinner with me tomorrow evening?' he added harshly.

Sabina was about to facetiously agree with him that

there wasn't, and then she wavered as she saw the intensity of his expression as he waited for her answer.

She drew her breath in softly, the tension between them now so heavy she felt as if she could reach out and touch it. 'Why would you want to do that?' she delayed huskily.

'Because it's too soon to ask you to spend the rest of your life with me!' he bit out self-derisively.

Sabina's eyes widened with shock as she stared at him disbelievingly. Had Brice just said—? Had he really just—?

She shook her head dazedly, couldn't speak, daredn't speak. Was Brice telling her that he loved her?

'I take it that's a no to spending the rest of your life with me,' Brice rasped hardly as he obviously saw that shake of her head. 'Okay, then I'll settle for the dinner together I originally asked for!'

He was going too fast for her—she was still trying to get over the shock of his last statement! How had he jumped from dinner to a lifetime together? Had she missed something?

'Could we just go back a few steps, Brice?' she said slowly, looking at him uncertainly now. 'I know you've flirted with me the last couple of months, that you've even kissed me—'

'Let me just put you straight about something before you continue, Sabina,' he cut in firmly. 'I don't flirt. I never have. I never will,' he stated flatly.

'But—'

'As for the kisses,' he continued as if uninterrupted. 'It was a question of kissing you or putting you over my knee and spanking you—I chose the more pleasurable option. For myself!'

Sabina swallowed hard, a bubble of happiness starting to build up inside her as she listened to him. A fragile bubble she was very much afraid would suddenly be burst!

'Brice, could we get out of here?' She frowned. 'Go

somewhere where we can talk less publicly?' The lounge of this busy hotel was still full of people, despite it being after midnight.

He looked at her for several long minutes before answering. 'Can I have your agreement to have dinner with me tomorrow first?' he finally said slowly.

If what she thought—hoped—was true, he could have her promise for more than that!

But she didn't say that, just nodded, still too stunned to dare to believe what Brice was saying to her.

'Good enough,' Brice bit out forcefully, standing up. 'Okay, let's go.'

Sabina shyly took the hand he held out to her as she got slowly to her feet, leaving her hand nestling within the warm confines of his as they walked out into the night.

CHAPTER SIXTEEN

BRICE had never felt so nervous in his entire life as he poured Sabina and himself a glass of brandy. Admittedly Sabina had left the hotel with him, driven them both back to his home, but he was still uncertain of her motive for doing so. Did she just want to let him down gently, away from that crowded hotel? Or was it something else?

'There we are.' He crossed the sitting-room to where Sabina sat in one of the armchairs, handing her the glass of brandy before taking a sip of his own. Although the fiery liquid did little to warm him; he felt like a prisoner awaiting sentence!

'Sabina—'

'Brice—'

They both spoke together, smiling ruefully at each other as they both stopped at the same time too.

'You first,' Brice invited, remaining standing, feeling too restless to sit down. Sabina might no longer be engaged to Latham, but that didn't mean he stood a chance with her himself. In fact, the comments she had made earlier about enjoying her freedom seemed to imply the opposite. Although she had at least agreed to have dinner with him tomorrow...

Sabina drew in a deep breath before speaking, her brandy remaining untouched in the glass. 'There are some things I have to tell you before—before—'

Before 'passing the sentence'? Brice wasn't sure, after all the weeks of tension, that he could get through this. Before he had been tied by the fact that Sabina was engaged to another man, that loyalty alone—he didn't even want to think about Sabina being in love with Richard

174

Latham—meaning she couldn't, wouldn't respond to Brice's interest in her. But now that excuse was out of the way, there was still no reason to believe Sabina might be interested in him!

'Then tell me,' he rasped more harshly than he meant to, wincing as he saw the way she tensed at his tone. 'I'm sorry,' he sighed. 'I'm afraid I'm not the most patient of men,' he acknowledged ruefully.

'I would never have guessed!' She gave a slight smile. 'Anyway,' she began again, 'as I've already explained, I am no longer engaged to Richard.' She looked straight at Brice now, blue gaze unblinking. 'The engagement was broken exactly three weeks ago. The moment we returned from Scotland, in fact,' she admitted ruefully.

'Go on,' Brice encouraged huskily, almost afraid to breathe now in case he broke the moment.

She sighed, taking a sip of the brandy before continuing. 'I was the one to broach the subject, but—Richard had reached the same conclusion. I—' She gave a pained frown. 'I saw a Richard that day I hadn't known existed. A man who will go to any lengths—any lengths,' she repeated with a shudder, 'to add what he considers unique to his already vast collection.' She looked up at Brice now, her eyes glittering brightly with unshed tears. 'You said earlier that it was too soon to know whether or not those horrible letters had stopped. I can assure you that they have,' she said gruffly. 'Because Richard was the one sending them!'

Brice stared at Sabina, unable to take in exactly what she was saying. How could Latham have been responsible for sending those letters? For one thing, there had definitely been a man last November sending her letters and making threatening telephone calls, because he had been put under psychiatric care after his attack on Sabina. Secondly, Latham was supposed to be in love with Sabina, and he must have known how much receiving those letters upset her...

Or was that the point? Brice wondered sharply. Hadn't Latham's own nephew warned Brice about ever tangling with him, that his uncle was a fierce collector of priceless objects? And Sabina, although certainly not an object, was certainly priceless!

Sabina gave a humourless smile as she saw the obvious bewilderment on Brice's face. 'Hard to believe, isn't it?' she said shakily. 'I still find it difficult to believe I could ever have trusted such a man!' She shook her head self-disgustedly. 'But it is true, Brice. Richard and I argued that day when we returned from Scotland. Richard said some things that were—' She swallowed hard. 'He was angry because he guessed— He was angry,' she repeated flatly. 'And in the course of that anger he told me that once I had agreed to marry him he had been the one to take up sending me those letters.'

'But why?' Brice rasped.

Sabina grimaced. 'Can't you guess?'

'To keep you dependent on his protection!' Brice suddenly guessed furiously. 'You would obviously have been very vulnerable after that attack,' he continued frowningly. 'Very susceptible to Latham's apparent kindness, I suspect—'

'Very,' Sabina confirmed heavily. 'The truth is, Brice, Richard and I were never in love with each other. We— we made a bargain,' she admitted huskily. 'Richard would protect me, and I—I—'

'You became the priceless object on his arm,' Brice finished incredulously.

'Yes,' she admitted with a grimace. 'I *was* frightened after the attack, Brice. Completely vulnerable.' She looked at him imploringly.

'And he wanted to keep you that way,' Brice ground out angrily as he saw the whole truth now.

The bastard! How could he? How dared he do that to Sabina...?

'Exactly,' Sabina confirmed heavily. 'You mentioned that I had probably received one of those letters that day you came to the house and I was ill? That was because— Richard had come home early from a business trip that evening I came to your house and ended up staying for dinner. He—he knew where I had been.'

'Clive!' Brice guessed disgustedly.

'Yes,' Sabina sighed. 'The letter I received was my punishment for seeing you without Richard's permission. I've had several weeks to think about this, Brice, and I realise now that I received one of those letters every time Richard thought I needed reminding that I belonged to him! In fact, that was what those letters always said, just ''You're mine''.' She swallowed hard.

'I'll kill him!' Brice's fists were clenched at his sides. 'Take great delight in tearing him limb from limb!'

Sabina shook her head. 'It doesn't matter, Brice.'

'Doesn't—! It matters to me, damn it,' he ground out furiously. 'I would like to—'

'It really doesn't matter any more, Brice,' Sabina told him huskily as she stood up. 'I became engaged to Richard for reasons that were just as wrong as his own,' she admitted gruffly. 'I felt exposed, vulnerable, after the attack, and, although I had known Richard for several months before that, it wasn't until after that I actually agreed to marry him.' She shook her head. 'For the totally wrong reason, I now realise. As for Richard, he wanted to own something he thought was unique—'

'You are unique!' Brice cut in harshly.

'Maybe,' she accepted heavily. 'But although I liked Richard, I was never in love with him. Not the way I love you,' she added so softly Brice wasn't sure he had heard her correctly.

In fact, he was sure he couldn't have heard her correctly!

*　*　*

Sabina looked across at Brice, sympathising with his stunned expression. As stunned as hers must have been earlier when he'd told her he was asking her out to dinner because he thought it was too soon to ask her to spend the rest of her life with him!

But she had come a long way in the last three weeks, knew that the knock to her self-confidence that she had known the night she'd been attacked would have healed in the naturalness of time—without the constant reminder of those letters that had started to arrive again only weeks later! As it had healed now...

It was still difficult for her to believe that Richard had become the perpetrator of those letters. Not that it had been too difficult for him to have done so; she had confided in him totally once they'd become engaged, even down to the fact that she'd always recognised the letters because they'd arrived in a green envelope. After that, it had been easy for Richard to simply take over sending the letters whenever he'd felt inclined to reinforce her dependence on him.

She moistened dry lips. 'Richard is—a strange man, in many ways,' she began softly, not quite meeting Brice's gaze. 'Do you have any idea what it was that made him decide I was no longer perfect, after all?'

Brice still scowled. 'Does it have anything to do with me?'

Sabina gave a rueful laugh. 'Everything to do with you! Richard, it turns out, is a man who likes to admire his possessions by simply looking at them. I—he—' She paused, her cheeks becoming red. 'Richard is absolutely horrified at the thought of physical intimacy with a person—any person!' she emphasised frowningly.

Brice looked more stunned than ever. 'But I thought—'

'I know what you thought, Brice.' Sabina sighed. 'By mutual agreement I had my own bedroom in Richard's house, my own room if we happened to stay at a hotel.' She shook her head. 'Which was why it was no hardship for us to have separate rooms at your grandfather's home,' she added ruefully. 'That was part of our bargain too. I believed it was out of respect for our friendship, but—it appears that Richard simply finds the whole idea of physical intimacy distasteful, a breach of a person's personal integrity.' A realisation that had stunned Sabina three weeks ago.

She had become engaged to a man who not only found a physical relationship between a man and a woman repugnant, but who stooped to sending her anonymous letters in order to maintain her dependence on him.

She still couldn't believe the lucky escape she had made!

Brice shook his head. 'The man is weirder than I thought he was,' he dismissed disgustedly. 'Although that still doesn't change the fact that I intend going to see him, want to make sure he knows he is never to come near you again,' he added grimly.

Sabina shook her head unconcernedly. 'He won't,' she said with certainty. 'Richard and I have come to an understanding—another one!' she added self-derisively. 'He will stay out of my life, and that of my family and friends, and I won't tell the police that he was the one sending me anonymous letters.' Her expression was bleak. 'I think that sounds fair.'

'Not to me,' Brice rasped. 'Never seeing you again isn't nearly punishment enough for what he did to you.'

She gave a rueful grimace. 'Richard doesn't want to see me again,' she assured him. 'He no longer considers me unique, you see,' she added softly.

Brice's eyes were narrowed. 'Why doesn't he?' he said slowly.

'Several reasons.' She shrugged. 'But the main one is

that he is aware of the—physical attraction, between the two of us.'

'That's because I find it hard to be in the same room with you for six minutes without wanting to make love to you, let alone six months!' he admitted impatiently.

She laughed softly; it was exactly the same way she felt about him! 'We've been here at least fifteen minutes now,' she pointed out provocatively, her gaze alight with the love she felt towards this man.

Brice looked at her sharply, slowly relaxing as he saw the mischievous expression on her face. 'Very remiss of me,' he murmured huskily even as he crossed the room to stand in front of her. 'I love you, Sabina,' he told her forcefully. 'I want to marry you.'

'Before I answer that, I need to assure you of a few things,' she said slowly.

'Yes?' he prompted impatiently.

Sabina smiled at that show of impatience. 'I want to assure you that none of my actions—and I mean *none* of them—are now made because of any lingering fear over what happened all those months ago. It was upsetting at the time, but I'm over it now. I would have been months ago, if not for Richard's behaviour,' she added hardly. 'Do you understand what I'm saying, Brice?'

'None of your actions now are made because of any lingering fear because of what happened all those months ago,' he repeated with obvious impatience.

'Right.' She nodded her satisfaction. 'Then my answer to your previous statement is yes,' she breathed ecstatically as she moved confidently into his arms, her head nestling against the warm strength of his shoulder.

Brice looked down at her quizzically. 'Yes, I love you? Or yes, I want to marry you?'

'Yes—I love you. And yes—I'll marry you,' she answered without hesitation, that love glowing in her eyes as she looked up at him unblinkingly.

He groaned, briefly closing his eyes. 'I'm not sure I can believe this,' he admitted huskily.

She smiled at him—she could hardly believe it herself! But it was true, she and Brice loved each other, were going to marry each other. 'I'm sure we can find a way to convince you,' she murmured throatily.

He raised teasing brows. 'Are you making an improper suggestion, Miss Smith?' He feigned shock.

'I am, Mr McAllister,' she confirmed without hesitation.

Brice's arms closed possessively about her as he swept her up, his mouth forcefully claiming hers.

But Sabina didn't doubt that it was with love, caring, desire, all the things there should be between two people who loved each other and wanted to be together for the rest of their lives...

CHAPTER SEVENTEEN

'I HAVE to say, Logan, that I think Aunt Meg is taking all of this rather well,' Brice drawled in amusement before taking a sip from his champagne glass.

The two men turned to look at Logan's mother, the actress Margaret Fraser, as she stood across the room talking to Logan's wife, Darcy, the two of them cooing over the baby boy Darcy cradled so lovingly in her arms.

Brice nodded. 'I thought it was bad enough when you and Darcy made Aunt Meg a grandmother, but now she has a stepmother who's only ten years older than she is!' He turned to look across the room to where their grandfather, newly married, was standing beside his bride greeting their guests as they arrived at the wedding reception.

Joan looked absolutely lovely in her cream satin suit, but it was to the beautiful young woman who stood at her other side, Joan's maid of honour, that Brice's gaze strayed instinctively. And stopped.

Sabina.

His own wife.

Of two weeks, four days, and—he glanced at his wristwatch—three hours.

And they had been the happiest two weeks, four days and three hours, that Brice had ever known.

The dazzling smile Sabina gave him as she caught and held his gaze told him she had read his thoughts—and that she felt exactly the same way about him!

There were no longer any shadows in Sabina's eyes, only the love and happiness that was the centre of their lives together. Brice intended seeing that it remained that way.

Although it wasn't something he ever intended discussing with Sabina—for obvious reasons—he had dealt with Richard Latham in his own way, the older man left in no doubt, after their brief meeting six weeks ago, of just how rapid—and official—Brice's reaction would be if he ever threatened or came near Sabina again.

'And what are you two talking about so cosily?' Fergus drawled as he strolled over to join them, a glass of champagne in his own hand.

Logan grinned. 'How different our lives all are from eighteen months ago,' he murmured ruefully. 'For the better, I might add,' he said firmly.

Fergus gave a leisurely glance around the room, nodding his own satisfaction. 'Logan's mother, Aunt Meg, married to Darcy's father, Daniel. Logan and Darcy married with an endearing son of their own. Chloe and I married for almost a year now, and our own baby due in three months. Even Grandfather surprising us all by finding happiness with Sabina's mother. And as for this sly devil...!' He slapped Brice on the back with cousinly affection. 'I'm still not sure how you talked that beautiful woman into marrying you!' He shook his head with mock incredulity after glancing at Sabina in her sky-blue dress.

'Charm and good looks,' Brice returned mockingly.

'Oh, yes?' Logan gave him a sceptical glance.

Brice grinned. 'I've been assured it runs in the family!'

'By whom?' Fergus taunted.

'Grandfather,' Brice answered with satisfaction.

'Oh, well,' Logan drawled, 'if Grandfather said so...!' He glanced over to where their grandfather was smiling down at his new wife, his expression softening with the affection they all felt for the patriarch of their rapidly growing family. 'It's good to see him so happy again, isn't it...?'

'Very.'

'Yes.'

Fergus and Brice both answered at the same time, the three men smiling at each other with family satisfaction.

'Well, you three are all looking very pleased with your-selves.' Chloe, Fergus's wife, looked at them enquiringly as she moved to stand beside her husband.

'Very,' Darcy added questioningly as she joined them, releasing the baby into Logan's arms as he struggled to go to his father.

'And why shouldn't they?' Sabina murmured huskily as she linked her arms with Chloe's and Darcy's. 'They're married to the three of us!' she added with a mischievous grin that encompassed all of them.

Brice glowed with love and pride as he looked at her, that love becoming almost overwhelming as his gaze in-cluded all his family.

The McDonald clan was complete!

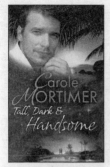

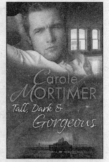

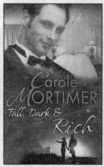

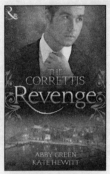

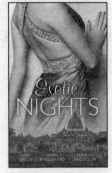